TABLE OF CONTENTS

FOREWORD:
POE IS FOR THE AGES
Clint Collins and Scott Woodward

Although Black Mirror Press originally conceived the idea for a 21st century updating of Poe's tales, it reluctantly had to abandon the effort. Yet the Raven would not be denied. It flew through many a midnight dreary before finding a light burning at Camden Park Press and tapping at Lyn Worthen's window. We are grateful she heard the tapping of the Raven and let it in.

The Raven taps for us all, doesn't it? After all these years we are still fascinated by the writings of Edgar Allan Poe. The house of Roderick Usher ever beckons, sitting by that "black and lurid tarn," and we wonder how that Amontillado would taste in a damp cellar. The power of Poe's tales and poems resonates through the decades and even the centuries, and in this anthology you will see his classic works come to life in our modern day.

Thanks to Camden Park Press the terrors and thrills of Poe's work now become even more real and present for us, and, as Poe wrote in "The Fall of the House of Usher," we will experience them "with a shudder even more thrilling than before." That tell-tale heart may beat beneath the floor of a luxury condo, but it still haunts us as powerfully as it ever did.

So we invite you to open your shutter to the Raven and take that midnight walk along the Rue Morgue with Annabel Lee. Poe is for the ages and Camden Park Press now brings you the 21st century edition!

Clint Collins and Scott Woodward
Black Mirror Press
August 28, 2018

Introduction:
The Call of the Raven

Lyn Worthen

Once upon a midnight dreary, while I pondered, weak and weary,
Over many a quaint and curious volume of forgotten lore—
While I nodded, nearly napping, suddenly there came a tapping,
As of someone gently rapping, rapping at my chamber door...

For over one hundred and fifty years, the raven has tapped at chamber doors, flown through open windows, and cast its baleful eye upon us from watchful perches. But why do we continue to grant him admittance, this bird who brings in his wake a cast of dying women, mournful lovers, and scheming murderers?

Is it our own fear of death that makes us such curious observers? Our unfulfilled desires for revenge that find us encouraging Montressor as he leads Fortunato down into the catacombs? Do we find comfort for our own grief in sharing Poe's lament for his lost love? Or is it his ventures into the realms of the mind that bring us back to his work?

For there was a side to Poe that left the macabre behind in favor of the psychological, the pseudo-scientific. Who could read The Unparalleled Adventure of One Hans Pfaall and believe it possible that the same hand penned The Pit and the Pendulum? Who reading Berenice (which you should not do before going to bed!) would recognize the author of The Murders in the Rue Morgue and the creator of Auguste Dupin, the less-famous predecessor of Sherlock Holmes? Indeed, many readers consider Poe the father of mystery and psychological-thriller literature.

From dismembered corpses, rivals bricked behind cellar walls, murders in back alleys, and detectives on the trail of devious villains, the works of Poe were dark and often disturbing, intense and creepy at the same time. They make you question your own sanity (or lack thereof). Yet for all that, his stories have had a profound impact on both the horror and mystery genres to this day.

And then there is the poetry. The melody and beauty of language is manifested so wondrously in poetry, and Poe was a master of the craft, creating poems whose rhymes and patterns are familiar even to those who do not consider themselves to be scholars of the form.

Whatever brings you to Poe, I believe it is the evocative imagery he paints in sometimes hypnotic lines of pen and ink that have captured our imaginations; the sensations of fear, loathing, grief, and despair that have bound his characters to our souls. And I believe it is those same elements that the authors in Quoth the Raven have so thoroughly captured.

Life events prevented me from submitting when Black Mirror Press first announced the idea of an anthology filled with contemporary reimaginings of the works of Edgar Allan Poe, planned for release to coincide with the 169th anniversary of the author's death. So when I saw the notice that Clint and Scott had closed the anthology, I could fully empathize with their decision. And that was when the raven came tapping on my chamber door. "People have already written stories," it whispered. "All that effort shouldn't be allowed to go to waste!" I ignored the raven at first, but it was insistent. I consulted my team, shifted things on the calendar, considered fleeing to a tropical island until the madness wore off. But in the end, I wrote to Clint and Scott, adopting their orphaned project, and put it on the fast-track to publication.

The volume you hold in your hands represents an enormous outpouring of effort on the part of all of the authors involved - and I include those who submitted but were not selected as well. The quantity and quality of the submissions I received was nothing short of amazing. I could have built an entire anthology comprised of reimaginings of Annabel Lee, and the various versions of both The Black Cat and The Cask of Amontillado - and mash-ups of the two - could have filled a second volume. Narrowing the choices to this small set of stories and poems involved many difficult decisions.

In Quoth the Raven, we invite you to answer the call of the raven and revisit Poe's work, re-imagined for the twenty-first century. In these stories, the lover of mystery and Gothic horror will find familiar themes in contemporary settings, variations on Poe's tales, and faithful recreations of the author's signature style.

And when you are finished reading, it is just possible that you'll find the raven has taken his place in your mind and heart as well.

– Lyn Worthen
Sandy, Utah
October 7, 2018

QUOTH THE RAVEN

*Contemporary Reimaginings
of the works of
Edgar Allan Poe*

A.A. Azariah-Kribbs lives in Maryland with her creative muse, Fuffle. Her work has been published in several venues, including Harpur Palate, Mystery Weekly, *and* The Sonder Review. *Her website, "Wallie's Wentletrap," features her original artwork and fiction. Visit it at https://wallieswentletrap.com*

About this story, Azariah-Kribbs. says: "The Accompanist *is a love story inspired by Edgar Allan Poe's dark romances, specifically* Ligeia *and* Eleonora. *If Poe's assertion that 'the death... of a beautiful woman is, unquestionably, the most poetical topic in the world,' then from a woman's perspective, the death of a beautiful man must be equally striking. I wrote this short story to explore the tragedy and beauty of love from a woman's point-of-view—true love that, even 'dead,' simply refuses to die."*

So much of Poe's work revolves around loss of a love, that it seemed only fitting to lead off this collection with this gentle tale of love and loss... and what comes after.

THE ACCOMPANIST
A.A. Azariah-Kribbs

Music is soft and full of memory.

He loved to sing.

That is how we met. It seems so long ago. He was a singer, and I his accompanist. The first time I heard him I was impressed—impressed, that anyone with a nervous stoop could manage more than a shudder. But singing was his strength. When he sang, he stood straight and looked up, up to Heaven, and forgot us, our place, until the song was done, and he stood like one surprised and ashamed.

His voice had a peculiar strain to it. Trained, skilled, there was still a tension or pressure in his throat that made his effort tremble. This was a fault to some. To me it made him all the rarer. I was obsessed with that tremulous strength. I tried to capture it in recording. I tried to preserve its paradox, the union of freedom and repression. But no matter how sensitive my device, his voice defied preservation. It was too light and nuanced to be played by machine.

I felt that some expression of his heart must be in his voice. His heart, after his voice, was a mystery. Unlike his voice, his heart could be learned in part and won entirely. I flattered him (not insincerely) and, like all artists, he began to depend on that flattery as an addict craves his vice. I worried at first that he would lose that curious weakness in breath if I were too eager. But he was rare. The more abject my love, the frailer and sweeter his song.

We married. The wedding was quiet. Our witnesses were a friend on one side and parents on the other. I thought it strange that he should have no family. I would have thought he, of anyone, would be a mother's darling. But there was none but one, a friend and colleague. My mother kissed him and my father blessed him. His voice, his heart was mine. That was enough.

Perhaps you think I did not love him. Perhaps you suppose that my fascination for his voice was a superficial thing and that he was, to all intents and purposes, my songbird in a prison of plaster. You do not know me. You did not know him. He was not a performer, no master of illusion and art. He *was* the art. To know his voice was to hear his soul invisible.

I said that I tried to copy him by machine. I have the discs still, the videos. I do not listen to or watch them. There was always a shrill discord in review; a hollow, tin edge, that preserved none of the real vibrancy, the waver and catch of hesitant life that were so singularly his.

*

It was our habit to review our repertoire together. I remember one evening, when we performed one of our favorites. I sat at the piano, and he sang. His voice had never been more beautiful, strung with melancholy, thrilled with love. But at the last he leaned heavily on the cabinet.

"What is it?" I said. "Are you tired? Sit with me."

He looked at me with veiled eyes.

"No," he said. "I shouldn't."

"Why? What's the matter?"

"I have done you wrong," he said. "You have been good to me, and I have brought you pain."

I couldn't understand him. Seeing my confusion, he came to me and knelt by my seat.

"I have not told you the truth," he murmured. "I said I was disowned. I did not tell you, my family is dead."

"Dead?"

"It is a thinness in our blood."

I pressed him. "You are unwell?"

He took my hands in his. He kissed my fingers.

"No," he whispered. "I am dying."

We went at once to the hospital. An examination proved a curious disorder. It was nothing the doctor could explain except a slow decease from within. There was a thinness in the blood, as he had said, that could not be helped by transfusion. The quality perplexed him. The doctor could not decide if it were a new type of disease and couldn't think how to cure it.

"Rest is what I advise," he said. "Complete rest."

My husband would not rest. He insisted we keep our engagement at Carnegie.

*

I see it now as if it were yesterday. The electric light was like the fire of an eye from above, turning on a scene unearthly as a dream. He stood and sang, and his voice was raw and weak as sorrow, and as tender. I could not see the music before me. My fingers moved over keys I did not feel.

I couldn't bear it. I couldn't bear that so soon after having it, I should lose his voice, my voice—*my* voice. He was wasting away, and I begged him to sing until I could commit his sound to memory. So he sang for me. Every day he sang, and his voice was a little thinner, a little more feeble, more precious. His finest chord was on a failing breath, when his soul rose to his eyes and did not leave, but burned there, a strange fury of death agony and passion.

He slept in my arms.

He died.

His voice passed with his life. My recordings and films were nothing to me. They did not hold his soul. Yet I wondered if his soul were not still in him. His heart had stopped so quietly that there had been no rattle, no gasp. The soul could have stolen away from him, like breath. But I did not believe it. He would not let me believe it.

They laid him in a plain coffin. His hair was raven-wild as before, with all its rich luster, and his dark brows were gently set, relaxed. What suffering had ravaged, peace touched with a fairer cast. I could not fool myself and imagine him alive. Sleeping, he had never been so still. But when was death ever young and composed, as if he might remember to breathe and feel again? When had death become beautiful and traded a bare grin for passionless lips?

I placed my hand on his cold cheek. I kissed his cold mouth.

His gift had been tongue, tooth, and breath.

My skill was in my hands.

*

It was hard to play to another's voice. For some time, I set aside the stage and worked as an instructor of finger instruments. I studied the flute. I prized the harp. I taught these, and my piano, to children. My income was poor, but I had time to myself. I was content to avoid any public performance and test my skill before a familiar, intimate audience.

My efforts were generally admired. It was my harp that truly made friends wonder. Its design was singular and elegant, smooth and dead white. There was a peculiar, brittle delicacy in the frame. They told me they had never seen

3

another to equal its weight and style. They asked if I wouldn't tighten the strings, to steady an occasional, tremulous twang.

I told them I had tried. It was a consequence of the model. Even if I replaced the strings, there was always that thrill and quiver. I teased that this idiosyncrasy had made it possible for me to afford the instrument. The same fault made me value it beyond price. I often felt when I struck a light note, that it wasn't I who played, but the harp itself that would sing.

Tiffany Michelle Brown is a native of Phoenix, Arizona, who ran away from the desert to live near sunny San Diego beaches. She earned degrees in English and Creative Writing from the University of Arizona, and her work has been published by Electric Spec, Fabula Argentea, Pen and Kink Publishing, Transmundane Press, *and* Dark Alley Press. *When she isn't writing, Tiffany can be found on a yoga mat, sipping whisky, or reading a comic book—sometimes all at once. Follow her adventures at tiffanymichellebrown.wordpress.com.*

About this story, Tiffany says: "Prior to this project, I'd never read Edgar Allan Poe's Berenice. *After discovering the story, devouring the text, and researching its critical reception, I knew I'd found my inspiration. When* Berenice *was first published in 1835 by the* Southern Literary Messenger, *readers were so disturbed by its graphic content that they complained to the editor, ultimately forcing Poe to self-censor his work. I despise censorship, so reimagining* Berenice *for a contemporary audience seemed like a perfect act of literary rebellion. In the end, writing* My Love in Pieces *was both thrilling and terrifying. I hope this story leaves you screaming."*

There's something to be said about those who willingly allow an author to lead them through fear and pain to the point where you wonder exactly when it was that you crossed the threshold and the madness crept into your own soul. Go safely...

MY LOVE, IN PIECES
Tiffany Michelle Brown

Cell phones were never allowed in the drop-off line at Bailey and Emily's school because, as the other parents were quick to say, they held everything up. I knew this, but there was something so out-of-place about a phone call before ten. Sure, you regularly sent me text messages, wishing me a good day or letting me know I'd forgotten my coffee on the kitchen counter, but you rarely *called*.

You only called if something was wrong, which is why I broke the rules and reached for my phone.

But it wasn't you. I didn't recognize the number.

Grasping for a safe, mundane explanation, I convinced myself that it was one of our Japanese investors with an urgent business matter. But that didn't make sense. The number had a local area code, and the hour wasn't optimal for business in Japan.

Unease slithered into my gut as I hit the answer button. As it turns out, reasonably so.

It was a medical admin at Madison County who was trying to reach me. In a raspy voice, undoubtedly the byproduct of years and years of chain smoking, the woman told me there'd been an accident. You'd been admitted to the ICU, and I should come quickly.

In slow motion, the bottom of the world fell out from under me. My stomach flip-flopped, and my blood ran cold in spite of the car heater belching out stale, warm air.

Bailey and Emily were carrying on in the back, completely unaware of my sudden concern, singing along to a YouTube video. No doubt you'd have scolded me for supplying them with "brain candy" right before school. But you… you weren't there to reprimand me. You were…

"Wait," I choked, a command directed at both the admin and our girls. I turned in my seat, waved a hand at our pink-clad daughters, and told them to stay put. Daddy would just be a minute.

I yanked the car into park, threw open the door, and stepped out into the bitter cold. It wrapped around me like an icy python, darting into every available crevice, looking to snuff out every ounce of warmth my body held. My teeth chattered as I shut the car door.

A school guard wearing a neon reflective vest approached me, but I growled, literally *growled* at her, which worked. She held up her gloved hands in defeat and trudged away to call out someone else breaking child drop-off protocol.

In a voice barely above a whisper, I asked the admin to repeat everything she'd said. In a patient, practiced voice, she told me your car had succumbed to the ice. It spun out of control and hit an oak tree. You'd suffered a number of injuries on impact, and to help you recover, the doctors had placed you in a medically-induced coma.

I leaned my full weight against the car, my heart racing, my brain spinning. "They did what?"

"It's the safest way for her to recover. You should come to the hospital. We can tell you more when you arrive."

"Of course, of course. I'll be there as soon as I can."

By the time I hung up, I was completely numb from both the relentless cold and the horrific news. In spite of the shock, my innate pragmatism took over, thank God. I made two more phone calls, one to Rhonda, asking her to reschedule all of my meetings and calls for the week, and another to Felicity, asking her to watch the girls.

The snarling heat of the car's interior should've been welcome—you always claimed I ran it far too hot—but as I climbed back inside and gripped the steering wheel to steady my nerves, the hot air felt suffocating.

I cleared my throat and willed my words to come out smoothly and calmly. I couldn't lose it in front of our daughters. "Change of plans, girls. No school today. Instead, you're going to have a fancy tea party and French toast with Aunt Felicity."

As the girls cheered from the back seat, my heart pin-wheeled and I swallowed bile.

*

I wasn't ready to see you like that, broken and bandaged and so very ashen. Your skin, once the color of fresh cream, was the color of dirty snow. Your face was swollen and bruised, a misshapen piece of fruit, thanks to the airbags. Your leg was broken in two places, but it had been reset and shrouded in plaster. The doctor said one of your lungs had collapsed, and you had a concussion. Your injuries were many. Thus, the medically-induced coma. They had you on painkillers and steroids and other medications that had so many syllables, I wondered if the doctor was making them up for my benefit.

The worst part was that wretched plastic tube down your throat, the contraption responsible for your breathing, since you could no longer manage that on your own. I couldn't *see* you. I couldn't see my wife, the shining constant of my life.

My chest grew hot as a branding iron, and I feared I'd spontaneously burst into flame. My flesh would drip from my bones, and then... then, I'd be unrecognizable to you, too. Maybe that would be better.

"She'll wake up, right?" I managed.

The doctor gave me a kind smile. "In time, yes. We'll take her off the barbiturates that keep her under as soon as possible, but she has a lot of healing to do. I can't give you a definite timeframe. Of course, we'll do everything we can to aid in her recovery."

It wasn't the answer I wanted. My fists curled and hardened at my sides, ready to fly, but I held the impulse in. They were just trying to help.

I told the doctor thank you and shook his hand, though my palm was cold and clammy. He left the room, and we were alone. I sank into a chair, ran my hands through my hair, and listened to the metallic beep of your heart.

It's cliché, but it all felt like a bad dream.

I thought of that morning, of the time before. You'd surprised me, climbing atop my hips in the gray light of dawn, bringing your finger to your lips while grinning mischievously. You bit my shoulder to keep from waking the girls. You smiled at me. You gnashed your teeth in the throes of our lovemaking. You were so warm and alive.

A fine pressure mounted in my chest, and I tucked my head between my knees to alleviate a sudden swoon. As I gulped in sour hospital air, an object on the floor near your bed caught my attention. It was blindingly white, slightly round with distinct grooves, no larger than a fingernail.

I lowered myself to the linoleum and crawled toward the object until your hospital bedclothes kissed my shoulders. I held it up to the light. It was a tooth, an incisor, freshly lost by the look of it.

But how did it get there? Was it yours? Did the doctors knock it out when they inserted your breathing tube?

I hoisted myself up and stared down at you. I rolled the tooth between my fingers. It was like holding a piece of a puzzle but not knowing if it fit anywhere. Of course, I had to know.

The action felt unclean, treacherous even, but ever so gently, I curled your lip up toward the ceiling. And there, along the top gum line, I found it, the absence of you. Mystery solved.

I started toward the corridor, ready to alert a nurse to my discovery, but I paused at the threshold. I looked at you, sleeping, shattered, soundless, and decided you'd been through enough for one day. I didn't want them touching and examining you again. I wanted you to rest. I wanted you to come back to me.

And perhaps most importantly, I didn't want them to take this piece of you away from me. I slipped your tooth into the pocket of my woolen coat, sat down, and took your hand in mine.

*

Felicity's eyes were swollen when I arrived home, and I was afraid she'd told Bailey and Emily what had happened to you.

"I wouldn't do that, Dan," she said. "I told them I've been sick. Plagued with allergies. After I made French toast and turned on the TV, they stopped asking questions."

I made macaroni and cheese for dinner—from the box, with extra butter because we were out of milk—and I told the girls that you'd been in a bad accident, you were asleep, and you needed lots of rest to get better. Bailey asked if you'd become Sleeping Beauty, and that made me smile.

"Kind of," I said gently. Their little faces were confused and half-sad. I could tell they didn't know what to make of the news. "The doctors are using all the magic they can to help Mommy wake up."

"She needs a kiss," Emily said matter-of-factly.

"From a prince," Bailey added, looking sullen and pushing noodles around her plate.

"Well, there aren't too many of those around," I joked, but I realized much too late that I'd made a very adult jest to our very young children. At a really terrible time, to boot.

You were always so much better at these things. You never faltered, never made a mistake.

"Daddy, did you kiss Mommy, to try to wake her up?" Emily asked.

I hadn't. I couldn't. I kissed your fingertips, your forehead, your cheek, but there was no getting to your mouth. No way to kiss you properly. I gulped at my wine before answering. "Of course I did, sweetheart."

"It didn't work?"

"No, Em, it didn't." That admission made me feel like a failure.

"Can we visit Mommy?" Bailey asked, her eyes growing wet.

"In a few days, sweetheart. She might wake up by then." I didn't want them to see you yet. I hadn't been ready, so how could they be? I needed more time to prepare our girls. "In the meantime, you don't have to go to school this week."

Bailey gave me a half-smile. "Can I have Oreos?"

And I knew I'd give them all the junk food, the toys, the TV time I could that week. I'd give them every material thing I could manage, because I couldn't give them you.

*

It was stupid and maudlin of me, but after I tucked in Bailey and Emily, I opened a new bottle of wine, sank down into the coach, and watched our wedding video. I remember balking at the cost and making comments about gutted bank accounts while you rolled your eyes at me. In the end, I never regretted forking over the cash for it.

I'd always loved that video so damned much, because I'd never seen you smile like you did on our wedding day. It's like you were filled with light. Busting at the seams with happiness. Every moment that was captured that day, whether on film or video, featured you grinning like a love-struck idiot, and it made me extraordinarily happy. The thought that I could make you feel that way, it was second to none.

Before I knew it, the bottle of merlot was empty and our decorative pillows, the ones you picked out, were dark and wet. The video came to an end, the screen went dark, and I was swallowed by nighttime silence.

Stumbling upstairs to our bedroom seemed a terrible idea, and climbing into bed without you beside me seemed impossible. I decided to sleep on the couch.

I took off my coat and draped it over our recliner. I slipped off my loafers and set my glasses on the end table. I'd be sleeping in the clothes I'd worn that day, but I couldn't care less.

I bundled up under the blanket your mother crocheted us for Christmas last year and tried to get comfortable. My body lazed and calmed, but my mind could not be quieted. The room spun. My mouth went dry. A new round of tears threatened to fall. Consumed by the easy darkness of the living room, I'd never felt so alone.

But then I remembered.

I was up like a shot, groping about in the dim. The moment my hand dipped into my coat pocket, I felt better. More steady. Less manic.

Your tooth felt cool in my palm. It glowed in the shadows, a brilliant fragment of you, and I know it sounds crazy, but it felt like you were there. Perhaps on some other plane of reality, you were. Or maybe you hovered over me like an angel or a ghost—though I didn't really like those comparisons.

For the first time since that morning, I felt like everything was going to be okay. I settled back into the couch, rolling bone between my fingers, until I fell into a deep sleep and dreamed of your smile at our wedding.

*

I woke to two sets of small hands tugging at my clothes. I fluttered my eyelids open, and two blurry balls of energy danced before me. My head ached, and my body felt pinched and cramped. I groaned a little, and the girls laughed.

"You sleeped on the couch?" Bailey asked incredulously.

"I did."

"And you lost a tooth," Emily said. She was holding my hand, and there in my palm, your tooth twinkled in the morning light. I closed my hand and jerked to a sitting position. My brain spun and scrambled as a hangover pressed against my temples. Emily pried at my hand, thinking it a game. I kept my fist tight and fished for an explanation.

"It's Mommy's tooth," I began, and it was the wrong way to start.

Emily's eyes widened, and she crumpled to the carpet, wailing. In support of her twin sister, Bailey followed suit. Their harrowing cries escalated the pounding in my head, but that pain was nothing compared to my shame. What had I done?

I'd scarred our children for life, that's what I'd done. Not twenty-four hours after breaking the news to them that their mother was in a coma, I'd shown them one of her extracted teeth. I was sure a child psychologist would have a field day with this.

"Girls, girls," I said softly. "The doctors taking care of Mommy gave me this…"

I'm such a liar.

"This way it doesn't get lost. I can keep it safe."

The crying continued, the girls inconsolable, and I had no idea what they were thinking. I grasped desperately for some semblance of an explanation they would understand.

I took a breath and tried again. "We don't want the tooth to get lost, because then the Tooth Fairy won't be able to give Mommy her prize."

Bailey's cries softened, and she turned her big green eyes up at me. "The… the… the…" she said between sniffles, "Tooth Fairy? She's coming?"

I scooted off the couch to sit on the floor. I smoothed Bailey's hair back. Emily continued to whimper, but I knew if I could calm one of them, there was a good chance I could calm the other. "Of course, honey. The Tooth Fairy always comes, when anyone loses a tooth."

"But Mommy isn't here," Emily croaked, and my heart sank to the carpet.

"The Tooth Fairy will still come here, and we can save the prize for when Mommy wakes up and comes home." Of course, I didn't know if you'd ever come back to us.

Oh, the trauma I was inflicting…

But it did the trick. Bailey crawled over and nestled in my arms. A few moments later, Emily joined her. It should have been nice, this family cuddle, but my skin felt slick and oily, and I was clutching your tooth so tightly in my fist, I could feel it biting into the flesh of my palm.

*

That week, your prognosis remained the same, and our little family fell into a new routine. Felicity came over in the mornings. She made pancakes and poured cereal, did the girls' hair—I'd always been a disaster at that—and, ultimately, kept them as calm and happy as she could. Every day she brought over something new—coloring books, puzzles, movies—and I was filled with such gratitude.

Her presence in our home allowed me the opportunity to be by your side. I was there the moment visiting hours began, and the nurses often had to kick me out of your room when night fell.

I talked to you while you slept. I spent hours recounting the early days of our courtship, how you'd hooked me from the very beginning with your easy smile and boundless energy.

You'd always shone, you know that? And everyone around you became etched in light. Perhaps that's why we all loved you so much. You made us better than were, more brilliant. Brighter.

Though, in your hospital bed that week, hooked up to gadgets that beeped and snarled, you'd dimmed. Your skin looked like brittle paper, and I could almost see through it. I could trace all your veins, your network of life, though the thought of following that pattern across the whole of your body made me queasy. The bruises on your face bloomed and changed color, from startling purple to lazy green.

Every day, the nurse on duty would say that you'd improved, that she'd seen new color blossom in your cheeks. It was a nice gesture, but I figured they said those things because they were sorry for me, not because you'd gotten any better. I decided they conspired together, because they all said the same thing.

I brushed your hair every day. We watched TV, though I felt guilty that I was forging ahead with the police procedural we usually enjoyed together. It was a small thing, but it felt like a betrayal. I decided I'd abstain from watching it the following week. I'd wait for you.

I read you poetry, which you'd always adored and I'd never understood. Nothing changed in that regard.

Except for the night I had to place your tooth under a pillow to satisfy the girls' belief in the Tooth Fairy, I kept it with me always. I'd become increasingly protective of it. It was part of you, and if you woke up—no, *when* you woke up—I knew you'd miss it. Sure, dentists can give you fake teeth, but there's something about having the original *you* intact, isn't there?

And with your tooth at the ready, I'd be the fixer you've always expected me to be. I'd be the one who could put you back together again.

Sometimes, I'd take the tooth out and marvel at it. You'd always had great hygiene, so it was impeccable—strikingly white, though you'd never used whitening toothpaste, completely intact, without so much as a chip or a blemish or a stain.

As long as it was whole, I was able to convince myself that you'd remain whole, too.

And since it never left my side, neither did you.

*

The bar was dark and dirty and perfect and close enough to the hospital that I didn't feel guilty about going. It smelled like stale beer and bad decisions. Peanut shells crunched beneath my shoes as I made my way to a vinyl stool. The seat had been torn open and duct-taped back together. I could relate. After spending a week watching over you, remaining a steadfast solider by your hospital bed, I was coming apart at the seams. I needed a drink.

I ordered some top-shelf scotch, and the petite bartender, an older woman with bleached-blonde hair and heavy makeup, had to get out a step ladder to reach it. I saw her wipe dust off the bottle, too.

You always hated it when I drank scotch. You said it made me taste like smoke.

That night, that's how I wanted to feel. Like vapor. Like I could disappear. Because life without you… well, the week had proven that was all kinds of bullshit.

After I'd downed two glasses of amber-colored liquid in quick succession, the bartender set the bottle on the counter next to me. "You can pour your own, but I'm keeping an eye on you."

I nodded and gave her a bleary wave. The alcohol had begun to lace with my blood. My body grew warm, my fingers tingled, the edges of the room softened.

I thought I was ready for what would come next.

To tell you the truth, I expected to cry. I longed for it. I wanted to break down in front of strangers and wallow in their pity. I'd orchestrated the whole night, played it out in my mind. I'd go to a bar and share my sob story with any poor schmuck who'd listen. I'd tell them about you, how great you were, and how broken my life had become without you. My tears would earn me sympathy, a free drink, a pity fuck—anything would do.

I never could have predicted that my sorrow would desert me in my hour of need. That white-hot rage would bubble to the surface in its place. That after I finished my fifth glass of scotch, I really wanted to punch something.

The world could keep its condolences. I wanted a wild and violent release. The yearning for destruction snaked down my forearms and through my wrists. The weight of the empty tumbler in my palms felt satisfying and heady. I pushed hard against the glass, wondered how much strength it would take to crack it.

The blonde bartender came over and wordlessly took the bottle away from me, but I didn't care. The alcohol was just a primer, and I'd had plenty. It was doing its job, bringing everything to the surface.

I thought of you then—your jet-black hair and your porcelain skin and your long neck and the way you could make me laugh even when the world was chaotic. I thought of our girls, who'd inherited your dark hair, witty personality, and fear of spiders. I thought of what their lives would be like if you didn't wake up. I thought of the doctors and nurses at the hospital who'd kept telling me all week to be patient and wait and let you rest, and it suddenly seemed like they hadn't been doing *anything* to help.

And then I realized that I might lose you forever.

I pushed back from the bar, growling, sending the vinyl stool tumbling. My arm made a swooping arc and threw something small to the floor. The object skittered and bounced. I stomped over to it and smashed it beneath my shoe. I heard a small, bright pop, and in that moment, it was the sweetest sound I'd ever heard.

Looking back, I have no recollection of reaching into my pocket for your tooth. I just remember the noise it made when I crushed it beneath the heavy sole of my boot.

Not long after, I was unceremoniously booted from the bar by a rough-and-tumble bouncer. I went quietly, meaning I didn't fight him. But I guess I wasn't all that quiet, because the tears had finally come. I wailed and blubbered and stumbled through the cold, finally experiencing the rock-bottom release I thought I so desperately needed.

But as I zigzagged across the parking lot, drifting toward drunken incoherence, I recognized that the cost had been much too high.

I locked myself in my car, tossed my keys in the back seat, reclined the driver's seat, and sobbed in confinement. I kept reaching into my pockets, hoping to find another piece of you, hoping what had just happened in the bar had been a fever dream. But, of course, I searched in vain.

In my madness, I'd made sure there would be nothing left of you.

*

The buzz of my cell phone against my leg woke me the next morning. My eyes flicked open and then demanded to shut again when bright light barreled into my skull. The vibration in my pocket continued, so with my eyes screwed shut, I rummaged for the device. I brought it close to my face, cracked an eyelid just enough to see the screen for a nanosecond, and hit the answer button. I brought the phone to my ear.

"Hello?" My voice sounded as if I'd gargled with glass.

"Is this Daniel Roberts?"

"It is."

"I'm calling from Madison County Hospital. I have good news. Your wife, Claire, she woke up this morning."

My heartbeat surged. "She's, she's… she's not in a coma anymore?" Heat welled behind my eyelids, urging them open. The morning light was unbearable at first, but I pushed through the pain. My sight was blurry, as if I was underwater. Through the haze, I registered the outline of a steering wheel in front of me. I was in my car.

I groped at the dash, hoping it's true what they say, and old habits die hard. My fingers scrambled this way and that and eventually fell upon the familiar shape of my glasses. I slid them up the bridge of my nose, then blinked wildly. The first thing I saw clearly that morning was a sign proclaiming that this parking spot was for patients only. I was in the hospital lot.

A wave of relief washed over me. I closed my eyes and let my body sink into the leather driver's seat. You'd come back to me, and I was close by. Soon I would gather you in my arms and the world would be right again.

"Yes, Mr. Roberts, your wife is awake." There was something wrong with the woman's voice, even as she recounted what was supposed to be happy news. There was a pause on the line, and then the woman's voice again, nervous but firm. "But I'm afraid there's been an incident."

I felt like I'd stuck my finger in a light socket. I jolted upright, and the seatbelt was the only thing that kept me from slamming my chin into the steering wheel. "An incident? What kind of incident?"

"It appears that your wife was attacked last night."

I unbuckled my seatbelt and reached for my woolen coat, which I'd thrown on the passenger seat. When I lifted the material, a fine tinkling sound filled the car. When my eyes lit on the sound's origin, I let out a strangled cry.

Of course, the hospital admin didn't understand. She couldn't see what I saw.

"Mr. Roberts, I promise we're launching a full investigation into the matter."

I flipped the driver side sun visor down and peered into the mirror. My face was speckled with blood.

"Your wife may have been conscious at the time of the attack. We've tried to question her—gently, of course—but she wouldn't stop screaming. We had to give her a mild sedative, for her own safety. She's calmed down, but she keeps repeating your name. We think you being here could really help her. Also, the police are here. You should talk to them."

"Of course," I said, my voice hollow. "Of course. I'll be right there."

I let the phone slip from my fingers.

Shaking, I forced my gaze back to the passenger seat. Medical instruments, silver, sharp, and spattered with blood, reflected the grey light of morning. Strewn among them were small pieces of bone, thirty-one individual fragments in total, all of them extracted from your perfect mouth.

And then, we were both screaming.

R.C. (Renee) Scandalis adores all things make-believe. Accents and costumes make her giddy, Halloween is her favorite holiday, and she is an avid attendee at Rennaissance Faires. A San Francisco native, she received a proper hippy upbringing which she attempts to bestow upon her two boys, Jacob and Dex, despite the different times and culture of North Texas where they reside. Renee loves to be out in nature and is fortunate to go paddle boarding from her backyard, although her cat, Mew, is still not convinced it is a good idea, and watches warily from the shoreline. Learn more at www.arceewrites.com

About this poem, Renee says: "I have loved Poe since I was first introduced to him as a child, so when I got the call for submission I knew immediately this was the perfect project for me. I decided instantly that I would write about my cellphone as it is the only thing that sets my heart to pounding and my palms to sweating like Poe's themes. At first I thought I would use The Bells as it has the repetition I was looking for, but in the end The Raven has such a delicious rhyming pattern, I couldn't resist it."

Like the incessant tap-tap-tapping of the raven at the windowpane, we tap-tap-tap at our screens day and night. What would Poe have made of our ever-present digital ravens, I wonder?

THE CELLPHONE

R.C. Scandalis

Oh my heart is sink, sink, sinking, as my cellphone's blink, blink, blinking—
Muted for a moment's peace, but ripped away from reverie
by the screen I can't ignore.
Calling with its light, its singing, even though I've silenced ringing,
Notifications' constant pinging, calling for my soul for sure.
Mindfulness is hard to muster without peace—
its calling for my soul for sure—
This unsettled feeling, I truly do abhor.

Doomed to check all night and day, to see what others have to say,
There was a time almost forgotten, a tranquility I knew before.
Now I must have it close to me, I must check it constantly,
Free from it I'll never be, never be, no nevermore.
Days and weeks and years go by, but freedom comes, no nevermore—
This shackled feeling I deplore.

Once a tool but now my master, I must answer, answer, answer.
A quick response is expected, is demanded, or they are sore.
"A moment please, my lovely flower, to read this text; don't look so sour,"
"What's that you say? It's been an hour? Please just five minutes more;"
"Answer, I must, my love, I need just five minutes more."
Nine to five is gone for evermore.

Oh my god! This cannot be! I can't be out of battery!
How do I find my way with no phone to take me to my door?
I left today in such a hurry, I didn't plan, but not to worry
Into this store, I'll just scurry for a charger—it's how I got my last four.
For the power it is worth it; I would buy so many more,
so many more than just those four.
When confronted with a blank screen, I'll do anything to find a cure.

It's ok now, just don't panic, it's ok, let's not get manic,
I know I saw it on the bedroom floor.
But in my throat I feel the bile, all day without will be a trial—
I must sneak home in just a while, all day apart I can't endure.
I'll turn around, I'll just be late; to wait 'til lunch
I can't endure—
You'd do the same, of that I'm sure.

Now I've put it on my wrist, now my messages can't be missed.
Convenience comes tho' with a price, a price we pay that's sure.
Just one thing I've come to do, but hours later I'm still not through;
'Twas just one task that drew, drew me to the screen once more.
I'd planned to stay away today but that one task drew me
to the screen once more—
I fear peace comes nevermore.

I knew a man whose baby drowned; right there he was, his head bent down.
Enraptured by the screen he was, engrossed in watching who would score.
And to my own? I must confess, it's easier to send a text
Than try to talk to my son Dex; getting through seems such a chore.
Dinner with his phone in hand—getting through is such a chore.
Maybe we will talk again.
We'll talk again, we talked before.

Out of sight I will put it; I have strength, I can do it.
From where it lies, its calling, calling, "Check me! Check me! I implore!"
It feels like hours since I've checked, to see the likes, the tweets, the texts—
Trouble focusing on what's next, it's shouting at me from the drawer.
What's that? Just five minutes passed?
It's laughing at me from the drawer—
Its call too potent to ignore.

Vicki Weisfeld's short stories have appeared in Ellery Queen Mystery Magazine; Betty Fedora; *and recent anthologies, including* Busted: Arresting Stories from the Beat, Murder Among Friends, *and Bouchercon 2017's* Passport to Murder. *Her short mystery* Breadcrumbs *won the 2017 Derringer award for "long" short mystery fiction. She writes for the UK website crimefictionlover.com and is a member of Sisters in Crime, Short Mystery Fiction Society, Public Safety Writers' Association, and Mystery Writers of America. She dances—ballroom and flamenco—and is a dedicated genealogist. Her active website offers book and movie reviews, articles on the writer's craft, and travel tips: www.vweisfeld.com.*

About this story, Vicki says: "This was a delightful excuse to reread Poe—some of the more famous stories and some of the more obscure—as well as a few essays and poems. Beyond his discursive style, I noted some features that might work their way into a present-day story: obsessions, classical allusions, familial tendencies (always bad!), the dead and the not-dead. I was especially struck by the story Berenice *and the groom's obsession with his wife's teeth. In his introduction to the Poe collection on my bookshelf, W.H. Auden laments Poe's petty and vengeful biographer Rufus Wilmot Griswold, providing a name for my character, Wil Griswold. Getting a little back for EAP."*

If you've ever found yourself slowing down and staring at an accident, you know the competing sensations of horror, fascination, and gratitude that the victims aren't among your circle of friends. This story delivers on two of the three…

TOOTH AND NAIL

Vicki Weisfeld

People called us "the beautiful twins," and in our early years, when our stepmother dressed us in androgynous rompers, close family members could not tell which yellow-curled toddler was Tommy and which was I, Liz. I wonder whether we ourselves knew the difference between us, totally wrapped up in each other, consumed by the longing to create a whole of two halves. They say we did not begin to talk to anyone else until we were four. We did not need to.

No wonder Tom's betrayal felt like a self-inflicted wound.

Our memories, which only dimly record those early years, flared into vivid life a few days before our eighth birthday, when those airplanes hit the towers in New York—the *Twin* Towers. We knew about the poor trapped people, the horrifying collapse, the dreadful aftermath we should not have been allowed to watch, though we were, and we heard that some of those people leapt to their certain deaths, wresting an agonizing sliver of control out of their hopeless situation. We remember what our stepmother called "the resurrection walls," with the hopeful homemade posters headlined *"Missing…" "Have you seen…" "Please!,"* showing smiling faces that families couldn't yet comprehend were forever lost to them, the words exposing the wounds across their hearts. All of that, we do remember.

Although we cannot provide a comprehensive picture of our early childhood, our recollections make up for this incompleteness with later lucidity. The same year the towers fell, shortly after our birthday (on the first of October), the household that had seemed so solid and permanent to Thomas and me began its precipitous disintegration. Our stepmother, like our mother before her, died in a tragic—and with a mature hindsight, I would say suspicious—accident. We were told she was in the garden shed alone, bending over a pile of tulip bulbs she was sorting, when a slick-bladed garden knife slid from the shelf where it had been carelessly laid and pierced her skull.

Only two midnight-black cars crept along the cemetery's gravel paths behind the hearse that bore her casket. The heavy clouds of that oppressively gray day befitted the state of my brother and me, dully watching the raindrops that streaked the limousine's windows. From that melancholy afternoon forward, our father drank heavily, which made him, if possible, even less apt to display the support, consistency, affection, integrity, or guidance expected of a parent. Instead, he looms in our memories like a malevolent giant. The destructive spirits he poured into our mother's crystal glasses unbottled something evil in his own spirit, turning our home into treacherous terrain Tomás and I were ill-equipped to navigate.

We learned to move stealthily through its many rooms and remain out of sight. The housekeeper completed her chores before he stomped through the back door. As if by magic, dinner appeared on the table, floors were scrubbed, laundry folded, lawn and garden tended. We strived to assure that nothing we did, or did not do, would inspire a complaint that would cause him to turn his attention onto us. In this, we were not always successful. Our drunken father's blows on Thom's back pained me and sharp words spoken to me wounded him.

When we reached adolescence, our father claimed he still could not tell us apart, and when he wanted to punish Tamás, would have me lift my shirt to prove I was not he. In my mortification at being required to reveal my tiny breasts, a choking disdain rose inside me, but our father held the snapping leather belt with the heavy buckle that slashed and bit, and I remained silent.

You may be inclined to believe that our recollections from before these difficult years were not recorded because they were too much a part of ourselves to note. You might ask, does a fish know the water is there? If we *could* probe those earlier memories, perhaps we would find they extend as far back as the womb, wherein two beings, limbs entwined, swam together, aware only of each other and that keenly, every movement of the one necessitating accommodation by the other.

But must *I* be the one to adjust to everything? To every assault on the relationship between Thomas and me? I think not. I cannot, and I will not! If you read this account and cannot bring yourself to forgive what I have done— and I assure you this is no apology—at least you will know my reasons, and I daresay, in my situation, you would have done the same.

When at last we were of an age when we could leave home, we employed our mother's ample legacy, held in trust for us, to enable us to attend the same university, where we studied side by side. My nursing courses demanded my presence in the laboratory, studying the weaknesses of the human body, while Tomas worked for a degree that he said focused on strength: strength and security.

Near the completion of our studies, our father died. Drunk, he staggered around numerous safety barriers and stepped in front of a commuter train. From the whisperings at the funeral, we believed his casket contained very little of him. Because it was easiest for us to follow convention, we agreed he would be buried alongside our mother and stepmother, though if you could give either of them the choice, I daresay they would not wish to spend eternity in his company, however partial. Tomi inherited considerable investments, and the house and the two hundred acre farm it sat on were mine.

On the day of our college graduation, Tamsin made a shocking announcement: "I'm going to work in Silicon Valley." In that moment, the mirror I had gazed into my entire life, shattered.

"That's three thousand miles away!"

"I know where it is. It's where the best jobs are."

"But I have the house and the farm. I can't just leave it."

"You should stay, enjoy the property. Be a nurse. You'll be a good one."

"Boston, New York, and Washington would be just as good." *Somewhere closer. For pity's sake.*

"Liz, I already have the job."

"How can you do this to me?"

I cried. I wrung my hands, but despite all my pleas, he *would* go, he was going, he went. I silently vowed to bring him home. I concede he seemed happy in his new work. Perhaps that should have brought me some satisfaction or pride, some reciprocal pleasure, but it did not.

You undoubtedly appreciate that acquiring a rambling, hundred-and-fifty-year-old country estate was practically guaranteed to keep me too busy to think about life's larger questions, and the reasons I had been abandoned—yes, I *will* use that word!—by the love of my life.

To me, Tomi still inhabited every inch of our home. It was as if he had just left every room I walked into. His shadow flickered around corners. His breath was the breeze at the windows. I found him in the garden where, as children, we'd caught dragonflies and nibbled wood sorrel, in the basement where we honed our mechanical and electrical skills, in the garage where he nailed together birdhouses for me to paint. Put plainly, I persisted in wanting Tamati to come home, but with every gain in the strength of my importuning, his responses grew vaguer and more distant.

Finally, one of Toma's emails revealed the worm in the apple, the rot at the core of our relationship. It bore a stranger's name: Veronica. Before long, he deluged me with photographs of her—suspiciously blonde hair, sunglasses that hid her eyes, a vulpine smile, blinding white teeth.

According to Tomasz, Veronica was a social media maven, whatever that meant, while my letters sounded as if they were copied from one of the antique books I read. Guilty. The books in our family library, with all their archaicisms, had flowed through our ancestors' consciousness and now flowed through mine to his, enveloping him in the mind-habits of our forebears, a past that—I hardly need tell you—included no Instagrammatical Veronica.

He said I should adapt myself to Twitter, but nothing I want to express can be encapsulated in 140 characters, or, as he said it is now, 280.

Except... I *could* convey how I feel about Veronica, this woman I have never met, this trespasser on my private mindscape. For that I only need five characters: B-I-T-C-H! Five plus one for the exclamation point and, I suppose, one more for a space. If I typed it 40 times, it would make a perfect Tweet. Not a blissed-out bluebird, it would be a crow squawking from the treetops. BITCH! BITCH! BITCH! Thirty-seven more times. Tom planned to bring her to meet me at Christmastime.

Since Tam decamped to Silicon Valley, I pull the old books from our library shelves. I read their tissue-thin pages and sniff linen covers faded to the green of lichens. One of my favorite volumes chronicles the life of heroic Mithridates Eupator, King of Pontus, conqueror of Asia Minor, defender of Greece, enemy of the Romans, expert poisoner. The third of Mithridates's many wives was Berenice, her name the antecedent of that which nettles my waking mind, the loathed Veronica.

In the daytime, pipes and roofs and wiring and horticulture have not been my sole occupations. I also had a part-time job as a nurse at a local hospice. Long before Veronica made her unwelcome debut in my awareness, a housepainter charging an obscene amount learned of this employment and seduced me into obtaining pills for him. At first I refused, but he recognized a lonely spirit and over a period of weeks ingratiated himself with me, flattering me first with words, then with unanticipated caresses, and teasing me with doses of the kinds of pills he wanted. These stratagems worked in concert to overcome my resistance. Before long, I was raiding the medicine cabinets and bedside tables of patients who died—"for proper medication disposal," I planned to say if anyone challenged me.

Oddly, I cannot recall the details of the painter's no doubt colorfully spattered appearance. My Svengali! I cannot remember him because he, and all other flirtations I might have had or wished I had, were erased by the man he introduced me to, the red-haired Wil Griswold.

While the now forgotten and anonymous housepainter had been a pleasant diversion, I was completely overcome by Wil. He flattered and cajoled me, filling my time in the months before and after I first heard the hated name, yet as much and in as many ways as I wanted him, he would never be my Veronica.

He carried himself with such a surfeit of confidence, it persuaded me I might borrow a little of it and use in it persuading Tomi to return. He was light as a moth, as air, and had an air about him, a bracing chemical tang that lingered after he left. That was the meth.

He needed every mote of his overweening confidence to persist in the dangerous work of cooking up methamphetamine in his cramped garage near town. A hundred yards from my house was an outbuilding that was much more suitable, larger and more isolated, a barn in fact, and he soon persuaded me to let him use it as his manufactory. In return, he provided me with free samples. When I say they were free, I mean money was not exchanged. I cannot say they were without cost. Oh, no. The cost was high.

My dalliance with the housepainter had proved that, while I carry a feminine simulacrum of Toma, also, either surrounding it or at its core, I cannot say which, I harbor my father's weakness. I needed Wil. My *body* needed him like my father needed drink, and it was a toss of a coin whether it was the affection he showed me or the drug that held me more strongly in his power. Well-informed through my nursing education regarding the risks, perversely, I persisted in following Wil's impish lead.

You will not be surprised to learn that I soon forsook my job. Before long the days when I loved my work were so far beyond recollection as never to have existed. When I told my employer I was leaving, she cried, and to make her stop I pulled an acceptable reason out of the air and claimed I was going back to school. My colleagues, who saw me more often than she did "in the field," gave me a surly celebration. I could tell they were jealous of my impending freedom yet suspicious enough of my recent behavior to be glad to see the back of me. They gave me a card in a bulging envelope that contained more than two hundred dollars they had collected to help me buy books. I gave it to Wil.

I suspect the hospice patients or their more lucid relatives passed the word that I made them nervous.

Ha! Don't talk about nervous!

They made *me* nervous with all their demands—demands I could not meet because I could not make them young and vigorous again. Nor could I heal them after their squadrons of doctors had done their best (or worst). Hoarders' paradises, their houses were, too hot and filled with miasmas of nasty smells. If you have a suspicious mind, you may suppose I skimmed their drugs before I went. I prefer to think I liberated them for a rainy day. By the time I would need the unnoticeably few pills I took from each of them, they would be long past needing them.

I picked at a sore on my arm and reflected on what Christmas would be like with a stranger in the house. However, as it turned out, Tom's plans changed. He sent me a selfie of them, a grinning twosome, and explained they could not make a Christmas visit after all.

"Veronica wants to spend the holidays with her family. Six brothers and sisters!" Did all of them have such big white teeth? It would be like a vacation with beavers, or maybe wolves.

"Take your sunglasses," I wrote back. Tom replied "?"

I did not answer. They would visit in the spring for certain, he promised. I printed out that picture and ate it.

In early December, a big brown UPS truck delivered a big brown cardboard tube. My present from Tomas! Inside was an enormous poster, Tommasso and Veronica. Life-size, Veronica inspired a suffocating revulsion that swelled in my chest, putting such pressure on my ribs they threatened to burst through my skin. Tom wore a Santa hat, looking like the old me—the me before I lost forty pounds—with a fluffy white mustache and wig. *She* held a sprig of holly in her frightening teeth. I felt I was looking into the headlights of an oncoming Mercedes.

With a sharp knife I pierced the thick paper and sawed all around her mouth, then taped her sparkling grin onto my own face. I took it off only at mealtimes. After a few weeks my new mouth was sticky with food bits and somewhat wrinkled. I liked it anyway.

*

March arrived, flinging undecided weather with abandon. Wil had occupied the barn for nine months, birthing his lucrative product. Tomé and Veronica's arrival was only a few weeks away. I surveyed the condition of the house. If Wil would give me an extra dose or two, I could clean it, attic to cellars, in a couple of days. Stripping the sheet off the full-length mirror, I surveyed the condition of my body. Not so quickly or easily dealt with. What to do? What to do? What would *you* do?

I'd hide my dull and brittle hair under a floppy hat, some scarves. Could I plausibly wear a hijab out of solidarity with my Muslim sisters? Did I have any Muslim sisters? No. Anyway, Te'oma was my brother, it wouldn't make sense. Sense! What about any of this makes sense? How could one twin steadily ascend in life, while the other rode the long escalator down?

Winter's padding—thick boots, bulky sweaters, down coats—had disguised how much weight I had lost. Now my clothes hung on me. I had to cinch one of Tomek's old belts around my jeans, its long end waving like a pit viper. I would order new clothing online. Loose flowy dresses, knitted vests, voluminous shawls. Anything to disguise how little of me clattered underneath. I did not need to be a cleromantic for these rattling bones to foretell my future. You hear heavy-set women joke about their weight as being "more to love," so, I asked myself, what did that mean for me?

Wil offered a ready answer, by deed and word. I had seen teenage girls sneaking away from the barn at night, picking their way through mud and dirty remnants of snow. I seethed and rattled pans and threw things for a few days and finally confronted him. He said I was having another of my hallucinations— what a liar!—but, "as long as we're on the subject," he said, "fucking you is like banging a skeleton. No offense."

I threw my bowl of oatmeal at him and locked myself in the bathroom. I swallowed the last of my stolen anti-anxiety pills and confronted a sight I usually avoided. My own face.

Sunken cheeks, sallow skin, lusterless eyes. Pulling away Veronica's no-longer-so-dazzling paper smile, I studied my mouth. My teeth looked like a destruction site, cracked, broken, and pockmarked with cavities. I'd stopped brushing them when the bathroom sink flowed with a river of blood.

When they arrived, I would smile with my eyes and firmly closed lips. I would avoid words containing the letter "s" because a broken tooth made me lisp. I gave myself fits of laughter saying "please pass the sugar." I must point and nod.

Tamsyn and Veronica planned to stay a week, though he needed to spend a few days in Baltimore at a meeting that involved an overnight stay. With that information, the spark of an interesting idea flared in the back of my mind, and, while I worked on external appearances, I stoked its flames until it blazed.

In one of my last acts before their arrival, I retaped Veronica's mouth onto the poster, hoping they wouldn't notice its ragged and curling edges. On closer inspection, I was sure they would. *She* would. I tore the poster into curling strips and burned them in a rusty barrel.

*

After a long dark winter of the soul, seeing Tomi at last was the first day of spring. Wil joined us for dinner the first night, though I ignored him, and

Veronica, too, come to that. She was exactly as expected, all kind smiles that failed to mask her devilish intentions. Meanwhile, Tom studied me, not in his familiar, affectionate way but with a look of concern. One morning we walked around the full extent of the property. Two hundred acres in all, most of it farmed by a neighbor whom we called Farmer Cashcow, whose rent of the fields provided a tidy supplement to my barely existent income.

When we were far from the house and yard, he said, "I don't like Wil." I, of course, already knew exactly how he felt.

"Why not?" I was all innocence, a word I could not say.

"I think he's a bad influence. He strikes me as untrustworthy, and the people who visit him look a bit… disreputable."

"Really?"

"You don't want those sorts of people on your property."

"Our property," I said.

"It's yours now. My life isn't here anymore. It's in California. With Veronica. We plan to get married."

I pressed my lips together until I could trust myself to speak. "I—" I wanted to say "miss you," but "mith you" lacked the seriousness I needed to achieve. "I don't like being without you. Alone here."

"I can see you're unhappy. You're skin and bones. How's your job? Did you have to take time off for our visit?"

"No." That part was truthful. "Work. You know."

"I mean it about Wil. What's he doing in the barn, anyway? It smells awful."

I almost giggled, thinking about trying to say the word "scientist." "Oh, chemical lab, kind of thing."

"In a barn? That's not like any laboratories I know."

I paused to select my words carefully. "Preliminary work. A real lab will come later."

He could detect evasion when he heard it and gave me a funny look. Fortunately, he had no interest in visiting Wil's "lab." Nor did he probe my relationship with Wil. Possibly he had already guessed what it was, even though this week Wil was staying with "a friend," he told me, and visited the barn only a few hours each afternoon. With Toomas in our house, the needle registering my interest in Wil had fallen to zero, nevermore to rise.

We moved through the days like pieces on opposite sides of a chessboard, until Tomos left for Baltimore. I channeled my inner Mithridates and added a few crushed chinaberries to Veronica's dinner. Throughout the night, every time the bathroom door squeaked closed, I sighed contentedly. I arose early, occupying the bathroom for my morning routine, which, if I was leisurely about it, required about ninety seconds. Elbows planted on the windowsill, I watched the morning mist rise over Farmer Cashcow's fields.

Veronica padded to the closed door then back to her room. A few minutes later she padded to the door again. A light tap. "Sorry to bother you, Liz. Will you be in there much longer?"

"Oh, good morning!" I said in a hurrying way. "Give me a moment."

"Of course. Good morning to you."

I contemplated the mist for another ten minutes, then flew out of the bathroom clutching towel and toothbrush, both perfectly dry and unused. She leaned against the wall, arms wrapped tightly around her stomach. She'd managed to hold it in. At least I wouldn't have to clean up after the bitch.

I cooked bacon and toasted frozen waffles. I could not eat such a breakfast, not with my teeth, nor could she with that queasy stomach. The smells drifting upstairs eventually summoned her to the kitchen. She was pale as paper. "Bad night?" I frowned, sympathetic.

"I don't know what it was. I'll just have some tea."

"Travel can do that. Different water."

"Maybe." She paused. "Liz, I was wondering. Why do you call Tom by so many different names? He thinks it's funny, but it's... different."

I shrugged. "Habit." I would never tell her the whole truth, that I clung to a childish superstition that I could hold onto him if I did not let his spirit slip past me in the guise of a Tomaž, Tàmhas, or Tomica. "I'll make you my herbal tea. You'll think you're drinking a chemical factory, but it will take care of a bad tum-tum like you wouldn't believe." It was exhausting to come up with sentences that didn't use the "s": tastes, smells, stops, solve, stomach, son-of-a-bitch were all discards in that last one. The medicine taste came courtesy of Wil. One part peppermint tea, six parts meth. Or was it seven? Possibly her body wouldn't be able to withstand it. We'd know soon enough.

She brought her empty cup to the sink and grabbed hold of the counter, swaying. "That was disgusting."

"Effective, though."

My fresh-washed instruments lay drying on a folded towel. Pliers, chisel.

"You certainly take good care of your tools," she gasped. Despite her growing distress and the string of drool reaching the counter, her teeth gleamed temptingly.

"Yeth," I said, and gave her my best, full-on, meth-mouth grin.

*

When Tom returned Saturday afternoon, I greeted him warmly. I'd made a strawberry rhubarb pie. "Your favorite," I said, having rehearsed "berry and rhubarb," if he didn't remember.

"Awesome! Where's Veronica?"

I looked around the kitchen as if she might be standing unnoticed beside the refrigerator. "Not with you?"

"Of course she's not with me. Why would she be?"

I scratched a scab on my shoulder. "When Veronica left, I thought... Baltimore with you."

"She left?"

"Friday." I gazed out the window, noticing Wil's pickup stop in front of the barn. Another grueling methology session ahead. I had a monster headache and swallowed a couple of painkillers with some coffee.

"What did you say to her?" Tomáš asked.

Wil exited the truck and pulled some supplies out of the back.

"Nothing, we got on fine." On the windowsill sat a jelly glass holding a collection of small rocks. Very shiny. Very white.

Wil trudged toward the barn door.

"Did she go back to San Francisco? Did she leave in a car? Who picked her up?"

"I don't know, Tuomo. A cab?" I shrugged.

Wil opened the barn door and went inside. I would know when he turned on the lights. Everyone would. I counted five seconds.

A fireball burst through the barn roof with the roar of all the thunder in the world. I screamed.

"What the—!" my brother shouted. We must have watched for a full sixty seconds, stunned, before he had the presence of mind to call 911. As it turned out, a passerby had already called it in, and cars were stopping along the roadside to watch and generally impede the access of the emergency vehicles.

The volunteer firemen found us huddled on the back stoop. I was hunched over, head in my arms, my shoulders shaking—crying, they might have believed.

Our barn was totally engulfed. The old wood snapped and crashed, sending up sparks. Dense smoke darkened the sky. The pungent smell in the air made it barely breathable. When I looked up, the flames had reached the high branches of a nearby elm tree, and a cluster of leaves was outlined with fire. Saving the barn was never considered. No one would go near it with the risk of further explosions. Someone backed Wil's pickup out of the danger zone.

The deputy sheriffs weren't long in arriving. I expected they would have a long list of questions, and keeping my mouth shut in a state of numbed shock seemed my most effective play, much better than laughing in their faces.

Tommi answered most of the questions—"Wil Griswold, that's his truck," "chemical lab," "a renter," "a few months."

"How well did you know him?" a deputy asked me point-blank.

"Wil? Friend of a painter I hired a while ago." I stammered, gesturing toward the exterior of the house and its still-bright shutters. "I needed the rent."

"It's a big place for her to keep up all by herself," my brother said in my defense, I believed, taking heart. *Exactly what I'd been telling him.*

"Did you know what he was doing in there?"

I shook my head. "I don't go back there. Other people did. I didn't know them." *Strangers.*

"So he had a lot of visitors."

I nodded. "They never bothered me."

"The ones I saw looked pretty sketchy," my brother said. "Not the kind of people my sister associates with." I envied him all those "s's." *My thithter athothiath with.*

The deputy studied the distance between the house and the barn. *Possible,* he seemed to be thinking. *It's possible she didn't know.* My scabs itched under the long sleeves of my sweater. I shrugged and briskly rubbed my arms.

"Cold?" Tom tightened his arm around my shoulders.

"Our detectives will be investigating and so will the Fire Marshall."

"Good," I said. *That's that.*

The next few days were chaotic, and I rarely bothered about what day or time it was. Coming down off the meth, I slept a lot, which Tom attributed to a stress reaction. I wouldn't be using any more of that drug, as I had no intention of making friends among the local lowlifes. Wil had been a one-off.

During those days following the fire, though, several events occurred that you might presume didn't involve me at all, except as observer, and yet were vitally important to me. The first was when the investigation determined Wil had been running a meth lab.

"Oh, my god. Is that… dangerous?" I asked the detectives, clapping my hand over my mouth to hide my risky diction.

By the time they explained to me in detail the many risks involved, they had convinced themselves that the conflagration was undoubtedly only a matter of time and if Wil had any sense at all, he should have known better, thus confirming their assumption that drug dealers are either stupid or careless or both.

"Why do that…?" I pulled my lips down over my teeth and trailed off, puzzled.

Equally eager to describe the politics and economics of drug culture to a citizen whom they by now considered rather dim, they enjoyed having a wide-eyed, courteous listener.

During these conversations, Tom was outside supervising the removal of what remained of the barn. Neither he nor I had needed to mention that I had trained as a nurse and should have had some experience of the world.

Imagine my delight when we were alone again, and Tom assured me he'd taken a temporary leave from his job, so he could stay with me "until this mess is cleared up." It was lucky for me that Tamsin couldn't read me like I could still read him.

Meanwhile, he called every person he could think of who might have seen Veronica or know where she was. There weren't many cab companies or car services in our area, and none had picked her up.

"A friend?" I asked. "If only Veronica had confided in me," I said. "Had told me *any*thing."

*

Tom and I and a pair of detectives were arranged around the kitchen table when he shared with them the mystery of the missing fiancée. Their interest visibly perked up.

"Well, sir," one said, "it isn't public knowledge yet, but we actually recovered two bodies from the fire. We knew the one near the door was Griswold, because your sister saw him go into the barn right before the explosion." I nodded helpfully. "But," he continued, "the other one... I don't know how else to say this... seems to have been nailed to the floorboards of the hayloft."

"My god!" Tuomas cried. "You must be..." but then he must have realized this was not something they would joke or be wrong about.

I clapped my hands over my mouth and moaned.

As gently as he could, the detective said, "That victim might possibly have been female... could be your missing fiancée."

"Occam's Razor," the other detective said.

Impressed? I was, though it was a touch cold-hearted.

"Can I—do I have to—would it help for me to identify..." Tom said.

"That isn't necessary, or even possible, in fact. The fire was... If it really *is* her, and not one of our transient drug addicts, which to me seems more likely, we may not be able to prove it."

"What about DNA?" Tom asked.

"Maybe. But the bone fragments were exposed to so much heat; the coroner doesn't think they would show anything."

"Why not?" I asked and reached out a hand to grip Tom's arm.

They loved an attentive audience.

"DNA degrades in a bad fire, and any test results aren't reliable."

The other detective spoke up. "There is one thing, though, that might help. We found part of a jaw, but no teeth."

"That's not Veronica then," Tom said. "Her teeth are beautiful." He broke down.

You can imagine how much will-power it took not to steal a glance at the windowsill, at the jelly jar and its gleaming white nuggets.

"But, Tom," I asked, "why would Veronica even have *been* there? And what happened to her luggage? Her handbag?"

"That's right," he said, relieved. "You don't take your suitcases to a barn. She wouldn't have done that."

And she hadn't. Her clothing and cosmetics were in my dresser drawers. I'd buried the rest in an unused, far corner of one of Farmer Cashcow's fields.

"Unless she and Griswold were planning to…" one of the detectives started to say and thought better of it.

I was silently grateful for the faint suspicion he'd draped over Veronica's memory. This would make it easier for Tom to forget her. I ran my tongue over my jagged teeth.

It will be so simple to glue her teeth onto mine. Wearing her clothes, flashing her smile, I'll make my beautiful twin mine again.

Penelope "Penny" Paling is fond of the odd. Her focus is on writing practical characters living in an impractical world. She is a relentless advocate of women—real and fictional—and aims to write female protagonists that women of all ages can identify with and believe in. She lives in the Phoenix area. Connect with her at pennypaling.com

About this story, Penny says: "This piece was inspired by Poe's Ligeia. I've mirrored many of the original elements in this update but have also opted to directly challenge a few. For example, the narrator here is neither unreliable nor male: rather, I've shifted the point of view from the widower to his new partner. The narrator, description, and situation are all updated to reflect a post-feminist, contemporary America. It explores the question, 'How would a modern woman handle loving a troubled man and the ghosts that haunt him?'"

No one goes through life without picking up at least a little bit of baggage—and sometimes that poses challenges for a relationship. So what do you do when the past isn't so easily dismissed?

MARCELA

Penelope Paling

I first saw Leo while on a bike ride through the town I grew up in.

It was the fall and homecoming activities were in full force. I was back home for the first time since my high school graduation eight years earlier. We were all in town to support my youngest cousin, Katherine, who was in the running for homecoming queen.

Things had grown stale between my parents and I after only a couple of days, so I pulled my old bike from the back of my dad's workroom, cleaned the rust off the gears, aired up the tires, and made my way down the driveway.

Without a truck or off-road vehicle, there weren't many places in town to go. Outside of my neighborhood, which was a cluster of about a dozen historic houses, you turned onto the main thoroughfare Bells Farm Road. Immediately, you passed the combined junior high and high school, as well as a single, official-looking building which was home to the post office, police station, and library. From the main road, the markers of farming were visible—infinite rows of berms ready for next year's planting—but very few houses remained. Most of the original farms had been swallowed up by a larger outfit in recent years. Still, my parents held tight to the community and often wondered aloud why I had stayed in Boston after graduating college.

The crumbling sidewalk gave way to gravel as I left the main part of town. The sun hung low. We'd raced this way on bikes a thousand times as kids, but now it made my legs burn and the seat felt too small.

I stopped for a moment at the top of a hill. Looking out in the distance, the road stretched on for miles before disappearing behind trees. To my left, a developer had razed an acreage to build new homes in the next town over. To the right was the town's original church-turned-schoolhouse. It had been abandoned after World War II when the new schools had been built.

Even from a mile away, it was clear someone had recently repaired the property's original stained-glass windows. A truck was parked down its driveway, and two dogs were wrestling in the field in front of it. It seemed as if someone was trying to turn it into a home.

The windows flickered colorfully as a light went on inside. The main door opened, and the silhouette of a man appeared in the doorway, whistling and gesturing to the dogs. He walked around the corner and into shadows. A tiny pop of flame appeared as he lit a cigarette. Except for the tiny orange orb, his face was black. Still, I could feel eyes on me.

With that, I could no longer ignore the chill that was settling in for the evening. The bike tires scraped harshly against the rocky dirt as I turned to go.

The ride home felt faster than the ride out had been. Even with the irritations it held, there was a warmth to riding back toward my childhood home.

*

The next day was the homecoming game. During half-time, Katherine—the most shining example of our family's trademark blonde hair and blue eyes— stood proud and glittering next to a tall boy of equal popularity. The game was a game. In the end, I could not tell you what was happening from moment to moment, but the home team won, which is the hope, right? And it was fun to sit in the stands with my extended family while my cousin, Jack, spiked and then knocked back warm ciders he bought from the same snack stand we had worked at together during high school. More than once, he leaned over and deftly passed the metal flask to me while our moms shimmied uncomfortably, if not disapprovingly, in their seats.

Immediately after the game, Jack and I grabbed our sweaters and walked to the town's only bar. Had I not already sipped enough from the flask to earn a small buzz, he never would have talked me into it.

The air in the bar was warm and thick: with body heat, beer foam, and nostalgia. It was also crowded. There was the standard din of the bar—beers opening, glasses clinking, and voices slurring happily—but there was also a frequent squeal or shout as one person recognized another they had not seen in some time. Other than family, it was doubtful that anybody would squeal upon seeing me, but anxiety mounted nonetheless.

Thanks to aggressive maneuvering, Jack secured an open spot at the bar, with one stool for us to share. He let me sit, mostly because my legs were still jelly from the previous day's bike ride, and we waited for service. We gossiped for a while about our parents; my aunt and uncle also wanted him to move home to settle down. We both laughed at the thought of him settling down at all. Two rounds later, Jack announced, "Gotta piss!" before disappearing into the throng of people.

I was not alone for long. The man sitting to my left lifted his head in contemplation of striking up conversation, then dropped it down several times before finally asking, "Were you riding your bike out near the old schoolhouse yesterday?"

I turned my head, but not my body, and half-smiled. I pulled my drink in closer to my body. Living alone in Boston had left me wary of strangers, men, and bars. "I was."

He nodded. "That's my place. I've been working on it for a couple of years."

I took a sip of my drink and fished for a reply. Remembering the stained-glass windows, I said, "It looks like a labor of love."

His eyes looked wet as he stared off into space. He said, "My wife loved it when she saw it."

I nodded and looked around. Partly for his wife, partly for Jack.

The ice in his glass settled into a new pattern. He swirled it and took a sip. He had yet to fully turn his head. From the side, I could see that he had a long, narrow face, high cheekbones, dark—black?—hair that was neatly trimmed. He smelled of smoke, which made sense. He also smelled of scotch.

He slurped the final drops from his glass. He was quiet for so long that I figured that was the end of things. I began to relax back into my seat and resume people-watching.

"Hi." Jack appeared then with a twinkle in his eye. He offered a hand to the stranger and said, "I'm Jack, Claire's *cousin*."

Leo began to turn and take Jack's hand. Before he could speak, I explained, "Leo is renovating the old schoolhouse."

Leo stood up to fully face us. He looked me square in the eyes, one corner of his lip curling upward. For a moment, it was as if the whole room was designed to color-coordinate with his hazel eyes and dark features.

Jack nodded in appreciation. "Very cool, man."

As if by magic trick, cash appeared by his empty glass and he said, "It was nice to meet you both. You two have a great night."

We stared as he disappeared into the crowd between us and the main entrance. Jack took the now-empty barstool and, smiling, announced, "Well, you did always have a thing for weirdos."

*

The next morning, Jack headed back to Indianapolis and I was alone with my parents once more. I tagged along with my mother on her errands. She browsed the stands at the weekly farmer's market for over an hour, talking about how much better the onions had been before so-and-so took over the community garden. "But the potatoes have improved," a fellow gardener who knew my mom, chimed in. This sparked a hot debate which I took as my cue to find coffee.

Outside a tiny coffee shop on the main drag were two familiar dogs leashed to a bike stand and waiting patiently. Inside, I saw Leo in line a few people ahead of me. His smile was easier in the daylight. He looked to be five or six years older than me. Even with paint-spattered work clothes on, he reminded me of the guys from my MBA program. If we had been in Boston, he was exactly the type of guy I would want to talk to. But here we were in rural Indiana.

He took his coffee and chatted amicably with the server without noticing me. It was just as well.

My mom came in just as my drink was ready. She spoke hurriedly about the friend she had just chatted with, relenting, "She is right about the potatoes." She spoke in a hushed whisper as if there were spies around every corner. Given the size of the town, this wasn't far from the truth.

Back outside, Leo was standing near the entrance. He smiled at us both and my mother immediately beamed. "Leo!"

"Sandy," he said with a nod toward her. Then to me. "*Claire.*"

She turned suddenly to me. "You've met? How wonderful! Leo is our favorite handyman. He's going to help us spruce up the house once we figure out what to do with it."

He smiled at us both. I didn't understand how this confident, smiling man was the same awkward mope from the night before.

"You should come by for dinner tonight," my mom said suddenly.

He and I both jumped a bit in surprise: me in my shoulders, him in the brow. He looked at me and I looked away as nonchalantly as I could. I knelt down to pet the dogs because neither of them made me nervous.

*

Dinner happened. My dad, my mom, the bright-eyed carpenter, and myself made small talk over a pot roast. My mom did almost all of the talking; I'm convinced this is how she stays thin.

After dinner, I gathered the dishes and headed into the kitchen for some quiet. Leo appeared before too long. My parents had put on *Jeopardy!* in the TV room. He picked up a towel and began drying what I had already washed in the rack. We didn't say much but the whole thing left me wanting to smile so when he asked me to come and check out his house the next day, it seemed like the right thing to do.

My mom was thrilled at the idea of Leo and I meeting again. She wondered aloud: "Maybe you'll come back home to stay after all?"

*

We met the next day at the gate of his property. The grounds were made up of ten acres, with one half of the land covered in woods and the other half meadow. We walked across the meadow to the main structures: a building and a barn. They sat on the meadow side of the property, were made of weathered wood paneling, and had a makeshift quality from so many different uses through the years.

He began walking toward the house and I followed. "I hadn't planned to move out here or stay this long." He chuckled to himself, reminiscing. "My wife had a thing for American antiques, so we'd go on road trips to find them. We came through town and she fell in love with the biggest antique in the whole town."

My body remembered that I knew nothing about this man. I hung back.

He looked back over his shoulder with a smirk. It faded quickly as he saw me standing steady with a firm grip on my bike handles. He turned halfway— one shoulder pointed toward me, the other toward the house—and announced, "It's not haunted."

"I know." I shifted my weight on my feet and steeled myself. "I used to hang out here as a kid." He put his hands on his hips, uncertain, so I asked what seemed to be the obvious question:

"What happened to your wife?"

I watched him as he measured his words. His gaze moved between the property, my face, and the ground. "She died unexpectedly. It was a brain tumor." This explained the wet eyes at the bar. "This," he gestured to the property, "has helped keep me busy."

The bike wheels squealed as I wheeled them down the hill to the house.

*

The front of the building was an add-on from when the building was a school. It had been recently converted into a small kitchen.

"Before Marcela died, I was an attorney. I worked long hours for a large firm and wasn't home much. After she passed, I decided to come out here and fix the place up. You know, in memory of her." He tapped his fingers on the kitchen counter appreciatively. I nodded.

"There's more." He continued into the main living area. The church pews

39

were long gone; they had been replaced with upholstered seating and rugs. The electrical was updated, too, with fans, blinds, and overhead lights all running on remotes. He was particularly proud of this.

The space was also filled with a motley crew of bold art pieces in antique frames. Stone Foo Dogs rested beside delicate crystal statuettes. One wall was dotted with antique cuckoo clocks all showing different times. There were pieces of pottery with cracks that had been filled with gold. The couches and chairs were draped with thick, woven blankets and embroidered pillows.

There were at least a thousand books in the room. The entire length of one wall was outfitted with floor to ceiling bookshelves, with a rolling ladder to reach the highest tomes. The shelves had no backing and some sections were vividly backlit by the stained-glass windows behind them.

The wall opposite the kitchen and loft area, the one which would have been home to a pulpit or blackboard, had been replaced with a sizable stone fireplace. Over the mantle was a large piece of art, a Gothic piece with a macabre orgy of monsters and humans. All I could do was stare. He said, "Family heirloom. It's creepy but I never get bored of looking at it."

Up the ladder, inside the loft, sunshine stubbornly worked its way through two tiny windows. The ceiling was sloped and fairly low. He squatted down beside me as we stood in the middle of the space. The bed was low to the ground and draped lazily in quilts.

The house fought a constant breeze and so was never totally quiet. Vivid tapestries covered the walls and rafters, woven with metallic-hued thread that glistened as they wafted.

The tapestries shimmied and rustled, the walls whistled, and the old church bell—which was closed up but still in the steeple—occasionally chimed lightly through the walls.

*

I flew back to Boston the next day, but Leo and I chatted continuously over the next couple of months. To my mother's satisfaction, I returned for the holidays. By spring, I'd arranged with my employer to work remotely from my hometown, with plans to commute to Boston once per quarter.

I found myself daydreaming about home improvement projects and world travel simultaneously. Perhaps it was from all the stories Leo shared.

I'd learned about his family—they were historically Romani, though not as interested in curses as the movies made them out to be—and about his marriage. He had traveled a great deal before and during his marriage. They had met during a semester abroad in college. "She was from Italy herself," he explained. "My family loved how much she reminded them of our heritage. She fit right in."

I tried to appreciate her through his eyes but it was a struggle not to feel envy for a woman so beautiful and so loved.

*

I returned home, both literally and figuratively, and set up a makeshift office on my parents' kitchen table. My mom was thrilled at my return, and, if nothing else, my dad seemed happy to have somewhere to send my mom's nervous chatter.

In the evenings, Leo and I continued our courtship: grabbing pizza or ice cream, taking long walks, and talking. For the first few weeks, he dropped me off each night at my parents. Eventually, I began to stay the night.

Most nights we kissed passionately and fell into bed together, if we even made it that far. Some nights were different, though.

He was already a quiet man but, somehow, on these nights he was quieter. It felt like a fog settled onto the property. Even the perpetual breeze halted. He would grab a glass of scotch, his guitar, and disappear onto the darkness of his porch with the dogs. A part of me wanted to follow him out there, but the rest of me knew better.

This was the only downside to our domestic experiment.

I lay in bed alone, working on my laptop or reading. He knew a lot of songs, but one always stuck out. It was a sad song I knew and loved, from an artist with a power to make even sad songs lift you up. Something in the way Leo sang it made my heart ache.

When I fell asleep before he came to bed, I always stirred when he crawled in. His footfall, the creaking floorboards, and the rustling of the tapestries sounded like thunder in contrast to the quiet of the house.

I would stare at the ceiling and wonder if I would ever get used to the music—both his and the house's.

*

One night soon after I began staying the night, I woke with a start. My body was coiled around the pillows with my back against the headboard. The sheets were drenched in sweat, as was I. Disoriented, I hit my head on the rafters above my pillow.

In the moments before I woke, I'd dreamt that I was lying in the same bed and a woman with piercing black eyes was hovering over me, nose to nose, staring straight into my eyes. She looked angry and her lips were moving as if she was shouting, but I couldn't hear a word of it.

I looked around the room as if the woman were still there. It was stone silent except for the usual rustling of the tapestries. Leo was not yet in bed and my

41

mouth tasted oddly metallic, so I headed downstairs.

It had become habit not to look directly at the awful painting after dark, and so I fumbled a bit as I made my way passed it and into the bathroom.

The taste had been that of blood. It wasn't much, and I couldn't find a cut in my mouth, but I thought about the woman's face so close to mine and opted to brush my teeth.

When I came back out into the dark space, I felt eyes on me and wondered if Leo had crawled up into bed. "Leo?" I whispered into the darkness.

There was a rustling from the loft. "Leo?" I asked again with no response. It was quiet, so I began to climb the ladder. As my head peeked over the floor of the loft, he was not there. Suddenly, there was the unmistakable thump of feet padding across the floor. I leaned back, tempted briefly to let go of the ladder out of panic. Still on the ladder, I looked around the entire room. It was decidedly empty.

Perhaps it was the haze of sleep, the newness of the space, or the hour, but it seemed as if it was the sound of feet running directly toward me.

*

The days we spent together were wonderful, and most nights were, too. We took turns cooking dinner for each other and, on the weekends, we'd partner up to build fencing, strip paint, sand wood, and so on. We often fell into bed the best kind of tired—after a job well done, a good dinner, and a passionate roll in the hay.

Not long after the incident with the footsteps, which he had assured me had a rational explanation such as raccoons on the roof, I was awakened by Leo sobbing and crying out for Marcela.

There was a bit of an accent to his pronunciation, as if he'd only ever pronounced it the way her parents had intended. That consideration made me smile because, yes, he was the kind of guy that would put that much effort into those he loved, even in his sleep.

After the third night straight of this, I gripped his shoulders as he thrashed. I ducked when he struck his arms out toward me. He stirred, and I explained why I'd woken him.

He looked around, disoriented at first. Then his eyes wetted, the same as the night at the bar, and he said, "I was dreaming about the night she died." Several minutes passed in silence before he pulled his knees to his chest, took a deep breath, and opened up.

He described her restlessness, medications she'd been given to help with her Bipolar diagnosis, vivid night terrors that left her screaming at night, and startling moments where she'd grab him by the wrists and recite poetry in Latin. When pieced together, it indicated a psychotic break.

"The last time she did that, I figured the meds just weren't working. She just kept repeating this same poem over and over. Most of it was in Latin, but I recognized some of the words from what I learned in middle school. It was about dying and immortality. I could not calm her down and when I tried to get her to go to bed, she grabbed a knife." He took a deep breath. "I panicked and called the cops." I rubbed his back as he fought back tears. "They took her to the ER where she had a sudden seizure and died. I wasn't even there." There was something new about the words he was saying. It was as if he'd thought them but never shared them.

Tears streamed as he cried for several minutes. All I could do was rub his back and listen. He looked through the window nearest the bed, beyond the fields, into his own past. "After she died, the doctors let me sit with her body for a long time. She just looked like she was sleeping."

He steadied himself and wiped his face with his shirtsleeve. He cleared his throat and, with the voice of a lawyer, said matter-of-factly, "They found a sizeable brain tumor during the autopsy."

"I'm so sorry, Leo." I reached out for a hug and we held tight for a long time.

*

I thought that, since we had bridged this unknown gap together, we would both sleep better. He was drinking less, sure, but the nightly cycle was not unlike the kind I'd had when I was a kid and became convinced that there were monsters under the bed, waiting to grab me.

In this case, there was nothing under the bed but floor. There wasn't even a closet for a monster to hide in. And yet...

First, we'd fall asleep. Then I would have a nightmare in which I was being smothered or held down by infinite hands, or I'd hear footsteps on the loft floorboards and jolt awake, sitting bolt upright.

Once awake, I'd hear rustling. Was it the tapestries, my imagination, or something else? My mind would run amok at this point, and I would chase after it with rationalizations. Just as I'd start to settle into the cool of the pillow, I'd feel the eyes from that creepy painting on me.

Sometimes I would grow queasy and lay awake wondering if I was going to vomit. The thought of trying to make it through the obstacle course of antiques to the bathroom before vomiting only added to my anxiety.

*

When the nausea followed me into the daylight, I was left to wonder if it was more than just nerves. A pregnancy test came up thankfully negative, but the next day I found Leo brooding over the used test I'd unceremoniously trashed in my sleep-deprived state. "Why didn't you tell me?" he asked.

It was time to come clean about my nights in the house.

He listened at length, first to my assertions that my end of the birth control deal was airtight, then to my experiences with the house. After I'd said my piece, he rambled for a while about rational causes—the house, the draft, wild animals, and so on.

I was losing weight, too. My mom was the first to comment. I told her it was from the manual labor. She paused as if she was about to argue but thought better of it. We never talked about it further. I'm not sure what was more irksome: her look of concern or the fact that she was voluntarily quiet. So I went to see Dr. Rand.

Dr. Rand had been the town doctor since I was little. She assured me that my vitals were good and ran some blood tests, just in case. She recommended a counselor two towns over and offered me two prescriptions: one to help me sleep, another to help with my nerves. I took the prescriptions, also just in case.

Before I headed out of the exam room, she said, "Your blood tests will be back in a few days. Maybe you should find somewhere else to sleep for a few nights?"

*

That night was a revolving door of the same nightmares I'd been having to date. I wrestled with an unknown assailant. I was held down, choked, unable to speak. Leo was convinced it was sleep paralysis. He'd seen it before with Marcela.

There were worse things than being compared to a beautiful, Italian woman with impeccable taste in men, but there were also better things to have in common with someone than debilitating nightmares.

*

One day not long after, Leo turned to me during dinner and said, "I think this place is just about ready to sell."

I nearly dropped my fork. Inside was a hurricane of relief and astonishment. The thought of getting away from this house brought me more hope than I would have imagined a moment earlier. My mind began to fill with visions of blissful sleep. "Wow! Really?"

He nodded, "I finished what I set out to do. I think I'm ready for the next project."

I set the fork down and chewed thoughtfully. "So… what's the next project?"

He lifted a small, black box from his lap and set it down—closed—in front of me.

I looked at him, then at the box, then at him. His grin was goofy; it was the happiest I had ever seen him.

As pragmatic as I am, my heart bubbled with the thought of a diamond inside. I picked up the box and cracked it slightly. Inside was confirmation in the form of a gleaming, antique diamond solitaire.

He didn't have any fancy words prepared, nor did he make any promises. He just said, "I love you."

In that moment, I had no doubts at all about him or our future. The only doubts I had were about whether I would survive another sleepless night. I decided to take one of the sleeping pills.

*

Thankfully, for the first time in a long time, I slept until sunlight. I rolled over to find an empty space on the bed, still warm from Leo. I heard him rustling around with the coffee maker and sat up to stretch.

"You up?" he called.

"Yeah," I sighed as I hoisted myself out of the bed and downstairs.

I was met at the base with a look of consternation. "Do you not like the ring or something?"

"What?" I immediately reached for my left ring finger, which was bare. I held up my hands in the morning light to inspect them. "Oh no! Where did it go?" I started to retrace my steps, wondering aloud about where it might have gone.

"Claire," he said as I raced to the ladder, muttering. "Claire!" he called, this time sharply.

I stopped in my tracks. My stomach rumbled as it often did at night. "Yeah?"

He pointed to the bulletin board in the kitchen. Protruding from it was a boning knife. Hanging from the knife was my ring. It sparkled innocently in the morning light.

My mouth fell open as I took in the scene.

His look of consternation faded. "You didn't do this?"

I shook my head and pushed the loose hairs out of my face. We both stared at it for a few minutes. He looked out the window and made for the door, which was locked. The dogs followed him out into the yard as he searched for evidence that somebody had been prowling.

He came back in, satisfied and masculine. He folded his arms. "Where did you leave the ring?"

I lifted my hand and pointed to the appropriate finger. "I was pretty excited about getting it," I reminded him.

He nodded. "Maybe you're sleepwalking?"

"You mean sleep-climbing-over-your-body-and-down-a-ladder?" He was reticent. I added, "Maybe *you* were sleepwalking?"

He scoffed instantly.

"So… I'm capable of crazy things but not you? Bullshit." My patience, like my sleep, was gone.

He lifted his arms as if he were calming a horse. "That's not what I meant. You've told me more than once you get spooked, and you've been having nightmares when staying here."

I folded my arms. "Yes, but you have nightmares, too."

He was quiet for a long time before he announced, "Let's assume it was one of us for now. We'll be sure to bring in the dogs and lock all the doors and windows each night going forward to be safe."

I nodded, went to the bathroom and immediately threw up. In the mirror, I looked downright gaunt. My hair was ragged and knotted after a night of battle and the thought of brushing it exhausted me. When I emerged, I announced, "I'm going to stay at my parents' tonight."

We both spent the rest of the day walking on eggshells: him to keep the peace, and me to survive the mounting anxiety.

*

One overnight at my parents quickly turned into three. I had underestimated how much I needed (and loved) to sleep. In my childhood bedroom, the sensations were familiar, and there were no nightmares. The only downside was that Leo was not with me.

My mother was ecstatic about the engagement, though perplexed by my request to stay at home again. My dad joked it was to "build excitement for the wedding night." Mom shushed him and made a show of pushing the thought out of her mind.

"It's hard to sleep out there," was all I could say to explain.

"Really?" she began, "But it must be so quiet out there near the woods-"

Dad was quick to interrupt: "I don't think either one of us would sleep any better in a house like that." That was the end of that.

Leo stopped by frequently and stayed for dinner on the third night.

On the fourth day—a Saturday—I headed to his place in the afternoon armed with a small overnight bag. He'd assured me nothing odd had happened in my absence. He'd even slept in twice, which he had not done since he'd taken up residence. He also mentioned that he'd been—as he put it—monitoring for changes.

Before I walked up to the house, I wasn't sure what that meant, but the tiny white apparatus pointing at me as I approached the front door made things clearer. He opened the door with wild eyes.

He waved a small, handheld device. The tablet allowed him to stream from multiple cameras positioned throughout the property. He beamed with pride as he cycled through each view. He explained that they were continuously recording and that any significant motion, as well as a designated panic button, would trigger various alarms and long-term storage of the recordings.

I couldn't tell if he was delirious from the promise of technology or drunk on the pride of having installed it all himself.

Being my dad's daughter, I wanted to ask if all this was really necessary. Yes, I'd had some rough nights, but we were effectively in the middle of nowhere. Besides, recording didn't really provide us protection. The only true upside was that, if someone hurt one or both of us, there'd be video for the police. Besides, wasn't he planning to sell the house anyway?

I kept this all to myself. It was very sweet gesture, and his concern made me feel a little more at ease. There'd be no more mysterious knives in bulletin boards; no more wondering about weird sounds and occurrences.

I reached out to hug him. We kissed, then fell quickly into the breathless, desperate desire of too many nights apart. We made it only so far as the kitchen table. Afterward, we went right to making dinner. My ring, which I now checked for compulsively throughout the day, was still on the correct finger. We made it through dinner slowly, spending more time talking than eating.

Despite the warm recoupling, we grew nervous as sleep loomed. Leo spent extra time locking doors and securing windows. He tinkered with the tablet while I settled into bed. The dogs settled into their own beds downstairs; normally they wandered in and out but tonight he wanted them nearby to help "keep an eye on things."

*

Around 3 a.m., I woke with a start. Not from a bad dream, but from feeling cold. I normally slept cocooned in a heavy quilt while Leo slept sprawled out in the open air. The quilt was gone. I reached around the edge of the bed for it with no luck. For a moment, I thought about my childhood fears and how afraid I was to let anything dangle over the edge of the bed due to the risk of being grabbed.

My hands continued to grope, hitting only the fabric of the fitted sheet and worn floorboards. I leaned over Leo, who was sleeping peacefully, to reach around his side of the bed. There was nothing but the fitted sheet beneath him. I sat for a moment, cross-legged, letting my eyes fully adjust to the limited light.

Air wafted through the room, stirring the tapestries as usual. There was no whistle, though, and no chiming from the bell. The tapestries continued to roll like ocean waves. The room grew colder.

I scooted backwards on my side of the bed until my back braced against the wood of the low wall. I pressed Leo until his body rolled slightly. Then I did it again. I patted his arm, poked his rib cage, and began to do anything short of shouting that would cause him to wake. The dogs stirred downstairs.

That's when the footsteps started. They were slow at first. Plodding. They circled the open floor of the room. They shuffled along the ladder, grazed along the wall, then pounded the rafters overhead.

I sidled up against Leo, shoving him urgently. If I had been a screamer, this would have been the moment for me to shine, but I was a breath-holder. He groaned.

The creaking of the floorboards got closer. Slowly at first, and then quicker. The footsteps receded again.

A chilly breeze enveloped my head and shoulders. "Wake up, Leo," I said. I reached out to shake him but was stopped.

An icy sensation wrapped tightly around my neck, then down my spine. The sensation tightened as the gust in my ear spoke in a language I did not know.

Through a tightening grip, I growled, and everything went black.

*

The next morning, I smelled the distinct smell of dirt and farm exhaust. I opened my eyes to find myself in the barn, with the dogs lying beside me on the ground. I sat up and the dogs stirred and stretched beside me.

I surveyed myself. My hands and feet were covered in dirt. My hair was in knots. My nightclothes were torn in two places. My ring was gone and there were red marks on my hands and legs.

Despite the situation, the dogs seemed at ease beside me. They followed me toward the house.

The front door was ajar. I hung back and called out, "Leo!"

I went inside. The dogs refused to join me; they opted instead to mill around on the porch. "Leo," I shouted, this time more panicked. The quilt I'd been searching for during the night was folded up, clean and neat, on the kitchen table.

I heard a groan from above and scaled the ladder in an instant.

My eyes narrowed as I surveilled the room. Leo was spread eagle on the bed. He was naked and looked quite relaxed. He held his head in his hand as he began to sit up. He smiled drunkenly before noticing my appearance. I stared at him with arms folded. His brow furrowed as he noticed my scowl, my clothes, and my hair. "What happened?"

"I can't stay here anymore," was all I could answer. I plodded back down the ladder to my overnight bag and disappeared into the bathroom. He knocked more than once calling after me, to make sure I was okay. I took a long, slow shower. It only got longer and slower as I recalled the last moments before I fell asleep. I pressed gently against my neck; it was tender to the touch. When I came out, he was sitting on the couch, with the tablet set beside him.

I began, "I don't know what happened but—"

He lifted the tablet in the air without making eye contact. I took it and pressed play.

On the screen was broken, greenish footage of us sleeping. I looked at him and he said, "Wait for it."

A few moments passed before the quilt began to move—as if being pulled—off my body, over his, and down to the first floor where it disappeared from view. I gasped and held my free hand to my lips.

He would not look me in the eye. "Watch the next one," he said. His voice cracked as he spoke.

I opened the next file, which offered a third person perspective of me: sleepily groping for the blanket; sitting up in the bed, watchful; grabbing desperately for him to wake up; and pressing up against the wall, arms flailing as if being attacked. Everything I was seeing to this point was familiar. My body went limp. The video then cut to an error screen.

I was quiet for a long time before he announced, "There's one more."

"Do I want to watch it?"

He shrugged. To the floor he said, "Probably not."

I pressed play. The video was from multiple angles. It was me, but not. The figure wore my pajamas and engagement ring, but my hair seemed different—darker, somehow—and my eyes seemed to glow like fire in the night vision. The figure looked right at the camera and walked around the house as if floating, touching the clocks, figurines, and books—things I was afraid to touch in daylight—with great care.

The camera angle changed as the figure scaled the ladder. It sat down on top of Leo and began kissing him. The figure had a much easier time rousing him than I did earlier in the night.

The figure pulled off his boxer-briefs and mounted him with a flourish.

I had to pause it for a moment to process this. It made no sense, but it felt like watching him cheat on me, *with* me. I looked at Leo then, who was watching me. He looked away.

After I finished the video, I felt a great many things. First, I wanted to throw the tablet at him, grab my bag, and leave without looking back. Then, I wanted to collapse onto the floor crying while he held me because it was all too much. Finally, I wanted to find some gasoline and burn this mausoleum to the ground.

Neither of us understood what was happening but it's almost impossible to carry on a relationship with someone who can't look you in the eye.

*

A few weeks later, I went to Boston for my quarterly visit and decided to stay.

I paid for my parents to come visit me in the fall. They brought news that Leo had held an estate sale that brought in antique hunters from all over the country and sold the renovated house for a big profit. I was mostly happy for him, but still found myself daydreaming about burning it to the ground.

I found a new apartment in Boston and got a cat. I met a guy named David. He did not want to get married, owned no antiques, and had a thing for blondes. It was all very nice.

Sometimes I had nightmares about the rest of the video. In them, I am pressed against the wall above the fireplace, as if trapped inside the video camera or—worse—that horrible painting.

The dream continues much like the video: Leo wakes up completely, touches the figure's cheek and seems to ask, "Are you ok?"

The figure says something to him and his eyes light up, knowing I am not me, and he takes over. He pulls at her hungrily, wrapping his hands around her long dark hair, all at once weeping and rejoicing. Even without sound, it's clear he has only one name on his lips.

"Marcela."

Brian Ellis is a writer and editor whose work has appeared in trade publications for more than a decade. He is still waiting to earn money from his more interesting work, however, which includes fiction and nonfiction stories, poetry and a half-completed screenplay. He currently resides in New Jersey.

About this poem, Brian says: "The spellbinding lyricism of The Raven *left an imprint on my adolescent mind when I first read it. As the years passed, I would return to the poem regularly, until one night the words for* Eleanor *began to form in the distinct rhyme scheme and meter."*

Just as the motion of the pistons and rolling of the tires move a car down the road, the rhythms of a poem are as much a part of the story as the words themselves, carrying the reader along with them on the journey.

ELEANOR

Brian Ellis

Deep into a late night's query, this one answer came so clearly
That I had to stop and think in fear there must be something more.
What I must do—yes, I knew it—there was really nothing to it,
What relief in that one moment, no more stress like months before:
I would bring her home for dinner and not think about it more,
This, my woman, Eleanor.

We had met one night, November, her appearing, I remember,
Lovely, lost, and oh, so tender to the feelings that I bore.
I had been a lonely fellow, native son to thoughts of sorrow,
Not sure how I'd last till morrow, when she knocked upon the door.
Welcomed visitor (I knew her!). How she healed the hurt I bore.
As did I for Eleanor.

Two months later we eloped, a small affair just as I'd hoped.
Then, our wedding night, I let the love within, through words, outpour.
"Stop your work," I said with feeling. "On my job we'll earn our living."
She refused, and I was reeling, with a pain not felt before.
"You're a fool," she said. "Your salary alone will leave us poor."
"I suppose, my Eleanor."

Otherwise our married life went by with ease and seldom strife,
Leading to the night of firm resolve: My folks must meet my Eleanor.
Late the next day she was napping, so I gently started tapping,
When this failed I started slapping, slapping worked but then she roared,
"Don't you slap me while I sleep!" She rubbed her butt and swore.
"Your words hurt me, Eleanor."

"What is it you want?" she muttered. "What is… so important?" she stuttered.
I could sense her temper flaring and declined to utter more.
"Don't you pull that crap with me," she spoke with utmost clarity.
"It is time," I said, "for you to see—for you to meet my brother Elmore
And my parents." "'Bout time," she responded, turned, began to snore.
She sleeps well, my Eleanor.

On the next day, which was Sunday, we both made dessert, a soufflé,
And before we left I put on handsome clothes from days of yore.
As I drove our beat-up wagon, which was nicknamed Mother Dragon,
That old, hellish thing kept lagging, and I pushed the pedal more.
Thirty minutes in, the engine puttered, fluttered and was heard no more.
"That's great work," said Eleanor.

Sitting in the cooling mobile, patience waning, in denial,
I conceived a plan to end our plight and save our night and more.
"Hun, this car is dead," I told her, steadily becoming bolder.
"Not a chance to fix the motor. Let's just curb it. Nothing more.
Listen, up ahead my parents' house is three blocks, maybe four—
We can walk there, Eleanor."

Walking led to more derision. "Damn these heels," was her emission.
"How much further? It has been at least a mile!" "Oh, not much more.
Trust me," I implored. A groan was her assent, followed by more argument,
Till I said, "Look up. Be silent." There, inside the window by the door,
Looming were two eyes, so still, like they had never moved before.
"We've arrived, my Eleanor!"

Three quick knocks, but not an answer, other than some muffled banter,
Soon replaced by footsteps steadily proceeding toward the door.
Creaking, as it opened slowly, breathless, as I sought for family,
Who was there before me, but the person (yes the person!) who'd done more,
More than anyone, to influence the man I had become since I was born.
"Mother…this is Eleanor."

Silence followed, which was broken as the door came slowly open,
Letting us inside my home until the age of twenty-four.
All the sights were so familiar: white-furred cat named Old Man Winter,
Father sleeping on the brown recliner, younger brother Elmore
Peering down the stairs and with one look hid fast behind a door.
He'd not changed much, that Elmore.

"Everyone," I said so all could hear me. Father woke, but still looked weary.
Slowly Elmore ventured near me, staying two steps from the door.
"Time for each of you to meet my wife, my Eleanor." Mother took a seat.
"There's my mother, Betty Lou. My father, Pete. And brother, Elmore."
"No, it's Edgar," spoke my brother. "He's a little crazy," whispered I to Eleanor.
"No, I'm not," returned Elmore.

Mother stood and to me said, "You selfish child. Two years ago you fled.
Not a sign. We worried you were dead." My father muted *Animals Galore*,
That old nature show reporting on some blackbird. Think it was a crow.
Was it truly? I don't know. "Nothing's changed," my mother said. "I bore
Your ungrateful hide into the world and still my feelings you ignore."
"Here's soufflé," spoke Eleanor.

Mother shook her head. "We finished dinner near an hour ago," she said.
"Could you not have called me? One of many decencies that you ignore."
Mother turned from us, and quiet followed, which from arguments it must,
Till my father, not so taken by the fuss, did look at Eleanor.
This was when he asked the question I had hoped to never hear, forevermore.
"What do you do, Eleanor?"

"I'm a lady of the evening." Silence. "Pleasing men earns me my living."
Mother gasped. And father sighed. And brother giggled. Then mother roared,
"You have always been a loser, like your Uncle Ted a boozer,
And the simple fact you'd choose her means you'll not be something more!
Both of you leave now—right now—before I wind up saying more."
This set off my Eleanor.

"Tell me—who are you to judge him? You pathetic, old curmudgeon!
Worthless bitch! You never loved him." Just a pause and then some more.
"You may not approve of what I do, but tell me who the hell are *you*?
Nothing but a loveless shrew, who drove away her son whom… I adore.
Call me what you will, but I am loyal. This I am, and so much more."
Spoke my mother, "Mangy whore!"

Eleanor lunged fast at mother, down they tumbled, pleasing brother,
Who was punching air just like a boxer. "Damn you!" mother swore.
"Damn you back!" returned my wife. Me and father tried to end the strife,
Which was far more rife with anger than I'd thought. "You've cut me, Eleanor."
When we got them parted, they both had a look that I had never seen before.
"Time to leave now, Eleanor."

But before we left completely, my eyes stopped upon my family,
Watching father tend to mother and my brother cry for more.
It was then I knew what I must say. I simply could not leave home in this way.
Gathering the remnants of soufflé, I threw away the shards and chocolate core.
Then, I added, "Family, our car broke down a mile from here... Um. I implore—"
Yelled my father, "Out the door!"

Standing in the darkness, yearning, melancholy in me burning,
Never would I be returning—one last time I stared upon my house of yore.
Ghastly light was flashing, taunting, shadows creeping, sickly, haunting,
As though evil within flaunting—thoughts I shared with Eleanor.
"Yeah, it's cursed," she answered. "Like the chamber in that poem... 'Nevermore.'"
"That's well spoken, Eleanor."

Hugh J. O'Donnell writes fiction, produces podcasts, and likes things. His work has appeared in Iridium Zine, Andromeda Spaceways, The Method to the Madness Anthology, *and others. He is also the author of the drabble-novella "The City: A Story in 140 Characters." His greatest achievement thus far has been winning Carl Kasell's voice on his voicemail. Hugh lives in Western New York with his husband, cats, and video game consoles. Find more of his work online at hughjodonnell.com.*

About this story, Hugh says: "The Montressor Method was inspired by a friend who worked in Special Collections for SUNY University at Buffalo. He often complained about one of the other archivists doing shoddy work and damaging the materials. I got to thinking about how you'd get revenge for something like that, and the idea of using The Cask of Amontillado *to lure and trap a Poe fan really appealed to me."*

We all have that one person we'd love to lure into a diabolical death-trap, don't we? While this story cannot truly give them everything they deserve, there's nothing to say you can't imagine yourself into the leading role, encouraging your own personal nemesis down the stairs...

THE MONTRESSOR METHOD
Hugh J. O'Donnell

Everything would have been simpler if we lived in an age that accepted the gentlemanly sport of dueling with pistols. If only I could have put a bullet in Roberts' malformed brain, or stabbed the boor in the heart. The whole affair with his death would have been far simpler. Unfortunately, I was forced to rely on more subtle and intricate methods to exact my revenge.

There was no single incident that I can recall that led to my decision to murder him. I cannot even remember a moment where I consciously reached a unified state of mind on the matter. It was a thousand little injuries, an endless stream of minor slights and overlooked mistakes. But somewhere, in the dark recesses of my brain, I kept the tally, and one day, I simply realized I was already planning the grim deed.

Roberts was a curator of rare books. His interest was primarily first editions, special collections, and that sort of thing. The lout somehow became a senior librarian in the public university system, specializing in eighteenth- and nineteenth-century horror. I myself have an interest in the genre, and studied library science before becoming independently wealthy. I continued to pursue the field as a hobby, and quickly amassed an enviable private collection.

It was through this shared interest that our fates became intractably linked. Unfortunately, I quickly discerned that he was the most lax, careless, and downright foolish librarian I have ever had the misfortune to meet. I had personally seen him stack first edition copies of Mary Shelly, Le Fanu, even a copy of *Tamerlane and Other Poems,* on their sides, one over the other. His carelessness did such damage to the spines that they soon cracked and needed extensive repair. Again and again I saw him err, and yet he walked unscathed from the ensuing damage, from job to job, promotion to promotion.

More offensive than his lack of professional skill, was what could be charitably called his social graces. The man was a slack-jawed lout, even sober, and he was very rarely without drink in him. But others claimed him to be friendly and charming, perhaps the same way that one would be enamored with a large, shaggy dog, which he resembled. And while he was always openly cheerful to me, it was in a manner that was almost instantly, thoughtlessly cruel. Perhaps it was the fact that he was unaware that was most maddening. I would, if such a thing were possible, have simply been the gentleman and extricated myself from the situation; but it seemed as though the man were following me! It soon became quite apparent if I risked an open confrontation with the boor, it would cost my social standing dearly. Thus it was that I wore a smiling mask and plotted the deed, first in the back of my mind, then the front. It did not take me very long to find the perfect opportunity.

*

It was during the carnival time known to the less interesting literary minds as 'convention season,' and I was obliged to make an appearance as a member of the literary community. I endured the event as best as I could, bearing the unwashed masses and their outlandish costumes and fashions. I knew Roberts was there, and that he would seek me out. He always did at these things, then subjected me to his ridiculous theories and opinions about Robert E. Howard and the New Deal or some such nonsense. He was always so pleased by the thought that he had hit upon some revolutionary new idea that no one else had before. It never occurred to him that the ideas were so foolish anyone else would have been too embarrassed to even write them down, much less expound upon them.

Unsurprisingly, I found him at the hotel bar on the last night of the convention. He was seated at a small table at the back, alone for the moment, but it was clear by the way he swayed in his seat, and the empty bottles lined up in front of him, that he had been holding court there for a good portion of the evening.

"Alex!" he shouted, beckoning with huge, red, waving fists, nearly punching nearby drinkers by accident. "Come, have a drink!" He had half a beer in his hand, but made a rather extensive, and somewhat rude, gesture, and a waitress arrived, looking put-upon and world-weary. Roberts asked for a beer. I ordered a glass of red wine. She disappeared without a word, taking a portion of the empties with her.

"You don't drink red wine," he said in the authoritative voice of a man already too far gone to care. I smiled, imagining the hangover he would have in the morning. Then I remembered that if all went well, he'd never have a hangover again. I couldn't help smiling even wider.

"Rarely," I said, "but I'm in the mood for it tonight."

"Why's that?" he asked, slurring. I heard a faint sound of jingling bells, and saw that an odd little painted bell on a string had been tied to his badge. It had been meant to resemble Cthulhu, I believe.

"Oh, I'm just thinking about something. I bought a new first edition recently, but I'm having my doubts about it now."

"So you're drowning your sorrows, eh? Whiskey's better for that kind of thing, ya know?"

"I was actually looking around, seeing who's still in town for the con. I was hoping I could get Dr. Laurence to take a look at it before she headed back to Seattle."

"Laurence?" He asked, offended. "I've got twice the experience of that bit, uh…" He was interrupted by the return of the waitress. He didn't want to swear in front of the young woman, although courtesy didn't extend to not staring down her blouse, I noticed. She glared at us, practically slammed our drinks on the table, and retreated again. I watched him watch her go over the rim of my glass.

"The piece is a magazine. She mostly archives 19th century periodicals, so I thought I should go to her."

"The only think you could get out of her is a cheap fuck." My eyebrows shot up. He was even more drunk than I had thought. If I wasn't careful, he would pass out before I got him out of the hotel. "What magazine is it?" he managed.

"Well, if you must know, it's a copy of *Godey's Lady's Book*, circa 1846."

"*Godey's Lady's Book*?" He asked, perking up.

"Yes."

"1846, you said?" Even he knew that the magazine regularly featured first printings of Edgar Allan Poe.

"Yes," I admitted. He drained his beer.

"An extant copy?"

"It looks good, but I have my doubts. I'm worried it's a forgery."

"What month?" There was a gleam in his eye.

"November, but what does that matter if it is a fake?"

"*The Cask of Amontillado?*"

"I have my reservations, but yes. You were busy, and I arranged it on short notice."

"I should say so. And you were going to have Laurence verify it?" His buzz was being edged out by manic excitement.

"I couldn't find you. I didn't know you were still in town."

"My plane leaves in the morning."

"There you go," I said. "I'd hate to make you miss your flight."

"For a first magazine run, complete, of Poe's '*Cask of Amontillado*'? I'd walk home." He shrugged into his coat. "Let's go take a look at it."

"What, now?" I asked, my smile slipping.

"Certainly. This isn't something you run across every day. This is a first edition Poe for chrissake."

"But it's nearly one in the morning!"

"Still early enough. Finish your wine." I let him bully me into leaving the bar with him. We managed to get into my car, his eyes shining, a huge grin on his face, and that damn bell ringing with every lurching, drunken step. I could hear him mumbling "*Amontillado,*" and chuckling the whole way.

I sighed, rather theatrically, and made a show of resigning myself. I took an effort of being seen leaving with him, both of us apparently two sheets to the wind.

*

The length of the drive, for my estate was a good hour from the hotel, I begged him again to reconsider. He would miss his plane, I said. It was already very late, and who would want to be working on the last night of a convention? As expected, Roberts dismissed all my protests. He said that getting a good look at a fine condition copy of a hundred and fifty year old magazine, with a Poe story, no less, was worth it. I told him that I could get Dr. Laurence to authenticate the piece, to which his response was a stream of profanity that I won't repeat here.

It was just past two when we reached the estate. I had, at the very least, managed to keep the man from worming his way into my home, so this was the first time he had ever seen the mansion. He whistled. "Not bad, Johnston." I thanked him, and punched in the automatic code for the gate.

"The whole place is state of the art. Electronic locks, automatic light and temperature controls, the whole bit. And wait until you see the library." I hurried him inside, and, realizing that he was starting to sober after the long drive, I offered him a drink. He took it, and we headed for the library.

"Sherry, huh?"

"I thought it might be apropos, considering."

"The thought occurs," he said wetly, "That this is a lot like the story." He grinned.

I choked on my drink.

"What do you mean?" I asked carefully.

"Well, here we are, alone in the dark of night, in your mansion, to take a look at this McGuffin of yours? How do I know that you aren't planning on bricking me up in your basement like poor old Fortunato, eh?"

I blanched. Had the ignoramus seen through me so easily? Were police already on their way?

He broke into a fit of laughter that went on for nearly a minute. "Man, Alex. You should see your face! Even drunk, you're so serious. Loosen up, man! Now, let's go take a look at that little prize, shall we?" He pulled out a cigarette and lit it. I smiled weakly.

We made our way to the library, a sizable portion of the house. It was a specially designed, three-story room with shelves stretching from floor to ceiling. He took in the scene with awe, only spilling a bit of sherry on the carpets. "So where is the *Amontillado*?" He asked, looking this way and that.

"I put in the vault, further on. The piece is very sensitive, given the quality of the paper, and its age. It needs better protection than I can give it out here."

"Didn't you say you had state of the art environmental control?"

"The stuff above ground is good, but wait until you see what's down below." I grinned and took a sip of sherry. It was excellent stuff. "Can I top you off, Dave?" He readily assented.

"Now, then," he asked, glancing around again like the attention deficient ape he was, "Where is this vault of yours? I don't see a staircase down." I strode to a bookshelf, which looked no different than the others, and waggled my eyebrows.

"I hope you'll excuse my flair for the dramatic," I said, reaching out for a hardback copy of Doyle's *The Lost World*. The hidden switch was activated, and the door swung inward on its hinges. Roberts brayed another laugh.

"Lay on, Macduff," he said. We descended a flight of stairs, overhead lights snapping on ahead of us and off after we had passed. He paused several times and backed up, testing the system. "There's one thing we have on old Montressor and Fortunato," he giggled. "We don't have to worry about carrying torches."

"Or trowels," I smirked. He thought that was a good joke.

The climate controlled vault was set in the wall behind a sheet of heavy glass. There was a computer station set up just outside the sliding door. Within was a table for examination and repair of my rarest books, kept at the back in row of sliding inset shelves. The humidity, light, and temperature could be controlled perfectly, so that the precious contents would be preserved forever. The books in the library were mere curiosities. This was where I kept my treasures.

Roberts stood impatiently at the door, shivering with anticipation. "The *Amontillado*?"

"In there, old friend. The system is very complex, and requires that an operator stay outside and man the controls," I said, gesturing to the console. "It's a safety feature." He leaned over to examine the complex displays, nearly spilling his wine on them.

"Don't you have a guard or something?" He asked.

"I have people here during the day, but it's the middle of the night. There's no one on staff now. Why don't we head back? You have a plane to catch, right?" Roberts almost screamed at me.

"After we've come this far? With only a thin glass wall between us and our treasure? You can operate the controls? It'll be fine." I affected trepidation. I told him I had made a point of being profoundly disinterested in the workings of the device whenever my assistant attempted to demonstrate them, that I had never anticipated the time when it would be myself at the controls. I eyed his cigarette. He cursed, and stamped it out on the tile floor.

"If you are sure. I really think we should call this off."

"Just open the damn door, Johnston!"

I pushed the button. A panel of glass slid sideways, and there was a rush of even colder, drier air. Roberts stepped through, and the door slid shut behind him. He laughed at that joke.

"I need to keep the temperature and pressure constant." I said over the intercom. "Nothing to get alarmed about. You'll find the *'Amontillado'* in drawer seven." He lumbered over. The wine glass was still in his hand. I wondered how much damage he could do in the vault with that little glass of wine. I checked the console. Drawer seven was unlocked, all the others were shut tight. It slid open at his touch, revealing a single sheet of typed paper. He looked at it stupidly, while I pushed the button that started the halon fire detection system. My revenge had already begun. He pulled it out, barehanded, and squinted at it in the light, reading aloud the words typed upon it.

"For the love of God, Montressor?"

"Yes," I said. I had imagined this day for months, years, but it was still more delicious than I had dreamed. "For the love of God." He crumpled up the note, and only then did he notice the fans, and the heavier than air gas that they were pushing into the room. He coughed.

"Is this some kind of joke?" He went to the door, and it gave a satisfying rattle when he walked straight into it after it didn't open for him. I turned the fans up. The air pumped out of the room faster. His damn bell jangled merrily as he beat his fists against the glass.

"Again," I said, slipping further into the role of Montressor the assassin. "I must insist we do this another time. You'll miss your plane at this rate." He shouted, but I pretended not to hear him. He beat more desperately on the glass, searched for something he could throw into it. I watched patiently. The oxygen was nearly gone, and the panes were specially treated three inch thick plates. They could stop a small car without shattering. I had chosen them specially, for security.

I watched Roberts pull at the door in vain. His face was turning such interesting colors. At that point, I couldn't open the door again if I wanted to. Once the fire suppression system had been activated, the vault wouldn't open for twenty minutes, to allow for the gasses to cycle through. It was a safety feature. I sat and watched for the full period.

*

Sadly, things were not so simple for me as they were for Montressor. After the gas had cleared, I entered and arranged the scene, removing the note and placing another cigarette in his hand. Then, I called the police and I told them that Roberts was dead. My vault was made of glass, and no brick on earth could cover the fact that we had been seen leaving the hotel together.

I had planned for this as well, of course. I explained how this horrible tragedy happened, how the staff had the night off, and I thought I could use the machine, and oh, God, what had I done? We had both had a bit to drink, and I let Roberts into the vault. I hadn't noticed his cigarette until it was too late. The halon fire suppression system activated, and I couldn't turn it off until it was too late. What a tragedy. No one who knew the curator's methods even questioned the story. It was just like him.

It was a good performance, but it was not without its critics. Roberts' widow absolved me, but I was still put on trial. My name was nearly wrung through the mud, but I bore it well, in silence and solemn dignity. Eventually, the charges were dismissed. My detractors could find no evidence that it had been nothing more than a tragic accident. I had been careful that in spite of Roberts' transgression against me, none were aware of it. I had no motive to kill such a good friend and colleague.

So in the end, I got away with it. I set up a memorial endowment 'to carry on the legacy of a friend lost too soon,' and went on with my life. I certainly never felt guilty. But sometimes, if I'm in the vaults at night, alone, I can almost see the fog of his last breaths on the glass, and hear the faint chime of a tin bell.

In pace, requiescat, indeed.

Scott Wheelock is a painter, writer and teacher living in Philadelphia .He has taught at: The Pennsylvania Academy of Fine Arts, Moore College of Art, and Tyler school of Art, and had many group and solo shows including Connors-Rosato Gallery, NY and the Pennsylvania Academy of fine arts museum. He is currently working on a series of illustrated magazines about a cult called: "The Face of God Church" which was located in the Deep South in the1930's. You can find out more about Scott and see his work at: scottwheelock.com

About this story, Scott says: "Many years ago, I had a recording of the Masque of the Red Death *that had been set to music. I used to listen to it over and over struck every time by how Poe's concluding words caused me to stop what I was doing and listen as Poe made the world and everything in it come to a full stop. 'And now was acknowledged the presence of the Red Death. He had come like a thief in the night...'*"

In an age where we have all but eradicated so many of the diseases that once regularly cut a deadly swath through the population, reports of virulent outbreaks still touch us at the most primal level. Who would we save from a global panedmic, given the opportunity? And how long can we, as a race, truly cheat death?

THE CRIMSON TEAR

Scott Wheelock

The Crimson Tear had long devastated the earth. No weapon had been so efficient, so decisive, and so indiscriminate. A foaming at the mouth was its avatar, proceeding to shortness of breath, then to bleeding from the eyes as if the individual affected cried tears of blood. These tears, which once inspired fellowship in others, now brought only fear and loathing, for the whole sickness—from the foaming at the mouth to the tears of blood—lasted but half an hour.

But Prince Abdullah was defiant of the scourge of the Crimson Tear, and from his tower above Qatar was determined to weather its reign of destruction. Once nearly an exile from his own country, he found his old ways, which had been called secular and heretical, served him well in this new world.

From a nightclub on the 97th floor of a tower of glass and steel, he and a hundred friends and companions not only sought shelter from the Crimson Tear, indulged in the raucous freedom prohibited them by their previous rulers. The Prince ruled the uppermost five floors of the tower, and from the penthouse roof commanded a fleet of helicopters and a half-dozen anti-aircraft batteries.

Below, the lower 90 floors of the tower had been cleansed by flames, leaving only their mighty steel beams intact.

From the rooftop, the Prince watched with morbid fascination as the world died around him. The fleet of helicopters that once brought revelers and supplies now lay broken or had never returned from treasure finding expeditions. It had been months since he had seen an aircraft flying above the ruined landscape; before that, the princes' guards had shot down many helicopters whose unwelcome occupants wished to share in his good fortune. There were only a few dozen missiles left for his anti-aircraft guns, but the Prince believed they were no longer necessary. The fires had long burned out in the world around them and the city had gone utterly silent except for the noise of his generators.

The Prince had been host and King to this crowd for almost a year, and while the food and water remained ample, the fuel which powered the generators would last no more than a few short weeks. It was the generators that made life possible at the tower's summit, for they provided not only the preservation of the food, but air-conditioning which, in the scorching heat, was an essential amenity. He knew the day they must push through the throngs of burned bodies that were stacked in the stairwell would not be much longer in coming.

Once the world below the tower had withered and died, every day became the same, and the date when Prince Abdullah and his revelers must abandon the tower arrived with a speed that surprised them all. Undoubtedly, descending from the spire would be arduous, but once accomplished, the world and everything in it would be theirs for the taking.

Perhaps to avoid thoughts of the descent, or possibly to commemorate their place of refuge, the Prince ordered a grand celebration, for after a year of retreat at long last there would be a rebirth. The celebration would start at midnight, and when the sun rose to its full height, they would commence their descent.

The Prince spared no expense of his precious fuel; the floodlights, the DJs, the music, all poured forth upon the vastness he surveyed beneath him.

And a glorious party it was! One hundred revelers upon the roof of the world, dancing as one. The beams of the floodlights cut through the air, illuminating first this part of the crowd then another. The night was an ecstatic celebration. Hope filled the partygoers' hearts in that place they had not realized had slowly emptied in their year of retreat.

But a night lasts but a few short hours, and when the sun appeared on the horizon, the morning light caused the partygoers to hesitate and fall into confused isolation. In a way it was as though time had stopped during their occupation of the tower, and with the rising sun, time was about to commence once again.

As the sun crested the horizon, the partygoers became aware of a speck in the distance, followed by the noise of a motor cutting through the air. Prince Abdullah ordered the music to stop. In the silence that followed, the partygoers beheld one of the forgotten helicopters that had been sent to loot the treasures of a dead world long months ago. The Prince felt a shiver—this must this be an omen, but of what he could not say.

The helicopter showed no signs of slowing as it neared the tower, causing the crowd to break apart, for it was clear the aircraft was not being directed to land in its customary niches. The wind of the rotors was deafening, and as the craft landed, the blades blew up the dust of a year of neglect.

When the blades stopped their revolutions, Prince Abdullah yelled, "Who dares? Bring him before me, so I may know who we will throw from the walls of the tower."

Reluctantly, the crowd dragged the pilot out of his aircraft and forced him to stand before Prince Abdullah. He wore a visored helmet, and to the horror of all, as the Prince removed the helmet the aviator's eyes shed a Crimson Tear.

Now the revelers knew it was the Crimson Tear itself that had come to them with the sunrise. In the span of a single day, one by one the dancers fell, the generators failed, the music stopped.

And darkness, and decay, and the Crimson Tear held dominion over all.

More than seventy of Gregory's stories have appeared or are forthcoming in such journals as Glimmer Train, The Georgia Review, The Florida Review, The Baltimore Review, The Pinch, Post Road, The Los Angeles Review, PANK, *and* Tahoma Literary Review. *His work has earned six Pushcart Prize nominations and has won awards sponsored by Descant, Solstice, Gulf Stream, New South, and the Rubery Book Awards. More often than not, his writing reflects Kafka's assertion that a literary work "must be an ice axe to break the sea frozen inside us." See more at www.gregorywolos.com.*

About this story, Gregory says: "This story was woven from three notable personal experiences: an idea for a point-of-view switch story involving one of Poe's 'buried alive' characters; a friendship-altering argument over the prospect that extra-uterine fetal incubation will in the future eliminate the need for abortions; and a joking insinuation to a Meals-On-Wheels acquaintance that she might be stealing from her clients' lunches. While fuming over the EUFI argument, I'd been trying (and failing) to write a Fortunato/Cask of Amontillado remix when my story's nameless ascetic/anorexic driver snuck in and took over the narrative, resulting in Oofy Baby *and its central concern, how does one construct a life?"*

We overhear random bits of conversation every day, most of which are as quickly forgotten. This tale takes some of these random conversations and weaves them together to form a whole that, while surreal and strangely disturbing, is definitely more than the sum of its parts.

AN OOFY BABY SEES FORTUNATO'S SIDE

Gregory J. Wolos

> *"For the love of God, Montressor!"*
> –"The Cask of Amontillado," E.A. Poe

The sweating teen boys with the basketball sit at a picnic table in the far corner of the park's only covered pavilion. They drink sports drinks they bought from the refreshment stand by the pool, which is hidden behind a fence. I can hear kids frolicking, water splashing, shouts, the shrill blast of a lifeguard's whistle, a hoarse command to "stop running."

I eat my lunch and eavesdrop on the boys' talk. Is it sports? It's got to be sports, though I'm not connecting it up yet, waiting for a recognizable phrase, like "slam dunk" or "home run." Their voices are low and serious. I'm eating a chocolate pudding cup with a plastic spoon. This is Mrs. Cuchinello's pudding. When I dropped off her "Meal on Wheels," she didn't notice that dessert was missing. If she complains tomorrow, which she's never done, I'll tsk-tsk and tell her I'll inform Administration. Mrs. Cuchinello isn't a caller. Only three of the eighteen people on my list would call if something was missing from their meals, and I keep them off my "special rotation."

"Implications of gestational location…" My head snaps up when I hear the phrase from the shorter of the basketball boys. His baggy shorts and tank top hang from him like hand-me-downs from a giant, and his yellow wristbands match the sweatband crimping his black hair. The boy and his lanky friend, whose blue jeans are fashionably torn at the knee, glance at me before I duck back down to my meal. Does my thinness confuse them as they measure my age? Am I as old as their mothers? A big sister?

Pudding done, I move on to the entrée—Mrs. Poulter's chicken broccoli alfredo with bowtie pasta. The tiny widow flutters around her living room to music she plays so loud her windows vibrate. I could probably take her entrée every day without her noticing, but that's not how my plan works. Mrs. Poulter will lose her entrée no more than once every three weeks, like everyone else in my special rotation. She still got her garlic roll, pudding, and three bean salad. This afternoon I've already eaten the roll I took from Mrs. Wong. It was soggy with alfredo sauce.

Gestational location? That's not sports talk or kids' talk. Did I hear right? Maybe it was rap lyrics, like "*just take a vacation.*" Maybe I'll try Mr. Silberbach's three bean salad before the pasta.

"It's called 'extra-uterine fetal incubation,'" Yellow Bands says. "They can grow a baby from scratch, outside the mother. E-U-F-I. 'Oofy'."

"'Oofy'?" Blue Jeans has got their basketball pinned under his arm. "That's goofy."

The boys snort ragged laughs at the rhyme. But which do they think is goofy, the name or the idea?

I never take more than one item per five day week from my fifteen non-caller Meals on Wheels patrons, and I rotate through their bread, vegetable, entrée, and dessert. Every weekday I wind up with a completely free, multi-course meal. The kidney bean I stab at with my plastic fork slips off, and I chase it across the picnic table where I finally spear it. The boys are too involved in their conversation to notice. I nip the bean and wince—it's too vinegary. Mr. Silberbach is lucky I've taken it off his hands. He was today's last stop. Before I carried his meal to his front door, I hunched down in the driver's seat of my car and pinched back the foil on his plate, then scooped all but one kidney, one wax, and one green bean into my Tupperware bowl.

My car has a permanent smell like boiled cabbage. At night sometimes when hunger nags, I sit in my car, inhale deeply, and pretend I'm eating.

Mr. Silberbach greeted me with his usual stained-dentures smile. "I'm hungry," he said. "You're late."

"Only five minutes," I lied—it was more like fifteen. Today being a Monday, I was fighting the headache I get from weekends without eating. On Saturdays and Sundays I only drink water. On Sunday nights I dream about food.

It was Mrs. Poulter's fault that I was late to Mr. Silberbach's.

"Come in, come in, I want you to listen to this," she said through her door. The music flooding past nearly pushed me off her stoop. Every day she listens to something from *Man of LaMancha*. Today's song, like on most days, was *"The Impossible Dream."* The singer's voice was muffled as if he had a pillow over his head. Mrs. Poulter looked at me slyly.

"It's Hungarian," she said over the singing. "This is from the performance Peter and I saw in Budapest in 1987. They were selling cassettes in the lobby, so we didn't have to use the recorder I had in my purse."

"Hungarian, nice," I said, hyperventilating slightly as I raised my voice. "Better than the Japanese."

"Not better than the first of our three Japanese versions, the one from Kyoto. Have I told you that we saw *Man of La Mancha* over two hundred times? In seventy-seven cities on five continents? Peter and I would play a game where we would try to remember a detail from each different performance, and we almost always could. Since he's been gone, all but the special ones are muddled together."

"Mmm." Of course she'd told me. Mrs. Poulter's meal, even without her pasta, felt like a lead weight in my hands. Stars swirled when I blinked. "Gotta go," I said. "Hungry folks are waiting."

Mrs. Poulter's head swayed to the familiar tune and its incomprehensible lyrics. With her eyes shut she mouthed the words in English: "*This is my quest, to follow that star, no matter how hopeless, no matter how faaaar...*'" Then she squinted at me with a suddenness as sharp as the swipe of a knife. "You look so pale, dear. And you're nothing but skin and bones. Would you like something from my lunch?" She clawed at the box, which, of course I couldn't surrender— if she opened the meal she'd certainly have noticed the missing entree. I clung to her meal.

"You know what I'd like to hear in Hungarian?" I asked. "That song about the prostitute. The part where she says she was left in a ditch after she was born."

Mrs. Poulter's frown of concern lifted into a smile. "Ah, 'Dulcinea': '*Naked and cold and too hungry to cry,*'" she sang creakily. She pivoted and, with a slow motion prance, headed for her cassette player across the room. While she had her back to me, I tossed the meal box onto her foyer table and hurried down her walkway to my car. *"The Impossible Dream"* halted abruptly behind me. I knew from experience that she wouldn't miss me.

Dark clouds blot the sun, and it's so dark in the pavilion I can hardly make out what's left of my meal. Rain would make basketball impossible. The boys are still discussing EUFI: "Oofy." The lives of boys who talk about extra-uterine fetal incubation are a mystery.

"There's *implications*," Blue Jeans insists. His knees poke through the holes in his pants. He's tucked the basketball inside his T-shirt and slaps it while he talks. Is he mimicking pregnancy on purpose? "If the baby's not inside, how does it get the mother's, you know, juices?"

Juices?

Yellow Bands is drinking his blue Gatorade when he hears the word. He wipes his mouth and frowns. "There's chemical fluids that supply those, whatever they are," he says. "Who knows what the set up would look like? It doesn't have to be a replica of a woman's..." He pauses, searching for the word, which is funny, since he knows "extra-uterine fetal incubation." I grin into my Tupperware bowl and pry a green bean from under a limp bowtie.

"Womb," his friend with the basketball belly supplies after a few seconds, though at first I worry that it's me who's answered. Do the boys notice how *womb* rhymes with *tomb*?

"Womb, right. Nothing has to look like a real womb. Probably something like a fish tank hooked up to a computer. There'd be tubes and wires. You'd see a wall of tiny babies in aquariums, like tropical fish in a pet store. Things will be rigged up to get them all the juices they need."

"But aren't the *real* mother's juices special?"

"How?"

"I don't know," Blue Jeans shrugs. "Maternal instinct? Isn't that a thing?" I think he's just realized he looks pregnant.

"That's mental. It's not juices. How do you *not* get attached to the thing that fills you up for nine months? But all the baby needs is, like, food and shelter. What, you think there's some kind of 'maternal instinct sauce'?"

The boys laugh.

I'm always famished on Mondays. If I were alone in this pavilion, I'd lick the alfredo sauce from my Tupperware. On weekends I look at food pictures in supermarket ads, but they don't fool my stomach as much as the smell inside my car. Meals on Wheels pays me fifty-five cents a mile for gas, three times what I need, but most of what's left over goes for rent. I could probably afford a box of crackers once in a while, but I don't want to create a dependency. There never seems to be as much money as there should be, though toilet paper I get from stalls at McDonald's, and I haven't needed tampons in a while since my period stopped last winter. I've stopped producing eggs. I'm empty. What would my Oofy boys think about that?

There's an ozone smell that comes before storms. The kids at the pool are whistled out of the water. Lightning flashes, and I get an idea—I could double my income with a second Meals on Wheels route! It would have to be at another location, because eighteen clients is the maximum for each driver. The boys are staring my way. Have I said something out loud? No, they're looking past me at the rain that's suddenly spattering the pavement outside the pavilion.

Two routes. There's an hour to deliver the meals, noon to one, and only one me. Impossible, right?

*

Mr. Silberbach's the one who got me thinking about time. He didn't really mind that Mrs. Poulter's Hungarian "Impossible Dream" made me late. Half a minute after I showed up at his door, I sat next to him on his sofa, looking at pictures of his granddaughter, who's with the Peace Corps in Madagascar, where she's teaching villagers how to raise bees.

"She's about your age," Mr. Silberbach said, though I'm sure I'm much older. Being starved-skinny makes me look like a kid. When I first volunteered at Meals on Wheels they checked my license to confirm my age. To my great relief, they didn't notice it was expired. Renewing a license is expensive.

*

When Blue Jeans stands, the basketball slips out of his shirt, and he dribbles it on the pavilion's concrete floor. There are two echoes with each bounce, a loud one off the roof of the pavilion, and a tiny buzz inside the ball like there's a bee trapped inside it. It's raining steadily, and thunder rumbles overhead like someone moving furniture. If I leave the shelter, I'll get soaked. My clothes will take forever to dry, like they do on Saturdays when I rinse them in the sink. I spend most Saturdays naked and waiting.

"There wouldn't have to be abortions," Yellow Bands says.

The beat of Blue Jeans's dribbling slows. "Why not?

"Because instead of throwing the baby away, you can just grow it. People need babies to adopt. They wouldn't have to go to China or Russia. There'd be tons of fresh ones."

Bounce-pause-bounce-pause...*Tons of babies. Don't throw it, grow it!* I snap the cover onto my empty Tupperware container and stare through the foggy plastic, half expecting to see a bee. How do I drive two routes at once? How does a body decide to stop making eggs?

"But is that it—is that all abortion is?" Blue Jeans holds the ball. He doesn't look at his friend. "Isn't there more to it than that?"

"Like what? If you're throwing the baby away anyway, what do you care what happens to it?"

"I don't know—just more." He stops dribbling, spins the ball like a globe on his index finger. "Maternal instinct sauce," he says, pronouncing each word like he's sharing a song title.

I feel the boys' eyes suddenly stuck on me like the mouths of sucker fish. I stare into my empty container. There's no genie inside, or even a bee, just bits of clotted food.

*

"You must be tired, all that driving."

Mr. Silberbach's words came to me out of a black void deeper than sleep. He thought I'd dozed off, but I'm pretty sure I passed out. Just for a second though, because I still held the picture of his granddaughter in Madagascar.

"You want to see something?" Mr. Silberbach asked. He took back his photograph. He rocked himself to his feet, his body hunched in the shape of a question mark. I rose like a lifting fog and followed him to his kitchen.

"Here," he said, stopping beside the kind of kitchen table I'd seen in Salvation Army stores. He was so stiff, he had to swivel his whole body to look me in the eye. "Did you ever read 'The Cask of Amontillado,' by Edgar Alan Poe?"

"Armadillos?" I knew what they looked like— rat-sized, armored rodents that could roll themselves into a ball. About Poe all I knew was that he wrote spooky stories.

"No, *Amontillado*. It's a kind of wine. Poe wrote about a man who feels insulted by an old acquaintance, so the insulted one lures the insulter, a man called Fortunato who's a very heavy drinker, down into the cellar deep under his house with the promise of some very special wine called Amontillado. Then the insulted fellow chains up Fortunato to a wall in the corner of the cellar and quickly builds a brick wall in front of him so nobody would ever find him. Fortunato is left there behind the wall in the dark. Forever."

The hair on the back of my neck tickled like someone was blowing on it. Very creepy. When I looked warily at Mr. Silberbach, he was gesturing at his kitchen table.

*

The rain drums on the roof, hissing on the concrete and grass outside the shelter where puddles are forming. A narrow stream leaks into the shelter from a big puddle like a finger sticking out of a palm. The boys have stopped looking at me.

I peek at Yellow Bands, who rubs his chin. "You think they could grow meat like that? Outside the cow? Could you pull out the calf right away, when it was just a couple of cells, and start growing it on the outside, and then get the cow pregnant again, you know, like, the next day? And then the day after that and the day after that? No waiting around for a birth. There'd be big warehouses with tanks where Oofy calves grew to birth size, and when they were ready, they could be harvested for meat."

"Does a cow have a cycle like a human woman?" Blue Jeans asks. "Does it get new eggs once a month? Or does it take a cow longer because it's a bigger animal?"

I wince, expecting the suck of their mouth-eyes, but feel nothing.

"Well, it's got to take less time than a whole pregnancy."

"And I bet you could speed things up by injecting the cows with hormones or something."

"I think they call them steers when they're for food." The boys speak quickly, excited by their idea.

"Whoever works it out, they'd be billionaires," Yellow Bands says. "But you've got to be an expert on how a cow's body works."

Cows have more than one stomach. Would the boys want to know that?

And then the boys' do look at me again, though I'm sure I haven't spoken. I focus on the splinter of wood I push at with my thumb. I'm trying and failing to force it through my skin. *I'm no expert at cow anatomy,* I want to tell them. *I don't even have a period. I don't eat enough.* Are they worried that I might steal their idea?

"The hell—" Yellow Bands mutters. "All of this Oofy technology won't be ready for decades, anyway." He catches the ball Blue Jeans tosses and rubs it with his palm and stubby fingers.

"Nope," Blue Jeans says. "Probably not. But this meat talk is making me hungry. I could use a double cheeseburger."

My shrunken stomach growls, even though I've filled it with a Meals on Wheels lunch.

*

"This is a model for a life-sized sculpture," Mr. Silberbach said. "If I get the materials, I'll build it in the yard. I thought of the idea one night when I couldn't sleep. I'm no artist. I was a school teacher."

The "model" on his kitchen table was under a dome—a turned-over glass mixing bowl, actually.

"I cover it with a bowl because of ants," Mr. Silberbach said. "They smell everything in the summer. They're after the dried apple, which I used instead of clay. My daughter was supposed to bring me some clay, but she kept forgetting. She's worried all the time about Sarah in the Peace Corps. There's no clay sitting around at Meals on Wheels is there?"

"None that I've ever seen," I said.

The apple part of Mr. Silberbach's sculpture model didn't look dried. The puffy brown lump sat in a pool of leakage. Mr. Silberbach lifted the dome with two hands, as if he was removing the crown from a king, and the sweet odor of rot hit me like a punch. Backed up against the rotten apple was a pink plastic doll. I rested my hand on the table's sticky surface and bent over for a closer look. It was one of those troll dolls—I hadn't seen one in years. Mr. Silberbach's bug-eyed, grinning troll stood naked and with open arms, like it was waiting for a hug. But the thing I remembered most about trolls was the long hair that burst from their heads like colored fire, and this one was completely bald. There were dots in its scalp where the hair had been pulled out. Had Mr. Silberbach found the troll like this or plucked it clean for his art?

Then I noticed that the doll was wired to the rotten apple: paper clips had been twisted around each spread-eagled arm and jammed into the rotten apple. And then I saw the wall of dominos stacked like bricks a few inches in front of the troll. I gasped, tasting a hunger burp.

"That's right," Mr. Silberbach whispered, admiring his own work. "It's Fortunato. He's been chained up and walled in by Montressor, the man he insulted. Fortunato will never escape. He would have been in total darkness, but we have to pretend that the light shining on him here is the opposite of light."

"The light is the dark?" I asked.

"If it was actual total darkness, how would we see him? You'd have to take my word for it. Besides, Fortunato eventually took care of the light. I call my sculpture *'Fortunato's Side.'* Because we're on *his* side of the bricks. Edgar Alan Poe didn't write about that. But this became Fortunato's whole world."

*

The basketball boys don't mention that there could be Oofy piglets or lambs, too. Any kind of meat could be grown. If I was a vegetarian and chose never to eat the meat from the entrees I deliver to my Meals and Wheels clients, I'd probably starve to death. The life-plan I stay faithful to doesn't leave me much of a margin.

The snickering boys sit together now. The rain has thinned to a drizzle. These are not kids I would have known when I was in school. These boys would have been in different classes, the ones for smart kids, classes where topics like "extra-uterine fetal incubation" came up. They would have eaten lunch at tables far from mine and taken school buses to and from homes on streets I never knew existed before I started driving for Meals on Wheels.

"One business not to put your money in would be rubbers," Yellow Bands says. His big grin and squishy body remind me of Mr. Silberbach's troll. "Everybody could have sex all the time and not worry about it. Women could sell the little embryos. Now *that* would be a business to get into."

I blush. I'd been looking at the puddles and thinking of the wrong kind of rubbers.

"Wouldn't the embryos belong to the men, too?"

"Maybe women would keep it secret and take all the money. There'd probably be legal hassles. Women." Yellow Bands shakes his head, looking more like a troll with every word he speaks.

"It would be the same thing as with the cows, anyway, wouldn't it?" Blue Jeans asks. "The technology won't be around for years."

The boys are quiet again. There's just the rain. I'm picturing a huge building with row after row of incubating human fetuses lined up in thousands of tanks: Oofy babies arranged in order of development, so if you ran down a row a long, long way it would be like time lapse photography. You could pretend you were watching a single baby grow from something the size of a pea into a fully ripe infant. In the very last tank in the row, I picture a full-sized baby troll, as bald as Mr. Silberbach's Fortunato.

*

"This is Fortunato after Montressor, the insulted man, left him chained up and walled-in," Mr. Silberbach said. "But what Montressor didn't know is that Fortunato didn't die. Nope. At first he was terrified, alone in the damp, cold blackness. Who wouldn't be? But then Fortunato figured it out. And after that, he lived a long time, relatively speaking. As happy and fulfilled as any human being has a right to be."

"What did he figure out?" Bent over and dizzy, I resisted resting my chin on Mr. Silberbach's dirty kitchen table. My gaze stuck on the bald, grinning troll doll's whiteless bug eyes.

"Out of the silence and darkness, Fortunato heard a tiny buzz. He wasn't alone—a fly was walled up with him. What did he know about flies? Not much, he'd never thought about them except to swat them away from his food. Minor nuisances. He listened to this fly circle his head, and he tensed—*all* of him tensed, his muscles, tendons, bones, even his skin. He was waiting for the fly to land on him—to touch his flesh. Where would it make contact? He was certain it would settle on his face, and his eyes and nose and lips twitched with anticipation. And, oddly enough, chained there in total blackness, Fortunato *felt* his features for the first time in his life. Because his face, his body, his senses— these were all he had."

Riveted to the face of the troll doll, my dry eyes burned. "What happened to Fortunato's fear?"

"Fear was a feeling, too, just like his other senses. Feelings were all he had. They were his treasures, he realized."

"Fear was a treasure?"

"Fear and everything else he felt."

"And when did dark become light?"

"Ahh—" Mr. Silberbach reached out and floated his palm just above the doll. "Light is supposed to come first, but it didn't for Fortunato. First came *time*— he was thinking about the rest of his life, and he measured it against that buzzing fly's. Neither had more than a day or two left, but to the fly, that day or two was a lifetime. And this was Fortunato's triumph. Chained up and walled in down in Montressor's cellar, he determined that he would live out his remaining time with the sensibility of a fly. If every breath was a week, if every heartbeat a day— I've figured this out—forty-eight hours times sixty minutes, times an average heart rate of sixty beats a minute—Fortunato had forty-seven years of fly life left—he'd die at a ripe old age."

I shivered. I no longer felt my legs. I stood up straight, but it was like I was a pencil balanced on an eraser. The slightest nudge would have toppled me. Did troll-Fortunato wink at me? I tried to imagine living forty-seven years in the dark.

"The light?"

"Simple. Fortunato had so much time, he invented it." Mr. Silberbach swiveled toward me, pointed at his head, and squinted one caterpillar-browed eye. "With the power of his mind. It didn't take him long. A thousand heartbeats, maybe—less than three of his years."

I heard my own heartbeat, which sounded like a dripping faucet.

"What did he eat?" I asked.

"Eat? I thought you were worried about the light. What did he eat? He licked the sweat from his upper lip: water, salt—plenty of nutrients to last forty-seven of the kind of years that were his to live. But the light—that he molded out of darkness. Like a bat's echolocation. You know what that is? Echolocation?"

"No."

"I told you, Fortunato had his *feelings*. He threw his treasure at his world, and what there was to see, he saw. He 'saw' the bricks a few feet in front of his face, and he saw the mortar between them. He saw the grains of sand in the mortar, the flecks of light in the mica. And you know what? He looked so hard, he saw the history of each rock and pebble and grain of sand—he gazed into the past, for millions of years, from when the rocks were bubbling lava that swelled into mountains and hardened. And then he watched as the mountains were worn away by rivers, wind and rain, then pounded into beach sand by waves. Fortunato saw the first creatures crawl out of the sea. On Fortunato's side of the brick wall he saw forward and backward for as long as there was time."

Mr. Silberbach's tongue slipped up to the little groove under his nose. When he pulled it back in, the skin over his lip glistened. "Fortunato was a god," he said. "And he never would have known it if he hadn't insulted somebody and gotten himself imprisoned in a cellar wall."

Then I must have fainted again, or fallen asleep, because I dreamed I was in a tent in Madagascar, and a young woman I understood to be Mr. Silberbach's granddaughter was talking about honeybees:

"When their hive is attacked by a Japanese giant hornet, the sting of which is fatal to bees, the entire population of honeybees surrounds the invader. And then they vibrate—a mass vibration that produces heat at a level that honeybees can stand, but that's intolerable to the giant hornet, which melts to death from the inside out. As if it was microwaved."

I heard singing—a familiar tune in an odd language, and then I saw Mrs. Poulter and a smiling old man sitting in folding chairs in another corner of the tent. They wore matching safari hats and bobbed their heads in time to the music.

"'The Impossible Dream' in Malagasy," said the man with Mrs. Poulter, who clasped a cassette player to her chest. Someone passed me a Meals on Wheels food container.

"We're going to have hornets for lunch," Mr. Silberbach's granddaughter said. "Toasted hornets. Yum."

I woke up sitting on Mr. Silberbach's sofa. I held a glass of water. How did I get there? He couldn't have carried me. Dust filmed the glass. Particles swam in the water. I held the cool, smooth glass against my forehead, then peered through it—walls and furniture were warped like reflections in funhouse mirrors. Did I dare look at Mr. Silberbach through the glass?

*

The rain has stopped. The sky is so white it hurts to look at it. The pavement around the pavilion is steaming. I suck at the thick air, pretending my shallow breaths fill me up. The basketball boys rise from their table and rush toward me as if riding a wave. As they come at me through the shadows, I see that they're younger than I thought—maybe late elementary school. The holes at Blue Jean's knees look less fashionable than worn from play. Yellow Bands' troll features are baby fat. Driven by hunger, they sweep past me without even a nod, boys I wouldn't have known who'll become men I won't ever know.

I hear their ball smack wetly on the pavement, but I don't turn to look. They're no more attached to me than any of the thousands of warehoused Oofy babies would be to the mothers or fathers who spawned them. No more attached to me than they are to each other.

They're going to eat. My stomach makes a fist, gives a small cry. I take another breath. Nobody hears that cry but me. The cry is triumphant. It announces the fulfillment of the life I have chosen to live. My plan. My creation. Like Mrs. Poulter's Hungarian *"Impossible Dream"* and Mr. Silberbach's sculpture and his granddaughter's Madagascar bees.

Everything is so clear under Fortunato's light.

Sidney Williams is the author of multiple novels including Disciples of the Serpent, Dark Hours *and* Midnight Eyes. *His early books include* When Darkness Falls, Blood Hunter, Night Brothers *and* Azarius. *Additionally, he wrote three young adult horror novels under the name Michael August. Sidney's short work has also appeared in* Cemetery Dance, Eulogy, Sanitarium *and in diverse anthologies including* Under the Fang, Demon Sex, Crafty Cat Crimes *and* Hot Blood: Deadly After Dark. *He teaches a creative writing course focusing on horror, mystery and suspense and wears an Edgar Allan Poe t-shirt when introducing the history of mystery. Visit him at sidisalive.com*

About this story, Sidney says: "A Cooler of Craft Brew began with news of an insidious act committed by a 'Florida man' which struck me at once as a Florida variation on an Edgar Allan Poe story. Since the news account didn't provide details, I wondered how the reported endeavor could have been accomplished to begin with. Then I tried to imagine how it might have been successful, and worked to mirror a few flourishes of Poe's while finding a reason for all of those bizarre 'Florida man' events. As I finished my tale, another, similar case cropped up, and so on it goes."

There are those who think that the works of Poe only appeal to readers of, shall we say, "refined sensibilities." Here to disabuse you of that notion is a character who is about as unrefined as you're going to find... and a man whose solution to his problem truly does Poe proud.

A COOLER OF CRAFT BREW
Sidney Williams

I put up with a lot from L'Heureux. It didn't start when he sent me out to Celebration. It goes back a little further, but I'm an easy-goin' guy, and that whole deal just pushed me a little too far—and I guess opportunity just woke me up to what might be possible.

But, like I said, for a while, I rolled with every crap assignment he threw my way. For ages. Just nodding once I figured out that when I complained he'd spit excuses and say we had a job to do.

I guess maybe it really started with the time he took me off the crew close to my house in Forest City and sent me to help with the excavation in Bithlo. I wasn't doing anything out there that any of our backhoe drivers couldn't handle, but he claimed it had to be me and it put me driving home in Orlando rush-hour traffic and clicking off Sun Pass charges on the toll roads to try and save time. Raina quit trying to keep supper warm after about the second day I worked that project.

Then it was down to St. Cloud because they'd run into a ground saturation issue. I asked him if he was just jacking with me after that one. It's not far as the crow flies, but the traffic's hell.

They just needed to do the dirt work right, and get some trenches put in, but he said: "Monty, it needs someone with your touch and your experience."

Raina was busy doing other things by the time I got home muddy and wiped out every night, and she'd be pretty chilly the next day, too. I couldn't blame her, but I was too tired to put up much of a defense.

I asked L'Heureux if he was trying to make me quit for some reason, but he said no, I was too good of a worker for that and he just couldn't trust some of the young guys to get the job done.

So it went on like that for a while. I tried just doing a good job, but it was one shit thing after another, and I finally went to the work trailer one morning and told him I'd had enough.

"Oh, come on, Monty. Don't lose that can-do attitude you've always shown us. I know you get tired some days, and I see what a good worker you are week in and week out, but those guys in the office the other day were asking me if you were slipping."

"What?"

"There are eyes everywhere, and the suits know if somebody's slacking or even if their heart's not in their work. I got asked about some of your moves at the Thornton sight. You know they send people behind us?"

"What'd they say?"

"Wondered if some of the dig was sub par, if the foundation was done right. I covered for you, said it musta been somebody else if something didn't look right."

"Crap, are they out to…"

"Just pull your weight. You'll be fine. Look, there's another job down in Celebration. Real mess. You go work down there a few days, get that squared away, you'll be in the CAT-bird seat again."

He smiled and chuckled, but I must have given him a blank look.

"You know, you usually drive a Caterpillar… never mind. Look, I'll move some money around. Get you a room. Won't be a great room, but you won't have to make the drive across town at rush hour."

"Come on, Celebration? I know there's a gig in Maitland that's way closer to me."

It got heated, as I mentioned, and L'Heureux had had to work a while to settle me down.

I hated leaving Raina for several days, but the way he described it, it sounded like a good way to shore up my job. So, I finally calmed down and said yeah.

I thought she might want to come along, but she had some things around the house she wanted to get done. So I went, and it turned out to be a bear of a job, with work needed to skew around groundwater issues, plus an area that needed to be set up for a retaining wall, and then another issue that cropped up.

Took a couple of days longer than expected, but L'Heureux said to put my brews on the tab and kick back, so I did. I sat and sipped and watched TV in the room, and Raina would just talk a little while on the phone then have to get back to some plants she was re-potting or somethin'.

I started to resent L'Heureux. He could have done more to protect me without having me living in a motel for a week, couldn't he?

I made it through it all anyway, and when it was finished, I called him.

"Come down and see it," I said. "We whipped this site into shape. Tell the fat cats I'm a good employee."

"Monty, I'd love to, but there's a ton of compliance paperwork..."

"Come on. If you can find a spot to bury just a little more brew in the budget, they have Abita Purple Haze down here. I can get us a cooler filled up. Just tell everybody you're at the office."

I'd picked up he liked that special brand of craft beer from a Louisiana brewery. It had a little touch of raspberry in it that the Yuengling lager he'd latched onto here didn't have. He'd complained not long ago Publix had stopped stocking Haze. I noticed later they changed that, but at the time, you had to go to a liquor store to find it. It served up a nice enticement.

"Cold as your ex's heart," I said. "And it'll help you forget her." He'd poured out his soul a few times when he'd first come down to Orlando about all that he'd been through, and I'd lent an ear.

But I didn't want to push too hard. "Forget it. I'll see if Ritter wants to drink it with me," I said as he thought things over. "He lives kind of close down here."

"Ritter's probably got a fridge full of Bud Light," he said. Did I mention L'Heureux was a beer snob? "He won't appreciate a good cold Haze. I'll see you when I can get through the traffic."

So it was about 7:30, getting toward dusk when he showed up wearing a goofy Hawaiian shirt he'd picked up when he came to town because he figured that's how we'd dress here. Maybe over at Cocoa.

The worst of the day's temp was dropping just a bit. I'd zippered a light hoodie over my t-shirt, and I had the cooler between two lawn chairs.

"This place does look great," he said, scanning the clear expanse of dirt, the trenches and the retaining area as he walked the perimeter.

"Took a lot of sweat," I said. "This is a tricky area, but then it's Florida, land of sinkholes and underground lakes. What the hell can we expect?"

I popped a bottle and passed it over to him.

"You told me that when I came to town," he agreed. "Limestone, clay. Interesting terrain. I was looking for a change, and I got it. It's different here. Even the lizards and squirrels are a little different. Just something different in the evolution."

"Or the water," I said, pulling a second bottle.

He settled into the chair beside me and wiped a few beads of moisture from the brown glass.

"Thanks, man."

"You got your phone turned off? Mine is. Let everybody go to voice mail."

"It's in the truck. It can just ring."

"Yeah, you don't want the big wigs bothering us, and I don't need a call from Raina right now."

He knocked back a pretty good swallow, and he acted for a while like he wanted to tell me something.

"You helped me out a lot when I got here," he said.

"Raina and I really felt sorry for you. Living in that long-stay hotel with nothing."

"You couldn't find a rental when I first came to town. I'd go to a store and look around and think `all of these people have homes, and I don't. I'm lost.'"

"Why do you think we started having you over to Sunday dinner?"

L'Heureux chugged a bit more and chuckled.

"It helped. I'd heard all of the Florida man jokes too, and I wasn't sure what to expect here. You showed me Florida folk can be friendly, just like Louisiana folk."

He chugged again, a long swallow, almost like he was trying to drown something inside him.

"You got me through the first few months, learning the company."

"You might not have moved up from assistant to foreman so quick, eh?"

"Maybe not."

We swilled more, talked about those early days and the current state of the company and all of the ups and downs of the construction business in Florida and life in The Sunshine Sate in general. When he was just at the edge of soused, I gave my head just a slight upward tick.

"By the way, there's something I want to show you toward the back of the property," I said. "Something we'll need to take care of, but it's not a huge problem."

We walked past the raised foundational dirt where the building was going, and then the past the work lights and on to the rear of the lot where an opening yawned. I'd found the depression by accident when I was helping look for a spot for a small concrete square they were going to put in where they'd sit a dumpster.

"What the hell?"

We stood at the edge of the hole, and I unzippered my hoodie. He didn't pay much mind to my T-shirt that pictured a big yellow backhoe with red lettering around it: *"Mess With A Heavy Equipment Operator/You're in for a Hole Lot of Trouble."*

He didn't even give that a second look. He was too busy peering down to try and see bottom. Then he dropped to his knees, but he didn't have enough light.

It had really been earlier as I'd checked the area out that I'd felt something snap inside me. For a minute I'd thought I'd inhaled some gas escaping from deep in the earth, that it'd triggered all the anger over everything I'd been feeling over my gigs and what work was doing to my life.

"You've seen something like this before?"

"Yeah, not the worst you'd think. It can be fixed."

"This is going to fuck up the whole project," he said. "We can't put..."

"I'm not sure it's a limestone situation," I said. "It could be related to what they call 'expansive clay.' Stretches of it go down a ways and just causes a dip."

"You can you fix that?"

"Yeah, yeah, we can fix... Shit, you can't really see the bottom. Let me pull a unit over. We can make use of the light on the cab."

I left him kneeling, peering down into shadows. I knew a lot had to be running through his head. Reports he'd have to file, reassurances, additional insurance, probably another survey.

Construction delays. Everybody that worked on the paper side of things hated those.

It wasn't his fault, but it'd be on his watch, and he'd been involved in some of the scouting of this site. He was so worried he just kept staring as I fired up a unit. He didn't even look back as I rolled his way, stopping just where I needed to keep the weight from getting too risky while I still had the reach.

He straightened and dusted the knees of his jeans, pivoting, but he didn't do it soon enough. I already had the dipper arm extended. I had the pins set for maximum maneuvering, and moved a couple of levers and gave him a nudge with the bucket, not too hard. He caught most of it in the chest, and spilled over the side with a quick shout of surprise.

I put things on idle and slid out of my seat to kneel at the hole's edge. It was about 15 feet to where he'd landed, if he was lucky. I'd created a little ledge there, at the dipper's maximum depth. The natural hole stretched on down from there.

If the blow from the bucket hadn't winded him, the landing probably had.

"You hear me?" I called.

The engine, even idling, made a good bit of noise.

"Yeah," he said after a second. "What the hell? Get me outta here."

I squinted and saw him at the first level. I'd pulled the opening back a little and made the ledge where he was as wide a landing spot as I could. If you're good, you can work with a lot of precision with a backhoe, and I'd been careful to keep the unit on solid ground. If the depression below him was a true Florida sinkhole, it might open all the way to God knows what's down there.

"Gosh, I'd like to help, kind of like you wanted to when you just had to assign me out in Bithlo."

"What do you mean?"

"It's kind of like that," I said. "You wanted to help, but you went ahead and signed the order anyway."

"I told you. You're one of the best."

"That's the damned truth. That's all's keeping you on solid ground right now."

I popped back into the seat and dipped up a bucket full of dirt, then swung it into the hole.

He was sputtering when I climbed to the edge again. I don't know how much had hit him, but he had a lot of red dust on him, and he was trying to climb up the pit's side. No go.

"Come on, Monty, work is work."

"Sure. Totally out of your hands."

I jumped back into the seat and dropped two more scoops in. One, zip, buzz, whump. Then another.

He was sitting when I looked in again. The falling clods had batted him around a bit, and he was breathing heavy. His eyes were like little white circles amid the grime on his face.

"I'm sorry, okay?"

"Sure. Sorry. Gotcha."

"What do you want?"

"Not much now. You're pretty much where I want you, and I'm pretty much where I want to be."

"Look, I know I'm partly to blame on this. Get me out, I won't say a word about it." He was taking heavy breaths between words.

"You're not going to be able to say much at all before long. You might catch an air pocket and last a while, but..."

"Come on, you've made your point."

I jumped back into the seat and dropped several more scoops.

He was up to about his waist now, trying a bit to dig himself out with his hands.

"How's the point looking now?" I asked.

"It's been driven home. When did you know?"

"Know? That I was going to do this?"

"About Raina."

You're probably ahead now of where I was then. I'd been stupid, and I'd missed the signs, or just hadn't let myself look at them.

I had to when he said her name, and everything all added up, starting with how she'd laughed at his jokes on those Sundays she'd fixed her blini and we'd all had a good time.

I felt like a real fool then and whatever was boiling inside me bubbled a little more. I knew my dirt, but not my own house. Of course, he'd wanted me to have a shitty drive so that if he popped over to the house he wouldn't be interrupted. Getting me down here for several days must have given them a wonderful week of romantic bliss. A lot of images flooded into my head now like water flushing into a construction trench.

Images I didn't want but couldn't help.

"I don't know what came over me. She was just so pretty, and..."

Raina with him. Naked. Pleasing him. Him touching her.

In my house while I was stuck in traffic?

I let a streak of curses fly, and then I was back in the driver's seat. A back hoe will work fast, especially if you know what you're doing, and like we've established, I am pretty good.

When I paused and stepped to the edge again, his hands clawed up through the dirt over his head. His face appeared, and he started spitting and gasping at the same time.

"You up there? You up there?"

His ears were probably full now.

"I'm here," I shouted.

"You don't have to do this." Sputter, spit. "Come on, Monty. Get me out of here. You know there'll be consequences."

"If they ever find you. I'll take your truck back to the office, put the phone back on your desk, leave it. They ask, I say, 'Yeah, he came down and gave things a look, went back to do some paperwork. Something about compliance orders.'"

I'd have to be careful of the security cameras, but I'd been thinking about that.

"Raina will be suspicious."

"They'll have to find her to ask her questions," I said.

"Jesus Christ, Monty."

"Good idea," I said. "Give him a call."

I was back in the seat then, and I didn't stop scooping until I was finished with some rip rack and a little more work. I didn't hear any sounds as I did a final smoothing over.

I called out a few times. "L'Heureux?"

No stirring below.

"L'Heureux?"

"L'Heureux?"

All looked good, and with all the filling and clay, no one should notice anything was out of the ordinary. If they did, he'd be down where whatever makes a guy turn into a Florida man seeps up from.

I popped one more beer, sipped a bit then poured a little circle on the ground. Maybe it would seep all the way down to L'Heureux.

RIP, Happy Man.

You shoulda known what a Florida man will do when he's pushed too far.

Karen Robiscoe's short stories, essays, & poetry have appeared in numerous literary journals including: Spectrum *at UCSB,* Lunch Ticket *at Antioch, Los Angeles, &* Steamticket Journal. *Fowlpox Press released her chapbook:* Word Mosaics *in 2014, and she currently writes a fitness column for several newspapers in Central California. You can keep up with Karen at her dynamic & popular blog: Charron's Chatter: https://charronschatter.com*

About this poem, Karen says: "I adore Poe's poetry, Much of it details the deaths of women he loved, and one night—upon a midnight weary, of course—I riffed on the possibility of Poe hurrying them to their graves. Poe-Po' Polly *is the result of a remixed* Raven."

Don't read this poem yourself—find someone to read it to you, loud and proud, so you get the full open-mic poetry jam effect of the words flying by. Find the right reader, and you'll swear you can see that birdee perched on the back of their chair and keeping his beady eye on you!

POE-PO' POLLY

Karen Robiscoe

It was the witchin' hour
a power tower glitchin' hour
a black as hell & bitchin' hour
in every sense of word.
Because a bit contrarily
and, yes, a trifle wearily
I'm here to tell you verily
the word is not the bird.

The bird in fact, is wordy
for all that he's a birdee
and though it sounds absurd
he roosts with boys in blue.
And sure as bells are knellin'
come midnight, he's a yellin'
putting me through hell
and getting all gumshoe.

He cackles and he coos
and parrot-izes news, and
asks me: where were you?
& then he spews some more.
Questioning embracing
some repeated phrases
people, things, and places
including poor Lenore.

A chick who I found sexy,
at least until she left me,
saying it was best, we
seek a separate road.
Didn't learn 'til later
she vanished at equator
just assumed she made
herself a new abode.

Now, worse than AWOL mistress
is I'm a peep of interest
(birdee's here on business)
raptor-captor style.
Searching through my mansion
perching on my transom
and though I offered ransom,
he's staying 'til the trial.

Donea Lee Weaver is a perpetual daydreamer who's been creating and telling stories since her elementary school days. When she's not writing about the things she loves (all things fantasy, romance, sci-fi and yes, even a little horror) she's playing with her daughter, her dog, and her husband somewhere in northern Utah. She also loves to read, travel and play games with her family. You can find her on Twitter @DoneaLee

About this story, Donea says: "When I saw the call for submissions I turned at once to The Black Cat. *Unlike my main character, I happen to love cats, and would probably own one, if my dog wasn't terrified of them, though we do 'have' a neighbor cat, who I've often caught staring in at me from a window ledge. And I also happen to have an unused brick fireplace in the basement... As I thought about these things and the cats I know, the story just came."*

Accidents will happen, and when they do, you have two choices: confess, or try to clean up the mess and make it look like everything is perfectly normal and hope nobody notices. Just don't leave any loose ends, or your whole scheme might fall apart at the seams....

THE CA(T)SUALTY

Donea Lee Weaver

They say cats have nine lives. I believe the same could be said about my marriage. Each year that ticked by marked a new age of regression in our failing relationship. Even the black cat I adopted when we first moved into our home together seemed to turn into a new cat, a darker cat. In fact, I'm not one-hundred-percent sure, anymore, if I'd initially bought a black cat. I think perhaps she had once been lighter, maybe a soft gray. But, she was a black-devil of a beast now. Just like my husband.

Music thumped through the speakers in my make-shift basement workout room as I mindlessly pedaled away on my stationary bike. Another thing that had slowly changed in the last nine years was my weight. The happy, svelte, one-hundred-and-twenty-pound beauty I'd been when we got married had somehow morphed into a two-hundred pound cheese-cake of a gal with a sad, home dye-job for a topping. I caught my reflection in the windows and gagged.

"Disgusting," I whispered.

A loud *thwack* and screeching mew rattled the windows, and I jolted. My left ankle bent sideways and slipped off the pedal, messing with my practiced rhythm. "Son of a..." I squinted at the windows and there she was, staring at me from an outside corner. Ms. Kitty Von Dee—my tiny nemesis. I bent sideways to pick up an exercise band and chucked it as hard as I could against the glass. It glanced off the ledge and Ms. Kitty smirked.

"Why are you being mean to my sweet girl?"

"Gah!" I jumped again and twisted in my seat to glare at my husband. "Why are you sneaking up on me?" I used the remote for my stereo, stabbing at the pause button a little too hard to actually stop the music the first time. "My exercise time is *me*-time. Go away."

"Make me." He looked me up and down, his nose crinkling, and then waved at the devil-cat, who responded to the greeting with a loud meow before she disappeared into the bushes. "And I didn't sneak up on you," he said. "I came down the stairs like a normal human being, making a normal amount of sound. It's not my fault if you didn't hear me. And you don't own the basement." He chuckled at his supposed cleverness. I rolled my eyes. "Why do you hate on Ms. Kitty, anyhow?"

He was kidding, right? *I* had saved the cat from the shelter. Not Eddie. Me. Maybe she hadn't always hated me, or maybe I'd blocked it out, but over the years I watched how she grew to adore my husband, yet devised new ways to torment me. I took my other foot off the pedal and ground my feet into the carpet.

"That thing is possessed. Why are you always taking her side?"

Eddie walked over by the windows, leaning against the ledge with his arms folded. "*You're* the one who adopted my girl in the first place." He stopped talking to point at me. "It was *your* idea to get a pet. All your lame guilt trips about how kids growing up with pets would be healthier and happier and blah, blah, blah. Fat lot of good that did us." He leaned forward and flicked my belly. "Didn't know I'd married a dud."

Slapping his hand away, I ground my molars and stared at him through squinty eyes. "How was I supposed to know we couldn't have kids, huh?"

He threw his hands up and then let them drop back down to his sides. "Well, thank goodness we didn't. You probably would have treated them about as well as you treat my poor cat!"

"You shut your mouth, Eddie. Shut your stupid mouth!" My chest tightened, and I felt the heat creep into my neck and head. This was an argument we'd had so many times over the past several years, and it boiled my blood every time he brought it up.

A hiss sounded behind me and I clasped my hands in front of me, for strength. As the cat stared me down, I laughed the crazed laugh of a woman at her wit's end. "Of course," I said. "Of course your little black protector has somehow found her way into the house to rescue you."

Ms. Kitty sauntered past me and leapt into the waiting arms of her cross-species lover. My nose twitched as my husband nuzzled his bearded face into that murky fur, and the cat purred like she'd just won the lottery for a lifetime supply of premium cat-nip. Eddie showed that sinister temptress more affection than he'd shown me in years, and the absolute patheticness of this realization hit me like a ton of cat kibble.

I cleared the phlegm from my throat. "Geez, why don't you two get a room."

"Really?" Eddie smirked at me. "You're jealous of a cat?"

I shrugged and huffed out a big puff of air. "If Ms. Kitty was a human, you'd be cheating on me with her and you know it."

The cat purred louder and kneaded her paws into my husband's chest.

"You're being ridiculous."

"Oh, I don't know. They used to believe that black cats were just witches in disguise, you know. I'm positive Ms. Kitty has cast a spell on you."

My husband repositioned the cat on his chest, so that they were face to face. "Are you really a witch, Ms. Kitty?" he baby-talked to her, while simultaneously mocking me.

"Whatever." My neck stiffened, and I stretched it to the side until it crackled. "Just go away, the both of you. I need to keep exercising. And you know I hate it when you watch." I put my feet back on the pedals and jabbed the play-button to restart my music.

"Who'd want to watch that?" my husband shouted above the bass-line. He tucked the cat under one arm and started to leave, but just as he passed me, and even through the music, I heard him say, "Maybe you can work a spell on her, Ms. Kitty, and make her butt ten-times smaller."

I'd heard that when people are in a state a rage, all they see is red. It was true.

"Hey!" I screamed. He'd already insulted my inability to have kids and now he resorted to fat jokes?

Eddie whipped around to face me, just as a three-pound weight collided with the cat's head. The beast let out a near human scream and flew out of her lover's arms. Eddie's face twisted into something almost unrecognizable.

"What did you do?" he shrieked.

"I. Missed." I picked up the next closest weight and lobbed it at him before I could stop myself. My mind was a raging fire I couldn't snuff out. All rational thought burned to a cinder.

The dumbbell smashed into his temple with a sickening thud and I watched him fall—in curious slow motion—the other side of his skull colliding with the edge of the fireplace hearth. Sliding off the bike, I ran to his crumpled body and gazed at the blood seeping from his wounds.

Check for a pulse, check for a blasted pulse.

I ignored the prompting and marched into the downstairs bathroom, instead. Eddie had left a bucket full of rags in there, and I grabbed the whole thing, along with some of the spare trash-can liners. My concern misplaced, I knelt beside him, layering plastic bags and rags on the floor before I nudged his head away from the brick ledge. One more mess of his I was left to clean up. But, blood would be easier to clean off the bricks than the carpet.

Call nine-one-one, Ginny. Call freaking nine-one-one.

I couldn't explain why I wasn't listening to myself. There was a chance Eddie was still alive. I stopped what I was doing, tilted my head and regarded him. His chest didn't move. His mouth parted open as if shock had frozen on his face at the moment of death. And his eyes were like doll's eyes, glass orbs that had never had a life of their own. Even lifeless, his dead eyes stared into my soul, and I sucked in a breath.

"I could say it was an accident," I whispered to no one. Wasn't it, though? An accident? Had I woken up today intending to kill my husband? I imagined his sister would never believe I hadn't killed him on purpose. Eddie told her everything, and she had to know that we hadn't been happy in a long time.

A gargled *mew* drifted from the dark corner of the room and my head snapped to its position. One glowing green eye stared back at me and I cried out. "You!"

Ms. Kitty limped forward, hissing and spitting her accusations at me, as if she was innocent in all this. Her left eye cavity appeared to have collapsed inward. A twinge of remorse pricked at the back of my neck, but I flicked it away. "This is your fault, you know." I accused her, satiating my own guilt. "If you hadn't been such a traitorous little thing. I gave you a home, and now look what's happened."

The cat ignored me, letting out a mournful yowl, and went to lick the side of Eddie's face.

Dead.

The blanket of numb that had encased me ripped away along with my breath.

Eddie was dead. I had killed him. I had... not the stupid cat. I'd delivered the crushing blow.

I pushed myself up and pointed at Ms. Kitty. "You stay there. I'll be right back."

*

"Hello ma'am. Welcome to Home Depot."

"I need some bricks." I fought the urge to pinch the annoyance perched between my brows. I never shopped here; I hated stores like this. Eddie had always taken care of crap like this—but I guess he couldn't home-improvement this mess away for me this time.

"What kind of bricks did you need?" The Home Depot guy stroked his nonexistent beard and sucked his lips into a thin line.

I clenched my eyes shut to get a picture of the fireplace in my head, but all I could see were those vacant eyes staring back at me. I coughed and shook the image away. "Umm, I don't know. They are kind of a burnt-red, rust color. Old. From the seventies, I think. You know. When…" I choked on that last word. *Crap. Which pronoun did I use? "My* house was built. I need the stuff that sticks it all together, too."

One of his eyebrows pitched. "Mortar?"

I scratched at the back of my head and my fingers snagged inside the matted brown curls. "Yeah. That stuff."

"May I ask what you need them for?"

No, jerk-face. My eyes narrowed. "A fire-pit, grill thingy for my backyard."

He nodded. "Okay. And you're going to build it?"

My hand clamped onto my hip. "Yeah."

"Well, you know, we have professionals here who can help you with that."

I blinked at him a few times. "No thanks. I'm good. That's what You-Tube is for, right?" I forced a laugh and I could swear he forced himself not to roll his eyes.

"Sure thing, Ma'am."

*

On the drive home, I felt the weight of the bricks and mortar dragging down the back end of my car. I wondered if Eddie's body would weigh it down the same way. Not that I thought I could successfully get his body up the stairs and outside to the trunk of a car unnoticed, anyhow. No. I was going to have to shove his body into the fireplace and brick up the entrance. We'd never used it anyway. That was it. The only choice.

I opened the front door and immediately heard the cat warbling her sad mourning song for her best friend. It was a pin-prick to my heart—the one I needed to feel something again, perhaps. My eyes felt wet and I swiped the back of my hand across them. This whole situation… well, it sucked. I wasn't heartless. Still, I wondered if the tears flowed now because of guilt, or loss, or fear.

"I do not have time to cry for him," I told myself. "For any reason."

And, yet, as I dragged the bricks and other tools down to the basement, the tears assaulted me with a vengeance. I could barely see a thing, except that I could make out my husband in a bloody lump on the floor, still dead, with the cat standing vigil by his side. The cat… oh, the cat. Her face was thoroughly mangled. I hadn't meant to hurt her. She'd just been in the wrong place at the wrong time.

Son of a…

I'd have to take her to the vet. "C'mon, Ms. Kitty," I tried to coax, my voice shaking. "I'm sorry you got hurt." Well, sort of sorry.

The cat, of course, wouldn't come near me. I shook my hands in front of me and grumbled to the ceiling. "Gah!"

When did I become this person? I used to love animals. *All* animals. Parakeets, chickens, hamsters… Growing up I had a Golden Retriever named Ruffles who used to sleep at the foot of my bed. That stinkin' dog had loved me to pieces, and I'd loved him back, hadn't I? The old feelings and the memories became watered down by my tears.

I inched closer to Ms. Kitty. "C'mon. Quit being stubborn. You need to go to the vet." I reached a hand out to her, and she swiped at it with extended claws.

I hissed at her. "You stupid thing! You'll die, too, if we don't get that eye looked at."

Honestly, I was surprised she was still alive now. I reached for her again, but she bolted upstairs.

"Fine!" I yelled after her.

My attention turned back to my husband. My heartbeat sped up and I found it hard to breathe, again. I went to touch him, but snatched my hand back. I needed gloves. Gloves, oh gloves. Where would I find gloves? How the heck did I get into a situation where I needed gloves to clean up a dead body? Sure, Eddie was some kind of special jerk, but wouldn't divorce have been a cleaner option?

A loud sob escaped my mouth and I fell on top of him, pinning my ear to his chest. Maybe I'd missed it? Maybe he was still alive and I could revive him and write this all off as just a horrible accident. But as I lay against his lifeless body, I heard nothing—no heartbeat, no shallow breath. The life that had resided in his body had flown away like one of those ravens Ms. Kitty was always trying to pounce on in the backyard.

My head ached and I felt ill. I needed to call someone, but whom? For the first time in my married life, I was actually happy that we didn't have kids. There was no way I'd ever be able to explain, to a daughter or a son, this horrible thing I'd done. I could barely explain it to myself.

"It's the cat!" I screamed. "It's the cat, the stupid, devil, *black* cat!"

My mind spun with justifications. The sobbing had clogged my nose, making it difficult to breathe. I crawled over to the bathroom to get some tissues. My face was a wet mess. As I stared at my mascara streaked reflection in the mirror, I barely recognized the person there. The girl on the other side of the glass looked maniacal, unhinged, and… something else entirely. Free.

I took several deep breaths until I felt a little sane again. I wiped my face with a tissue and straightened my shirt, forcing myself not to blanch at the blood stains on it. I'd burn these clothes, along with any other evidence that proved my husband had ever died in this house. Straightening my back, I marched to the dead man on the floor and blinked at him once, before moving around him to take away the foam insert we'd used to cover the fireplace cavity.

I stared at the space behind it. It would take some creative shoving to get his body pushed all the way in there, but it was doable. I glanced at the time on my phone. It was barely mid-day. By the end of the night, he'd be gone—walled away and unable to affect my life ever again. I could do anything I wanted, and that thought ignited a spark in me. I took one more deep breath before I bent down to hoist his body up onto the hearth. There was no turning back now.

*

It turned out that sealing bricks together to create something was rather cathartic. I took care to line the bricks up perfectly and then I scooped a little mortar onto my trowel and shaped and scraped it until it looked the way it should. I finished with the fireplace in record time, for a beginning brick-layer. Sunlight still filtered in through the windows, and I remembered that I needed a new project that people could see, just in case I was ever questioned about buying bricks in the first place.

I moved outside and after a little effort, something started to take shape in the corner of my backyard, although it wasn't the round type of fire-pit I'd first envisioned. Circles were hard. This square version would support a grill rack a lot easier.

"Ginny?"

I closed my eyes before answering. "Back here."

Eddie's sister, Sara, strolled up to me with a tentative smile on her face. The crease between her brows told me that she wasn't here on a social call. In fact, I wondered if she'd been the one dinging a ton of notifications on my phone all day. I glanced at the cell phone I hadn't bothered to answer, sitting unused on the grass.

"Hey," she said.

"Hey." I forced my eyes to stay expressionless.

She looked at the nearly completed fire-pit, then at me, and then at my phone. "So, I've been trying to call you. Is your phone not working?"

I picked up the cell and pushed a button to turn it on. "Hmm. Wow. Sorry. I guess I missed them." I waved around at the bricks and tools I'd been using. "This project has taken more of my attention today than I thought, I guess."

Her nose wrinkled. "What is it, exactly?"

"Fire-pit. Grill."

"Huh." She rocked on her heels, like she was unsure whether she should sit or not. "So, I've also been trying to get ahold of Eddie. We were supposed to go on a bike ride tonight, but he's not answering his phone. Do you know where he is?"

Yes. "No. Sorry. He took that cat for a walk this morning, and I haven't seen them since."

"He took the cat for a walk? Who takes their cat for a walk?" She cleared her throat.

I pushed myself off the ground so that we were both standing. "We've had that cat for nine years, Sara. Surely you know by now that she follows Eddie everywhere."

She waved a manicured hand at me. "Yeah, well. It's still weird. Their relationship is a little…"

"Right!"

Sara shrugged. "And they've been gone since this morning?"

"I guess they went on a *long* walk."

She frowned. "Well, when he gets back, will you please have him call me?"

The memory of me smashing Eddie's cell phone with a hammer and slipping the pieces through the last hole in the fireplace wall, before I sealed it all up, flitted through my mind. "Of course. You bet. I'll tell him the minute he gets home."

Her brow creased again as she scanned the yard, and for a minute her gaze settled on the big window at the back of our house. I almost fell over, stretching to the side to see around her. What was she looking at? Did she see the cat? I squeezed the brick in my hand and for a moment, I wondered if I could get away with killing two people? Sara always was a nosy…

"Okay, then," she said, glancing back at me. "Oh!" She stumbled back and raised a hand to her lips.

"What? What is it?" My breath caught.

She pointed down at my hand. "Your fingers are bleeding."

I looked down at my hand, the one that gripped the brick so hard that, yes, I'd cut my fingers on the jagged edge. I dropped the brick and tucked my injured hand beneath my shirt. "Shoot. Sorry. This project is kicking my butt. Eddie was supposed to help, but…" I shrugged.

"Help?"

I noted the sarcastic note in her tone. We both knew that I never worked in the yard. Building a fire-pit was absolutely something Eddie would be doing, not me.

I picked up the trowel and pointed it at her. "Anything else you want me to tell Eddie?"

She backed up a step or two. "No, just to call me. Soon, please."

"You got it." I forced a smile.

"Ok. Thanks. I'll see you, I guess."

"Yep. See ya."

As she sauntered away, I fought the urge to vomit. I wasn't out of the clear, yet. At some point, I would have to report my husband missing. I would have to dig deep and play my best version of the worried, grieving widow. No, wrong word. Wife. I was still his wife, as far as the rest of the world knew. And if that traitorous cat ever showed up again, I could play her injury off as proof of some nefarious attack. Surely they'd been mugged while out walking or something, right?

I knelt back down to put the last few bricks in place. Then I grabbed the kindling and starter fluid I'd set out. Starting a fire in the center of the pit would help speed up the curing process and set the bricks. But, the fire would serve a dual purpose. As it roared to life, I took my husband's wallet from my pocket and dropped it into the flames. One more piece of him gone. So far, so good, but I'd have to keep an eye on that sister of his...

*

The doorbell dinged and I whimpered. I hadn't slept in two solid days. Too many sounds and words and thoughts running through my head—I couldn't make them stop. And interspersed between the police interviews and news stories and visits from worried family members, I heard Ms. Kitty. She hissed, unseen, from every corner of the house. Her mewing floated into the bathroom when I showered. Her claws scratched on the backside of every closed door. I'd see her phantom tail whipping around, from the corner of my eye. If she was dead, she was certainly a relentless ghost out to haunt me for the rest of my life. If she was still alive... well, she'd become a master at hide-and-seek.

I smoothed my hair down before opening the door. It was Detective Poe. His sullen eyes and twitchy, dark mustache greeted me with what he would, no doubt, deem "bad news".

"Hello, Mrs. Allen."

"Detective." I pulled my lips into a frown and rubbed my eyes as if I'd been crying. The dark circles under them would sell this lie, for sure. "Any news? Have you..." I paused to gulp, for effect. "Found him yet?"

"No, ma'am. I'm afraid we haven't. There's been no activity on any of his accounts or his cell phone. I'm sorry. We're kind of grasping at straws here."

I pulled a tissue from the pocket of my furry blue robe and wiped my nose. "Is there anything else I can do to help? I just... I mean... I feel so useless."

He gestured to the space just past me. "Would you mind if I took a quick look around the house again? Maybe we missed something."

Yeah, you did. My eyes started to narrow for a second, before I stopped them and nodded. "Yes, of course. If you think it will help? Come on in."

I followed him around as he looked behind couches and in cupboards and behind doors all throughout the house. He held a small flashlight in his hand that he pointed at all the dark corners. Although I was tired, I was also calm. My color-matching skills had proved spectacular and the You-Tube tutorial on how to lay bricks had been top-notch. The wall I'd created for the fireplace looked like it'd always been there. And the tall, ugly fern I'd placed on the hearth helped hide things even better.

"Have you had a chance to talk to all of his friends?" he asked.

"All the ones I know, yes. They haven't seen or heard from him."

"Yes, they told me the same thing." Detective Poe tapped a mechanical pencil to his lips. "And his family?"

I re-knotted the tie on my robe and shook my head. "They haven't heard a peep from him. His sister even went up to the family cabin to see if he was there, just in case, you know. Nothing."

"Is it like him to just wander off for days?"

He'd asked this question before. "No. I mean, he has his job, so… no. He's pretty responsible about stuff like that."

He looked at me and raised his eyebrows. "Oh, yes. Yes. You'd mentioned that before."

When he'd made his way around the top level of the house, he stopped at the head of the stairs to the basement. "I'll check down there, again. If that's okay?"

"Yes." I tapped the railing. "Go on down. I'll be right behind you."

The detective turned on every light in the basement before he started his search. He checked the creepy furnace room and the laundry room. There was a space under the stairs, which we'd always kept empty. Detective Poe checked under there, too. Still empty. He checked the work-out room and the closet just off the work-out room. He checked the spare bedrooms. Really, they were just empty rooms because we'd never needed them.

As he ambled around, I found myself sniffing the air like a bloodhound. I'd sealed up the body pretty darn good. The stench of decaying flesh couldn't seep through solid brick, could it?

He checked behind the big-screen TV in the family room. And finally he came to the fireplace. My calm started to crack a little as he inspected this spot a bit more thoroughly than any other space in the house. He bent down and ran a finger over a spot on the hearth and pushed aside the fern. He dragged the toe of his wing-tipped shoe along the crease where the carpet met the brick. When he shined his flashlight on the newly constructed wall, my breath caught.

But, then he merely shrugged and turned back to face me. "Well, I don't see anything new here that I didn't notice the last time."

"Oh."

"I'm sorry to waste more of your time." He stepped past me and started to climb the stairs.

"Don't be sorry, Detective. I really appreciate everything you guys are doing to find my husband." I cleared my throat as if I tried to hold back a sob.

When we reached the front door, he turned and gave my shoulder a quick pat. "I hope we find a lead, soon. When we know anything new, I'll let you know."

"I appreciate that."

"Take care, Mrs. Allen."

"Thank you."

I gripped the door handle until I heard the detective's car start up and he drove away. And then I bolted the front door and sighed. A chuckle escaped my lips. And then the chuckle turned into a deep belly laugh. I laughed long and hard, until the muscles in my stomach ached and my jaw was sore.

"I'm getting away with it." I boasted, out loud. "I'm actually getting away with it! Ha!"

Adrenalin rushed through my veins and I jumped back down to the top stair that led to the basement. I gripped the railing until my fingers hurt and leaned forward, yelling into the darkness. "Do you hear that, Eddie? I'm going to get away with it! You're not going to take me down. This isn't going to ruin my life. I get to live and you get to rot. So, what do you think about that?"

A sad mew sounded behind me and I whipped around so fast, I nearly lost my footing on the stairs. I gripped the railing with both hands as I fell to my knees and froze.

"Alright, Universe. Well-played. I get it. I'll quit bragging." I pulled myself up and balanced, moving away from the stairs and squinting into the dining room. "But, I better be hearing things. If I find you, Ms. Kitty, I'll knock a space open in that new wall just large enough to shove you in there with him."

*

"How you holding up?"

My best-friend, Liz, was a gem for coming over one week after I'd killed my husband. It'd been several months since I'd seen her at all. There'd been months and months between every visit, in the past few years. Not like it used to be. I'd missed her.

We used to get together every month for a game night, back when I was perfectly sane, newly married, and hadn't yet adopted a demon in a black-cat disguise.

"I'm doing okay. I just… you know. I wish they'd find something already. Even if he ran off with another woman or something. I just need closure." I clutched the front of my shirt, as if I clutched a broken heart.

She leaned in for a side hug and patted the back of my head. "Yeah, I get that." She pushed away from me and took a pack of playing cards to shuffle. "You're not a little happy about it, though, are you?"

I feigned the biggest shock of my life, my mouth dropping open so my jaw almost collided with my collar bone. "No. Oh my gosh, no! How could you ask that?"

She pulled fists in front of her lips and winced. "I'm so sorry, Ginny. I just, well, I know you two haven't exactly been on the newlywed track in a long time, and…" She shrugged and threw her hands out to her sides. "I'm sorry. That was totally insensitive of me."

A spitting hiss echoed behind us in the kitchen and my eye twitched in its direction. "Did you hear that?"

Liz looked around, straining her neck longer to get a better look at absolutely nothing. "Hear what?"

The hairs on my neck pricked up like a… well, a cat.

"I guess it's nothing." I rubbed my temples before patting my friend on the shoulder. "And, it's okay. I mean, you're not wrong. We weren't happily married. Still, I never wished Eddie dead."

Liar.

"Of course not."

We silently shuffled our cards, cut our decks a few times, and set up for a game of Hand and Foot. "Don't forget to get rid of your red threes."

We played a few hands in silence. I paused our game to get up and refill the spinach and artichoke dip, just as there was a loud pounding at the door.

"Do you want me to get that?" Liz asked.

"If you don't mind? Thanks."

I heard the door click open, and then it was like every sound around me molded into one deafening screech. Before I could react, or refill the dip, I'd been surrounded by Sara, Detective Poe and two other cops in uniform. Liz stood frozen by the kitchen door.

Sara looked like something from the Exorcist—her eyes wide, her hair wild and unruly, and the look she gave me was nothing short of murderous. I would know.

"He's here," she shrieked. "I know he's here." She grabbed the collar of my shirt and yanked me closer to her. "Where'd you put him? Huh, Ginny? Did you chop him up like wood for that hideous new fire-pit of yours?"

I should have killed her with that brick…

"Fire-pit?" Detective Poe asked.

Meowing started like a slow gurgle, cutting through all the noise, slowly building until I had to cover my ears with my hands. Sara tried to tug my arms away from my head, but Detective Poe stopped her.

"Fine." I assumed she screamed this, because I could hear it through my hands.

She tugged the officers away, out my back door and into the yard. I walked to the sink in the corner of the kitchen and watched them from the window.

Liz touched my shoulder and I jolted.

"Sorry!" She ran her hands over her short blonde hair and gaped at me. "But, what the heck is going on here?"

My hands limped down to my sides, and I sucked in a breath. "Sara has clearly lost it. You know she never liked me. I think she's taken Eddie's disappearance harder than anyone."

"But, why does she think he's in the fire-pit?" She scratched her chin and leaned past me to look out the window. "When did you *get* a fire-pit?"

My shoulders hunched up around my ears and then relaxed. "I built it last week."

"You." She pointed at me. "You *built* something? Since when did you get crafty?"

A growl came out of me and I felt the fire entering my face. "I wanted a fire-pit and Eddie wouldn't get me one, so *I* built it, okay! I'm not a complete idiot, you know."

"Okay, okay. Geez."

The quartet of accusers came clomping back into the house, and I noticed the detective held a baggie full of ash. I pointed at it and laughed. "You're not going to find my husband's bones or flesh bits or whatever in that. Because I DIDN'T kill him. Are you even allowed to take that?" Would they detect the leather of his wallet or the plastic of his ID and credit cards? But those things didn't add up to a body. I had old wallets and old cards of my own to burn.

Detective Poe pulled a paper from the inside pocket of his jacket. "Standing search warrant. We obtained it when he first went missing. I thought I'd explained that to you? It's still good for a while."

"Fine. Whatever. Take your ash and get out of my house now, please."

Sara balked and stood her ground. "You'll have to drag me out of here. I'm not leaving until you find my brother."

Liz joined the other two officers, becoming spectators.

"Did you buy the fire-pit like that, Mrs. Allen?" the detective asked.

"What?" I looked out the window again and shook my head. "No. No, I bought some bricks at Home Depot."

"Bricks?"

I didn't like the sudden glint of knowing that shone in the detective's eyes. He turned silently and headed toward the front door... or to the top of the staircase that led to the basement. The two entrances stood mere feet from each other. I held my breath as we all followed him and he made his choice. Down to the basement we went, and my heart dropped into my toes.

"When did you buy the bricks, Mrs. Allen?" he asked while I watched his feet, hoping he might slip down the worn carpet on the stairs.

"I don't know. A few weeks ago, or so?" I forced down a gulp.

As we all piled into the space at the bottom of the stairs, Detective Poe once again took care to turn on every single light in the basement. Only this time, he didn't go from room to room. He stared at the fireplace as if he had laser vision.

Sara gawked at it, too. "What did you do to it? What happened to that ugly slab of foam you used to block that air from the flue?" She stumbled up to the hearth and grabbed the fern, chucking it across the room so that it crashed against the dry bar in the family room. She bent over and started hyperventilating.

"Is this new, Mrs. Davidson?"

Sara couldn't find her voice, but she nodded.

"No, it's not. That fireplace has been bricked over for years." I lied.

Everyone in the room looked doubtful, and Sara choked on her breath.

"Don't look at me like that. It's my house." I pounded my chest. "I know what is and isn't true about it." I shoved Sara out of the way and pounded my palm against the brick covering. "You see? It's solid as rock. Solid as a wall that's always been here. Sara doesn't live here. She doesn't have a clue what she's talking about."

Mewing and hissing sounded throughout the room, and I tried to push it from my mind. The phantom cat wasn't going to make me crack. No. She wouldn't get me now. I wouldn't let her. But, as I resolved to ignore the cat sounds that only I ever seemed to hear, I noticed that everyone else was staring at the wall in horror.

Sara's face paled to one shade whiter than a vampire's. "Oh, my goodness. Is that a cat?"

My world blew up. "What?" I stared at the wall. "You mean you hear that?"

Detective Poe motioned at the other officers and they advanced on me and pushed me up against the wall.

Liz had backed herself into a corner and blubbered as Sara went into hysterics. "Is that Ms. Kitty?" She rounded on me, pure vengeance etched in the lines of her face. "What did you do, Ginny?"

I hadn't noticed that Detective Poe had left the room, but he reappeared from the staircase with a crowbar in hand. At the first swing against the wall, I cracked a smile. At the second swing, a chuckle gurgled up from my belly and escaped my lips. When he swung the metal bar against the bricks a third time, I laughed out loud. I kept laughing, until I started crying, all the while watching Detective Poe destroy the one thing that would have given me a new life.

I felt like I was under water—everything slightly out of focus, words and voices like soggy echoes. The wall crumbled to the ground, smothering my freedom. The smell of rot wafted into all of our senses.

And that black devil cat, with its one good eye, skinny—but STILL alive— stood atop my husband's corpse, triumphant.

Ed Ahern resumed writing after forty odd years in foreign intelligence and international sales. He's had over two hundred stories and poems published so far, and three books. Ed also works the other side of writing at Bewildering Stories, *where he sits on the review board and manages a posse of five review editors.*

About this story, Edward says: "My title of course is a little homage to E.A. Poe's The Purloined Letter, *but I tweaked the tone of the story to give it a bit of a sideways sense of humor."*

No madness or mysticism here, just a simple case of a missing painting, an abundance of suspects, and an investigator with plenty of attitude and a unique set of skills... Then again, maybe there's a bit of mysticism here, after all.

THE PURLOINED OIL
Edward Ahern

"Somebody stole my picture."

I pretended to type a note on my laptop. "How valuable?"

"*Fungus Riddled Iris* by Emma LaRue. It's appraised at seven million"

"I've seen a picture. Nasty looking ergot." I focused in on her. Sylvia Peterson. Off-blonde hair. Attractive mid-thirties striving for that twentyish look. A bodacious emerald ring. Clothes tailored to fit her petite frame.

"Have the police made progress?"

She let out an annoyed hiss. "Don't be dense. If they had I wouldn't have to be here. The cops are as clueless as you seem to be. I'm only here because the insurance company assigned you to the case."

"With a payout of seven mil, Pound & Elias is having palpitations in the money chest. They bring me in when they get these anxiety attacks."

"And won't pay me until you're done poking around." Sylvia snapped the card I'd given her between thumb and fingers. "The Lost and Found Department? You need to hire a marketing firm." She glanced again at the card. "What kind of weird name is Adalson?"

"Obscure. The seven million, I assume, is replacement value? So an auction value would be around six?"

She gave me a hard stare. I sucked in my stomach. "That's none of your business."

"Ah, touchy. So maybe only five million. Tell me about the theft."

The story she told echoed the police report. Only the painting taken, no signs of entry or exit, no one home at the time, alibis for Sylvia, her soon to be ex-husband Willie Stevens and her sister.

She was being taped, so I slid past her words and focused on reading her. Pretty much the same as what a medium does during a séance while conning a grieving widow, but I did it better. Probably because I could reach out and, usually, sense the emotions of the speaker.

The painting's really off the wall. And she's lying by omission. And she doesn't like me, despite my charm. And she despises her live-in sister, who owns half of everything.

"… and then, excuse me, but could you not stare at me with your mouth open?"

"Ah, sure" I gave her my 'fond of children and pets' smile. It flunked.

"There's an excellent chance I can recover the painting."

Sylvia scowled. "There's an excellent chance you can fail and die from syphilis."

She bounced up, didn't offer her hand to shake, and turned toward the door. "You're wasting our time, Stokes." As she opened the door to go I called out. "Why do you hate your sister so much?"

"What?"

"You're concerned about the painting and repulsed by your almost ex. But you despise your sister."

"I never said…" She turned and strode back up to my desk. Nice legs.

"My sister's of no concern in this matter."

"And I'm going to join a monastery later this afternoon. You've never mentioned your sister's name."

"Margot Olsen."

I raised an eyebrow.

"Our father had four wives."

"Any other children?"

"None. After breeding with the first two women he relied on latex."

"Who else comes and goes?"

"The staff had the day off. Only Margot, Willie, and I were in the house. It's got a museum-grade security system, and the alarms weren't tripped while we were out"

"Why do you think it was taken that afternoon while you all were gone?"

"Because the maid reported seeing it at noon. Didn't you read the police report?"

"What about your boyfriend?"

"What—what boyfriend?"

I gently shook my head from side to side. "Sylvia, if we're going to find this diseased plant, you have to struggle for honesty. You pulled off your wedding ring maybe two weeks ago, so you and hubby aren't best friends. And your makeup doesn't quite cover the hickey on your neck."

She sat back down, glared at me, and shrugged. She had an attractive glare. "Okay, let's get this over with. What do you need to do?"

"Inspect the house and interview you, Willie, and Margot." I pulled two sheets of printed paper out of a drawer and handed them to her.

"What's this?"

"Your agreement to allow all reasonable investigation. Putting things on paper reduces bickering." I heard the whir of her thinking, warped gears lubed with cold cream.

"All right," she said finally, "but try not to get any creepier."

I keyed the intercom. "Sara, could you please come in and witness something?"

Sylvia held the two sheets in her fingertips like they carried HIV. Sara came in.

"Sylvia Peterson, meet Sara Trumbull. Sara, Sylvia."

Sylvia skimmed through the agreement, signed it.

"Are you going back home?"

"Yes."

"I need to check out the house. Could I stop by in an hour and a half?"

Sylvia hesitated, and I sensed why. "I need to talk to Willie as well."

She nodded. "Okay, but wash your hands afterward."

Once Sylvia had left I asked Sara to come back in.

Sara listens in—it's part of her job—and she raised an eyebrow at me. "She's just your type. Manipulative and elegantly slutty."

"Isn't she? Also rich and soon divorced. Should I upstage the boyfriend?"

"Don't. I'd tip her off that no one can live with you. My antennae aren't as sensitive as yours, but I don't think she likes you."

"There's that. How're we doing on the checks on hubby and sis?"

"Close. I've already sent you the material on the painting. Apparently, childlike rendering of plant rot qualifies as high art. There's about a dozen collectors unscrupulous and rich enough to buy the painting, None of them appears to have had contact with the family, nor to be making any unusual arrangements. Why don't you ever let the client know how much you already know?"

"Because if they think I'm ignorant their lies get sloppy and easier to pick apart."

*

I guessed that either Willie or Margot would avoid me, and got to the house an hour early—just in time to block Willie from backing out of the garage. He hopped out of his car and strode over to me.

"You're blocking me. Get out of my way."

I did a quick study. *Pear shaped. Bully boy attitude, big, forties, no scars, serious pudge, bad muscle tone. Voice just a fraction of an octave higher than he wanted it to be.*

"Right after we talk."

He put his hands on my open car window and leaned in. His cologne smelled expensive. "Get out of my way or I'll make you sorry."

"Bad line, Willie." I grabbed his left index finger, pulled it in and twisted. He screamed, which pretty well demolished the image he was trying to project. I kept a strain on his finger while I opened the door and got out, then let go.

Willie gingerly massaged the finger. "You broke it!"

"Not yet. Let's be friends. I need answers and you need your fingers for golf. How bad is your pre-nup arrangement?"

He scowled. "None of your damn business!"

"Okay, so not more than half a million. Good reason to steal the painting."

"Where the hell would I sell it? It's too well known."

I took him back through his statements to the police. A bad liar repeats his story verbatim, afraid to vary it. Somebody remembering forgets things, and changes his wording. Willie meandered. I read him while he talked. *Still the bully boy front, but he's afraid, of all 170 pounds of me, and of Sylvia for some reason. And something else...*

"Tell me about Margot Olsen."

His body stiffened. "Ah, Sylvia's half-sister, lives here, Not married, not working."

"And not normal."

"I never said that!"

"You did, sort of. Does she ever leave the house?"

Willie paused. "No. She has anxiety attacks, high strung artist."

"Why does Sylvia let you stay here?"

"I run the estate for her."

I stifled a laugh. He wasn't the diddler anymore, but he was still the butler.

"Okay, Willie, I want you to take me on a quick tour of the house."

He clenched his fists and took a threatening step closer. I got another whiff of rare spices. "Do it yourself, or get Sylvia to do it. Now get out of my way before you get hurt."

I looked down at him and put on a glare. "Willie, if you take a swing, I'll break your kneecap."

He wilted. "You're an asshole."

I nodded. It felt satisfying to be a bully, especially since I had no idea how to break a knee cap.

Willie tried to quick-step me through, but I slowed him down, paying minimal attention to the details of the rooms, sighting in on his wordings, eye movements and body language. Halfway through the tour, we encountered a slender, well-proportioned woman.

"Stokes, this is Margot Olsen. Mary this is…"

"Adalson Stokes, Margot, delighted to meet you."

"What an interesting name."

"If it's easier, my friends call me Dali. I'd like to talk with you a little later."

"Of course, that's my suite over there. Just knock."

Willie and I continued our tour. The mansion, a hundred and fifty years old, held lots of cubbies and cul-de-sacs, and was paneled almost everywhere in oak wainscoting. There were twelve bedrooms and fourteen bathrooms, so more opportunities to defecate than to sleep.

We finished up in the two story entry hall. "I'm leaving now, Dali."

"You don't get to call me that. When are you returning?"

"For dinner. Don't come back."

"Not planning on it."

What I didn't tell my tour guide was that I wasn't leaving. I zigzagged back to Margot's rooms, paying more attention to the layouts and furnishings. She answered my second knock.

"Margot, I'd like you to also give me a tour of the house."

"That's silly, Willie just gave you one."

"I know, but I need to see the place through your eyes as well."

Margot showed me her studio, crammed with oils executed in the realistic styles of Edward Hopper and Jacques-Louis David. I made polite sounds about them and she glowed. "Willie and Sylvia don't like them, but I think art should show the world clearly."

"What do you think of 'Fungus Riddled Iris'?"

She cringed. "Sylvia says I can't talk about it, that's it's a police matter."

"It is, but it's okay to tell me what you thought of it."

Margot leaned in toward me, her breath gently blowing on my ear. "I thought it was truly ugly."

I laughed, the sound echoing off the wood. "What do you know about the disappearance of the painting?"

"Nothing. We don't normally go through that hall. It was there earlier that day, gone when we got back from the theatre."

"Whose idea was it to go to the theatre?"

"Nobody's. We have a foundation that contributes to the performances, and have to put in appearances once or twice a season."

She was telling the truth about the disappearance. Seems to always tell the truth, which means I need to figure out the right questions.

Margot moved through the house with a doe's hesitant steps, her moods evanescent. She registered strongly at the empty space where the painting had hung.

"Thanks for the tour. Would Sylvia be in the office you showed me?"

"I think so."

Silvia was. I knocked and entered when she called out. She didn't get up from her desk. "So sorry that Willie left—"

"Actually, I was able to grab him before he took off. We had such a nice visit. Margot as well."

She scowled. "So that's that."

"Not quite. I need to have you give me a tour of the house."

"I don't have the time to spare for you."

"You need my verification before you can collect on the insurance. Let's play nice."

"I checked with some other Pound & Elias clients Your mind reading act has annoyed some important people."

I smiled winningly. "There's no bad publicity. Shall we start?"

Sylvia's glances were possessive, nodding slightly at the expensive artifacts. I threw out pedestrian questions while I studied her. She spiked several times with bad memories, but I couldn't tell what of.

"Are you always this boring, Stokes?"

"Depends on the company. Let's go back through the study."

"We were just there."

"Humor me."

"You're as cracked as Margot." But she turned around and led me back into the room. She kept her eyes rigidly forward, but her body strained in another direction.

Once back at her office door, Sylvia turned around, blocking me from entering. "We're done," she blurted.

"Not quite. I need to go back through the house on my own, although I'd be greatly pleased with your company."

"Not a chance."

"Okay. I'll go alone, then wait in the library until dinner time. I'd like to join you, Margot, and Willie for dinner and tell you all what I've learned. Please inform the cook."

"You patch of back alley slime. I'm not eating with you."

"You should, if you want to hear my recommendation. Just picture me as a truffle garnish."

She pursed her lips so hard they almost disappeared, then nodded curtly and entered her office, slamming the door behind her.

*

I finished a little early, and sat in the library reading a leather-bound book that probably cost more than my college education. Margot found me there. Her smile was the most genuine thing I'd seen all day.

"You're like me, aren't you?"

Her feelings flew off her like dandelion seeds in a gust of wind, and I didn't need an explanation.

"Yes. Same gift box, different side." I hesitated before continuing, choosing my words carefully. "Margot, what I'll say at dinner isn't meant to be hurtful."

"I don't think you want to hurt me."

"Probably not, which complicates things. Shall we go in?"

I was seated at the foot of the table, with empty places between me and the other three diners. Fortunately, I have a loud voice. "Why don't we dine first?" I suggested, "and then I'll describe what I think should be done."

Margot and I chattered pleasantly through the meal, while Willie and Sylvia were deaf mutes, understandable since they didn't like anyone else at the table. I began after the maid had cleared the dishes.

"Let's deconstruct the puzzle. Assume for the moment that the maid *saw* the painting but didn't *look* at it. The painting is too famous to be sold to anyone but a private collector willing to hide it. There are few people in this category, and none of them seem to be making the preparations necessary for a purchase. Nothing else was taken, so our presumed thief wasn't a generalist. And there's no word out on the street that it's available cheap.

"Let's also posit that the painting never left this house." I paused to read expressions and got the affirmations I wanted. "But why? And why file on the insurance when it's much easier to just auction the painting off? Maybe because the painting was no longer salable."

I looked up the table with gentle eyes. "When did you over-paint the picture, Margot?"

Margot gasped, but Sylvia interrupted before she could say anything. "Shut Up, Margot! Don't say a word."

"She doesn't have to. She's walked past an art work she hated at least twice a day for years. As a talented artist—"

"Do you really think so?"

"Shut up, Margot!" chorused Willie and Sylvia.

"Yes, I do. Anyway, one day she brings her palette to the hall and redecorates."

"That's slander."

"Not since it's true. During the tours Willie and Margot each had mundane tics and tells. You, however, reacted enough to indicate where the picture was hidden. I regret to say I couldn't find the release, and had to break open the latch on the wainscoting."

I stepped over to the sideboard, lifted aside an end curtain, and took out a framed picture.

The cobalt blue of the iris was bright and healthy. I set the painting atop the table so they could see the alteration.

"Now, what to do? Let me tell you. First, you tell the insurance company that it's all been a mistake, that the painting had been misplaced. They won't believe you, but since it's costing them no money, and it's hard to prove attempt to defraud, they won't pursue the matter.

"Second, find a discreet restorer to lift off Mary's layer of paint. If he does a bad job you can claim that the painting aged badly, and settle for four million on the sale."

Sylvia actually smiled. "Or, we get rid of you and just carry on."

"Such a cliché, Sylvia. Like everyone else, I have a cell phone and uploaded shots of the painting to my cloud files this afternoon. They would be examined if I die."

"So that's that."

"Not quite. You've committed insurance fraud, and there's a fee for my silence."

"The insurance company already pays you."

"To recover the painting, true. This is a separate—private—matter. To keep you out of prison scrubs requires $50,000, payable to an offshore account."

"You'd just keep blackmailing us."

"Please, I have principles. I suspect the people you talked to about me told you that I keep to my word."

Willie leaned in. "Sylvia..."

"Shut up, you dripping spigot." She stared at me like she needed a can of insecticide, then glared at Margot. I sensed that she couldn't think of a way to dispose of us that would help her cause. "All right."

I laid a business card on the table. "The account number is written on the back. I'd suggest burning this after use. Thank you for a predictably bland meal. I'll see myself out."

But Margot jumped up from the table and glided over to me, taking my arm. "I'll walk out with you."

Her demeanor was innocent, with no guilt blemishes. "Do you really think I'm a good painter?"

"I do." An urge struck. "You should maybe do my portrait."

She giggled. "I want to. When?"

"Let me call you."

*

Sara was waiting for me at the office the next morning. "And?"

"Check the offshore account, but it's safe to say your 401k is in no danger. The painting has been found, and the family restored to full dysfunctionality"

"I'm so happy for them. Pound & Elias have sent over another case, something about a castrated show dog."

"I do love animals." As Sara turned to leave I added, "The sister is a painter. I'm thinking of having my portrait done."

"Interesting euphemism."

Chris Abela started writing at nine years old, but spent many adult years pursuing other careers, including psychology, counseling, and usability research, just to prove that nothing could be as satisfying as writing—and darn it, she succeeded. She resides in Maryland with her husband and two children. On weekends you'll often find their house full of caffeine-and-pun-addicted friends who share a love of books, games, and great barbeques. Visit Chris at authorchrisabela.com and look for her other work in the forthcoming Cursed Collectables.

About this story, Chris says: "I wrote Kiss and Tell *because I was interested in exploring the psychological trauma of punishment. Like Poe's protagonist in* The Pit and the Pendulum, *I imagined a character who faced a series of recurring trials. I was fascinated by what these trials might do to someone's psyche and what the end result would be if, unlike Poe's protagonist, she could neither escape or be saved."*

What obligation do we have to those around us to stop the pickpocket, report the abuser, testify against the killer so they don't go on to hurt someone else? And when we find ourselves powerless, how far will we go to see that justice is served—and what lines will we cross in the process?

KISS AND TELL

Chris Abela

I remember when a Kiss was an expression of love, a form of sexual desire—perhaps a reverence or salutation. I try to ignore the couple sharing my park bench and their incessant display of affection, while I swallow the sharp, semi-sweet bite of asiago bagel and chase it down with bitter coffee.

A breeze stirs the fallen leaves on the path in front of me. The morning paper at my side rustles, reminding me that my jitters are from the headline, not the caffeine. I rest my lidded cup on the big, bold words: *Mother convicted in death of 3-year old.* Without reading the article, I know the details. For my own eyes saw the drowning. And the sight is not one so easily brushed away in dreams when it replays itself—over… and over… and over again. Justice found her, and this gives me reprieve, but only for the briefest moment. For I know this headline means I will be called again—to bear witness and enjoin Justice.

My fingers pick incessantly at the half-eaten bagel, tearing it to crumbles, like the time left in this reprieve. I fling the bready remnants on the footpath. The furor of flapping wings fills the air. Pigeons swarm and nab every morsel in mere seconds. I am aghast at the rapidity, although I shouldn't be. Isn't it always so?

I hear a cat-call among a group of passing joggers. No doubt for my benchmates, but I stand and adjust my skirt, just in case. I grab my cup and begin on my way. Breakfast bites and coffee churn in my stomach like stones in acid.

It's not long before the familiar light-headedness overtakes me, stopping me in my path. My mind becomes a prisoner that transcends to another place. This one is of darkness. I am sitting—surrounded by the soft vibrations and gentle rocking of a car, rolling along a dirt road. As my tunnel vision fades, I see I am the front passenger at night, and the path ahead is lit only by headlights. *Again?* I ponder. *Nothing good ever happens to me in a car.*

The driver brakes to a stop and the side of my shoe grazes a glass bottle or two. He steps out of the vehicle and my mind calculates the reality before me: scary, strong man, dark night, middle of nowhere. Several sounds follow in succession—the opening spring of a trunk, the rustling and clatter of metal tools, heaving grunts. I feel the slight bounce of the car as something heavy is freed and dropped to the ground. Immediately, the intermittent scraping begins. It grows louder by my door as he drags the five-foot canvas bag in his slow wake. I'm certain it's the body he's come to dump.

He reaches the stream of headlights and what I think I see makes dread swallow me whole. My heart lurches when I see it again—movement inside the canvas bag—becoming erratic. I hear a woman's muffled screams, and he bends to meet them.

"Stop!" I plead, banging my hands on the dashboard. "Don't do it!" One of my hands claws at the door handle. The other pinches the lever for the automatic window. Both, to no avail. I pound on the window in time with my heartbeat.

"WHY?" I know my guttural roar is muted by more than this stuffy casket of a car. But I don't care. "Why?" I scream again, followed by the crying in my head: *Why can't I persuade them? Why can't they ever hear me?*

Is it because I couldn't persuade her—I couldn't stop her? My sister's hysteric wails echo in my mind. I glance to the driver's seat and remember the way she swerved the car, whizzing in and out of traffic.

I hear the faint rip of a heavy-gauge zipper. My attention zags back to the stranger. A flash of downward movement registers in my sight and I bury my head. I refuse to watch; for what I already know is too much: Abducted. Alive. Alone. Conscious, beaten, and… things I will not allow myself to repeat.

Why me? Why must I always know the gut-wrenching truth?

Is it because I knew about my sister's break-up? The spiraling meltdown? Her suicidal intention prior to flooring the gas petal?

The passenger door opens.

I lean back in the seat, holding my breath. By the cabin's light I see the twelve-inch hunting knife not far from my shoulder. I hear the snap of a cloth and watch him wipe the partially serrated blade. I can't pull away as he turns over the dark-stained handkerchief with a careful fold and wipes again. When he leans in to pop open the glove compartment, I inhale with sudden unexpectedness. I cram myself further into the seat as his sweat assaults my nostrils much like cumin and onion. Before he shuts the compartment I glimpse three blood-stained handkerchiefs, maybe more. A shudder strikes deep in my core. It reverberates up my throat and into my mouth with the sour taste of vomit. Surely, I'm going to be sick.

The door slams shut with a swoosh.

The air vacuums away and I jar out of place.

On my feet, the surroundings reveal themselves more quickly this time. We are now ascending in a private elevator no more than three feet by four. The scent of cumin and onion wrestles with my senses. A trench coat covers his clothes, and he carries a briefcase. I worry what could be inside. My back presses against the cold, steel corner of this confined space. It doesn't matter that he cannot see me, for my mind still awaits an instant when those brown eyes turn on me.

The door slides open, and we are greeted by a spacious, white flat. I cautiously step out after him. There is a lounge area ahead with an adjacent kitchen on the left. The lounge area is furnished with a grey chesterfield sofa, matching side chairs, and glass table resting on a silver frame. The city lights twinkle behind a wall of glass. Even from this vantage point I can tell that by day, there is a view to die for. One that makes worries meaningless and people small and insignificant.

By the time I reach the spotless kitchen, he is gone. I think I hear running water somewhere beyond the nearby hallway. I listen more intently as my sight crawls along the ceiling-high, molded cabinets. A shower door bangs, confirming my suspicion, and now I'm left to wait.

A chill tingles my hand as I drag it along the marble island. I come to a perfect line of items—spoon, sugar, mug, bowl, knife, apple. His life begins to unfold in front of me. I imagine the way he spoons sugar into his mug before he pours the coffee. The way he completely finishes the cereal before ending breakfast with sliced fruit. The images swim around my head before I think to cast them away.

It hits me: *I'm waiting; I'm patient; it's like I've become the stalker.* I can't escape the chill that leaves my hand to travel down my back. *No,* I insist, jetting down the hallway.

I glimpse him crossing in front of a stately, four-poster bed, a towel wrapped about his waist. I stop in the doorway and my eyes cannot help but follow his statuesque figure to a mirrored dresser. I surmise his victims felt the same draw. And who can blame them? For how easily his body hides the abominable truth.

He spends minutes at the horizontal dresser folding and refolding, arranging and rearranging, the same briefs, deodorant, t-shirt—collared shirt, dress pants, rolled-up belt. He works like a frenzied child to calm the tsunami of chaos that must be ravaging his mind.

Just like my sister.

"I know you're listening," I say to whatever deity forces me into these situations. "She was a teenager at the time." Old enough to feel as deep as the ocean, but still too young to have perspective. "And I couldn't do it..." Even though I was her passenger, I couldn't bring myself to corroborate the surviving father's accusation that she plowed into the SUV on purpose, killing the pregnant mother and two children. *But I know she did.*

I am quick to move away from the door, leaving behind the memory. Standing at the side of the dresser, I see his frantic hands finally come to rest. He leaves, and I walk past the dresser, avoiding my reflection. Instead, I spy him as he chucks the towel and climbs into bed. When he's settled, I turn and slink forward. And I wonder if he knows he's being watched and studied like his victims.

He lays there, his silhouette appearing no different than an ordinary man. He could be a teacher, counselor, or security official and the majority of us wouldn't know the difference. After he drifts to sleep, I press my lips into the supple flesh of his forehead, leaving behind the mark of my Kiss. I do for his victims what I wouldn't do for my sister's: I brand him the killer that he is so that Justice may be blind no more.

My shoulder nudges forward and the tranquility of the room transposes back to the morning rush of Central Park. My hand is wet from sloshing coffee. I react, but not in time to stop spills down the lower half of my shirt. "What the—"

"I'm sorry. Are you all right?" a male jogger calls out. He turns to face me, and I can't decide what annoys me more, his bobbing up and down in place or the florescent yellow shorts. Both make my brain ache and I am relieved when he finally stands still.

I don't respond, and he steps forward, touching my elbow. *What's he touching me for?* I wonder. *Is he crazy? What if I'm the psycho nut wondering the park? What if I were a killer? Wait! What?*

His fingers poke the smartphone attached to his armband. He pops an earbud out of his ear. I notice the small, metal skull adorning the earbud and it reminds me all too well of the things I've seen and the secrets I choose to keep.

"Are you all right?" he asks again.

"Fine. Yes." I pause to examine the stains on my shirt, giving my mind the time it needs to regain clarity.

"Let me buy you another coffee."

I try to wave him off with my hand. "Oh no, that's not necessary."

"You're wearing coffee on your shirt because of me. Come on. It's the least I can do."

I hesitate and his smile widens. He tells me about his favorite coffee shop, *Brewed Awakenings* just across 5th Avenue.

"Okay," I say.

"Really?" He bounces from foot to foot, repeating my answer. "Okay!"

I reel back from his enthusiasm, and he is quick to apologize and explains that he is a programmer and likes to run, both of which are solitary activities. But he likes people, so it's exciting when he finds opportunities to interact.

As we walk to the coffee shop, I don't talk much. Mark is more than willing to take up the better half of the conversation—even through the mad rush of crowds, honking vehicles, and distant sirens. Luckily, once inside *Brewed Awakenings*, I snag the second bistro table along the front window while Mark stands in line. The name of the shop is emblazoned on the window, obscuring the view. Eyelashes shoot up from each 'e' in the word *'Brewed'* to make them look like eyes. *Kinda eerie.* I turn my head and focus on Mark. I guess sometimes it takes an affable and gracious person to remind me the world is not divided solely into criminals and victims.

This eases my mind as we sip our coffee and continue to chat. The more he talks, the more I like his genial, blue eyes. When he smiles, it's wide, forming deep lines around his mouth and exposing his straight white teeth. He's charming—even for someone who owns skull earbuds.

When he turns the conversation to me, the questions feel like rapid fire: Are you from here? What do you do? Family? I fight the urge to freeze. My answers, succinct nonetheless: Yes, consultant, estranged.

"Oh, consultant for what?"

A montage of perpetrators and Kisses sail through my mind. A swell of tension grips my body. "I... should really go." When I stand to leave, Mark pulls at my wrist.

"Wait—numbers."

"What?" *I don't have an exact number! Too many!*

He borrows a pen from a woman sitting at the table behind him. "We exchange phone numbers, I call you or you call me, and we go out." He scribbles on a napkin and hoists it in my direction with a chuckle. "That's how it works. There's an order to it."

I take the napkin. "Of course there is." My vision sinks into the white of the napkin as I recall my past mistake with the gunman in the high-rise hotel. He couldn't hear my pleas to stop as he prepared his semi-automatic rifle. He knelt at the open window and the desperation to stop him bled through every pore of my being. In haste, I pressed my lips into his forehead. Foreboding fired through me when he readied himself to shoot as if I weren't there. He pulled the trigger—continuous explosions tore at my eardrums faster than I could cover them. Details I couldn't bear to know slumped twenty-seven floors below.

I remember the fling of the backpack over his shoulder along with the determined steps that carried him to the door. Then the abrupt stop and turn, eyes that searched the room, and the hand that touched his forehead.

I gasped, feeling exposed. "Can you see me?" I asked with hesitation.

He staggered toward me and dropped the backpack onto the bed. He retrieved a pistol from the pack and placed it to his temple.

"No," I screamed. "You don't get to-"

The shot cracked and I jolted.

"Hey," Mark says, shaking my shoulder. "Where did you go?"

"What?"

"You have that far-away look in your eyes again—like when I bumped you in the park."

"Nowhere," I lie. "I'm thinking about what you said. There's always an order to follow." *And my mark must come after the crime or Justice can't find them through space and time.*

*

My finger swipes down the smartphone and news feed headlines scroll across the screen. I tap at the word 'canvas' before it disappears, looking for Canvas Bag Killer updates. But the sentence reads: Police canvass museum for missing girl. *No.* Not it. My finger swipes up, down, up.

I sense Mark's presence beside me. "One asiago bagel. Black coffee."

A plate and cup appear on the bistro table just above my smartphone. It's been our morning ritual since we met in Central Park three months ago. I read at the coffee shop, and he shows up bearing gifts. My head tilts up, but my eyes shift back to the headlines.

"Can't stay this morning. Important meeting."

"Okay," I say, glancing up at his navy blue suit. "Must be."

His posture straightens. He uses his reflection in the front window of *Brewed Awakenings* to adjust his tie. "Yup. So I'll let you get back to your obsession."

Obsession?

"As if you don't have your own, Mr. Fitness."

He chuckles and grabs the messenger bag from the chair opposite me. "Hey, I'm not judging."

I watch him leave out the door, but he walks along the front window and stops where I am. He displays his stellar smile, and I hear his muffled voice through the glass. "We all have our vices."

He turns and disappears into the sea of pedestrians.

Within no time, my finger swipes the smartphone—up, down, down. Headlines scroll fast, faster, and super speed like the reels of a slot machine. I poke dead center to find out if I've hit my jackpot. And I have. Near the top reads the headline: *Canvas Bag Serial Killer sentenced to 203 years in prison.*

By the time I swallow my third bite of asiago bagel, light-headedness overtakes me, and I transcend to another place.

I begin to smell the rich, earthy scent of leather and feel its smooth texture against my back. The tunnel vision fades and am sitting in one of two wingback chairs. A lavish office comes into focus before me. Behind the classic mahogany desk is a matching credenza with hutch. Along the left wall short glass tumblers and hatch-cut decanters sit atop a bar cabinet. I twist back, over the right of the chair, and my eyes follow a row of bookshelves the length of the wall. As I stretch, my foot slips, kicking into something on the floor. When I turn back, I see a nylon messenger bag. A thin, white cord spills out from the under the flap. My eyes follow the cord and it splits in two, ending with silver skull earbuds.

I jump to my feet and spin around, remembering Mark has an *important meeting* and I see him enter through the door.

"Mark, stop! You need to leave." I round the chair and follow as he makes a beeline to the desk. "I need you to hear me. You're in danger." My hands grab the sides of my head, and I want to pull my hair out. "Gahh! Why can't they hear me?"

I watch Mark round the desk and pull open the center drawer.

"That's it!" I yell at whatever unforgiving deity put me here. "I'm done, you bastard. I'm not watching him die. I'm not." I feel the sting of tears.

I slam my hands on the desk and lean toward Mark, willing him to hear me. "Get up. You need to leave. Now." My eyes dart between him and the door; my heart jumps to every flash at the door, expecting to see someone new. "Whatever you're looking for, it's not important." I clap my hand on the desk repeatedly. "Come on."

The seconds feel like eternity before he stands.

"Okay, let's go," I say.

His gait is unnervingly slow across the Berber carpet. Pins and needles dance on my skin as he stops at the side bar to pour a drink.

"We don't have time for that." I step around the center drawer he pulled out and throw myself into the lush office chair. As my hands rub the sides of my temples, my eyes catch on the collection of four-by-six photographs splayed inside the center drawer. The circular motion of my fingers stop; my hands drop to my cheeks. "What... the... is this?" Every color picture displays an unconscious person in various unclothed stages—some bound and gagged.

The world spins. "Wait. Just wait," I tell myself, desperate to regain my bearings. I look away from the ghastly photos and focus instead, on the neat stack of papers resting in the middle of the desktop. The paper on top is ivory. The body is blank, but there is a letterhead and Mark's full name is scribed along the top followed by E-S-Q.

"Esquire?" *Not computer programmer?* I freeze and can't bear to breath. *I… can't believe this is real.*

Ice clanks against glass.

"WHY?" I cry—fists pounding the desktop. My eyes cast daggers in his direction. And it's just in time to see him flick the side of a manila packet no bigger than his palm. White power sprinkles over the ice. My body seizes. My mind screams, *And how many times have I let you bring me coffee! Stupid. Idiot.*

"Great. You're here." A woman's voice cuts through the suffocating air, stealing my attention. Everything about her is tight and neat: charcoal pencil skirt, white scoop top with three-quarter sleeve, peek-a-boo shoes. She's carrying a folder in one hand and her long, brunette hair sweeps back as she pivots to grab the door.

I leap to my feet. "Stop! Don't shut the door!" But she does anyway as I round the desk and rush to the wingback chair.

She holds up the folder. "I have the brief you wanted."

"Excellent," Mark says. "I just poured us a couple." I turn and watch him walk back to the desk, sipping his drink. He sets his tumbler on the letterhead. As he sits, he drops the manila packet into the center drawer and slides it closed.

A pang of epic failure hits my chest. *That's what you were looking for?* I let out an exasperated sigh. "And here I was, worried about you." I flail my arms. An exaggerated laugh escapes my lips. "I was trying to save you."

I hear a faint click, and I know Mark has just locked away his secrets.

"Here you go," she says, passing me. She reaches out her hand with the folder.

Mark stands with his signature smile and rounds the desk to meet her.

I detest the way those lines frame his mouth. And I loathe his soft gaze. I grit my teeth, wanting nothing more than to pound his chest. I lunge forward.

A flash of blackness.

My hands smash the hard wall of his chest.

"Whoa," he says, staggering back. He looks as stunned as I feel. He rubs his chest and bends down to pick up the folder.

I look at my tingling hands and instantly decide to push again, but harder. I catch him unbalanced, before he gets a chance to fully stand.

Mark stumbles sideways into the bar cabinet. "What's that for?" he growls after he catches himself.

What for? My breaths rush through my nose and my face is on fire. I march to the bar cabinet. "For this," I say, grabbing the second tumbler. I hurl it at his head.

He reacts, but not fast enough.

"For everything," I continue as he doubles over. I pelt him with whatever I can grab. "For your lies." My hand grips the neck of the crystal decanter.

I repeat everything over and over—the words and the assault—so he'll remember *for what*. As I remind him, the words echo so loud in my head it hurts, and the pain is all I can focus on.

I stop only when I tire. I drop the decanter and roll back up onto my feet. It's then that I realize Mark and I are the only ones in the room. I can't bear to ever look at him again, so I don't. I inhale a slow, cleansing breathe. My body relaxes as I focus on the slowing thumps of my heart. *Tha-thump. A fast thump-thump-tha-thump. Tha-thump. I listen again: thump-thump-tha-thump.* I realize that between my own steady heartbeat, my ears detect a faint, foreign beat.

A loud gasp blasts my ears and I recount from where it came. It's *out there*, my mind thinks, but also *in here*.

"Ohmigod... Oh My Gaawwd!" stutters a voice that is not mine, but fills my head.

I step back, wanting to escape the voice. My footfall is heavy and clumsy and my arms prickle. *What is happening?* I wave my arms and hands in front of me like I'm treading water. I feel the extra weight in my limbs that is not my own.

"Ashley," a female voice says. "Where's Mark?" Another gasp. Flurries of activity. Distant shouts.

But all I can think about is *what is happening to me? And which part is real and which is not?* I wait. And I wait... for that relentless deity to snatch me back up. "*Brewed Awakenings*," I say. *I should be sitting at Brewed Awakenings.*

Hands grab my shoulders and wheel me around. A woman with bobbed, blonde hair and a tailored dress glares at me. She squeezes my arms. "Ashley."

No, I'm Jessica.

All I can think to do is tear myself from her grip and flee from the room. I hear her calling for Ashley as I zigzag down hall. All I know is that I must outrun Ashley. I dash to the door with the stairwell sign. Down I go. My shuffling feet spiral me down, down, down as rapid breaths ricochet off concrete walls around me. I reach the ground floor, and shove open the metal door with all my might. Outside air smacks my skin, crisp and cool against beaded perspiration. I scan the alleyway and run left toward the thick flow of pedestrians.

The sun is blinding when I emerge onto the sidewalk. The surroundings familiar. 5th Avenue. With haste, I head left again. I skip, charge, and jump through pedestrians. I do whatever it takes to keep moving.

I fly through the door of *Brewed Awakenings*, not sure what I'll find. My entire body shakes as I take baby steps to the second bistro table by the front window. The closer I get, I see: black coffee, a partially eaten asiago bagel, and smartphone. The chairs are empty. I stop and my feet are cemented to the ground. I glance at the people sitting at the first and third tables, wondering if they can see me. My head turns slowly to the line behind me, wondering if anybody can see me. I swallow hard and push through the fear holding me in place.

I take a seat at the second table. My hands rest in my lap, waiting for something—anything—to happen. Times passes, but I don't know how long. Nothing changes except for the forward momentum of the line and the cycling of to-go customers.

Without thinking, I pick up the coffee.

The cup is halfway to my mouth when I freeze, staring into the black abyss. Images swirl, showing me what I've done to Mark.

I jerk the cup down—cold, bitter coffee splashing and wetting my hands. I push the cup across the table and reject all I've seen. I twist away for good measure.

It wasn't me, I lie to myself. I rest my head back on the front window and close my eyes, praying I don't recall more images of Mark.

I wait. And I wait… until finally… I feel the burning brand of a Kiss upon my brow.

John Kiste is an Edgar Allan Poe impersonator who has studied Poe's works all his life and performed them throughout northeastern Ohio, in warehouses and chapels and even on moving trains. John's own fiction has been published in such works as A Shadow of Autumn, Modern Grimoire, Dark Fire Fiction, Theme of Absence, *and the latest Unnerving Press release,* Haunted Are These Houses.

About this story, John says: "It is a wonderful experience to study works paying tribute to the author my father often chose for my childhood bedtime stories. The Black Cat *was a particular favorite, as I knew that in reality Poe was quite fond of his tortoise-shell cat, Cattarina. Updating this piece to reflect the oddities of modern times was a thrill."*

One of the enduring qualities of Poe's work is his distinctive storytelling style, and any collection honoring him is almost duty-bound to include at least one story replete with the rhythms and nuances of the original, and in which the reader can almost hear Poe's own voice reading the work, in spite of its contemporary facelift.

THE BLACK, LONG-HAIRED DOMESTIC
John Kiste

For the most weird yet most homespun narrative I am about to relate, I neither ask for nor want acceptance. But I get the *true* needle in the morning, and wish to spill my ulcerative guts ahead of that. I do admit that I doubt my own mind; my long abuse of opioids and alcohol has brutalized not just my stomach and my liver, but also the clarity and focus of my brain. Thus the remembering of what many might call this simple series of daily happenings has fogged into an exercise of terror and madness as my faculties have faded and faltered.

My story, bleak and dim though it becomes, begins in warm sunshine. I attended a small eastern university where I was known for my math skills and my docile temperament. My sports teammates often chided me over my excessive fondness for animals. One spring day, a small raccoon was grievously injured by a mower on the football field, and I eschewed practice to attend to the dying creature. The rest of the squad laughed and hooted at my tenderness, but a freshman girl who had been studying in the bleachers rushed to assist me. The laughter stopped as the team became enthralled by her beauty and kindness. I was most enamored of all. She and I spent the rest of the afternoon and evening talking of animals both wild and domestic. When I graduated a year later, we were quietly married.

It was inevitable that we would surround ourselves with pets, many of which we acquired from local shelters. I had taken a position as a low-level stockbroker at a well-known eastern firm, and we purchased a condominium where pets were permitted, although the popular goats and pot-bellied pigs were frowned upon. Soon we had goldfish, however, and two rabbits, and a springer spaniel.

What my wife most desired to complete the menagerie was a black cat. I told her on many occasions that cats, especially black ones, were considered bad luck. Not so, she would reply. Not by all. Her knowledge and understanding of these animals was extensive. Each time I would berate felines, she would counter with a different tale or myth. She would tell me how the tabby cat had comforted Baby Jesus in His crib and had received the *M* on its forehead when a grateful Mary petted it there. Again, she would tell me how Odin's wife Freyja had her chariot pulled by two great gray cats. And how fishermen's wives kept black cats to control the weather far at sea and thus protect their mariner husbands.

She claimed cats had been called lucky for centuries in Russia—and this was not even noting how the ancient Egyptians had thoroughly worshipped them. I countered that all cats had been declared witches' familiars in the Middle Ages. That was true, she agreed. And when they were killed en masse, rodents with plague-bearing fleas ran wild, spreading the Black Death to the four corners of Europe and killing seventy-five million people. I argued no further.

It should come as no surprise that we obtained a large, black domestic within the week. He had no color on him anywhere, and we named him Eris in honor of the most massive of the distant Trans-Neptunian planets which orbited in utter darkness. This creature became the master of our menagerie. He was well fed and never attempted to eat the fish, but he herded the rabbits savagely and even lorded over the spaniel. Eventually he determined that my lap was the best perch for his throne and he would reign there statue-like until my legs were numb. He was transfixed by old Heathcliff cartoons on the television, and would listen for hours to a recording of Rossini's *Cat Duet* that I had found at a record exchange.

Our domestic life continued in this fashion for some time. All the while, however, my market returns slowly diminished. The national financial outlook was bleak, and my own talents more meager than I had envisioned. The downturn exerted more and more pressure on my feeble abilities, and the occasional draft beer with friends turned to a more than occasional whiskey alone, which devolved in turn to a frequent opiate in seclusion. I raised my voice and—dare I tell it—eventually my hand to my wife. She suffered silently and no longer shared her tales with me, but retreated to another room whenever I came in. The animals knew better than to cross my path at such times, and more than once the spaniel was kicked into the wall. My psyche, even now, is chided when I think back upon the wretched villain I had become as drugs and alcohol vied for true oversight of my soul.

I finally agreed to allow my wife to rid us of the little zoo; she feared for the safety of the creatures, and I was personally glad to be rid of them. I was reluctant to part with Eris, however. He still attended me cautiously and had not yet been a victim of my madness and fury. He would remain in my lap of an evening, large green eyes transfixed by the glowing TV, and I could tell, even with my blurred vision, that my wife would watch me sidelong nervously from another chair across the room.

She began to suspect that my business was suffering when I was forced to bring work home each evening just to avoid falling farther behind. My hopes for monetary salvation now rested on a shaky stock-hedging scheme that I was operating without my employer's knowledge or approval. Each night found me in my study, hunched over my laptop keyboard for hours, desperate to make every necessary calculation to perfection. Much of my fate was now beyond my control, but I was determined not to fail due to any lack of effort on my part.

One after-midnight bout with these figures felt especially promising, and I was about to save my iPad calculations for input the next morning when the markets opened. As I aimed my stylus at the correct button, Eris leapt unexpectedly into my lap and deleted my night's work. I shrieked wildly and thrust the tip of the stylus into the cat's right eye. He howled as he fell to the floor and scrambled from the room, wailing in pain. My wife burst into the study with anger and confusion on her features, but I pushed past her and left the condo. I sought a den of more than iniquity, and remained there for several days.

When finally sober once more, I attempted to smooth over the incident by assuring my wife that the maiming had been an accident. In truth, I had not been especially intoxicated when I had struck the animal, and I was somewhat remorseful in the aftermath of the assault. Of course the cat could not be persuaded to attend me any longer, and though my wife at length began visiting the rooms I occupied, the cat never did. When I would glimpse it from the corner of my eye, I always observed the maimed socket, which presented a fearsome and unwholesome appearance and never failed to increase my self-loathing. I began to resent intensely the very existence of the little familiar. I detested the idea that it was lurking in the next corridor, or perched in a hall closet, reminding me of the vile deed.

One morning when my wife was out, I brushed white powder from my nose as I exited the bathroom, and found the cat sitting on my best pair of purple suspenders. It fled as I approached, but its claw snagged the expensive fabric. I caught the beast in the hall and used the ruined galluses to strangle it. After a minute it hung limp in my hand and a monstrous fear washed over me. I had had no compunction in killing the thing—and felt little regret now—but I was dreadfully afraid of being found out. I must hide the furry pelt so that no one would know what I had done.

I dared not place it in the communal dumpster or hurl it into the street. Then I remembered that the plumbing access panel for the entire complex was just outside my back door. No one was about; I slid free the panel and stuffed the carcass far down behind the main pipes—heavy pipes that would never require maintenance. A sense of security swept through my soul. I would tell my wife that Eris had rushed out when I opened the door. She knew how the animal hated me—I could make her believe this.

This feeling of security did not remain long. As I went through my morning ablutions, I could think of nothing but Eris's one green eye. The fire of that eye consumed me. I was truly physically haunted by the cat's spirit, though I could not fathom if his ghost wished vengeance or merely remembrance.

Hungover, I dressed and left the condominium for the office. Two blonde girls held two jump ropes, and sang *Three Little Kittens* as a third skipped between them. I hastened to my coupe, head throbbing. In town, I passed the hulking structure of the Lambert Theatre, where the off-Broadway performance of *Cats* had found its way to the marquee. My throat tightened. My progress was halted at the railroad crossing as an old Chesapeake & Ohio train rushed by. One logo after another of the *Chessie Cat* dashed across my sight, blurring into a sort of millwheel as my eyes streamed tears of terror. This was madness; I had not seen a Chessie train for a decade. I turned my face to the construction lot beside me and immediately my vision fixed on a piece of heavy yellow earthmoving equipment. All was out of focus except the logo that spelled C-A-T resting on a lemon-hued pyramid. That I saw with crystal clarity.

Thus haunted, no possibility of work remained. I spent the day at a dealer's apartment comparing the effects of various pills. My wife would suffer tonight.

She seemed to accept my story of the cat's disappearance. We never spoke of Eris again. We had little opportunity. The very next day my stock hedging scheme collapsed. I was unceremoniously dismissed and our condo was rapidly repossessed. Creditors swooped upon us like pterodactyls and disabused us of any belief that we required material items. In miserable poverty, we sought an apartment that was little better than a slum in the poorest quarter of town, and I consigned myself to manual labor. Gradually, we adjusted to the new squalor and began to grudgingly acknowledge one another. I drank some, but strove mightily to ignore the call of opiates, with moderate success.

In periods of sobriety, I admitted to myself that I missed Eris. He had been my boon companion. I knew my wife longed for a living presence that could comfort her. Without being conscious of doing so, I began to scout a replacement for the departed pyewacket.

My travels took me to dark places even in my lucid moments of penance. An evening of bourbon and Texas Hold 'Em in the bowels of an ancient gambling establishment led me at length to a pillow in a cobwebbed niche for respite. I discovered as I reclined, however, that the pillow was not a pillow at all. It uncurled itself to reveal a large black cat the same size and color as Eris. No patron of the place had ever seen it, and as it followed my footsteps toward my tenement apartment, I was delighted to have found a double for that creature I had so ill-used.

No one could have imagined what a true doppelganger it was. My wife was delighted to meet it the next morning, but as she cuddled it closely, I observed that its right eye was missing. I shuddered in consternation. This could not be a coincidence. I would not be induced to accept a supernatural explanation, but I did feel that someone was playing a bad joke on me. This I would have continued to believe, had my wife not pointed out that this new cat had an undistinguished patch of white on its throat. That was true—and there was no doubt that Eris had been completely black. We had remarked on this fact many times.

In a matter of days, this new long-haired domestic had settled into its role as my assured nemesis. It made itself at home, and set out to destroy me by tracing my every step. It would brush past me in dark hallways and dash around me on the stairs, and I saw its solitary green eye glowing from every poorly-lit corner and cranny.

The logical remnants of my mind knew that my guilt and my weakened mental faculties had combined with alcoholic intemperance and opioids—and probably some degree of natural chemical instability—to create the neuroses and anxieties that I was experiencing. I was not an uneducated rube of a century past. I knew that my apprehensions and misgivings were baseless. I knew that the apparition at the heart of all my disquiet was nothing more than a simple midnight mouser.

Still, I cannot deny the mortal fear I developed toward this new animal. My wife also observed how I shrank nervously from its advances. Its oppressive presence hung about me even in my absences. I drank frequently and mused methods of ridding myself of the black beast. My thoughts constantly dwelt on the horrors wrought by this new demon—when a helping of side terror was linked to the old one.

I learned from a tavern mate that my previous condo was being demolished. This news wracked me with an innate fear that the corpse of the first animal might be found and identified by a neighbor still in nearby habitation. Such fears were certainly absurd, nor had the crime been one that would carry much weight with, or demand much attention from, the authorities, but this distress and uneasiness continued to press on my abscessed soul. The living beast stood in my presence whenever I was home, while the deceased one curled in my thoughts when I was away, and lingered in my nightmares when I slept—when I could, in fact, sleep. I was gradually driven back to my former haunts and in due course I awoke with needles in my arm.

My wife would have abandoned me, had any options been left to her. Her parents were dead, and she had never completed her college courses once we wed. Moreover, my gradual dehumanizing of her soul had bereft her of hope and self-worth, and my homecomings often found her curled in a corner with the black demon on her lap. She would slowly stroke its dark fur and watch me from under dark brows, knowing her only protection from my wrath was my utter dread of the beast.

One night, returning to our rooms sluggishly after a bout with a poorly cut drug of choice, I found my wife and the small monster slouched in a corner of the kitchen. My sleeve was still rolled above my elbow as I stood at the table, and my wife, eyes straining through the dimness, kept looking in horror from the track marks on my arm to the white patch on the throat of the cat.

I followed her gaze. The fuzzy area was no longer indistinct. It had focused to attain an uncanny resemblance to a hypodermic needle. This insignificant, though bizarre, development broke the spell of angst the animal held over me. I could tolerate the archfiend's presence no longer. Drug-addled insanity seethed through my very being. I rushed below to our storage area and stumbled back through the deserted halls carrying a chainsaw. It roared to life as I stepped into the kitchen and threw the bolt on the door.

The cat leapt from my wife's arms at my appearance and scrabbled across the wood floor into the next room. As I turned to follow its flight, my wife rose calmly from the floor and blocked my path. I revved the engine furiously and, goaded into a demoniacal rage, advanced upon her.

Of course my wife's screams would have been drowned in the banshee howl of the chainsaw, but she did not make a sound. She simply stared at me with moist eyes as I drove the whirring blade through her skull. She dropped silently to the kitchen floor in a pool of blood and gore. I powered down the machine, realizing at once that I would have to concoct a story to explain the noise—and her absence—as soon as I concealed the corpse and used our little shop-vac on the puddles and splatters and sprays of blood. My thoughts got no further than this, for the moment the chainsaw quieted I heard heavy fists pounding upon the door and strong shouts demanding ingress.

I was shocked; the neighbors had previously given me a wide berth in their terror and repulsion of my character. The police could not have been alerted so quickly. Indeed, they were nearly nonexistent in this tenement quarter. I stood, therefore, watching in stunned silence as the hinges splintered and the door collapsed inward. The chainsaw hung at my side. I made no attempt to restart it as four large men burst into the kitchen. One of them rushed in vain to my wife's body. The others bore me bodily to the floor and tore the weapon from my grasp. They stared at me, their fishlike mouths gaping in horror. Peripherally, I glimpsed the cat in the doorway, watching me with a single fiery eye and exposed fangs.

It was some moments before I could offer the men congratulations on being police officers of such alacrity. One of them shook his head and corrected my misconception. They were members of the SPCA from near my old condo, and they had come to question me in regards to my dead cat.

Tonia Kalouria is a former actress, recently returned from L.A. to "The North Coast" (i.e., Toledo), and considers herself a Midwest Gal at heart. Writing poetry helps her maintain her sanity in this topsy-turvy world, and she is a strong advocate for rhyming poetry. Her poetry has appeared in numerous publications, including The 5/2 Crime Poetry Weekly *(vols. 2, 5, and 6),* Common Threads, The Senior Years, The Litchfield Review, Planet Green, *and her own book,* Aerobic Poetry.

About this poem, Tonia says: "My poem is a metaphor for–actually, against– the MFA advisor's edict: "no rhymers need apply!" The black bird's declaration that nothing mattered save word count is tantamount to said advisor's submission admonishment that "if it rhymes, don't waste your time!" Since Poe also wrote satire, I thought this might be a way to get my point across, and concomitantly, to be an homage to Poe's Raven *masterpiece. (Two birds, one stone, so to speak.)"*

Poe aficianados are familiar with the Raven's pithy, "Nevermore." And while quoting that single statement was enough for Poe, what other words of wisdom might the bird have for us?

ADVICE IS FOR THE BIRDS

Tonia Kalouria

A sweet Bluebird of Happiness
flew down to visit me,
whenever I'd take quill in hand
to scratch my poetry.
Upon my Dutch door she would perch,
and chirp! chirp! chirp! with glee.

But came the day her sweet song ceased:
I missed her company.
I loved her blithe encouragements
and thought: "Where can she be?"
When her predator revealed himself,
I then knew why she'd flee.

A squawking, bully, blackbird "bard"
became the Dutch door's guest.
He groused about my writings:
Short rhymes, penned just for *jest*.
He daily screeched out *his* advice,
and did so with great zest.

I longed to share wry epigrams.
"No!" screeched the raven bird.
"Write sonnets, odes, and epics, so
Your pay is by the word."

I yenned to write great Senryus.
"No!" screeched the raven bird.
"Write villanelles, and ghazals, so
"Your pay is by the word."

I fancied witty, playful rhymes.
"No!" screeched the raven bird.
"Write elegies, and free verse, so
"Your pay is by the word."

My Muse was gone; my words, in wads:
All life became a bore.
Those daunting, haunting, blackbird barbs:
No, no, no, no… NO MORE!
Must silence bleak-beak bird for good…
My Duck Tape! This means WAR!"

EPILOGUE
Shrill raven shill shall shriek no more!
And Happy Bird's back on my door.
In peace, I now write with no dread,
and for us *both*, I earn my bread.

Having spent a great deal of time near Baltimore, it's possible that author Steven R. Southard has somehow absorbed a measure of the still-lingering aura of Edgar Allan Poe. During the night's darkest hours, by the light of a single candle, Steve pens tales of fantasy, science fiction, horror, and alternate history, which have appeared in more than ten anthologies and one series. The bravest and most curious among you may venture to his website at stevenrsouthard.com, where you may discover Steve waiting, lurking, and hiding behind his codename: Poseidon's Scribe.

About this story, Steven says: "I'm a huge fan of Jules Verne, who, in turn, enjoyed the writings of Edgar Allan Poe. When Verne noted that Poe's The Narrative of Arthur Gordon Pym of Nantucket *begged for a sequel*, he wrote An Antarctic Mystery. For my own part, I observed that Poe's The Unparalleled Adventure of One Hans Pfaall *left too many ends dangling*. When a strange being arrives in Rotterdam by balloon and delivers a letter describing a voyage to the Moon by the town's missing citizen, we simply can't leave it there. If rescue is possible, let's go."

For readers who believe Poe's work to be exclusively dark or mysterious, the story of Hans Pfaall may seem somewhat out of place in the canon. But closer inspection will reveal the same wry, narrative wit that colors many of Poe's mysteries, together with his unique brand of inventive, pseudo-scientific fact—elements which this story utilizes to excellent effect.

THE UNPARALLELED ATTEMPT TO RESCUE ONE HANS PFAALL

Steven R. Southard

By a knight of ghostes and shadowes
I summon'd am to tourney
Ten leagues beyond the wild world's end.
Methinks it is no journey.
– Tom O'Bedlam's Song

History is unlikely to record the name Hans Pfaall as the first explorer of the moon, but if it somehow did so, posterity would also regard him as something of a hero. It should be understood that I, however, loathe him with a hatred beyond all cosmic boundaries.

*

Borne along on the lunar wind, their balloon swept westward. Von Underduk and his companions gazed down at the line marking the boundary between day and night. On one side lay a desolate landscape of barren land interrupted by lifeless lakes and rivers. On the other lay the invisible darkness, receding before the onslaught of day.

"We should see it soon," Pfaall said, after an exchange of signs with Prime.

Their balloon travelled faster than the moving line of daylight. The line still lay ahead of them, creeping forward as they approached. Soon they would overtake it.

Prime raised his arm and pointed into the darkness. Von Underduk strained to peer into the inky gloom, but noticed nothing at first. Then a slight lessening of the blackness, or a hint of this, became just perceptible. As the thing resolved in a most gradual manner, it took on a deep gray cast and became a vast, raised tableland, a high plateau.

Van Broon dropped some ballast weights to ensure the balloon would pass over the mountain's edge. Squinting, Von Underduk saw a high central crest, dimly visible, a raised pinnacle jutting from the plateau's surface.

*

May 4th, 1835

My name is Mynheer Superbus Von Underduk, and I am the Burgomaster of Rotterdam.

Yesterday, the town's serenity was disturbed by the appearance of a small balloon. The gondola contained an earless dwarf about two feet tall. Before drifting on his way and out of sight, he dropped a sealed letter.

The letter was signed by Hans Pfaall, a former citizen of Rotterdam and a repairer of bellows by trade. I say former, since no one had seen him for the past five years. In the letter, he claimed to have constructed a special balloon and made a trip all the way to the Moon.

Arguments erupted over the authenticity and accuracy of the letter. Most people, me included, were skeptical that any man, especially one so common as Herr Pfaall, could undertake such a voyage. Yet the letter was so detailed in its descriptions, so meticulous in reporting every facet of the journey, that it made its falsity just as difficult to explain.

Rumors held that Pfaall was being held captive on the moon, and that this was the reason he had not returned. The gossip became so intense, it prompted calls for action. Many proposed a rescue mission. Others countered we were being taken in by a clever hoaxer.

July 5th

I am cautious by nature. A nobleman never risks destruction of his reputation by rash and imprudent action. I have carefully considered the matter and now authorize the expedition.

*

As the balloon drifted toward the plateau, Von Underduk became aware of a slight but increasing discomfort, which gradually strengthened into an indefinable foreboding. His stomach tightened into a knot of worry, his spinal nerves rippled with prickly sensations. He found himself sweating in rivulets that stung his eyes and ran into his mouth. An inexplicable fear seized him, causing him to breathe greater draughts of the sparse air.

"We shouldn't have come," Rubadub said, his voice quavering. He gasped for breath and glanced about in a frantic manner. "We must leave. Can't you take the balloon away from here?"

He'd said aloud what Von Underduk felt.

"No. It's the *thing* causing these feelings, somehow," Pfaall said. "That's how it keeps the Lunarians away. I feel it, too, but we must press on to discover what it is."

Their balloon surmounted the dark mountain's edge. Soon the dawn line reached its base and crept upward. What Von Underduk had taken for a flat plateau was in fact a rounded upper surface, smooth and curved. As the sun's rays uncovered more and more, vague features became clearer: here a long, linear trench between lengthy, raised mounds; there an ovoid valley with an arched ridge marking one side; and in the central region that strange, proud-looking ridge.

"My God, it's…" Rubadub backed away from the view.

"It's a *face*," Van Broon said.

*

March 15th, 1836

We built the balloon according to details in Pfaall's letter, though ours was larger since it must hold many occupants.

The rescue crew will have the most eminent men in Rotterdam. I will lead the group, accompanied by Professor Rubadub, Claude Oort, Beltt Van Aallen, and Verner Van Broon.

April 1st

Departure. Our mission begins.

April 10th

Journey continues without incident. I am quite tired of hearing Rubadub and Van Broon marvel that breathable air exists in the gap between Earth and Moon. They'd supposed it to be vacuum. True, the air is thin, forcing us to use our portable hand-cranked air compressors and suck air from tubes on occasion, but I think the gentlemen should be grateful rather than amazed.

April 13th

Reviewed Pfaall's letter again, particularly this paragraph:

"I have much to say of the climate of the planet; of its wonderful alternations of heat and cold; of unmitigated and burning sunshine for one fortnight, and more than polar frigidity for the next... of the people themselves; of their manners, customs, and political institutions; of their peculiar physical construction; of their ugliness; of their want of ears—those useless appendages in an atmosphere so peculiarly modified; of their consequent ignorance of the use and properties of speech; of their substitute for speech in a singular method of inter-communication; of the incomprehensible connection between each particular individual on the moon with some particular individual on the earth—a connection analogous with, and depending upon that of the orbs of the planet and the satellites, and by means of which the lives and destinies of the inhabitants of the one are interwoven with the lives and destinies of the inhabitants of the other; and above all—if it so please your Excellencies—above all, of those dark and hideous mysteries which lie in the outer regions of the moon..."

Much heated discussion ensued among us regarding the 'incomprehensible connections' and 'hideous mysteries.' We could only conclude Pfaall had embellished some aspects of his story to the point of absurdity.

*

There was no mistaking it, Von Underduk thought, but also no believing it either. A face is one of the first patterns babies learn to recognize, and its endless variations become imprinted in some mysterious way in every human brain. But to see a face—something so commonplace—*here*, where it should not be, on a scale impossible to grasp, that chilled Von Underduk to his core.

A mile wide, the face sent its frozen stare upward into space. For a terrifying instant Von Underduk imagined the face waking up, looking at him, then rising out of the ground to reveal an entire head atop a body twelve miles tall. But the stony face didn't move.

Was it human, or Lunarian? The face was too far buried to tell if it had ears or not. The nose displayed a slight hook, more than was common for humans, less than that of Lunarians. Probably any member of either species would see it as their own, but it could somehow represent both, or neither.

"Why did Prime's people build this?" Van Broon broke the deathly stillness.

After a few finger motions, Pfaall shook his head. "They didn't build it. They thought *we* did, many ages ago. They have no records of a time when it wasn't here."

That deepened the mystery.

*

April 19th

Arrived at the Moon. Floated above a strange landscape. Grayish-green vegetation grows everywhere, sustained by a series of parallel rivers flowing east to west. Towns and villages are closely spaced and thickly populated, though buildings are low and crude wooden structures.

How ugly the inhabitants are! They stand two feet high on average and from each face protrudes a long, hooked nose. But their strangest feature has to be an utter absence of ears. I feel nauseous just looking at the sides of their heads. The human ear might not be its most beautiful aspect, but its lack, *its replacement with a smooth, uninterrupted wall of skin, disturbs me greatly and causes me to look upon those creatures with unalloyed revulsion.*

I gaze about to ascertain where they might have confined Herr Pfaall, but none of the structures suggests a prison. My companions urge me to allow a landing, saying we could ask any of the creatures the whereabouts of a five foot tall Earthman, likely to be a well-known bit of news on the moon. I prudently take my time in deciding.

April 20th

We alit and just after planting the Dutch tricolor flag, we were approached by a large number of the unpleasant-looking lunar denizens. They gave no response to our queries and instead approached closer and closer, all of them flailing their fingers in a most threatening fashion.

Outnumbered and fearing for our safety, we fired a warning from our muskets. When this failed to influence them, we shot several of their number. One had neared Beltt Van Aallen to within a short distance before Van Aallen hit him in the chest. Inexplicably, Van Aallen himself was suddenly seized by a massive chest ailment of mysterious origin, and he died on the spot.

The moon beings departed the scene, dragging away their dead. Grieving over the death of our fellow voyager, we buried Van Aallen in the gray lunar soil, marking his grave with a crude cross of wood.

To our surprise, a short time later a single one of the moon people then approached us with great slowness and evident trepidation. He bore a sign, written in poorly-spelled, but unmistakable, Dutch, saying, "I will take you to Hans Pfaall."

*

Von Underduk felt small and insignificant in the presence of the colossal, ancient face. He disliked that feeling, especially when compounded with the peculiar horror he felt already.

Their balloon had floated above the nose and now drifted over the face's left cheek.

"We must land and explore it," Pfaall said.

The others looked at each other, but Oort spoke for the group. "Not for a million guilders would I go any closer to that monstrosity. We've come. We've seen your mystery. You yourself said it's causing the fear we're sharing. Little wonder the Lunarians won't come near it. I say let the wind carry us on, as far away as possible."

Von Underduk gauged the sentiment of the others from their expressions. "I quite agree. We go on."

Pfaall opened and then shut his mouth. He glanced at each of the elders of Rotterdam but could not have found any sympathy. "We're landing!" he shouted, lunging for the gas release cord.

Van Broon tried to stop him, but only caused him to lose his balance as he grabbed the cord. As he fell, he pulled with his full body weight and the cord ripped free.

With the gas spewing out of the envelope, the balloon began a rapid descent.

"Can't you shut that valve?" Rubadub called out.

"No!" Van Broon replied, "but we can drop ballast."

Detaching all the weights only delayed and softened their eventual landing. The balloon hit the ground fifty yards past the base of the facial structure. The balloon's gas envelope deflated into an empty sack lying on the dirt.

"Herr Pfaall, I hope you enjoy the scenery," Rubadub said as he stood up. "You've stranded us here. We can't make more gas, even if we could repair the valve."

"The discovery of a lifetime," Pfaall said, "and you talk of trifles? We must go to it, discover its secrets."

Ten minutes of argument ensued. In the end, Pfaall, Prime, Von Underduk, and Van Broon left the damaged gondola to go exploring while Oort and Rubadub stayed to salvage what they could.

The mountain loomed before them. Von Underduk shivered, not only because of the lingering frigidity the night had left behind. He felt his terror brimming to the point of nausea. Nonetheless, the quartet of explorers approached the gigantic artifact.

"This holds the key. I know it does," Pfaall said.

*

April 20th (continued)

The moon-person who bore the sign led us to a group of miniature elephants on which we rode for several hours through towns and fields. Finally, we stopped near a circular park in what we concluded to be their capital city. Within the park, a figure was writing on a mounted chalkboard—in Dutch—while thirty or so earless midgets copied on small slates. The figure could be none other than Hans Pfaall.

We greeted him and expressed our surprise to find him not imprisoned. He appeared amused that we'd thought he needed rescuing. He said he was quite happy on the moon, teaching the Lunarians to read and write, and said the entire population of midgets treated him as a sort of god. Little wonder that he who was but a common bellows-repairman on Earth was disinclined to return there.

He said he'd wanted to visit Earth a year earlier, but was reluctant to do so unless assured of a pardon for crimes he'd committed. Therefore he'd sent a messenger—the one he called Prime. Alas, Prime had become too scared to linger for a reply, and had returned to the moon without the pardon, whereupon Pfaall resigned himself to stay.

Pfaall then squinted at us with suspicion and asked if we'd harmed any lunar inhabitants. We admitted to having killed a few by necessity. Pfaall glowered and scowled. He raged at us, chastised us for not reading his letter.

I firmly informed him to respect his superiors, and it was some time before my fellow voyagers could calm Pfaall down enough to converse in a mannerly way.

Herr Pfaall explained what we'd taken for aggressive behavior—the waving of hands and fingers—was nothing more than the earless Lunarians' method of communication.

Odder yet, it seemed there existed a strange and invisible connection, which Pfaall called a 'life-link,' between each human on Earth and a particular Lunarian. For example, there existed a Burgomaster Von Underduk Prime, a Hans Pfaall Prime, and so forth.

The two paired individuals are born in the same instant and die at the same time. If female, they become with child at the same moment and give birth simultaneously. Although humans have lived in ignorance of this life-link, the Lunarians cannot. They feel the bond as part of their very core make-up. They even feel the pains and emotions of their paired human.

The existence of this life-link explained at once the puzzling death of Van Aallen. He had unknowingly killed his own lunar twin.

*

Arriving at the mountain's base, Von Underduk saw a featureless wall rising up and stretching away to both sides. The surface, off-white in color, looked impossibly smooth, smoother than any mirror.

"What now?" he asked.

"This is a machine," Pfaall said, gazing at the wall. "We must determine how to operate it."

"A machine," echoed Van Broon in an awed voice.

"Yes," Pfaall strode to the wall and touched it before anyone could stop him.

An opening grew in the wall, centered at Pfaall's hand. No door swung in or out; rather, a rectangular hole simply *grew* until it was tall and wide enough to accommodate all of them walking together. Beyond the portal lay a well-lit, empty room.

"We enter here," said Pfaall, as if expecting it all along.

"I suggest caution," Von Underduk said. "It might be a trap."

"The machine is making you—and all of us—fear it," Pfaall said. "We must fight the feeling, transcend it." He walked through the hole and into the room. "Come in, Your Excellency."

Prime walked in and stood beside Pfaall.

Van Broon tilted his head toward Von Underduk and whispered, "I agree with being careful, Your Excellency, but this *is* the most astonishing artifact in history. It's all right to take a few prudent risks."

Von Underduk hesitated, uncertain. Finally, he walked in, followed by Van Broon. "Herr Pfaall, do not touch anything else unless I agree first. Understand?"

"Yes, Your Excellency."

The Burgomaster didn't like the room. Four smooth, blank walls surrounded them and the ceiling somehow glowed without any visible gas lamps or candles.

Without a sound, the wall-hole closed behind them.

"We're trapped!" Von Underduk cried in dismay.

*

April 20th (continued)

Plainly, our mission to rescue Herr Pfaall was unnecessary and unwelcome. It was time to leave the Moon.

But Pfaall implored us to assist him in one matter first. He asked us to transport him to the far side of the Moon, the side always facing away from our Earth. The Lunarians had told him of some mysterious object there, but provided no details. For inexplicable reasons, they felt a deep terror about it. Reportedly no plant or animal lived in that hemisphere, and the Lunarians refused to go there.

Pfaall had taken hold of the notion that the enigmatic 'thing' had something to do with the human-Lunarian life-link, and that only by exploring it could we discover the link's secret. He believed the link exhibited strong effects on the Moon, because its source was the far-side object. Despite his pathetic pleading, most of us remained doubtful of Pfaall's plan. Nevertheless, he rode with us on the undersized elephants all the way back to our balloon, entreating us over and over.

Just as we were about to depart for Earth and leave Pfaall behind, Van Broon leaned to me and mentioned what an honor it would be for the Burgomaster of Rotterdam to lead a brief trip to the Moon's unseen side. I pondered this question for less than an hour before deciding I should not deny the great city of Rotterdam such an honor. If one travels two hundred forty thousand miles to see a new world, one should take in all the major sights.

*

After the hole in the wall closed, Von Underduk felt a slight sensation of movement, of the floor shifting.

"What madness is this?" he asked, gripped by horror. "Is our room moving?"

No one had an answer.

They continued to endure sensations of movements in various directions, each being minor enough for them to remain upright with ease. After a minute, the room stopped and a hole opened on the wall opposite the earlier hole.

Peering through the new hole, they saw another room of similar size, also unoccupied. But its walls glowed with colorful symbols and pictures.

Pfaall stepped through the portal before Von Underduk could say a word.

"Don't touch *anything*," the Burgomaster reminded Pfaall.

They all entered, but this time the hole behind them remained open. They marveled at the strange scene. The walls seemed solid and opaque, yet figures and icons illuminated the surfaces. Directly beneath each picture, one or more rounded bumps of indecipherable purpose stood out from the wall.

Each picture—with lines and angles and curves of extraordinary precision—looked as if drawn by an artist using colored light itself. Some sections of these lighted drawings *blinked*. One image depicted various views of the giant face itself, its internal spaces and machinery layouts shown in incomprehensible detail.

"Here it is!" Pfaall had wandered to look at a different section of the wall. "Here's what we're looking for."

He stood before a drawing of two standing bipedal creatures, one tall and one short, connected to each other by a blinking blue line.

"You see? This mechanism controls the life-link. As Archimedes would say, this is a lever for moving worlds. You *must* allow me to operate this knob, Your Excellency."

All eyes turned to Von Underduk, awaiting his decision. He detested such moments and therefore took his time weighing pros and cons, various potential outcomes and consequences...

"For God's sake," Pfaall said, and pushed on the rounded bump. It moved inward and the blinking blue line vanished.

"I *told* you not to—" Von Underduk began, then felt a slight shudder. He felt it only *inside* his body, an electrical jolt to some indefinable inner organ.

"Did you feel that?" Pfaall smiled. "I suspect we all did. I think everyone on both Earth and Moon felt it. The life-links—all of them—are broken. Here, observe." He stared at Prime and punched himself in his stomach.

Prime's eyes widened. He moved his hands slowly to his stomach, shaking his head.

"You see, he no longer feels what I feel," Pfaall said. "We have broken the life-link."

*

April 20th (continued)

I seethe with anger, that Pfaall disobeyed my order and that his action did something wonderful, both for the Earth and the Moon. That miserable bellows repairman is not the only one capable of magnificent acts of lasting greatness. It is time I acted without dithering, without hesitation.

Here before me is another pictograph with its own controlling knob. It hardly matters what the thing means, this strange drawing of two round bodies—one large and one small—with a ghostly oval encompassing both.

I reach for the raised bump. Pfaall is shouting, lunging. His hands fall on me, trying to stop me, but I'm too quick. This time I alone will get the credit and the glory. I press the bump into the wall.

In the picture, the oval shrinks in size to a circle that only covers the bigger circle. There is a whistling of wind, at first faint but now raising in volume.

"Your Excellency!" Van Broon is shouting. "The machine was sustaining the Moon's atmosphere! We must hasten to the balloon!"

We run through the hole into the moving room. We're breathing in deep draughts as the air becomes thinner by the minute. The room moves as before and soon opens a hole to the outside. We exit and see our balloon in the distance.

A fierce windstorm blasts us with gray dust as it flies upward into space. The air is so sparse, so thin. I'm gasping, forced to crawl.

Behind me a deep, monstrous noise becomes louder than the gale of escaping atmosphere. I turn to see the titanic face, that ancient alien Sphinx, lifting from the ground. It's rising, rising high above the Moon and bound for somewhere else in space.

The balloon is still so far... too far. My companions have all collapsed.

My last view as I lay down my head is of Herr Hans Pfaall, turning to look at me. That damnable, loathsome, detestable Hans Pfaall!

As a child, Melanie Cossey delighted in reading stories that left her feeling disturbed, like Shirley Jackson's The Lottery, and Poe's The Telltale Heart. Her love of the Victorian period combined with her penchant for impactful, unsettling stories nurtured her desire to create troubling tales of gothic horror. Melanie is a member of the Horror Writer's Association, and her short fiction has been shortlisted in numerous contests. Her story, The Nymphalidae won Honorable Mention in the Storm Crow Tavern's 2015 Tales from Beermat Microfiction Contest. Learn more about her, and her gothic horror, A Peculiar Curiosity, at regalhousepublishing.com/melanie-cossey

About this story, Melanie says: "I learned of the call for this anthology only two days before the deadline. Being a Poe enthusiast and a gothic writer, I could never forgive myself if I missed the opportunity to submit. Grabbing my tales of forgotten lore—aka my copy of Edgar Allen Poe: Complete Stories and Poems— I set to work scanning the offerings on which to base my submission. When I read The Blackwood Article and its companion piece, A Predicament, I knew I had found my story. My character, who endeavors to write a Blackwood article against a tight deadline, was quite literarily, me."

Authors have long been encouraged to follow this model or that method of researching and writing their work. And while Mr. Blackwood's advice certainly has its merits, it seems no stretch of the imagination to also consider its limitations...

THE BLACKWOOD ARTICLE
Melanie Cossey

And so sat I, bereft of spirit and soul, on this, the final morn directly preceding the evening upon which submissions were due. Oh!—time be damned! These ever-blinking, ever-proceeding digital timepieces of doom, how you dash my hopes, my dreams with your silent advancements! A multitude of lamentations did expel from my lips, thrust from my most treacherous of sorrows. Until I did then recall the quaint and curious volume of forgotten lore upon my chamber shelf.

Oh, dear and dreaded Mr. Blackwood, who did once instruct writers of most desperate and desolate spirits to advance themselves in high measure, come hence! Aid me in this, my most urgent hour of need.

The dog did scramble. The cat did screech. The chairs did spin. Yes, *spin!* As I, giddy with the delight of a hundred—nay!—a thousand schoolgirls, did clamber to my library ladder and pluck from up high, my most secretive and sinister of weapons: *How to Write a Blackwood Article.*

With greedy eye and brain most ravenous did I devour those sacred words of dread and delight. Word upon word! Instruction upon instruction! Until my head was a veritable storm of ideas, clouds so burdened they threatened to explode in torrents.

Ink! Blackest of ink. Pen! Abused and broken. These two things and nothing more, Mr. Blackwell insisted. Yet no pen of yore, nor ink of midnight had I. Curse this modern world! This killer of craft, handicapper of horror. With wistful sweep of determined wrist, I seized upon my tablet, near choking the wretched device with my vexatious demands to tap the ink to bold, and sweep the font to *Brush Script,* as unreadable as any Mr. Blackwood could prescribe:

ótan to cheirógrafo boreí na diavasteí
den axízei poté na diavasteí

That's Greek for '*when manuscript can be read, it is never worth reading.*' Oh, but would Mr. Blackwood not smile at my clever manipulation of the reader with my unmatched skill at employing Google Translate?

*

With time an ever-rabid dog, snapping at my heels, I raced, heart an incessant drum in my throat, to consume every concept, every miniscule detail of the teaching. Oh, my whirling mind, seduced by knowledge, tantalized by excitement, by ever-growing visions of magnificence, like a kaleidoscope, spinning with sounds and colors. Until I at last came to the crux of the matter, the dreaded finality of the instruction, the *coup de grâce.* To achieve the pinnacle of horror, I should—nay, I *must!*—acquire experimental knowledge. In short, dear reader, I must suffer a most horrific mishap, and thereby render myself intimately associated with death to record, forthwith, the sensations of horror.

Mr. Blackwood, being a man of unquestionable charity, has provided tips by which his student may go about the task. One must, he instructs, be sure to get oneself into a scrape of such magnitude as to be unparalleled by any other.

Being of most sharp and imaginative mind, I could not contain the realization that mine was a world of infinite technology, surpassing in brilliance and ingenuity the bygone days of Mr. Blackwood's time and era, when such conventions knew only basic and rudimentary function. How much greater would my own era be in affording me the opportunity to capture the rising horror of an advanced and modern deathly experience?

*

And so, my adventure had unwittingly begun as I, with steady mind, heart, and intentions set upon my wardrobe and pulled from within a most suitable costume—a three-hooped underskirt, a black taffeta skirt, and purple velvet blouse, held taut by a corset of silken finery.

Never looking the finer, I took up my cloak and tablet, exited my rather quaint lodgings, and entered the populous and pleasant streets of Vancouver city. With all the sincerity of a student freshly learned and eager to apply their knowledge, I looked to the goddesses Soteria and Athena to guide my steps. As I continued my solitary walk, my thoughts leapt to the myriad ways I could succeed at my terrible and exhilarating task.

Mr. Blackwood had been most forthcoming with ideas in which to achieve the utmost in sensational descriptions, but alas—the conventions that were used in his day were no longer valid in mine. For example, it was suggested that a student place his head in the oven, and presumably, suffer the unimaginable fate of inhaling gasses of a most lethal description. But the modern advent of a carbon monoxide detector, and thus an automatic shut-off valve, made such an experience decidedly obsolete.

With great resolution, I considered the example of throwing myself into a yard of dogs, but to my unfailing dismay, there had been an addendum to ancient bylaws in recent years, banning the owning of large and ferocious packs of canines within city limits.

Mr. Blackwood had so helpfully suggested that an aspiring writer get herself lodged in a giant bell, of the type that adorns a cathedral, but sorrow of most sacred sorrows, years of damnable gentrification had robbed Vancouver city of cathedrals and their citizen-trapping bells.

By way of my ever-vigilant cellphone alarm, I was made aware that the deadline hour loomed precipitously close, and I, determined writer—Oh, most dedicated of writers!—was unconvincingly far from my morbid and menacing journey of precipitous consequence. My heart quickened at the cruelest images, featuring myself failing at my task, my outbox cold—nay!—most frigid and wanting.

I commanded myself to think. *Think!* Then at once it struck me. If I couldn't throw myself at dogs, I would throw myself at a train. Oh, how brilliant I was, how crafty and clever. If ever there was a poor unfortunate Blackwood student who had succeeded at writing such an article, my sensations would be far greater, far more explicitly and intensely horrific than theirs. No such trains of yore could ever compare with the high-speed trains of today. And so, I, being of sound mind, did lift my skirts and dash through city streets, brazen in my movements, uttering barely an *excuses moi*, or a *pardon madame et monsieur,* as with ungodly haste, I arrived at the train station. With darting eyes that fairly ate up the view, I searched the crowded platform for the very clearing upon which I might attend to my journey, my feat of experimental knowledge.

But frustration of unholy frustration, every possible access was safeguarded with impenetrable fencing! Damn our modern-day bubble-wrapped world! What madness this was, that I should be so thwarted by steel and shock, when there were profound sensations to describe.

As I was in great hurry and had not a moment to spare, I turned on my heel and took my leave. Finding myself back on the grey and gracious streets of Vancouver city, I did readjust my plan of hurling myself into the path of a train, and therein decided to embrace the rather lesser sensations of being struck by a motorcar of most powerful and speedy description. I briefly wondered, as I took a determined step off the curb, if the color of the car would be of influential factor to the experience, and noted it was a crimson car with a wide bumper that filled my wide-eyed vision.

Oh, gentle reader, I cannot even speak of my unutterable frustration, my ever-eternal disappointment, when I felt my tender neck meet with the resistance of the knot of my cloak's cord, as, with the rebound of an elastic band, I was snapped back to my former place on the curb, to totter in the wake of wind and exhaust. And that stranger—Oh, most cursed of strangers!—thrust his concerned face into my countenance of anger, of seething indignation.

"My heavens, good woman, how do you fare? Weren't you watching before you stepped off into traffic?"

"I assure you, I was," I uttered in a manner most ungracious.

"Well, then, I imagine you'll be forever in my debt. In the future, may I most highly recommend, you do not neglect to look in both directions to determine when it is safe to attempt such a crossing?"

"Indeed," I muttered. "Most assuredly I shan't be attempting that again with you here to offer your most timely interference." And with that I thrust my head down and hastened with measured step down the pristine sidewalk, leaving the brazen gentleman in a wake of confusion and disbelief.

With great dismay, I trudged along the well-worn sidewalks of this lively city, weaving my way amongst fellow city dwellers, who no doubt considered it of great personal accomplishment to survive life's fate. I pondered, weak with the burden of a looming deadline, so heavy it threatened to turn my measured step into one of great effort, and weary from the burden of taxing my mind to think of ways I might seek to be united with experimental knowledge.

Then, like great Zeus' bolt, I was struck by the words of my most formidable mentor, propelling me headlong into a twisted maze of thought, one I was not so easily extracted from. Mr. Blackwood, in his unmatched wisdom, had mentioned a *chicken bone*. Oh, sweet happiness! Miracle of most revered miracles. It was by some blessed fate that I should remember these words in my most reverent and exquisite hour of need. Although the deadline was approaching expiry by the second, I had yet time to procure for myself one ever-so-delectable and timely meal of common fowl.

It mattered not how such a beast was prepared, be it roasted or fried, stewed, or rotisseried—all that mattered was that it provide me with but a tiny bone, so that I might at last brush up against that dark shadow which shall at last whisper to me its own great secret. And should I be so blessed, I shall be rewarded with the most powerful and scintillating prose, just as a maiden who feeds a bird throughout winter's cruel hour is rewarded with sweet birdsong come the blush of spring.

I quickened my pace, observing the ever-advancing hour, and dear reader, I admit my soul cried in terror, spurred on by the hopelessness of my want. For even if I should procure for myself the aforementioned chicken bone, I would still be required to ink the most perplexing, intricately detailed sensations, such that I have likely never experienced before, and should, no doubt, have the most difficult time setting them to screen.

And as Mr. Blackwood lays out in his rules, the most studious student is required to languish in the sensations, to extend them for as long as might be possible under the circumstances. I did not know if I would succeed at the task straightaway, or if I should need to take time to decipher my thoughts to reach for the most precise wording, or if I should be able to write in a fit of ecstasy, having all words come to me as an angel welcomes a saint who has freshly crossed the veil. In truth, dear reader, there wasn't much time remaining to pursue the former and so as I hastened through the city streets, I prayed that I would have the experience of the latter.

But alas! Through my most weathered and worn prayers, I could find no such source of chicken bones. As twilight began to fall, my desperate pleas through locked restaurant doors went unheeded. Until at last, collapsing in the street I all but admitted defeat. There would be no fanfare, no hope of publication—nay! Certainly, no dollar shall line the pocket of my cloak, where once tablet glowed in hopeful anticipation of receiving those blessed descriptions of sensations most dark and disturbing.

With the weight of a dozen millstones, I resigned myself to such a grand failure as is unmatched by any preceding one you can name. So convinced was I that not only should I not complete my task, but that, yes! I might never write again, as tragic as that may seem. For biting at my soul was an unrelenting mantra that I was a dark and dismal failure of grandiose proportions. And now, I could do nothing more but limp away into the dark of night, all hopes of making the deadline dashed on the rocks of broken dreams.

My dusty and city-worn shoes thus carried me through the vibrant streets of my once-loved Vancouver, where the indigo fall of twilight threatened, poised on the edge of day. A blood-red sun, dying on the horizon filled my vision, and

I could scarcely turn away. Paired couples, their laughter falling heavy on my burdened heart, passed me, ne'er once gracing me with a piteous half-smile, and I knew then that I wore my disgrace like a banner for all to witness.

At last, my feet refused to wander any more, and I came to rest in the shadow of a colossal wreck. There, exposing itself to me, with all the modesty of a woman of ill repute, was a Gothic manor house. Here, thought I, was at last my refuge from this night, from the weeping disappointment of a soul's desire crushed. Two gargantuan windows stood peering down on my presence, their slumping shutters like winking eyes, and the door, a wide-gaping mouth that invited me inside with its crooked smile. With nothing of my soul left to wager, I proceeded inside and was met with a stretching staircase.

Perhaps, thought I with a deep bemoaning wistfulness, my fate lies up these steps. And I went begrudgingly to my destiny. But mine was not a fate in which I disappeared into obscurity after first dissolving into a pit of worthlessness— Oh no! For I was yet to embrace what the celestial bodies had ordained for me in their eternal and infallible wisdom.

I was seized with an inexplicable desire to lunge skyward, up the rickety steps, forward into my destiny, although I knew not why, for surely I had already failed. There was but a half hour left until deadline. Yet on I went, step after tremulous and hesitant step, until I had surmounted the derelict staircase and stood, voluminous breath ragged in my throat, my gaze forging a path down the barren hallway into the chamber door beyond.

I hastened forward, and in a fit of furious exuberance, threw open the wooden door. Around me, the air was as silent as a tomb and my heart thudded at a curious pace, one more in keeping with a sudden terror than a purposeful ascent into an abandoned room. I stood in peaceful solitude for unspecified moments, inhaling of the breeze that alighted through the warped and weathered slat siding.

Of a sudden, I was pulled from my reverie by the faraway sound of a bird in flight. A gentle flap of wings grew ever closer, until I started at the unprecedented *tap, tap, tapping* against the glass. Was this at last, my celestial visitor, coming to console me, in my darkest hour? I hastened to the window, and without thought, without any compunction or hesitation, unlatched the stubborn beast and with all the might God gave a lion, threw up the sash.

Horror upon unmitigated horror! Oh ghastly demon of the fiery depths of hell, I at last make your acquaintance. Here was my fate, which had so eluded me this day, which had caused me to hate my very soul. And now, this spinning, whirling machine was at last before me, circling me, its singular eye blinking in a mesmerizing cadence. Oh, how it held me transfixed, shivers blanketing my translucent skin. Then, at once, the drone charged, dropping like a lightning bolt to collide with my head, and like the rush of an ocean tide, I was alive with sensations as the machine exacted vengeance. It fell and rose and fell and rose again, smashing my face until I felt the unmistakably sticky warmth of blood begin to trickle upon my most concerted and furrowed brow.

Then I learned of a pain like no other as its tiny, raven-colored blades wrapped around my golden tresses, tearing free ribbons of bloodied locks. Renewed with the sensations of the moment, I thrust a hand out to swipe at my most faithful companion, my tablet. Under assault from the jet-black drone, I dove upon the floor, and hastened to power on the tablet, and with all the will I could muster, I pressed the record button.

Then I surrendered myself to pure sensation, calling out all the definitions that I could draw to mind as I described for the camera my most treacherous of experiences. Word upon word, sensation upon sensation flooded my mind, then took the short plunge to my lips, as the drone descended upon my battered and bewildered body. My flesh tore asunder at the *whap, whap, whapping* of mechanical blade, and oh, how I rejoiced at a story well captured, at this terror that was most surpassed in all of histories finest battles.

I thought on my mentor in those my most grand and final moments, and it was then in my divine and giddy passing, that I uttered my final words:

> "And if I died, at least I died
> For thee—for thee."

Horror of most wonderful and sacred horrors, with my last burst of energy, I gazed down at my tattered skin, my exposed innards and with clear mind, delivered my final act, a gracious, most sincere, award-winning smile. Then I reached across the floor, shut off the tablet's camera and uploaded the video to the contest's website.

All at once the mechanical beast, my raven, did retreat, and I watched as it departed from the window, to fly, dripping my blood, into the inky night.

And I, did I not rush into the arms of death that night? No, dear reader, no! I had to live on, for I had more tales of horror to pen, more sensations to endure…

Matthew M. Montelione is an American Revolution historian who focuses on the local experiences of Loyalists on Long Island, New York. His work on the subject has been published in Long Island History Journal *and* Journal of the American Revolution. *Matthew also writes horror and fantasy stories which have been published in* Gravely Unusual Magazine *and* Fantasia Divinity's Midnight Masquerade *anthology. He lives on Long Island with his wife.*

About this story, Matthew says: "Edgar Allan Poe is my favorite short story writer, and so I was thrilled to have the opportunity to reimagine one of his tales. I chose The Facts in the Case of M. Valdemar, *a sinister story that fascinates me with its compelling blend of science and horror, and its exploration of the idea of arresting death. My reimagined version is set in the twenty-first century and examines the possibility of combining hypnotism with machines to transfer a dying human psyche into a robotic host."*

We routinely accept death as the cessation of all bodily function, but are often stymied in discussions of the soul or consciousness. Does it exist? Does it dissipate at the moment of physical death, or continue on in some other form? And if it lingers, can we take hold of a soul and keep it from slipping away...

THE FACTS IN THE CASE OF M. VALDEMAR
Matthew M. Montelione

The extraordinary case of Valdemar has recently excited discussion in many scientific circles. Even the common plebeian who sits in front of a television set all day long might have heard of and pondered on the horrid sequence of events. Although I tried my best to keep these matters private, away from the public's scrutiny, hell hath no fury like the internet. Misinformed and exaggerated accounts of Valdemar's demise are posted all over the web, and, quite naturally, ignorance and a great deal of disbelief have taken root around the matter. This current situation has made it necessary for me to explain the cold facts regarding Valdemar, as best as I can comprehend them myself.

For the last three years, I intensely practiced the art of hypnotism. From the onset of my interest, one particular question burned in my mind: if a dying person was hypnotized before they truly expired, could the trance repel the unwanted encroachments of death? I wondered if there could be some sort of complex connection between hypnotism and death. Nobody had ever attempted to answer such a question, doubtless because of the macabre nature of the quest.

My training as a robotics engineer spurred my interest a step further. If hypnosis could indeed arrest death, could a human consciousness be transferred from a failing body and into a robot in that moment? I reasoned that if there was ever a time in one's life when the transference of the human psyche was possible through the combined powers of science and hypnotism, it would be at the point of decease. Such a scientific breakthrough would be revolutionary! I needed to find out. I am sure at this point you can understand my wonder about the subject and its endless possibilities.

Alas, I was limited by funding and technological constraints, and forced to wade through droves of religious zealots who wished to shut my research down. Still, I am proud of what I created with what was available to me: a fully functional robotic human head, which, in theory, could download someone's consciousness through connected wires. I only needed to convince a test subject that he would be making the right choice if he volunteered for my experiment. After all, if successful, the volunteer would live on—albeit in a machine—but he would live! He would see the world just as any human being saw it, except he would be able to zoom in on faraway sights and sharpen his vision with built-in binoculars. He would have the power of the internet at his complete disposal, and thus would possess the key to infinite knowledge! He would speak in hundreds of different languages, and never tire of conversing in all of man's tongues.

Despite all these advantages, I knew that I would be hard-pressed to find a willing test subject, but I did have one of my older friends in mind. His name was M. Ernest Valdemar, and he was for forty years a professor of Psychology in New York. Valdemar had lived in one of the boroughs of that great city his entire life, and had made quite a name for himself in his field, publishing many scientific articles throughout his long career. He had a striking appearance, which was not altogether for the better. He was easily noticeable for his extreme gauntness, and for the whiteness of his face whiskers, which contrasted quite obviously with his exceedingly dark hair. Most people thought that he dyed it, but he vehemently denied the accusation.

Valdemar was also interested in hypnotism. In fact, I had put him under my sway on three occasions with little difficulty. I had hypnotized him most recently to calm his nerves. About a year ago, he was diagnosed with an aggressive form of lung cancer. Despite his impending doom, after I hypnotized him he usually spoke calmly of his approaching demise. Given our warm relationship and his particular circumstance, it was natural that I thought of Valdemar as a perfect candidate for my experiment. What was more, he had no living relatives to speak of, and therefore none would cause any interference if I was to have my way.

One day, after we had a fine lunch and talked about trivial matters, I spoke frankly to him on the subject. To my surprise, Valdemar was rather excited at the entire prospect. To make matters smoother, his doctor had given him a specific window in which he could expect his coming death. It was thus arranged between us that he would call me about twenty-four hours before the period announced by his doctors as that of his decease.

*

About three months ago, I received the anticipated telephone call. He pronounced to me, weakly yet clearly: "My dear friend, you may as well come now. My doctors are agreed that I cannot hold out beyond midnight tomorrow. I feel in my bones that they are right."

After I hung up, I raced straightaway to Valdemar's apartment in East Harlem, where I arrived to a very sad, yet excitable, sight. There lay my friend, propped up by pillows in bed. Wires already ran from his head to the robotic one, which was propped on an end table next to the dying man. The procedure was all ready to go, thanks to Dr. Davis and Dr. Finch, accomplices to my experiment, who had prepared the area. Two hospice nurses were also in attendance when I arrived. I greeted them all and sat near Valdemar.

The poor man had deteriorated rapidly in the span of a few weeks, succumbing to the summons of death in a most obvious fashion. His face was a dull gray color, and his eyes lacked the light so present in the living. His gauntness was so extreme that his skin was broken by his cheek-bones. His pulse was barely existent, and he coughed excessively in a most violent fashion. Yet, for all his failings, Valdemar exhibited a remarkably cool demeanor, and some degree of physical strength remained in him. Indeed, he wrote in his notebook a few times during my initial visit.

After greeting my friend, I took the doctors and nurses aside and obtained from them a detailed account of Valdemar's condition. The cancer had spread rapidly to both of his lungs and his lymph nodes. He was a doomed man, and only time would tell how long he would last, though the doctors and the nurses estimated that Valdemar would likely die around midnight the following night. At that time, it was seven o'clock on Saturday evening. Dr. Davis and Dr. Finch soon took their leave, and I requested that they return on Sunday night at ten o'clock.

Upon their departure, I spoke for a short time with Valdemar. I asked him if he was still willing to go through with the experiment.

"Yes!" Valdemar suddenly cried out, startling the nurses. "What are you waiting for? I will not be a part of the physical world much longer. Hurry, hurry," he said anxiously, gripping my arm tightly. It perplexed me that he still retained enough strength for that, but it showed me that he was still very much alive.

I had no choice but to ignore his request, for I could not begin the experiment without the other doctors. However, upon Dr. Finch's early arrival at Valdemar's around eight o'clock the next night, we started the procedure

155

immediately, not only to appease the dying man's wishes, but also because I knew without a doubt that I had not a moment to lose. Any second now, Valdemar would take his last breath. I prepared myself to mesmerize him while Dr. Finch made sure the robotic head was still operating properly.

"All systems go," Dr. Finch said with an excited smile.

I sat next to my dying friend and took his hand. "Valdemar, are you still willing to be mesmerized?" The nurses looked at the scene with suspense and a bit of uncertainty.

He replied weakly, but clearly, "Yes, I wish that. But I fear you have waited too long."

As he spoke, I began the passes which I had used in the past to put him under my sway. He was certainly influenced, but to what extent, it was hard to tell. Dr. Davis arrived at ten o'clock, and I explained to him the current situation. It was around this time that I continued my passes, gazing especially into the right eye of the dying man. I checked for Valdemar's pulse and found it was barely there. He breathed heavily, and slowly, at intervals of about thirty seconds. His chest heaved as if a fatal burden were upon it. This sad scene continued for about twenty-five minutes.

Suddenly, Valdemar let out a deep sigh, and his breathing ceased. His extremities went ice cold. At that same moment, bright blue lights flickered from the robotic head. It had registered Valdemar's brain waves! But, before I knew it, the robot went dark again. Dr. Finch ran over to the robotic head and analyzed it.

I vigorously persisted in mesmerizing Valdemar. About five minutes before eleven o'clock, I noticed clear signs of the mesmeric influence. His eyes rolled back lazily in his head and back out again, and his lids flickered here and there. His disgusting dark tongue stood straight out. Dr. Davis adjusted the limbs of the sufferer, placing his legs at full length and elevated his head slightly off his pillow.

I continued my work until exactly midnight. Dr. Davis ran some tests on Valdemar to examine his condition. We found that he was completely under the mesmeric trance! Our giddiness could not be contained, for we knew we were on the verge of a scientific breakthrough. The doctors and nurses elected to stay with me all night to help monitor the situation, and we left Valdemar entirely undisturbed until around three o'clock in the morning.

*

Upon our next examination, we found that he was in exactly the same state that he was at midnight: he breathed sparsely (his breath was only discovered by putting a small mirror to the lips), he had an undetectable pulse, and his body was stiff and cold as marble. Despite all of this, his appearance was not one of death. Had the hypnotic persuasion arrested the Grim Reaper? I checked the robotic head, but there was no activity. I started feeling drained and almost disappointed in the entire experiment, but I could not give up—not yet. I sat next to Valdemar and repeated the same mesmeric passes. I fully expected him not to follow me. To my astonishment, his eyes twitched! I then decided to ask him a question.

"Mr. Valdemar," I said, "are you asleep?" He did not respond, but I saw him move his lips slightly. The robotic head did not flicker. Twice more I repeated the question, and on the third repetition, his body started to shake. His eyelids opened wider, displaying the whites of his eyes. His lips curled slowly, and out of his mouth came a low and unnerving reply.

"Yes, I am asleep. Do not wake me! Let me die so!"

"Do you still feel pain, Valdemar?" I questioned him.

"No pain... I am dying!"

We all looked at one another gravely. There was something about Valdemar's tone of voice that made us uneasy. For a few hours, I did not think it wise to disturb him further. However, at around seven o'clock in the morning, I asked him the same question.

"Valdemar, are you still asleep?" Just like before, the dying man did not answer me right away. Rather, his lips twitched, and it appeared that he slowly gathered his energy and answered in a low tone.

"Yes, still asleep. Dying." His tongue flickered about his mouth briefly, then stopped moving entirely.

The doctors and I collectively decided that we should leave Valdemar undisturbed in his present mesmeric state until death finally claimed him. We went off to observe the robotic head, which to our chagrin had remained unchanged since the initial flash of light. I carefully checked the connecting wires, making sure all was as it should be. Dr. Davis penciled away in his notebook. The nurses stood far from the bed, as if they feared the dying man.

I admit I am not a patient man, and after a few minutes had passed, I could not resist repeating my question to Valdemar. I anxiously sat back down next to him and continued my work.

"Valdemar, do you sleep?"

When I spoke, a terrible metamorphosis overcame the dying man. His eyes rolled backwards into his head, his skin assumed a deathly pale hue which resembled white paper, and the circular spots in his cheeks, which had previously been well-defined, collapsed. It reminded me of the extinguishment of a candle by a puff of breath. His upper lip curled upward, exposing his yellowed teeth, and his jaw dropped wide open, exposing his hideous blackened tongue. It was truly horrid to behold. The doctors and nurses gasped at the sight of it.

After this, Valdemar exhibited no signs of life. We assumed him dead. Dr. Davis peered behind Valdemar's head, contemplating the best way to disconnect the wires that ran to the robot. However, not two minutes later, Valdemar's blackened tongue started slowly thrusting in and out of his mouth again! This behavior continued for about a minute.

Then, to the terror of all present, out of the motionless man we heard a most unearthly voice. It was deep, jarring, hollow, and reverberated around the entire bedroom. Valdemar spoke in reply to my question I had asked numerous times earlier.

"Yes... no... I *have been* sleeping... and now... now... *I am dead.*"

Hell itself could not have conjured a more cryptic tone. Dr. Finch fainted, and the nurses ran out of the apartment in fright. Dr. Davis ran to Dr. Finch and helped him up. I stood motionless, my blood running cold, my heart pounding out of my chest. A mere moment after Valdemar spoke those horrible words, the robotic head again lit up! Was Valdemar's psyche being transferred? The entire cranium lit up and bathed the whole room in blue!

The situation remained unchanged for nearly an hour. The robotic head was still illuminated, but it seemed to be in a static state. Valdemar's motionless body lay on the bed and the mirror no longer detected his breath. An attempt to draw blood from him failed. The only hypnotic influence I now observed was the twitching of his disgusting, decaying tongue. After a while, the robotic head's lights dimmed and then ceased altogether. At this point, we were all completely exhausted and retired for about eight hours.

*

When we again returned to Valdemar's side, we were shocked to see the patient virtually unchanged from last we left him. Apparently, the chilling events that transpired were too much for the previous hospice nurses to handle, and one new nurse had replaced them. The doctors and I discussed the feasibility of trying to awaken Valdemar, but we realized that no good would come of it. For all intents and purposes, the man was dead. Yet, there was no doubt that death— or what we perceived as death—had been arrested by the mesmeric influence. Whatever trance Valdemar was in, he was not in pain, at least. Our metal head remained unresponsive.

From this period until the close of last week—an interval of almost *seven months*—we all made continual visits to Valdemar's apartment. All this time, to our absolute amazement, he remained in exactly the same condition as when we left him many months ago.

Eventually, we all sat down and discussed what our next move should be. We agreed that the only plausible next step would be to try to awaken Valdemar. In this decision, we were certain we would receive backlash from the public (if they found out) for disturbing the peacefulness of a man's last moments on Earth. Still, the experiment had to go on.

*

The doctors and I next met at Valdemar's on a rainy September evening. To awaken him from the mesmeric state, I performed my usual passes. At first, as per usual, these were unsuccessful. However, after a few minutes, I noticed a slight response—a twitch in his right eye! To my disgust, in that same moment, from under his half-closed eyelids oozed a nauseating yellow ichor. For a second, I pulled back from Valdemar, truly sickened. I remained somewhat at an impasse, unable to decide what approach to take next. Dr. Davis then proposed that I ask the dying man a specific question.

"Valdemar, can you explain to us what are your feelings or wishes now?"

Instantly, the circles where his cheeks had been collapsed returned, his dark tongue rolled violently in his mouth (but still his jaw remained rigid), and the same demonic voice which we heard that horrific night near seven months ago echoed throughout the bed chamber.

"For God's sake! Quick! Quick! Put me to sleep, quick! No! Waken me! Quick! *I say to you that I am dead!*"

I was completely unnerved and quickly backed away from him. The robotic head lit up again and started shaking violently on the table, but I could not find it in my bones to move to it.

Then the bright blue light that was once contained to the head suddenly leaped through the wires connected to Valdemar's brain. Dr. Davis and Dr. Finch stood in horror, also unable to move. I gathered my courage and shook my old friend most violently, trying to awaken him. When that did not work, I set about vigorously performing the mesmeric passes again.

What happened next will probably not be believed by anyone who was not present on that dreadful evening, but I say to you, it is the cold truth. A truth that no human being—doctor, scientist, or otherwise—could ever have been properly prepared for.

As I rapidly made the hypnotic passes, Valdemar's foul-smelling tongue started thrusting in and out of his mouth most aggressively. A hollow voice bellowed out of his putrid mouth more clearly than ever: "Dead! Dead! Dead!" It burst from the sufferer's tongue, but not at all from his lips, which did not move!

At that same moment, another unearthly voice resounded through the room. It was that of the robotic head! It repeated the words of the screaming man who lay before me!

"Dead! Dead!" it yelled, and then in many different languages, warping in and out of lower and higher frequencies! "Dead! Morto! Muerto! Mort!" The dual voices pierced through our hearts in a most deplorable fashion.

As both man and machine wailed violently, Valdemar's entire body began to crumble, completely rotting away beneath my very hands in a matter of moments! Dr. Finch again fainted at the grisly sight. Finally, Dr. Davis ran to the robotic head, which clanged in harsh tones as it short-circuited and sent sparks flying everywhere. To my absolute horror, upon the bed, where Valdemar had laid, there sat an almost entirely liquid mass of repulsive putrescence.

I stared, motionless, at the disgusting puddle of rotted flesh and blood, thoughts racing through my mind. Dr. Davis screamed in fright when he saw the mess, but quickly took up his notebook and picked up his pencil. His hands were shaking as he scribbled down whatever details he could recall about the experiment. Dr. Finch lay unconscious on the floor. The lone hospice nurse was nowhere to be found.

The situation was altogether unholy, but I admit that I smiled grimly after we revived Dr. Finch, cleaned up the horrid puddles, and processed what had occurred. I now realized, without a shadow of a doubt, that I was correct in thinking that what we perceived as death could be arrested by a combination of hypnotism and robotics. And that, indeed, the consciousness of a human being could be transferred into a machine.

Oh! Think of what wonders this process could do for the twenty-first century person, if we were allowed to continue our research further and perfect the transition! Although Dr. Finch has since left his practice, Dr. Davis and I eagerly await the next dying friend who I may convince to be transferred into a new and improved robotic host. I dare say that Valdemar will one day be known as the first martyr of such a brilliant feat.

Amber Fallon lives in weird cave in a small town outside Boston, Massachusetts that she shares with her husband and their two dogs. A techie by day and a horror writer by night, Amber has also worked as a bank manager, motivational speaker, produce wrangler, and apprentice butcher. Her obsessions with sushi, glittery nail polish, and sharp objects have made her a recognized figure around the community. Amber's numerous publications include TV Dinners from Hell, Dead Bait 4, Horror on the Installment Plan, *and* Painted Mayhem. *For more information, follow her on Twitter @Z0mbiegrl or visit her at www.amberfallon.net.*

About this poem, Amber says: "I have a deep and abiding love of Poe. My mother used to read to me from a large leather bound compendium when I was very small, and I've been a fan ever since. While his short stories are fantastic, it's his poetry that sticks in my heart... especially The Bells *which I fell in love with it upon realizing how beautiful and subtle it is, invoking the stages of life through a single, simple object. Now that we've all but forgotten bells in our daily lives, I hoped to bring that same feeling into the modern era.*

There's a little madness that takes hold when the alarm goes off in the pre-dawn hours, the phone rings in your hand, a buzzer sounds from an overhead speaker, or a siren blares behind you on your commute. Injecting a shot of adrenaline and demanding our attention, they take us from the comfort of our modern lives, throwing our back-brain headfirst into the primal, fight-or-flight mode and waiting for our response. The strangest thing? We created these artificial masters ourselves.

THE TONES

Amber Fallon

I.

Hear the alarm clock with its tones—
   Jarring tones!
What a world of work and wakefulness accompanies their vibrant horns!
   How they shriek, shriek, shriek,
    From the stand beside your bed!
   While the birdy voices speak
   All the notes seem to cry
    Full of bright cacophonous dread;
   You're calling why, why, why?
   While your body begs to be fed,

To the to the triumph of your alarm clock's drones,
  From the tones, tones, tones, tones,
    tones, tones, tones,
From the screaming and the beeping of the tones.

II.

  Hear the iPhones with their tones—
    Sprightly tones!
What a world of likes and comments their pinging condones!
  How they chime, chime, chime,
    In the pocket of your pants!
  While the lights around you shine
  All the notes seem to gleam
    In a tinny, tuneful dance;
  Keeping theme, theme, theme,
  Like a sort of musical meme,
To the to the jubilation of your cellular phone,
  From the tones, tones, tones, tones,
    tones, tones, tones,
From the pinging and the singing of the tones.

III.

  Hear the messenger's calling tones,
    Strident tones!
What a world of communication their singing intones!
  Through the quiet of the day
  How their voices call and bay!
    From the dull buzz of vibration
    Since you've pressed mute,
    What constant inundation
 Of coworkers, friends, and familial relations
    Follows suit!
  Oh, from the speaker's groans,
What a gush of contacts pour through your headphones!
    How they drone!
    How they moan
    On your free time! You bemoan,
    Of the duty those messages become,
  To the chirping and the burping
From the tones, tones, tones, tones,
    tones, tones, tones,

162

tones, tones, tones—
To the whirring and the blurring of the tones!

IV.

   Hear the piercing fire alarm tones—
     Raucous tones!
What tale of terror, now, their bleating forewarns!
  In the startled ears of colleagues,
  How they scream out their cautious call!
  Too much annoyed to talk,
  They can only walk, walk,
    Out of doors,
In a clamorous awareness to the presence of the fire,
In a mad chorus with the dubious uncertain pyre,
  Looking tired, tired, tired,
  With heat, they perspire,
  And a calm careful measure
  Now—now to sit or never,
  By the side of the building down the block.
  Oh, the tones, tones, tones!
  What a tale their terror intones
    Of delay!
  How they scream and yell and roar!
  What a horror they outpour
In the monotonous Monday air!
  Yet the ear, it fully knows,
  By the beeping,
  And the bleeping,
  How the danger ebbs and flows;
  Yet, the ear distinctly tells,
  In the silence,
  And the balance,
  How the danger comes and goes,
By the coming or the going of the clamor of the tones,
    Of the tones,
  Of the tones, tones, tones, tones,
  tones, tones, tones,
In the shouting and the hollering of the tones!

V.

Hear the bleating of the tones—
  Fire truck tones!
What a world of security and protection their calling owns!
  In the loudness of the fire drill,
  How we pool and share our Advil,
At the fire truck's loud approach!
  For every sound that moves,
  From the speakers on their roofs
    Is a cry.
  And the crowd—ah, the crowd—
  Gathered in that human cloud
    Drawn together,
  And who, waiting, waiting, waiting,
  In the designated safety zone,
  Feel a break has been allowed,
  Before they are due back inside—
  They are neither man nor woman,
  They are neither free nor working,
    They are Employees—
  And their king it is who falls;
  And he calls, calls, calls, calls,
    calls, calls, calls.
  A summons from the tones!
  And his happy punch card owns,
  Their daily iterations of the tones!
  And he audits, and he frowns;
  Keeping time, time, time,
  As if they were committing crimes,
  To the summons of the tones,
    Of the tones:
  Keeping time, time, time,
  As if they were committing crimes,
  To the peeping of the tones,
    Of the tones, tones, tones,
  To the demanding of the tones;
  Keeping time, time, time,
  As he owns, owns, owns,
  More and more of their free time,
  To the pleading of the tones,
  Of the tones, tones, tones,

To the beckoning of the tones,
  Of the tones, tones, tones, tones,
    Tones, tones, tones,
To the needing and the pleading of the tones.

Ken Goldman is an affiliate member of the Horror Writers Association with homes on the Main Line in Pennsylvania and at the Jersey shore. His stories have appeared in numerous publications, receiving seven honorable mentions in The Year's Best Fantasy & Horror. *He has compiled three short story collections of his own work—*You Had Me at Arrgh!, Donny Doesn't Live Here Anymore, *and* Star-Crossed (Vampires 2); *a novella,* Desiree, *and two novels:* Of a Feather *and* Sinkhole.

About this story, Ken says: "As a former high school English teacher, Poe was a regular part of my curriculum, and I have taught every Poe story mentioned in my own tale. The incident that occurs in Josh Hooper's classroom is an exaggerated version of an event that once took place in mine, when, having just read The Raven, *I then jokingly said, 'Wouldn't it be something if I could make Poe appear right now here in class?' Everyone in the room focused on the door—and it swung open!"*

The unusual events of this story wrap themselves around a brief tour-of-sorts of Poe's work, resulting in the temptation to lead off the collection with this piece by way of introducing newcomers to Poe—such as the students here depicted—to the author's canon. But the story's somewhat lighter tone suggested that this placement, between darker entries, might provide a momentary respite for the reader. Or perhaps not. After all, high school isn't all fun and games...

GET THE DOOR FOR ME, WILL YOU, EDGAR?

Kenneth C. Goldman

The thunderstorm increased in ferocity tenfold, thick veins of white light fracturing skies too ominous for an early spring morning. Outside, in the Wednesday world beyond Carver High's eighty-seven yammering instructors, nature's bass drum hootenanny rumbled in the distance. But a good teacher was industrious, and if the flittering light show proved distracting, then it created an effective backdrop to Josh Hooper's lesson.

While reading aloud Edgar Allan Poe's raven's first immortal utterance of "Nevermore" from the author's most famous poem, the sky went *Ka-Boom!* and the lights inside Hooper's classroom flickered. The wind, coupled with the erratic strobing, established a respectable film noir effect, a genuine Poe moment any English teacher worth his spit would have relished.

"*Woooooooooooo...*" ghost-wailed Raphael Jones from the back row, taking advantage of yet another teacher-baiting opportunity. Whatever didn't come from a boom box Jones wasn't interested in hearing, and whatever came from the mouth of a teacher immediately turned the kid stone deaf. Hooper knew that Mr. Poe was no match for the likes of Heavy D and Lil' Kim, but that only meant he would have to try harder.

"Quoth the wise-ass, hopefully nevermore," Josh offered Raphael as his rejoinder, and the teacher's clever comeback won over the class enough to shut Jones' mouth for a moment. Once Carmella Caparelli laughed, several others followed her lead. Among Hooper's students the girl seemed the most capable of thinking outside the X-Box, a rare circumstance, considering her body could open doors for her even if she were brain dead. Since Carmella's intelligence impressed Hooper as much as her ample tits percolated the testosterone of every boy in class, he counted the girl's approval as a win.

A teacher was only as good as his last successful minute, especially with seniors. Upperclassmen felt above anything their middle-aged instructors offered, so Hooper readied himself for those moment-to-moment improvisations whenever he needed to keep yawning students from completely zoning out. In the adolescent world of iPod people, an educator did more than educate; he entertained with the in-your-face aplomb of a Richard Pryor. Teaching had become a daily stand-up in a room of persistent hecklers who, if you didn't deliver the goods, might decide to trash your Toyota. That had happened three times last semester, and some industrious prick had balls enough to scratch POE SUCKS into Hooper's paint job. That hurt, and not so much because of the vandalism. Excepting a good blow job, American Lit was Hooper's passion.

The Scarlet Letter? Adultery aside, maybe Nat Hawthorne didn't quite make the cut. Fitzgerald's less-than-*Great Gatsby*? Okay, a little heavy for George Washington Carver High's pimpled party animals. Ditto those more modern clowns, Steinbeck and Hemingway. But Edgar Allan Poe? The creator of so many tales of terror... sucks? Poe ... *sucks?* What alien breed of cretins occupied these seats?

Bullets of windswept rain pelted the windows. Still reading aloud Josh peeked down at the courtyard. This morning even the cutters had sought shelter from the downpour. No one liked to fuck with thunder and lightning. No one, of course, except ol' Edgar.

"'*And the silken sad uncertain rustling of each purple curtain ...*' Hear it? Do you hear those rustling curtains going *SSSSSSSSSSS?*"

Nothing. Nada.

Not so much as a changed expression to demonstrate these kids shared oxygen with him, although Carmella Caparelli's eyes remained clearly fixed on his while she grinned her little half smile.

Finally kissass Billy Silverman spoke.

"The hissing sound of the curtains ... It's called *a-little-ration*, right?" Billy probably required detailed instructions just to put on his socks, but for some reason Hooper liked the kid's die hard attitude.

"'Alliteration,' asshole!" some teacher's helper from the back row called out.

"Alliteration, that's just what it is," Hooper said, not missing a beat. "A literary device that works like a sound effect. It's like that thunder and lightning out there. It sets the poem's tone nicely. Poe's use of alliteration, don't you think? *'Silken sad uncertain...'* HISSSSSSSSSSSSSSS. Hear it?"

Sensing another opportunity, Raphael rejoined the game with his finest shuck and jive impersonation. "Like 'Big bulging busty boobs.' That's 'literation, ain't that right, Missy Carmella?"

During moments like this Hooper considered cutting out the kid's heart and placing it beneath the floor boards where it could beat tell-tale hip-hop for all eternity. Still, like any good narrator of Poe's words, Hooper offered a cynical smile.

"Right, Rafe. Except boobs don't make much sound. Not unless they're going for a cheap laugh."

Raphael smiled, too, offering his toothy grin while completely missing the irony of Hooper's absolute sincerity. That was good. Cracking jokes had become a tough call in an age of political correctness, when one misspoken word could earn a teacher his walking papers before the final bell. But Hooper had made Poe's point, and that earned him one more minute of acceptance by the most demanding audience on earth.

"Like all of us, Poe questioned death. He hoped there was something more than 'Nevermore,' something beyond the finality of the grave. As he pines for his lost Lenore, Poe's raven outside his narrator's door might well have been a manifestation of just that. '... *Deep into that darkness peering, long I stood there wondering, fearing ...'"*

Ka-BOOM-BOOM!

The lights flickered wildly, seeming almost to glow. Then they went out. For a moment there was quiet in the darkness, an absolute, surreal silence—an especially infrequent occurrence in a class of thirty very vocal kids. It didn't last long.

"Woooooooooooooooooo..." This new howl came from Kenny Greene.

"Oh my God! They've killed Kenny!" from the back. The inevitable laughs followed.

"Can't read much in the dark, can we, Mr. Hooper? We'll have to wait for power to come back, huh?" The fat fuck Sam Peterson spoke fluent wise-ass.

"Not to worry, Sam. I have the poem memorized. It sounds even better in the dark."

Carmella lit up. "Do you really, Mr. Hooper? You memorized the whole poem?"

[Thank God for you, Carmella.]
Hooper took that as his cue.

"'So that now, to still the beating of my heart, I stood repeating,
'Tis some visitor entreating entrance at my chamber door—
Some late visitor entreating entrance at my chamber door ...'"

"Nah, Mr. Hooper," from the fat fuck. "It don't sound no better in the dark."

Another crash of thunder. A knock at the door. Then another two. And a third round.

Knock... knock-knock... knock-knock-knock...

Hooper smiled at the perfect timing.

"Who dat knockin' at my chamber door?" from Raphael.

"Who dat who say 'who dat?'" Jeff Lynch, whose classroom of honor students sat next door, entered. Hooper hoped he wasn't going to complain about the noise again. "Just got the call from the office, Josh. Power's out all over the neighborhood. Looks like it's going to stay that way for a while, too. So no one leaves class when the period's over, and no piss breaks either, not while the school's dark like this. Security reasons, yada yada yada. Okay?" He turned to the rest of the class. "You okay with that, Poe-philes?"

Some kid proficient in both ventriloquism and the look of innocence muttered "Okay, you big fag."

"I'll take that to mean 'yes.'" Lynch left to spread the news down the corridor. Hooper turned towards his young prodigies, waiting for the groaning to die down.

"Looks like it's just us and Edgar for a while, gang. So let's see how that raven is doing. We'll take it from the top, okay? Listen and you can almost feel the narrator nodding off. '...weak and weary... nodded nearly napping.' Kind of like you guys right now. Listen closely to Poe's words." He shut his eyes to recall the words.

"Once upon a midnight dreary, while I pondered, weak and weary,
Over many a quaint and curious volume of forgotten lore,
While I nodded, nearly napping, suddenly there came a tapping,
As of someone gently rapping, rapping at my chamber door..."

Three rapid knocks again at the door, more urgent than Jeff's the last time.

"'Literation again, right?" Raphael asked. Laughs all around encouraged his toothy grin to widen.

"*Wooooooooooooooo...*" Someone else had picked up Raphael's mantel. Half the class joined in, even some girls. Fucking Lynch really knew how to kill a mood. Hooper went to the door.

[Darkness there ... and nothing more ...]

Hooper looked down the corridor, expecting to discover some pimply gremlin scurrying around the corner, maybe ducking into another classroom. But the hallways remained dark and empty.

"See any ravens out there?" from Peterson.

"No ravens, Sam. No pits. No pendulums. No lost Lenores." He shut the door hoping to return his class to some semblance of order.

Carmella voiced her take on the matter. "Maybe it's Poe himself. His spirit, I mean."

"*Wooooooooooo!* Carmella, the Ghost Whisperer."

The girl wasn't the type to capitalize on the occasional lapse into chaos so common among high school kids. She sounded damned serious, in fact. Carmella's comment recalled a moment during this very lesson on another rainy day, but not quite this morning's gully washer. Hooper decided he could go off the lesson plan a little. What was the harm of a colorful anecdote, some enrichment to goose his Poe lecture a bit during this extended class period when the kids' attention spans were likely to wane anyway?

Hooper paused for dramatic effect.

"Funny you should mention that, Carmella."

He waited for someone, anyone to bite. Denise Daniels, the skinny sad-eyed girl who sat in the back and was the least likely to utter a syllable in class, spoke first. That she had decided to speak at all startled him, along with half the class.

"My sister was in your class last year, Mr. Hooper. She told me all about what happened that time. She told me she couldn't sleep for a week."

The girl's remark roused every kid's attention. Anything suggesting the macabre became catnip to a kid.

[Denise, you may have just earned yourself an 'A'...]

Hooper faked brief indecision as if hesitant to share some forbidden tale. "All right, then. But what I tell you doesn't leave this room. Okay?" Playing his disciples with the precision of a concert maestro, he waited for the telling cue of kids leaning forward in their seats. Locking eyes with the stragglers, he waited until he had them all.

"I was teaching this same lesson, reading *'The Raven'* aloud just like today. There was a knock at the door, like just now." He knocked on his desk for effect. "...and when I looked, no one was there. I didn't make much of it; kids are always looking to make trouble in the halls. But it happened again at the same moment I read the line. Just like this." Slipping into Vincent Price mode Hooper enunciated the stanza. *"As of someone gently rapping, rapping at my chamber door..."*

KNOCK! KNOCK! KNOCK!

The class froze. All eyes went to the doorway. Probably Lynch was again playing hall monitor, or maybe another asshole kid was capitalizing on the darkened corridors. But that was okay if it set the desired mood.

"Who's there?" Hooper called out.

Nothing.

"Yeah, it happened just like that. So I'm figuring either someone is playing one hell of an elaborate joke, or maybe… maybe there's something else going on. So I say in front of my class, 'Get the door for me, will you Edgar?' Just like that, calm, cool. 'Get the door, Edgar.' And do you know what happened?"

Silence. He expected it. This time he enunciated the words slowly.

"'Get-the-door-for-me-Edgar.' That's what I said. 'Get the door for me'…"

All eyes returned to the door. Nothing happened. No one said a word. Everyone waited. Waited some more.

Again nothing.

Hooper looked embarrassed. "Guess sometimes the magic just doesn't happen. Anyway—"

The door creaked open.

"Dude, how the hell did you do that?" from Raphael.

"I didn't." A look of skepticism from just about everyone. "Hey, really. I swear. And I'd prefer you not call me 'Dude,' okay?"

All eyes returned to the door.

"Close the door for me, Edgar!" Hooper seemed more insistent this time.

The door slowly swung shut.

Several gasps rose from around the classroom. Hooper felt an odd satisfaction, as if he had performed some inexplicable magic trick even he didn't understand. But he had them now, and he wasn't about to relinquish the moment.

[Voila! gang. And for your amusement, here comes Mr. Poe to say howdy!]

"See, I think what I'd done last time was—maybe I'd managed to channel Edgar because of this poem we were reading together. But that's as far as it went, just the door opening and closing. I didn't think it could happen so easily a second time. Which means…"

"…he's inside the room with us right now!" from Carmella.

Hooper's eyes darted about the classroom. He knew a dramatic moment when he saw one. "Is that true, Edgar, old pal? Are you in here with us as I speak? You feel like giving us a sign or something?"

"Hokey," said Peterson. "Very hokey."

Raphael spoke in an uncharacteristic undertone. "Think maybe you can get Selena in here, too?"

"So now what?" Carmella again.

An answer came quickly—a relentless successions of death knell gongs, a harsh and persistent sound of thick metal reverberating inside every kid's brain with painful thuds. Several students pushed fists to their ears but the echoes persisted. Hooper recognized the sound.

"Christ. Can it be…?"

[…the tintinnabulation that so musically wells…]

"Mr. Hooper, what's…?"

"*'The Bells.'*. Poe's poem. We read it last week."

[…from the bells bells bells bells bells bells bells…]

Here was a literary illusion—and an allusion, too—from the dead poet himself. But as quickly as it had begun, the clanging stopped. An uneasy stillness hung over the class. Kids looked at each other as if searching for answers, but no one moved nor said a word. The silence didn't last long.

Something scratching, some creature clawing, trying to get out from behind…

"*…the wall! Look at the whiteboard!*" Raphael's voice had lost its wise ass edge while the kid pointed with shaking fingers. Heads turned towards the board behind Hooper, eyes bugged, and in a gesture from a bad B-movie, Sondra Winograd threw a hand to her mouth.

Hooper looked at the board behind him and felt his jaw go slack.

Any Poe-phile knew about Edgar's fixation concerning walls. The man had this claustrophobia thing going during his entire life, and wall symbols popped up all over his writing. It was the kind of detail only a teacher would notice or even care about, but Hooper sensed Poe's wall obsession was about to assume some big time significance.

The shadowy image of a large cat appeared on the board, a bloated creature struggling upon hind legs to scrape its way out as if the surface were made of smoked glass. But the terrified animal wasn't really *on* the board. The feline seemed trapped *behind* it, dates of Mr. Poe's birth and death with a listing of his works superimposed upon the cat's writhing torso. The animal screeched loudly in fright, enough to chill the blood of everyone in the room.

Poe's famous cat. Black. And here it was, the poor entrapped creature screaming for its life inside Josh Hooper's classroom. If the idea hadn't frightened the bejeezus out of him it might have given the teacher a genuine sense of celebrity.

EEEEeeeeeeeeeeeeeeeeeeeeeeeeeee! EEEEEeeeeeeeeeeeeeeeeeeeeeeeeee!

The cat was not alone in her screaming. Several of the girls took up the shrieking chorus, but it was the screeching performed during a good funhouse ride, not of terror; at least not yet while pieces of this puzzle remained to be put together. Carmella Caparelli remained silently stoic, staring at the proceedings with curiosity and mild bemusement. The creature disappeared in the next instant, but Hooper knew The Poe Show was far from over.

"*Rafe! Holy shit, man! Look at Rafe!*"

The funhouse ride ended that instant. Mr. Poe's theatrics took an ugly turn.

Raphael's face leaked bubbles of blood from open wounds that appeared from nowhere. His flesh had turned blood-red; almost crimson upon his dark skin, but the kid seemed unaware any transformation had taken place. His classmates' expressions indicated to him that something had gone seriously gonzo.

"What you mean? Ain't nothing wrong with—" Raphael put his hand to his cheek. Lunchmeat-thick shavings of flesh peeled off into his fingers. "Oh fuck... Fuck, man!" Raphael slid his hand toward his ear, but the appendage slipped from its cavity like a sliced cheese, plopping upon his desk in a bloody pool. The boy stared at it. Then he gagged.

"*And then was known the presence of the Red Death,*" from Carmella, as if the girl were reciting text for Brownie points. "You know what you got there is *The Red Death*, don't you, Raphael? You would if you'd done your homework." But Raphael Jones was not up to playing Twenty Questions while rotting skin flaps hung from each cheek. The boy was decomposing in his seat.

"I gotta get outa this room, man! There ain't gonna be nothing' left of me but balls and hair!" Raphael took to his feet. A rat the size of a small dog nipped at his Nikes. Several more plump rodents appeared on the floor, squirming throughout the classroom in furry heaps. Raphael stumbled back to his desk, trying to keep his nose attached to his face. Mutters filled the room, but not a peep from Carmella.

A clap of thunder from outside. A burst of lightning speckled the room.

Carmella's voice remained steady. "I don't think Mr. Poe wants us out of our seats. Look up there." She pointed towards the ceiling where a huge pendulum swung, its sharp metal blade catching flickers of storm light. As if having a mind of its own determining its tracking and movement, the razor edge swung down, the gleaming blade brushing past Raphael's head managing to nick a thick wedge off his remaining ear.

"Shit, man ... Oh shit ..."

[The rats of a pit below. The pendulum above. Mr. Poe was playing hardball.]

Kids froze in their seats. On his feet, Hooper did not move, either. One thing was for certain. On this stormy morning, his students were witness to the best Poe lesson in the history of the world.

Someone asked, "Mr. Hooper, can you do something? Can you stop this?"

A single word, whispered from somewhere in the shadows, yet heard by every kid in the room.

"*Nevermore ...*"

A cawing raven fluttered across the room, then vanished like a dark ghost.

"I don't know. Yes. Maybe." In the midst of Mr. Poe's signature terrors Hooper struggled to think.

[The relentless tattoo of a beating heart from the floorboards below. Twelve beats, then gone...]

"Unnghh..."

There was a rattle of chains, the death moan of an imprisoned man dying behind the wall who never did find that cask of Amontillado...

Hacking and wheezing, Denise Daniels' lips had gone blue, her skin pale. She was shivering as if the classroom had suddenly fallen into a deep freeze. A wind that affected only where she sat blew through her hair. Her reed thin body shook in a burst of spasms.

"I'm cold... So cold..."

[Killing and chilling my Annabel Lee...]

"I'm outta here!" from Sam Peterson, already on his feet and headed for the door. He managed a few steps before the floor opened beneath him, a giant maw exposing a darkened pit that went on forever.

"Sam, get back to your seat, get back now!" from Hooper, but too late. Fat Fuck fell into the abyss like a dead weight, his screams echoing the whole way down until they abruptly broke off with a thick *thud.*

This was no longer a day in the fun house. Several girls screamed and their shrieks were the real thing.

"Mr. Hooper. Do something for him! Please, do something!"

"Mr. Hooper, please..."

"It's not real," Carmella tried explaining. "None of it is real. Can't you see that? Mr. Hooper, tell them how he's trying to fool us! Poe is trying to trick us!"

From Raphael, still leaking blood gobs from every pore, "Forget Peterson, man. All of us in deep shit now!"

"I'm so cold..."

"DO something!"

Hooper understood it was his move. For some unfathomable reason Poe had selected his classroom to reveal himself. Hooper was in charge—it was time to act like he was. Taking a seat behind his desk, folding his hands as if he were about to deliver an elaborate speech, he looked every bit in complete control, even if it took a great effort to create the effect. His gaze circling the room, he kept his voice steady, calm.

"I know you're here with us, Edgar. And I know what you're trying to do. It's all about the fear, isn't it? The terror? It's what brings you here, and it's what keeps you going, isn't it, pal? And it's my job to keep that terror alive, isn't it? Because as long as your words and memory live, in that sense, so do you. It's your claim to immortality. Death is what you fear the most, isn't that right? And you know full well it's what we all fear."

The pendulum reappeared, swung right at Hooper's head. The teacher did not budge. The blade whooshed past him once, twice. Then it disappeared.

"Nice try, Edgar, but no cigar. Am I nervous? *'True!—nervous—very, very dreadfully nervous I had been and am; but why will you say that I am mad?'* I know all about that *Tell-Tale Heart* trick of yours, Mr. Poe. About the illusions you create from our worst fears. I've been teaching your words to kids for years!"

[The piercing scream of a woman buried alive, Madeline Usher's death shriek.]

"Oh, I can't say I don't admire your work, but I don't really buy into it. It's illusion, my friend, smoke and mirrors masking as reality, just like this little show you're putting on. But it's not real, is it? I'll give you an 'A' for the special effects. Because death IS real and it doesn't matter if you don't personally care for the grave. Because you're *dead*, and despite your little display here you're going to remain dead. As dead and buried as your gal pals: Annabel Lee, Lenore, Madeline Usher, and Ligeia. Have I left anyone out?"

A plump rat nibbled Hooper's shoe. He kicked it aside.

"No one wants to face death, Mr. Poe. But we really don't have that choice, not even those whose words live after them. Dead you are and dead you must remain. Your lost Lenore will have to remain lost, and so will you. Your own utterance says it all. That word says everything you need to know..."

The teacher allowed the moment to sink in for his unseen audience of one, and when he spoke again he whispered. "So, 'Nevermore,' my good friend."

Hooper had had his say. While his little speech had satisfied him, it had also distracted him from noticing the event occurring before his eyes. His class had grown strangely silent, and now Hooper understood why. Peterson had returned to his seat from the Pit, and Raphael Jones' face showed no indication of a lingering Red Death. But each boy's expression was vacant, their eyes cold as moonstones. Looking around the classroom Hooper saw the same look on every kid's face, as if each student had gone into some trance-like state.

Only Carmella Caparelli's eyes remained alert and fixed on Hooper, her knowing half smile firmly in place.

"You know what Mr. Poe has done to our class, don't you, Mr. Hooper? I mean, what he's done to everyone else but us?"

It didn't take very much brain work for a man familiar with Poe's tales to figure it out. The renowned author was pulling from quite an impressive literary arsenal.

"*'The Facts in the Case of M. Valdemar.'* Mesmerism. Or more modernly, group hypnosis. But the story wasn't on your reading list, Carmella."

The girl smiled. "You know me better than that, Mr. Hooper." She looked around at her classmates. "They won't remember any of this, will they?"

"I doubt it. At least not consciously they won't. But they'll sure think twice next time anyone tells them Poe sucks."

A movement caught his attention and he turned. For a moment, he had to focus just to be certain he saw what he did.

A dark figure stood by the door. It seemed a cloudy image, a murky semblance of a man whose somber expression could not be mistaken.

Hooper turned to Carmella. "You see him, too?"

The girl could only nod her head.

Hooper approached the doorway, kept his voice low and properly respectful. "I'll see to it that your words will be kept alive, Edgar. I can promise that much. You have my word on that. Close the door on your way out, will you?"

Perhaps the man smiled. Hooper could not really tell. He knew the shadowy figure did not require opening the door to take his leave, but he did so anyway, closing it behind him before fading into the darkness of the school corridor. A class act, no doubt about it, even if the late poet's methods of communication were a bit unconventional.

Hooper and Carmella exchanged knowing smiles.

When the door again sprang open, both teacher and student flinched. Jeff Lynch stood in the entryway, frowning at Hooper's class, all staring dead-ahead like zombies. The lights came back on that same moment, as did the bell signaling the end of the class period.

"Thought it was getting a little noisy in here, Josh, but I can see I was wrong. Hey! Wake up, people! This is still school, you know!" He clapped his hands together sharply, "Chop chop! Looks like this period's over!"

Raphael spoke first.

"What happened, man? Feels like I've been zoning for a week."

The other kids laughed right on cue, but Billy Silverman sat scratching his head. "Did Edgar ever get the door for you, Mr. Hooper?"

Hooper and Carmella exchanged glances.

"Nope, Billy," he said. "Sorry. No magic this time around." He turned his attention to the rest. "Pack up your books and move on out, gang. Fun time is over."

His students shuffled out of the room, but conversation among them seemed noticeably absent.

Lingering behind her classmates, Carmella was the last to leave. "Can't wait to see what you do with your lesson on Shakespeare, Mr. Hooper."

The teacher had to laugh.

Outside the rain had stopped, and the sun made a valiant attempt to come out from behind the remaining dark clouds.

Hooper opened the window to allow the sun's warmth on his face. The rain had actually made everything outside smell fresh and clean, no mean feat for an inner-city public school. He waited a few minutes before heading down the corridor for the teachers' lounge.

He hoped he could find someone who smoked. He needed a cigarette.

Aryan Bollinger lives and writes at the top of a steep gravel drive in North Carolina, where his wife and four-legged children bravely endure his cryptic murmurings. Aryan's work has appeared in the sci-fi horror ezine, Allegory, *as well as the college literary journal,* Catawba. *Most recently, his fiction has been featured in the Frith Books anthology,* Restless, *and in the* Dead Mule School of Southern Literature.

About this story, Aryan says: "I wrote this story because MS. Found in a Bottle *was the first Poe story that I discovered on my own. I had, of course, been assigned Poe's works in middle and high school, but* MS. *has always been special to me, opening my eyes to how wonderfully weird and evocative Poe could be."*

The mad prince Hamlet mused, "To die, to sleep—to sleep, perchance to dream—ay, there's the rub, for in this sleep of death what dreams may come...." But how deeply can a person dream before the dream takes over, leading them farther and farther along the dark and convoluted paths of the mind to that place where only madness survives...

THE DREAMING INCUBUS

Aryan Bollinger

"But when that which is perfect has come, then that which is in part will be
done away... For now we see in a mirror darkly, but then face to face."
1 Corinthians 10:12

Until recently, my life had travelled not just on track, but also upon the only track for which I had allowed. Life beyond high school had been planned with a degree of certainty I'd inherited from my father. Among other things, I would be employed in a relatively well-paying profession, and I would marry a reasonable woman. I had been vaguely proud of these milestones as each was achieved, but, lately, I'd become weary of the one and disaffected from the other. My employers' expectations were exhausting, and Karen had left, claiming I'd become a celibate bedmate, a distant relative whom she cared for, but with whom she saw no future.

Now, Cybil.

I opened my laptop once more, anticipation burning. I shouldn't look at Cybil's email again—I was being irrational. But, seeing the login screen appear, typing my password, and accessing my Gmail account, I felt something of giddiness. Nostalgia wasn't it—or wasn't all of it; there was something else inside Cybil's messages. Something of haste and worry, perhaps, but, more importantly, of longing. Maybe I was mistaken. Likely, I was.

But I intended to find out for sure.

*

Hey,

Heard things didn't work out with Karen—I'm sorry. Please come back to the old place if you can. I've missed you. We need to talk.

—C

*

I realized that deviating from my schedule might stress me further, but I desired the comfort of something well-worn. Restlessness deciding me, I drove the fifty miles or so to Cybil's childhood home.

I hadn't seen my old friend in over ten years—since her mother's funeral. The last time had been in the damp underground. A place meant for spiritual development, but something else had happened…something far more terrestrial. We'd been so heavy, so close—moments of excitement I'd tried to relive with Karen and had never been able.

Much of the recent weeks' tension lifted as I turned off the interstate and drove along the two-lane backroads. Sunlight warmed as I passed old markets and the elementary school, crossed the uneven bridge over railroad tracks that probably hadn't shook under a freight car in decades. Many of the sights were dilapidated, but I welcomed them nonetheless.

Cybil had never married and had never left town. After her mother died, I'd gone to college, and she'd kept house with her grey father who, I'd read, had also recently died. Thinking of how geographically close she'd been—and how alone—some of the lightness I'd felt began to fade.

Still, as I turned onto Cybil's gravel drive, I looked fondly into the woods on either side. We'd played together there, weaved between tree trunks, shot each other with Super Soakers and imaginary laser guns, crunched leaves and crooked twigs underfoot. We'd dreamed, set impossible things into motion through Cybil's uncanny imagination.

But weren't childish things meant to be put away?

Now, around a washed-out bend, Cybil's house loomed before me. Shadows puddled under warped boards along the front porch and the house seemed to lean, as if the roof was uneven and its walls lay askew of their foundation. I parked next to a brown sedan with a cracked taillight and exited my car. Narrow, blue strings of some strange material swayed from the gutters and porch railing, as though a fungus grew and dripped. Edging to the left and right, I saw that much of the house's sides were also covered in the dangling blue substance,

180

spreading even to the greyed pines surrounding her house. Chilled air pricked my skin.

An abhorrent fetor radiated from the house—like rot or mold, but somehow *beyond* these things, a sense of excess decay for which death, air, and time could not be solely accountable. Yet, oddly, what concerned me most was the air's utter stagnation. There was something intrinsically horrible about the sensation, as if Nature herself had taken notice of my intent and held her breath.

Stairs leading up to the porch groaned beneath my feet, and I saw a piece of blue-lined paper taped to the front door. Two words written:

Come in.

Jaws tight, throat burning, I did not want to enter the morbid house. The thought of retreating to my car and regaining the relative comfort of my daily routine crossed my mind. But thinking of our last moments, and the way I'd left... A sense of responsibility soon dispelled my misgivings—if nothing else, I owed Cybil one last decency.

I knocked on the door, not expecting an answer, and received none.

The door was unlocked. I left the still outdoors and entered into what I knew would be the loathsome stench of a charnel house.

But I was wrong.

No scent of corruption greeted me; if anything, the place smelled pleasant, like patchouli and, perhaps, mint. Though silent, the interior held none of the overgrown yard's awful portent. Somehow, though Cybil was nowhere in sight, I felt more at peace having come inside. I had spent many mornings on the couch beside the stairs, wiping crust from my eyes, smelling Cybil's mother cooking bacon, and avoiding her father who always seemed quietly imposing. Now, glancing over the furnishings, I found them well-kempt, if frayed and outdated. The living room led into the kitchen which was nearly spotless.

Her bedroom was down the hall. Door closed.

I strode through the kitchen, came to her threshold, and swung open her door, my expectation dire.

Cybil lay on her bed, motionless. Going to her, my breath caught sharp, for I knew she was dead. Pale skin, eyelids so soft and still.

But, grasping her hand, I felt warmth! Unbelievable. I felt her wrist. A pulse beat within! Why, then, did she lay in such dreadful suspension? Why did spindly cobwebs drift from her earlobe to the pillowcase beneath?

I saw the note then, as well as an old thing I'd nearly forgotten.

*

The Dreaming Book was a spiral-bound notebook Cybil's mom had bought at Walmart, green covered and three-subject. At an age too young for suspicion, I slept over at her house, and Cybil had written wild fantasies within the Book's pages. Worlds of fungus and light, of darkness and sand—places we'd discussed and others I'd assumed were of her own creation. We'd stay up until after the grown-ups had closed their bedroom door, and Cybil would ask me to touch her, just a hand on her shoulder would do. She'd told me to empty my mind and let the Book do its work. We travelled then, exploring alien vistas only hinted at within the Book's pages. Together, we'd talked to segmented creatures one night and barely escaped death the next. I always assumed there was a reasonable explanation—some subconscious mechanism for the dreams over which Cybil seemed to have control.

Sometimes, I'd wake up with scratches or bruises I couldn't remember going to bed with. Of course, our parents weren't suspicious—we played in the woods for hours on end—and again, I just assumed I hadn't noticed the scratch before, or maybe the bruise hadn't had time to develop.

Then, over the years, my visits to her house dwindled. I understood this to be the normal course of things—conservative parents of opposite-sex adolescents rarely allow sleepovers. I found that, with the end of our perceived innocence, came also an end to the closeness I'd allowed myself to forget in adulthood. It seemed the Dreaming Book had bound our intimacy, and the secret love we'd made in darkness had sealed our fates apart.

*

Now, the Dreaming Book lay opened on the bed beside her, about three-fourths of its pages to the left of its spiral, with words bursting across the right—words materializing too quickly to have been written by hand. Then the page flipped and I stared aghast as the next filled with words.

Glancing at the note lying next to Cybil, I realized it was stationary, in both page and text.

It read: *Find me inside. I am waiting.*

Finally, I saw an open bottle of Ambien lying on her opposite side. A couple of tablets had spilled onto the bedspread.

Calling an ambulance came to mind… but *the Book!* It was ours, and I didn't want to share it—and whether I came to that decision based on some awkwardly-built sense of loyalty or from shame, I don't know. But I couldn't leave. Not again.

I disregarded the pills—never liked the things—and slipped into the bed beside her. I placed one trembling hand on her shoulder and closed my eyes, realizing how quickly one can reassume wistful positions. I heard another page turn and felt a caress, as if dozens of eager fingers had been lurking just under the bedsheets in anticipation of a long-gone dreamer.

*

I blinked, and for a moment thought the transition hadn't taken place. The walls of Cybil's bedroom were still visible, she continued to lie just beside me, but then those images faded and I saw *beyond* them. Instead of the crooked, grey pines outside, I saw bright metallic slabs set strangely against the bedroom's angles, and an amorphous, bent figure shuffling away from me. Like an apparition, it walked through my friend's wardrobe, her bed, then disappeared through the bedroom's far wall.

As my eyes adjusted to the dazzling light, I realized I lay in the middle of a square hallway. The walls and floor were plated in sickly green alloy squares, about ten feet by ten, each held in place by a bolt at their four corners. I felt an odd sensation as I propped myself into a seated position: heat radiated gently from the floor, and for a moment, I felt a vibration... and then it was gone.

Looking around, I realized Cybil, too, had disappeared.

Positioned high above me was a set of blinding fluorescent bulbs. I couldn't look directly at them, but they were positioned directly in the middle of the ceiling. Shielding my eyes and looking further down the hall, I saw these bulbs were in a double row and that the ceiling itself was composed of the same green squares.

I stood, supported by shaky legs, but the simple act proved enough to bolster me. I moved to the left side of the hall and looked forward and back. I could see no discernable difference between the two directions, as both extended for an infinite distance, narrowing to a focal point of uncanny darkness in contrast to the harsh light surrounding me. I felt a chill of panic scuttle around my neck—I had expected to meet Cybil in the dream. Her absence was not only disheartening, but disorienting as well.

Shuffling footsteps came behind me.

I turned, and saw nothing but an unnerving void at the end of the corridor, and I began frantically scanning my surroundings for a hiding place. I noticed a shadow in the uniform nature of the hall: an indention on my right. Moving closer, I realized it was a door, recessed into the metal. With the shuffling growing ever louder, I examined the door, trying to find a way through—a doorknob, a lock, a latch. But there was only a narrow rectangle of glass showing darkness in the space beyond.

In desperation, I pushed against the door with both hands, and it shifted wholly to the right, like an airlock in a science fiction movie. I gave the interior a perfunctory glance, then heaved myself within. The door shifted back into place behind me with a hiss.

I turned quickly, sure something had entered the room with me, but I was alone, and saw only shadows moving beyond the door's small window. Hands shaking, mind revolving, I tried to gain my bearings. I had entered a small, darkened room, illuminated only by the lights beyond the window. On my right, three cribs were built in a row against the wall. Above each was a mobile in various stages of decay: wires protruded from smiling animals hanging askew, vomiting cotton. The alphabet encircled the room in large block letters, painted in primary colors, while crayon drawings of dogs and less identifiable things peppered the walls at random intervals. To my left was a narrow ledge: a changing table.

I'd slept and drooled in this very room as an infant and had wished dearly to spend time here as a youth. Every Sunday at Granite Hope Baptist, a mother was assigned nursery duty. When it was my mom's turn, I'd always join her, much to my father's displeasure, and play with toys too small for my hands. But I enjoyed being away from the worship service, even if the pastor's dreary voice could be heard through the antiquated intercom above the nursery's doorway.

Sometimes, when Cybil's mother dropped her off at church, we'd come into the nursery and play during the intervening period between Sunday school and preaching. We'd laugh at how idiotic the infant's toys were and giggle whilst playing with them, as if the irony of our condescension was lost on us.

Now, I crept to the narrow window in the sci-fi door, barely registering its disparity in such a familiar place. As I neared the glass, the intercom above me clicked. Nothing at first. Then soft, indistinct words, the harsh friction of cloth on cloth. A zipper pulled, a moan.

A figure slipped into view through the door's window, staring directly at me. Eyes black as the corridor's void. I stumbled back, throat constricted. Wrinkled jowls dangled from the thing's sunken cheeks and lank hair drooped across face and shoulder. The figure's height led me to assume him male; yet, he was unmistakably ancient, scrawny, and bent. He breathed moisture on the glass as he gazed within, obscuring further detail...

And then was gone. I glanced fearfully through the window after him, saw him shuffle away with the meticulousness of infirmity, as if afraid the next step would send him tumbling. The figure didn't look back. I touched the door and it shifted open immediately, just as the voices from the intercom above began to distort and crackle.

I stepped hesitantly out into the hall and saw that the walking creature had disappeared. Looking both ways, I observed nothing but a deserted, metallic corridor. Then I heard a voice coming from my right. Though barely audible, it was distressed, angry. I strained my ears, trying to make out the words, but they were unintelligible.

I went toward the sound, hoping to find Cybil. The voice sounded not only angry, but terrified as well. I walked with head lowered due to the fluorescent bulbs' brightness, but quickly leveled my gaze, eager to shed the unconscious mimicking of the bent man. As more of the strange hall's features became apparent, I realized the figure must have disappeared into another room or along a hallway that branched from the one in which I'd appeared. Each branching hall gave birth to others at odd angles, and I passed innumerable doors. I explored a dozen or so at random, but most were locked or opened to rooms containing only nailed-shut windows or trash—here, empty, cobwebbed cardboard boxes; there, Polaroid snapshots filled with grey fog, their subjects long overexposed. With each passing moment, the distressed voice became louder, but I could not understand what it said. As with many dreams, distances and time became abstract and unrelated. The hall was at one moment infinite and stretched; the next moment, I'd reached a dead end, smacking painfully into a metallic wall.

I called Cybil's name, but I now seemed to be alone, other than those distant, desperate shouts, the source of which seemed to be around each corner I turned. Hearing this constant acidic litany made me desperate to find her, comfort her. My thoughts returned to our last moments together, when I'd found her in the basement. Her tears had poured and poured—grieving someone she'd lost. I wanted her to stop crying, due as much to my own discomfort as to the desire to see her smile again. I'd sucked her lower lip into my mouth, and she'd wrapped her hands around me in the dark.

And yet, the thought of saying goodbye had been too hard, and leaving had always seemed a foregone conclusion.

*

Just as the network of corridors began to panic me in its complexity and claustrophobic isolation, I began noticing slight differences down certain passages. Some of the hallways had the slightest indication of damage—scorched places where the greenish alloy had loosened, blackened. The floor bubbled and buckled were it met the wall. A violet discoloration proliferated around these deformed areas, a viscous shadow of some monstrous force. I found that not only had the green plates been distorted, but many of the fluorescents had also become defective—in some sections only a few of the high-intensity bulbs remained functional.

While walking along a particularly dilapidated corridor, I heard the sound of splattering. I turned as motion from above caused me to look up. Dark purple, nearly black, bubbling footprints bled through the dimly-lit ceiling. Disembodied, stationary. I walked toward them, unsure, but curious… then the bubbles ruptured and from them poured a glutinous violet fluid, burning as it dripped, changing everything in its path. For a moment, I recoiled from the exudation, but I felt intense heat and found that a few small drops had landed on my left arm. I feverishly wiped the fluid away, but only spread the caustic material across my opposite hand.

More splashing. The footsteps advanced—one, two, another—each step puffing and hissing like peroxide across a bloodied knee. Then they changed course, curving downward from the ceiling onto the wall, then descending to the floor. I watched, amazed, as the disembodied steps moved away from me, retracing the path I'd just travelled. They turned along a left corridor and disappeared.

I stood in place, unsure. Deciding simply to keep my distance, I trailed the steps as they meandered down several corridors, avoiding their burning residue, hoping they would lead to answers.

*

After an indeterminate length of time (how malleable our dreams, how repulsively fluid and disproportionate!), I turned a final corner to find the bubbling footprints had halted. I paused, undecided, until another of the decrepit men appeared several yards ahead, stumbling out of another room. He tilted his head back and forth, as if listening for something. Short stabbing screams punctuated the air around us, and after a moment, the figure walked down an adjacent hall, from which the screams had emanated. The violet footprints before me began to fade, and soon nothing was left of them but misshapen metal and disturbing residue.

Alone once more, I walked forward and glanced down the adjacent hall, but seeing nothing but flickering light, continued on toward the place from which the bent man had come. There was a doorless entryway, narrow, with nothing inside but shadow—the light from the hallway seemed unable to reach within.

I nearly turned away, intent on finding Cybil—hoping her screams were not the ones I currently heard—and would have gone if her scent hadn't come to me from within the blackened place. A breath of her. A memory I'd kept in places too dark to recall.

Groping within the room, I ran my hand along what seemed to be a smooth, glassy surface, seeking a light switch. I found it and light erupted within the room, while extinguishing simultaneously from the hall. There came a hellish chorus of screams, seeming to originate from scores of throats. As I stood between places of dark and light, the sound of dozens of feet, quickened to a frantic run, advanced from every direction.

I entered the room, hoping to remain unseen by those in the hall, and felt immediate vertigo—the floor beneath me quivered, as if I were standing on deck of a rickety ship.

Cabinets lined the walls, each covered by clear plastic. They contained tubing and less identifiable medical items. A stretcher tottered before me, its wheels squeaking as it shifted upon the unsteady floor. A pulsating oblong shape lay atop, covered by a pure white sheet, and held in place by crisscrossing straps and buckles.

The room gyrated with more ferocity, and my location now seemed obvious… I was in the back of a moving ambulance. I approached the stretcher apprehensively, certain the scent had come from under those sheets—for couldn't I smell her sweetness now?

The room jolted as a truck might when hitting a pothole, and, losing my balance, I lurched forward, sending the stretcher forcefully into the wall.

I looked down upon the oblong shape and immediately backed away. Points along the material poked outward (*as if dozens of eager fingers had been lurking just under the bedsheets*), straining (*in anticipation of a long gone dreamer*) against the straps binding it.

Brightest scarlet blossomed along the fabric, erupting from underneath. Slowly, with deliberateness from which I could not tear myself away, letters stretched and dripped across the sheet's pristine surface, defiling, forming a simple word.

DISCOVERY

As the sweetness within the room mingled with the stench of copper, black spots formed in my vision, threatening unconsciousness. I willed myself to back farther away from the bulging gestational mass even as it grew and the fetor of slaughter replaced what had been left of her. The pulsations halted when it reached nearly the size of a beach ball, and I heard something from within—not words; whimpers and suffering melodies.

No words.

Sorry. Didn't know…

…she'd been pregnant. Didn't know she'd lost it.

The blood-inked word expanded upon the sheet until unrecognizable, and I turned and ran back to the narrow doorway. I took a single backward glance at the stretcher and saw the shape collapse. I heard nothing, smelled nothing; for there was nothing left.

Heaving myself across the threshold, I tumbled into near darkness and heard a sound to my left. I turned to see more of the shuffling men, a group of five or six this time. The bent figures were stimulated—their howls and gesticulations increasingly crazed, and their incoherent voices, once mere mutters, now turned to shrieks and heavy retches.

They passed, then rounded a corner on my right.

More static-laced sounds came from the hall down which the energized men had walked. Yet another change had come over the staticy voice: the original soft whispers I'd heard in the nursery had turned to angry shouts, but had changed again to agonized sobs: the sound of a thing trapped and injured.

I turned the corner and a monstrous hall yawned before me, where men writhed in shadow. The burning steps had been here—large swaths of buckled metal hung loose from both walls. The frenzied men ripped and tore at the distorted metal fragments, pulling the squares away until fingers and mouths dripped black under the weak, flickering fluorescents. Harrowing wails grew ever louder from down the hall, and the figures' excitement grew with each removed piece of alloy.

A man holding a long strip of metal in his fist raised it high, in obvious victory, and its end lodged between two elongated bulbs. There was an immediate scent of burning as blue light arced through his spasming body, and the man burst into flames. Under the new, brighter flamelight, I clearly saw what lay beneath the greenish squares. Viscera throbbed, fell, and leaked through the wall's broken places. The network of corridors seemed carved from living meat—and just as the flesh seemed eager to break into these uniform, metallic confines, the bent men seemed eager to assist it. Revulsion drove me forward, toward the hall's end.

I walked, trying to avoid thrashing men and spilling warmth. Fluorescent bulbs flickered ahead of me, strobe-like. In the momentary illumination, groups of men huddled around a traditional wooden door with an intercom fixed above it. I brushed past several of the screaming figures, pulse pounding, certain the hall would elongate in its prior detestable fashion, but it did not. Men jostled desperately at the door, and as I pushed through, I found the entryway locked; its knob present, but held fast. Wretched squalls blared from the speaker box. Then, for the first time, I felt the men's fingers against my skin. I pounded the wooden door with clenched fists—so many of them and voices so loud. Hoarse, phlegmy, rattling throats, suffocating, drooling. They scratched and tore my clothes, bringing my flesh bare. Blood ran warm across my back and sides. Collapsing to my knees, they pushed, crushed, and reached. I couldn't breathe—

"Cybil!" I cried as fingernails dug into my cheeks and their wet breath cascaded over my neck. "Cybil, please!"

A *click*. The door breathed open an inch.

The men shrieked, but I did not hesitate, and crawled through the doorway. Kicked it closed, but one man's hand was caught in the jamb. Lying on my back, with one foot against the door and another bashing the frail appendage, the door soon shut resolutely, and I heard a thump of flesh land beside me.

Turning away from the door, I found myself alone in a downward stairwell. After a long moment, I stood, ignoring the pain in my neck and back. And though my ears still rang from the intercom outside, I now heard soft sobbing, this time free from static—seemingly from the source—and a renewal of the indistinct words I'd heard in the nursery. I walked down, wondering how many things or people I would find below. Soft carpet underfoot. Light from below lit the stairwell diffusely, casting layered shadow. And something else… an odor—

I followed the stairs to the left at an angle. Continued down.

Reaching the bottom, I stood in Granite Hope's basement, where I'd found

Cybil years ago, tears pouring, needing someone and finding only me.

The place looked nearly the same. Foosball, air hockey, and ping-pong tables. Board games, sofa, and loveseat. A boom box across the way, emitting those muffled words. Yet stagnation and frigidity pervaded the place, as well as an odor I recognized, but had never associated with the Baptist church. The exterior of Cybil's house had been seeping with it too, eager to enter and defile the home, though for whatever reason, it had been unable. The word for it spilled into my mind: *consumption*. There was a disease in this place that had festered, proliferated, and fed incubi.

Brown-painted poles supported the ceiling, spaced about ten feet apart. Each child in the youth group had been allowed to choose a pole to decorate, make their own. Upon each was attached a series of quotes, Bible verses, art, and snapshots. The top of each pole displayed a different child's face. I passed them—dusty, unsought capsules of time. I remembered the picture Cybil had put atop her pole, how she'd smiled when she'd placed it there. I remembered writing messages under it, taping drawings.

I looked for Cybil's face.

I never found it.

Yet, while defeated sobs and hushed breathing sounded from across the room, her pole held my full attention. Blue tendrils of fungus swayed from it, met and meshed, split and severed, covering the pole in its entirety. Pictures from summer camp, Sunday school, and lettered insults were overgrown, barely recognizable through the awakened consumption. Yet, she was there—at least in part—breathing, pulsing, imploring.

A groan issued from my left, followed by a stifled scream. I looked to the sound and saw the loveseat facing away from me. Someone was in it with long hair, struggling to come upright.

"Cybil!" I cried, and rushed over, noticing her gaze fixed to a point in the corner of the ceiling.

Two of the foaming footsteps appeared on the nicotine-stained boards above. Their bubbles burst and splattered, running violet down the wall in creeping rivulets, melting paint from the wall. The footsteps moved toward us, raising smoke from the foosball table. The yellow and blue plastic men oozed and mixed.

I turned to the slouched figure, aghast at the depth of agony one must hold to become split three ways—for weren't the Disease, the Screamer, and the Walker all one within Cybil? Breathing heavily, expecting the worst, I peered at the final piece of my friend.

An old, bent man lay there, wrists and ankles bound in tight, fibrous twine.

I stood, dumbfounded, as the figure gazed up at me with rheumy eyes surrounded by wrinkled skin. His hair lay in matted tangles over his face and shoulders, and an odor came from him. Unlike the Disease, this one was a mixture of fear, sweat, and offal. Upon my arrival before him, the man began to thrash, and blood dripped from his fingertips where the twine binding his wrists had worked their way inside. He cried, a hopeless sound, like someone being pushed deeper and deeper into flame.

Footsteps drew ever nearer, the boombox hissed and I heard a familiar voice say, "It's ok. You're ok, right?"

I turned to the bound figure, realization dawning.

It was me. Wasn't it? Though many years older and prior stoutness grown frail... I remembered those shoes. Nikes. I'd thought they were so cool in eleventh grade. Why hadn't I noticed them before?

Why hadn't I—

I stepped toward the sobbing, helpless man, my hands trembling. Shame throbbed in my throat, breath painful. I'd had enough gall to tell her everything was fine *(It's ok)* after I'd pushed myself inside, then, in the next breath, *(You're ok, right?)* asked her for reassurance, despite my misgivings. It wasn't supposed to happen like that. We were supposed to... I don't know.

(Didn't know she'd been pregnant; didn't know she'd lost it)

Lost ours.

I walked backwards, away from the boy I'd been, and perhaps, out of which I'd never fully grown. The footsteps sizzled just behind me, carpet dissolved under purple fluid. My aged reincarnation arched his back over the loveseat, repeating a woeful sound.

(Please)

Over...

(Please)

...and over.

Just before the footsteps were directly above him, they paused... and the man's sanity broke. It wasn't the animal sounds he made or the fact that the cuffs of his jeans dripped with urine that convinced me of it. His wrists came free of their ties. The bound boy had been in that basement for a long time, and the binds must have gone deeper than I could have imagined. In a final demonic frenzy of strength, his arms separated freely, leaving their hands behind, still dangling in bits of twine. Spurting stumps rose upward, beckoning the footsteps closer. His tongue lurched and surged, seeking a draught to quench glowing coals.

It came.

The purple fluid splattered and hissed upon his contorted face and the flesh fell away. No blood, no time for that. Bone surfaced and my old, unsure tongue disappeared in acrid steam. The bent thing lay smoking and still.

I felt a sudden draft behind me, and the stillness broken by the air's movement was extraordinary: as if Nature herself had breached some long-held depth. I turned and saw a black doorway. In another world, that door led to a single row parking lot outside Granite Hope Baptist. What lay beyond it now I didn't know, but I knew my path lay not above with the bent and mindless; neither was it here with a sickness I couldn't affect with apologies or feeble amends. I wanted to know what lay on the other side of creation, what may ripen if allowed to grow.

I walked to the black doorway. I knew my time had come to an end, and that furtherance would result in dissolution—a life so lived cannot hope for continuity. I had wanted the resolution to secrets; now, I wished only for hope.

Through the threshold I saw ebony chaos, formless feathers reaching forever onward, my place within less than nil.

Now, Cybil. I glanced behind once more and wondered if the Walker would ever free the Disease—burn it, destroy the unfathomable pain. I didn't know. I couldn't know.

I walked through the black doorway.

*

My face grinds on sand, rough and dry.

I sit up, taking in my surroundings. On my left, water laps gently along the shore, white foam crests and stretches. Blue-lined notebook pages, half buried in sand, pepper the beach at seemingly random intervals. On my right, a dense, wild wood, trees whisper and huddle in abstract secrecy. Behind me, a rock formation reaches skyward, upon which something strange perches. The animal seems dead, shriveled and still... now it turns, stares for a moment, then skitters out of sight.

Prints in the sand lead away, diminishing in the distance before me, between surf and forest. I gaze on them and recognize a woman's tread, compact, deeply turned. I know they're hers and I want to find her. She has never been closer; nothing stands between us.

A sudden gust ripples the pages, loosens them, and carries them into the sea.

To my left, the lulling surf and the undertow.

To my right, the forest ending never, forever blooming unknown.

I look toward where she's gone, between, and I wonder if we'll ever be found. Good night.

I'll say that, at least, as much for her as for myself. The left and right matter little. Good night.

Emerian Rich is the author of the vampire series, Night's Knights, *and writes romance under the name Emmy Z. Madrigal. Her romance crossover,* Artistic License, *is about a woman who inherits a house where anything she paints on the walls comes alive. Her short fiction has been published in a handful of anthologies by publishers including Dragon Moon Press, Hidden Thoughts Press, Hazardous Press, and White Wolf Press. She is Editorial Director of* SEARCH *Magazine and the podcast* Horror Hostess *for HorrorAddicts.net. You can connect with her at emzbox.com.*

About this story, Emerian says: "My favorite Poe poem is Annabel Lee, *so when I saw the call for reimagined Poe stories, I had to take a stab at reworking it. Although the original is presented as a poem, I chose to write my version—a heartbreaking tale of the deep bond between two surgeons caught in a global pandemic and their fight to stay alive for one another—as a short story, set in the modern age, but which retains much of the same flavor of Poe's work."*

Who has not mourned with Poe for the tragic loss of his beloved Annabel, shared the grief expressed so eloquently throughout his writing? Is there one of us who would not have wished for her to have returned to him...

MY ANNABEL

Emerian Rich

They blamed me, but I couldn't stop it. Annabel was going to die from the moment she hugged that poor sick child and I knew it. She knew it too, but neither of us vocalized it. It was more of an exchanged look, a silent message as she smoothed back the hair of that poor homeless waif.

The virus had been loosed on a plane flying in from London, but the passengers didn't start getting sick until they left the airport. By then, they'd had time to infect others. Patients streamed into the ER faster than we could care for them. The rules? Stay four to six feet away, use the protective gear, and make no contact. We followed the rules... except that once.

Just like an unexpected pregnancy from casual sex, it only takes once.

I can't explain why Annabel picked up the child whose sneeze infected her, only that it could have just as easily been me. Perhaps it was the child's pleading blue eyes, too young to know the severity of what her innocent-seeming cold meant, or maybe it was those cute, chubby cheeks covered with tears. Maybe it was because we'd talked of having such a child, of finally being ready to give ourselves up to parenting, of allowing our lives to be taken over by the mixture of joy and stress of being parents. Diapers, late night feedings, no rest. After all, if two doctors couldn't function without a little sleep, what good were we?

And so Annabel allowed herself to be infected because of a sudden lapse in judgment, an urgent wish to ease a little girls' suffering. Who could fault her for that? No one. But they blamed me.

She'd waved me off when a few of the interns in hazmats swooped in to handle the girl. The interns washed Annabel, too. They worked quickly, shedding her of her clothes and wiping her down as I watched from the other side of the glass.

"She can be saved," they murmured. No way the great Doctor Lee—one half of the greatest medical team ever known to the West Coast—could succumb to the virus as the result of simply embracing a defenseless young soul. We were brilliant surgeons, but our bodies were still human. The physical laws of biology and virus still applied.

By the time I'd been installed in a hazmat suit, my Annabel was naked and shivering, more from fever than cold. Unembarrassed by being on the patient side, where modesty was nothing compared to wellness, her teeth chattered as she fell into my white-shrouded arms. I embraced her, gripping the body I knew as well as my own, wishing I could smell her hair, wanting nothing more than to rip off my mask and succumb alongside my love. But when I moved to do so, she pleaded with me to protect myself, that it was she who made the mistake and she who must pay the price.

"You must live on," she said. "You must live this life for us both." I obeyed, but I regret it and have every day since.

I stayed by my love's side, caring for her until the moment my beauty could shiver no longer. Until her last breath passed and even after, when her skin became so cold, I could feel the chill through my protective gear.

I denied my medical obligations, screamed when the interns reminded me of them, and fought those that tried to come between me and my love. No matter what I did, Annabel would die. Did die.

In those last hours as I held her on my lap—me in my hazmat, she in her hospital robe—Annabel reminded me of our life. Not the life we lived then—each trying to be strong for the other, trying to concentrate on the love not the loss—but our life before. When we moved to San Francisco fresh out of medical school, against her parents' wishes, to be interns in a new city on the West Coast. She spoke of the little apartment we could barely afford. Of love-making between shifts, or on breaks, or whenever we could. In the car, in the on-call room, and sometimes in our own bed, exhausted but craving each other's touch. She reminded me of those rare days off when we'd take a picnic to the park and roll in the grass, enjoying the sun on our pale, indoor skin or running along the beach letting the freezing water tingle our toes in the sand.

"We loved with a love that was more than a love," she said, her weary, red-rimmed eyes looking up at me from her curled spot on my lap.

"That we did and will always, forever more," I replied.

After the light was gone from her eyes and her heart stopped for good, I held her still, willing my love to revive her. You'd think it would. For why would the heavens give us such a gift of love if not to make it powerful enough to bring back life? Oh, but I know the angels have always been jealous of our love, and now I get to be jealous of them, because they have her and I am alone.

*

Her kin came to collect her. They'd heard of her illness—she made me call them—and they came. Her father the judge, her mother the lawyer, and her brother the neurosurgeon. All practical thinkers, but in a situation of a lost loved one, there is no practicality involved. They blamed me. I could see it in their eyes.

You did this. You killed her. They were right—and wrong. The virus had chilled her to death, but had I not taken her away, had I not loved her, she would still be alive. She would still be on the East coast, the *right* coast. The unspoken blame was almost worse than if they had yelled at me. At least then I could yell back.

They weren't happy when I told them we'd bought plots in a cemetery up north. They were hoping to take her back East.

"Back home," they said. *Where she belongs,* I read in their eyes.

But Annabel had been adamant about us being buried together in the little cliff side community by the sea where we had once spent a glorious vacation. And so they complied with her wishes.

It was all done to their schedule. They took her before I could even say goodbye, and she was buried within a day of her death. So fast, I felt they kidnapped her from me.

Before death, it had been all about us, about me and her, alone. After, it became about *them.* What they wanted, what they thought Annabel would have wanted. The Annabel they knew, before I poisoned her.

They left shortly after and I was alone, but I felt her there with me and reminisced on the trip when we'd bought the plots. It was the most memorable trip we'd ever taken together. Winding our way there on that deserted two-lane road, serpentine and dark. Admiring the tall trees and absence of life in the woods. We fantasized buying one of the seemingly abandoned cabins we came across every mile or so. Living alone in the woods. A place where we'd be together with no one to separate us. They were fun fantasies. Ones you make on vacations, but never believe will really happen.

Settled in our hotel, gazing out the window at the torrid sea beating against the rocky cliffs, Annabel squeezed close to me.

"It's paradise," she said, kissing my neck. "Let's never leave."

But leave we must, and on the last morning, after packing the car and having lunch, we walked to the coast and along the cliff line. The wind blew back her hair as she smiled, looking out at the sea. As the sun shone bright, lighting a glittering path across the water, a church bell rang. We turned, spotting a little white chapel, boarded on one side with grave stones.

Annabel grabbed my hand and ran so fast I struggled to keep up. A marriage party exited the church, all smiles and well wishes.

"How happy they must be. Remember our wedding day?" she asked, and I did.

We had met on the beach alone, with only a priest and his wife as witness. Although no one else stood with us, it was exactly how we wished it to be. After the vows, we walked along the shore, bathing our feet in the cold water until they grew numb. Then Annabel led me to a deserted cove and in a sandy cave, we made love to the sound of the waves crashing against the shore. All that history showed in her bright smile as she asked me if I remembered.

"I could never forget," I said and embraced her with a force I could not control. A magnetic, hypnotic force powered by the strength of our love and a destiny we'd never denied.

"Let's die here," she said.

"What?"

She laughed one of her, *Don't be silly, Allan,* laughs and blinked toward the church cemetery.

"Let's be buried here together," she said, and then ran to the church before I could answer.

The priest thought us quite mad, I'm sure, wishing to be buried in a small town where no one knew us and where the last interment had been a century before.

"Don't you want the nicer cemetery up the hill, with the shiny new gates and million-dollar crematorium?"

"No." Annabel was adamant. "It must be here on the cliff."

He couldn't argue with her heart so set on it, and his church in need of costly repairs.

So, with our plots purchased, we headed back to the city, back to real life.

*

I had not looked at the paperwork until after her death.

Two plots sharing an upright headstone in the style of the old cemetery. Grey granite, matte not polished. Names to be etched, dates to be added later. Paid in full.

It all sounded very legal and unemotional. The loss of her love hit me in a rush once again as her delicate signature came into view.

"This is what I want, Allan." She'd looked into my eyes with such conviction that day, I could not deny her.

*

The day I met Annabel, she'd had the same look of conviction. We'd been thrown together in Anatomy class and had to dissect a corpse. I was understandably a bit queasy, but Annabel had taken up the scalpel and dug right in. I was floored by her courage and suddenly felt the need to outdo her. We spent the next hour arguing about technique and scientifically removing ourselves from the fact that we were cutting through a person. A dead person, but a person nonetheless.

After class, I yearned to get the smell of the cadaver off me, but I couldn't leave without asking Annabel to drinks.

"Sure," she said, with that little smile she had, and I was hooked.

From that night on, I was hers. It was no longer me and her. It was us. I never knew I'd like being part of an *us* until I met her. If I didn't know better, I would say she cast a spell on me. After all, how did a level-headed, driven, med student become a man so attached to his girlfriend that he chose his intern program with her in mind?

If you've never been in love—true love—it isn't something I can explain. It just *is,* and you either go along with it or suffer in agony over the loss of someone who finally makes your life whole.

*

Annabel once asked me if I believed in ghosts, and I'd answered with a definitive *no.* She'd been less sure, and brought up the idea of haunting.

"If I should ever die and you live on, I would do everything in my power to connect with you."

"You mean haunt me?"

"Well, why not? What else have you got to do once I'm dead?"

I loved her sense of humor.

*

Memories of her haunted me so severely, I swore she was there in the room.

Take a deep breath love. It will be fine. Her imagined voice soothed me like the time I had performed my first heart transplant. *You know what to do. There is a system to this. Just follow through.*

I obeyed and put on my black suit. I walked alone to the cemetery, craving the serenity of the walk and the memories of Annabel being there with me.

Prayers said and her family gone, I found the strength to approach the newly packed grave. The priest stood some distance off for a while, but eventually he retired into the chapel.

I stared at the headstone.

Annabel Lee.

The letters bore into the stone with startling finality. Mine was there beside it, and although no dates were carved, I knew they soon would be, for how could I go on without my precious Annabel?

I sat down next to my love and listened to the waves crash below us. I told her I loved her in so many ways, I soon made no sense. Me, a doctor of medicine, spouting poems and sonnets. What did I know of such things? The answer? Nothing. Until Annabel came into my life, and then every day was a gift of glory and bedazzlement.

*

Back in our hotel room, I felt her with me again. A whisper in the curtains, a shadow across the room. Was she haunting me? Truly? I wasn't scared, I was intrigued.

A pounding came at the door, and I startled out of my day dream. If only I could open the door and find Annabel simply returning with ice from the vending that we'd use to chill the champagne we'd brought to celebrate. I glanced at the table. The champagne was gone. I snapped out of the memory and remembered. It wasn't that trip, it was her burial day and there was no champagne, only cheap mini-bottles of liquor I'd swiped into the basket at the corner store.

The bang came again and I went to answer.

The door swung open to my Annabel, and I squinted and blinked, thinking it a dream. No, it *was* her, but not the Annabel I knew.

True her skin—although pallid—was in her form, and her clothes—although soiled—were in her style, but her eyes lacked the light they'd had and the brilliancy of her hair had gone grey.

I stood, staring at my love, not sure of what was going on until she lunged forward, her teeth intent to latch on. I jumped back, avoiding her attack. With one last look at my love, I ran across the room, through the sliding glass door to the beach, and away from her stumbling pursuit.

I kept running, unsure if I was dreaming or if the nightmare was real. The path was dark, lit only by moonlight. No one was out, the silence broken only by the waves' crash.

And then the events of the previous days came to me in a rush, like fast-forwarding a video.

I remembered being at the hospital and notified of the virus. Patients dying quickly, their symptoms setting in within hours, with no hope of a cure. Annabel dying the same way, unable to be cured. Then her family came and took her away, leaving me in the chaos of a hospital overrun by mourning families and the corpses of their loved ones. In shock, I wandered through the din like a sleepwalker, unable to process any of the voices.

I'd found my way home at some point and packed, heading out the door as my phone rang incessantly with calls from the hospital and pages to come back. Driving through the chaos of the streets, I avoided one check point after another. I had to get to Annabel! I had to see her one last time before she was buried.

Arriving in the sea side town, I drove directly to the church, where her family was having the hole dug. I swung open her coffin and kissed my little Annabel, pleaded for her to come back to me. Her family pulled me away and promised to wait while I cleaned up. I checked into the hotel, flipping on the TV while I got dressed, needing the white noise so I didn't go insane.

Virus. Widespread panic. Fleeing the city. Highly contagious. Do not approach. Stay in your homes.

The words hadn't sunk in, but they came back in a rush and I understood. More moments sewn into the story solidified my new reality.

I am in a world overrun by reanimated corpses and now, my love, my Annabel, is one of them.

*

She only comes out at night. And in the weeks she's been undead, I've become an undead stalker. No new reports come from San Francisco, so I assume they are all dead—or undead like Annabel. I haven't seen Annabel's family since the burial, but I assume they left town as soon as she was interred. They may be dead as well, for all I know. In town, they are all dead: the priest, the corner market sales clerk, the nice little old lady who runs the hotel—all dead. All hungry.

And I'm hungry, too. I've run through what little supplies the town had, and I've scavenged most of the homes in town. I've found no other living humans and don't wish to go in search of any. If I left, I would have to leave her, and I'm not prepared to let her go. Yet.

Perhaps it's delirium from hunger, but I can no longer go on. I'm tired. I can no longer live without the Annabel I loved. I can no longer live alone. I'd rather be by her side for all eternity as one of the walking dead than live this half-life of a starving, grieving human.

So, I am going out this afternoon to lie down by her side. When the sun goes down and dims the glittering sea, she will rise and make me her own, as she did when she first set eyes on me. My darling—my wife and my bride—I'll lie there, by her tomb, by the sounding sea.

Kara Race-Moore first leaned about Edgar Allen Poe when her sixth grade teacher did a dramatic reading of The Tell-Tale Heart, *complete with stamping and yelling, and has been hocked ever since. She studied history at Simmons College as an excuse to read about the often scandalous lives of British royals, and worked in educational publishing, casting the molds for future generations' minds, but has since moved into the more civilized world of litigation. When not distracted by the day job, she writes fantasy, horror, and science fiction, holding up the stories as a fun house mirror to the real world.*

About this story, Kara says: "The Masque of the Red Death *has always been one of my favorite of Poe's works, with its sharp contrasts between luxury and decay, safety and terror, rich and poor. The 21st century offers plenty of similar contrasts, and changing the main character from a Renaissance prince to a Wall Street hedge fund manager struck me as a perfect parallel. Having recently learned that luxury underground bunkers are a trend among today's super wealthy, I realized I had the perfect setting for today's elite to wait out a plague. Yes, the underground beach-pool is real."*

Today's society places great emphasis on the differences between us—rich and poor, this race or that, gender preferences, religious beliefs, educational differences, national background, haves and have-nots. Too often overlooked are the things we all have in common, such as the desire to survive, to thrive, to seek justice…

DARK POOLS OF LIQUIDITY

Kara Race-Moore

The Ebola virus mutated from a horror film serial killer that only managed to kill a few lonely, marginalized victims into a war drama dictator that caused the death of millions. The virus then brazenly crossed the seas and began to lay waste to the population before people even comprehended they were in danger.

Evolving into an efficient killer, the mutated disease caused its victim to progress from general fatigue, to a high fever, to bleeding from the eyes, to death in less than two days; in the worst cases, in less than two hours. Hospitals were instantly overwhelmed, and all over the country, from the Atlantic to the Pacific, people succumbed en masse to the virulent disease.

But for Gerald Dorado, President and CFO of Renaissance Investments, one of the most successful hedge funds on Wall Street, times were good. Times were very, very good. There was always more money to be made in a time of chaos, when uptight bureaucrats and self-righteous reporters were less likely to pay scrupulous attention to what you were doing. Perhaps some crusading civil servant might tilt at him in years to come, but in that case he would just pay the fine for whatever small charge they could make stick, shrug, and move on to make more money.

Dorado already had several investments in treating symptoms (not cures, there was no money to made curing people), and, as the Ebola virus began to mow down Middle America, he threw almost everything he had into the businesses that supplied the pandemic's needs. He invested in the factories that produced bio-suits, body bags, and rubber gloves. He saw his portfolio swell with profit from his stocks in various patented drugs; none of them helped the victims, but hospitals still stocked up on anything that promised even a glimmer of hope. The surge in sales of medical supplies tripled that year's original projected revenues. And the money he would make from the rollover of the dead's mortgage and student loan debts was going to make all the profit from the living pale in comparison.

As the pandemic spread wider, there were so many afflicted people that the hospitals turned many away, telling the sick to stay home until mobile help could be arranged. Any minute now, they promised, the government would have medical units on the move. In the meantime, those with the tale-tell red eyes were shunned by the public and—in a few cases—even killed by mobs whose helpless fury overcame their fear.

When actual rich people started to die, and the chaos began to outweigh the daily profit margins, and the stock market was put on temporary hiatus, Dorado gathered up those in his network who would be most useful to have owe him favors later. Flying to an undisclosed location on his fleet of private jets, they descended into his luxury bunker to wait out the pestilence.

The bunker was a former missile silo, deep in the earth, renovated and refurbished to his own design, following his exquisite tastes; a palace of luxury surrounded by nine-foot thick concrete walls with a door that could stop a nuclear bomb. It had all the needed features to produce air, water, and energy, and keep out any weapons, diseases, or mobs—in short, it was all that was expected for your standard underground bunker. Dorado had seen to it that, once everyone descended the forty-nine stories from ground level and the door was officially sealed, he and his were well provisioned to wait out the outbreak in comfort and style.

Every floor was a marvel to behold. There were the necessary areas for the grimy engines that ran everything tucked away deep on the ground floor, and above them were the bunk bed stuffed levels for the requisite staff, but the rest was as luxurious as any five star hotel. Safety was the least of the features Dorado had designed into his bunker; this was a building built to impress, and impress it did. His chosen few marveled as they were given the grand tour, beset with luxury from all angles.

All of Dorado's guests were provided with charming suites, each king-sized bed made up in the morning with a mint on the pillow, and turned down at night. Laundry was picked up nightly and returned, fresh and clean, the next morning. There were restaurant areas on the common floors, and each suite had a small, private dining area for when one felt the need to dine in and have room service delivered, any time, day or night, in the day-less, night-less bunker. Each suite had a wet bar for self-serve drinks, a granite fireplace, tended to by the butler service, and marble bathing tubs with dolphin-shaped faucets, as well as his and her sinks in the bathrooms so couples would not have to endure the indignity of knocking elbows when brushing teeth after a sumptuous private breakfast in bed for two.

Naturally, not all suites were as luxurious as others, but of course it as expected there would be a hierarchy in room assignments so everyone was sure to know their place in Dorado's favor. It was rumored Dorado himself slept on an emperor-sized bed with silken sheets, surrounded by priceless works of arts from the Smithsonian and the Met that he had negotiated to keep safe, for a reasonable fee, while the country was gripped in the current emergency.

But the number of activities for all to while away their time that were fitted into the shelter was astounding. Two floors alone were dedicated to a gigantic swimming pool simulated to look like a beach with the shallow end sloping up to meet an expanse of soft white sand imported from a far-off island and a 360 degree screen wrapped around the walls programed to display an idyllic Caribbean vista. There was a bowling alley, a gun range, squash courts, and a four-story rock climbing wall. The gymnasium featured multiple jogging, stepping, biking, and stretching machines, as well as every variant of weight possible, so Dorado's guests would have no worries about getting out of shape during the pandemic.

Those preferring more sedate pastimes were invited to spend their time in the leather chair furnished library with shelves of hardcover books taking up two floors, or the green-velveted billiard room. An old school arcade room offered all the old two-bit games, and there were two movie theaters, one showcasing all the latest arrivals, the other showing all the old classics. The Spa was a fully-staffed facility, with a steam room, sauna, Jacuzzi, and several masseurs on staff to massage away any tensions caused by the tedium of waiting.

There was sushi freshly prepared from fish in the giant aquarium that decorated most of one side of a level, and crisp fresh salads from the pleasant hydroponics garden where one could take a stroll and inhale the delicate fragrances. The staff tending the plants would be happy to have a bouquet of your favorite flower delivered to your suite. Pastry chefs prepared delicate confections of the most artistic sweetness, and various frozen or dried foodstuffs were daily turned into amazing dishes that rivaled the menu of any Manhattan restaurant.

Should guests require aid for their relaxation, they could have their favorite cocktail shaken up by the award winning bartenders in one of the many bars, each decorated in a different theme. Guests could wander into a bar made to look like a 1920's Speakeasy or visit one that resembled a Victorian brothel. For the more 'hip' guests, a 1960's psychedelic paradise beckoned, or they could take their libations amid the same sleek lines of a well-known fictional spaceship.

And if one wasn't in the mood for hard liquor, there was one level that held a wine vault, filled with thousands of the finest vintages, overseen by a sommelier available to help pick the perfect bottle to accompany any meal from the well laden kitchens.

*

It was at the end of the first month of seclusion that Dorado decided to throw a masquerade ball in order to keep everyone from growing bored amongst the static splendor. The masquerade was arranged to be an extravagant event, made even more so by the sumptuous setting. Dorado set the party all on one level, with the partitions rearranged to form seven large rooms, each decorated to a specific mode. The digital screens along the walls were programmed to a specific color theme, with matching lighting installed.

The first room the guests entered when they got off the elevator was all in deepest sapphires, the screens showing underwater footage, as if dark fish glided calmly just outside the concrete walls. This lead to the next room, were the energy brightened as strobe lights of purple painted giant flowers on the walls, and the screens displayed geometric shapes of dark purple flying over a lighter purple background. The following room was all done in jungle greens, the screens back to a more realistic portal, this time of a shimmering rain forest, with a hint of movement in the leaves now and then, suggesting a large predator on the hunt.

Orange was the hue of the next room, in all the warm shades of the most succulent hand fruits, and here were the buffet tables, piled with every sort of delicacy, sweet and savory, to satisfy all tastes. This, of course, lead to the room where the drinks were being served, the decorations done in shades of bitter white frost and cold clear ice, the screens a pure, cold white of winter's deepest chill. The next area was all in bright, neon pinks and violets, the space and lights and music encouraging the costumed revelers to carelessly dance the night away.

The last chamber was darker than a movie theater, with black velvet hung all over the walls, and dark reds pulsing on the screens. Here Dorado had set up a large screen projecting the death toll ticking upwards, the numbers pulled from the CDC's scrupulous, up-to-the-minute, online records. Few guests lingered in this room after a mere glance inside. Everyone knew once the number ceased ticking up, then the pestilence would be over and they could reemerge. Still, no one wished to look at it for long.

But even with the reminder of the hold Death had on the outside world, the party was magnificent and said to be a complete success—and not just by those who wished to be heard praising their host. Dorado's tastes were held up as exemplary. Only Dorado, they said, could have had the vision to imagine such luxury amongst the ruins. Even though almost no one ventured into the seventh room, dancing and talk and laughter pulsed in the other six chambers.

But in the early hours of the morning, ripples of disquiet began to spread. Amongst the costumed crowd, no ordinary appearance would have caused a stir, but one of the masked figures was dressed beyond the realms of all good taste.

The unrecognized guest wore the tattered remains of a health care worker's protective uniform, the blue tunic and pants dirty and frayed, the blue gloves stained with dark brown patches, the paper slips over the shoes gone ragged, and the paper mask over the mouth, grimy. The dark skin of the face was tinged a corpse-like grey. Worst of all, the eyes had been made red with clever contacts, and drops of blood had been artistically painted on the cheeks.

The costume made it appear as if Patient Zero, Mayinga N'Seka herself, walked among them.

As Dorado's gaze fell upon the gauche reveler, he shuddered with revulsion, and then his face reddened with rage.

"How fucking dare you?" he demanded. "How dare you insult my generosity with this mockery? Someone grab this motherfucker! If they want to mock everything I've done for them, they can see how funny the mobs outside find them!"

He was standing in the blue suite when he decreed this, but his bellow echoed throughout the entire floor, for someone had turned off the music as soon as he started to speak, and now all his guests were silent.

There was a stir of movement as some of the brasher young people who made up Dorado's numbers thought to follow his orders, but none could quite get up the courage to lay a hand on the figure. And so she passed unimpeded though the rooms, and people shrank back as the embodiment of all their fears moved from one shade to the next. Many shook their heads in slow confusion, skin prickling with a vague, prescient fear.

Dorado followed the figure, moving through the crowd which had parted to let them pass. Just at the entrance to the final room, she turned to face the enraged billionaire.

Removing the paper mask from her mouth she smiled grimly at him. "What a lovely party you put on. Or rather, what a lovely party you ordered your staff to stage for you and your guests."

"You're one of the staff, aren't you?" Dorado spat out, seemingly enraged more by the fact he was forced to converse with someone he deemed so beneath him than at her insolent behavior. He panted heavily, as if his anger was consuming all his energy.

Her smile twisted up, sharper. "Do you have any idea what my job even is? Do you even know my name?"

"I don't need to know your name," he snarled, "that's part of the point of being rich. What are you doing crashing my party? Isn't it enough that I'm saving your life by letting you work down here and paying you?"

She shook her head. "No. It isn't enough." She gestured with a hand to indicate the bunker in general. "All of this could have gone to such a more useful purpose than making sure you all had canapes and cocktails, while above people are dying like flies."

"You're breaking my heart," he sneered; his face was more purple than red now. "That's the way the world works, bitch."

"No, that's the way the world *up there* works," she pointed skywards. Everyone in the vicinity look upwards involuntarily. "Down here, however, when there is literally an 'on/off' switch to the oxygen? Down here things are different. Oh, and by the way, I disabled the oxygen before I came to party." She grinned. *"And lo, the engineers shall inherit the earth."*

It was only then that Dorado realized the prickling in his fingers wasn't just from his anger at this shocking confrontation. Even in the various colored lights, he saw his guests' skin was gaining a bluish tint. Those nearest Dorado, who had heard the engineer's words, panicked. People screamed and ran, although there was no extra air for screaming, and there was nowhere to run.

"Why?" Dorado groaned, as he sank to his knees. "You'll die, too!"

She nodded as she knelled next to him. "The last of my family died of Ebola yesterday, choking on their own blood, alone, and un-helped. The people you wouldn't allow in because you only wanted your chosen guests and helpful staff."

She smiled serenely at him. "So why not take everyone down with me? I am sorry about the rest of the staff, but it might shake up some change if there are a few less of you assholes in charge of the money."

"You don't... know what... you're talking about," Dorado heaved out. "People like you... need people... like us. Like me. You *need* me."

She put an arm around him, as if they were drunken chums. "Silly rich man. No. You needed *me*. You just didn't know it, because your money blinded you. Your money bought you time, but it could never buy you knowledge of what you really needed to know."

"And so what? Suffering made you better? What do you know that I don't?"

She chuckled with the last of reserves of her strength. "I don't know much, but hey, let's end things on a good note and say 'love is all you need.'"

At that, there was no strength in either of them for any more talking, and they both slumped all the way down to the floor, with her arms still around him. Dorado and the engineer were two of the first to die, the rest dropping soon after, the corpses gently bathed in a multitude of colors as rigor mortis set in, and the bunker of safety became a tomb.

And so death had come after all, invited in by someone so overlooked no one could see the danger. The death counter in the darkened chamber was slowing down, and soon the pestilence would pass, as plagues always do, but this selfish percent of the population would never emerge into the new world.

Stephanie L. Harper grew up in California, attended college in Iowa and Germany, completed graduate studies and gave birth to her first child in Wisconsin, and now lives with her family in Oregon. She is a Pushcart Prize nominee, and author of the chapbooks, This Being Done, *and the upcoming* The Death's-Head's Testament. *Her poems appear in such journals and anthologies as* Slippery Elm, Isacoustic*, Rat's Ass Review, Panoply, Underfoot, Stories that Need to Be Told, *and elsewhere. Follow her work online at https://www.slharperpoetry.com.*

About this poem, Stephanie says: "Poe's timeless masterpiece, The Raven, *has been singing the mesmerizing beauty and heartbreak of nevermore to my psyche since my earliest exposure to the poetic arts as an adolescent. I've come to believe there's a healthy dose of that iconic bird's dark wonderment living inside every heart, so it was only a matter of time until my creative expression would follow this conviction to its logical conclusion…"*

A seldom-acknowledged fact is that Poe did not limit the animals featured in his writings to ravens and black cats. Among others, an orangutan was a major character in The Murders in the Rue Morgue, *a scarab beetle was featured in* The Gold Bug, *and penguins waddle through* The Narrative of Arthur Gordon Pym of Nantucket. *So why shouldn't a rabbit have his chance at the limelight… or the garden!*

THE RABBIT

Stephanie L. Harper

Once upon a midday gleaming, as the sun perched, eager-seeming,
above my homestead's weedy patches of forgotten sod.
Whilst I sighed, wondrous with gloom—oh, how that sky did fiercely loom!—
on my yard's bedraggled flora a grayish rabbit gnawed—
with a certain pluck & gusto, chose its clumps & briskly gnawed,
ever mindful where it trod.

I presumed it was a visitor from lettuce fields abroad,
for it was fuzzy, quick & small, cute as a little cotton ball,
but unlike any other rabbit that I'd ever seen before…
I distinctly don't recall if it was springtime, or late fall—
where I live, these stark environs kind of always look like fall—
lacking features to enthrall.

Soon, my feelings started seeping, the way shadows take to creeping
from their places of safekeeping, 'til they lumbered into view
(as for that moment's peace I'd sought, when with my sanctuary wrought,
I'd crawled inside to stay—& stayed much longer than I knew;
it could've dried & blown away, for all I really knew...)—
& there was nothing I could do...

Now, the rabbit, on grasses chewing—my soul eschewing—is my undoing:
My vain attempts to woo it hither churn up far too much ado,
so, I'm here, just sitting, stewing, my years accruing (*they keep accruing!*)
of the untold days' ensuing—garish sunlight streaming through
(when all is said & done, I'll bet that sun just seeps right through!);
also, I'd swear that fur-ball grew!

With such a craving so unnerving, I'm apt to wither undeserving
of even one, small, savory serving of Hasenpfeffer stew—
my wee compadre, to be sure, won't soon be rapping at my door:
I could with tears & snot implore, writhing prostrate on the floor,
but it wouldn't give two shits if I dried up here on this floor—
yet to hunger, evermore!

Susan McCauley has an MFA in Professional Writing from the University of Southern California and an MA in Text & Performance from the Royal Academy of Dramatic Art and King's College in London. An award-winning short film was based on her story, Alma; *her stage adaptation of Nikolai Gogol's,* The Nose, *was produced at George Bernard Shaw Theater in London; and scenes from her play on Elizabeth I were produced at HMS Tower of London. Her short stories* The Snow Woman *and* The Nest *have been published in anthologies. You can find her at www.sbmccauley.com*

About this story, Susan says: "When I learned that a publisher was looking for retellings and modern twists on the stories of Edgar Allan Poe, my mind went immediately to The Cask of Amontillado, *which I'd taught in some of my college English classes. The tale both captivated and horrified me, but I was always left wondering: what made Montresor so vengeful and murderous? We never knew his motivation. So, when I had the opportunity to give the story my own spin, my aim was to create a story faithful to Poe's original, while answering my question and adding a modern twist."*

When you finally give in to your baser nature and decide you've had enough, it's important to plan your revenge to the last detail. Because in much the same way that it was the accumulation of little things that pushed you to the edge, it's the little things that will be your undoing...

THE CASK
Susan McCauley

Jack drummed his fingers against his thigh as he waited for the latest shipment of booze to arrive. Every tap of his mortar-covered fingertips left dusty prints on his jeans. Charles Fortunato, his so-called best friend, had done it again. Lied. But this time, the lie had caused both insult and injury. Well, he'd had enough. There would be no 'next time.'

Jack checked his watch: a quarter past twelve. The delivery was late.

He squinted down the tree-lined country road that wound its way to the historic tavern where he spent most of his waking hours. Jack inhaled, the scent of pine trees and fresh air invading his nostrils. The surrounding forest called to him, the leafy shadows summoning him to the darkness. Maybe after tonight he could walk freely under the dense canopy and search out the buck that kept eating his garden. Maybe after tonight he'd have not one, but two heads to hang above the mantel.

The squeak of an axle drew Jack's eyes back to the road. Ronnie Taylor's truck. *Finally.*

The truck squealed to a halt before reversing toward the kitchen's service door. A cloud of smoke issued from the driver's side window, soon followed by the door opening. A tubby, gray-haired man climbed out.

"Jack." He nodded. "How's things today?"

"Not too bad, Ronnie. Just trying to get the place in order for our reopening."

"How're the renovations coming?" Ronnie took a long draw from his cigarette.

"The contractors are finished, but they made more work for me. One of the men accidentally knocked a hole in the cellar wall. It's not bad, but it needs re-bricking."

"Won't the weather get in?" Ronnie glanced at the thick clouds darkening the sky.

Jack shook his head. "We found an old storage space in the cellar. What we thought was the outer wall is really a second interior one."

"Humph."

Jack nodded. "We even found some old casks stuck between the walls. Uncle Larry figures it was part of an old wine cellar, and the previous owners forgot about the casks when the new wall was put in."

"What are you gonna do with 'em?"

"Uncle Larry wants to leave them. No reason to move 'em. Too old. They'd probably just break. Besides, we'd have to remove more stones to pull them out."

"It'd be better if the contractor hadn't damaged that wall in the first place." Ronnie stomped out his dying cigarette butt.

"I'll have it fixed by Monday." Jack shrugged. "Well before the festival and our reopening."

Ronnie opened the back of the truck and grabbed a box of wine. "Better get this shipment in before the rain really starts," he said, wiping the spittle of rain from his cheeks.

"What do you have for us today?"

"The usual—Chianti, Cabernet, Merlot, a nice Fumé Blanc. I've also got a case of sherry here." Ronnie's gray eyebrows rose, and he licked his lips. "Larry wanted to give it a try. It's Amontillado. See if he'll let you have some. It's delicious."

"I'm sure I can crack one bottle. He likes me to know our products."

Ronnie helped carry the boxes into the kitchen, then drove off with a wave, leaving Jack to do the rest of the heavy lifting. It was a full shipment, and it would take Jack the better part of the afternoon to lug everything to the cellar and sort the wines into their appropriate racks.

A boom of thunder crashed, shaking the narrow windowpanes at the top of the cellar. Fat droplets began to fall, cascading down the glass like tears. The winter storms of the East Coast could be brutal; still, this one seemed a little early.

Jack set down the case of Amontillado, cracked open the box, and picked up a bottle to inspect. He studied the white-and-gold label, a faint smile forming on his lips. He'd invite Charles for a drink this evening. His friend could never refuse any get-together that involved alcohol, and Charles would be especially pleased to try the Amontillado. He fancied himself a connoisseur, but Jack knew better. Charles was simply an arrogant idiot who drank too much.

*

The rain pattered steadily on the roof overhead. It'd been raining all day and was supposed to rain through the night. Thunder boomed outside and lightning illuminated the clouds through the tavern window. Tonight was a good night for wine.

"To life!" Charles grinned, clinking his glass with Jack's.

His smile was more annoying than ever. Charles Fortunato was too handsome and charming for his own good, even when he was drunk. *Charmed the pants right off my fiancée, then embarrassed me with their little secret in front of my best customers. Tore my heart out and made me look the fool.* Jack forced a smile and hoped Charles would believe the lie.

"To your long life." Jack took a sip of wine. He swirled the fruity, aromatic liquid around his mouth before swallowing it. He held his glass to the light and gazed at the deep-red liquid within, then refocused on the distorted image of his friend. "Nice vintage."

Cabernet. A nice wine for an evening in, Jack mused. *Even if it's with him.*

Tinny notes of *Für Elise* interrupted Jack's thoughts. Charles's cell phone. He claimed to appreciate the classics, but Jack knew he used his basic knowledge of composers in an attempt to impress women.

Charles looked at the phone, grinned, and silenced the ring. "It's Cindy, that cute little piece I met last night. I'll call her later." He shoved the phone back in his pocket and picked up his glass. "Delicious!" He shot it all at once, the wine dribbling down his chin like a bloody stream.

"Slow down. Enjoy it." Jack took another slow sip. *Charlie goes through booze like he goes through women, and no one seems to pay any attention. It's about time someone handled it.* "And there's something new I haven't tried—an Amontillado."

"Amontillado!" Charles lurched to his feet, then steadied himself on the table edge.

"Easy there. Maybe you'd better just sit for a few minutes." Jack gazed out the window. The rain was still pelting down, causing a small flood in the parking lot. Perhaps he'd have to stay here tonight. The last time he'd spent the night at the *Montresor* was with his now ex-fiancée. He shrugged away the memory. The thunder crashed again and the lights flickered out. "Why don't you sit for a minute? I'll get a flashlight if you're up for going to the cellar."

"Naw, I'm fine, Jack." Charles teetered on his feet. "Grab the light and let's go see this load! Maybe I can do a taste test for you."

Jack grinned and collected the flashlight from behind the bar. "Maybe. You are knowledgeable about your beverages."

"Only the best, man. Only the best." Charles steadied himself again at the top of the stairs.

Jack led the way down the darkened stone steps, cool air pressing in around them, with only a narrow beam of light illuminating their path into the cellar.

"You keep it all down here?"

"The wine," Jack said. "And if we have extra inventory, we store it here."

Charles coughed. "Kind of musty, isn't it?"

"If the damp's too much for you, don't come. I can bring a bottle of Amontillado back up." Jack's light passed over the ancient stone wall as they moved deeper into the cellar. He would have to fix the mortar; water trickled in from the downpour, making it very damp.

Charles coughed again, struggling for breath.

"Really, Charles. Your health is too important. Go back upstairs."

Charles stifled another cough. "A little cough never killed anyone."

"I know," Jack whispered, grinning in the darkness. Charles must not have noticed he'd had most of the bottle of Médoc himself. Jack had only one glass. He led Charles toward the Amontillado.

His beam of light illuminated a case of liquor.

"Amontillado." Charles stopped by the crate that had yet to be unloaded and reached for a bottle.

Even in the dim light, Jack could see the strands of Charles's thick, brown hair, dust angels dancing in the ray of light above his head.

Fist clenched around cold metal, Jack raised the heavy flashlight and waited for the next boom of thunder.

"Hey, put the light back over here, I'm trying to read this," Charles complained.

Jack raised the flashlight higher.

A boom of thunder reverberated through the stones, and Jack landed a crushing blow to the top of Charles's head. Charles fell to his knees before careening forward and collapsing on his face.

Jack smelled the metallic tang he knew so well from hunting with his father as a boy. Blood. He'd never liked it. He swallowed back bile. He knew what he had to do. There was no running. No going back. Charles had insulted him for the last time.

He gazed down on his guest, quickly wiping the blood from the flashlight onto Charles's shirt.

Charles moaned; he wasn't totally unconscious. Jack had to hurry.

Jack set the light on a workbench he'd erected for the remodel, dragged the wounded man to the stone wall, and hefted him over the damaged edge. A muffled thump sounded when Charles hit the earth between the walls.

Jack peered over the ledge and angled the light downward to where Charles lay on the packed earth, legs splayed between the old casks.

Leaving the flashlight and crowbar on the edge of the damaged wall, Jack pulled himself up. He tossed the crowbar to the floor and then hopped into the cavernous space below.

It was dark, but his eyes were adjusting. The steady beam of light helped. Besides that, he knew this cellar well enough to find his way in the dark. Jack picked up the crowbar and freed the two top rings of the nearest cask until they slipped off. He loosened a couple of boards and pried open the lid. The barrel was empty, dry.

Jack hoped the cask would remain airtight after he resealed it. It wouldn't do to have a suspicious smell seeping through the wall. Still, it was usually cool down here, and if any smell did seep through, anyone would just think a rat had been trapped inside the wall during remodeling. Maybe he'd add some lime he had left over for mixing the mortar; that should help with decay.

Jack hefted Charles over his shoulder.

"What're you doin' with me?" Charles asked, his voice like gravel against sandpaper.

"Just putting you in your place, Charles. Just putting you in your place." Jack grunted and lowered his friend into the barrel.

"What the...?"

"Shh, now," Jack hushed. "It'll be just a little longer."

Jack climbed back over the wall and searched the workbench holding his tools. The storm raged outside. The sounds of wind and rain battering the trees issued through the timeworn fieldstone walls like a discordant orchestra.

Charles started to laugh. "I know... I know, this is one of your jokes." His voice, muffled and garbled through the stones, made Jack's stomach drop. He'd have to add dirt or sand to mute the noise.

Boom. The thunder rumbled again.

Jack grabbed a hammer and dropped a couple nails in his pocket before turning back to his task. The garden. There were several bags of dirt and sand out there for a new garden bed he was planning. Jack nodded; that would work. It would have to. He scrambled back over the stones, landing atop one of the empty casks.

Charles blearily smiled up at him, blood running from the wound on his head and into his eyes. "Very funny, Jack. Now help me out of here."

"Oh, no. It's time for a nap, my friend." Jack placed the lid atop the cask. "Nighty-night, Charles."

"What—" Charles began coughing again. "What are you doing?"

Jack slipped the rings back around the outside of the cask to hold the lid in place. Pulling the nails from his pocket, he then nailed the boards he'd loosened securely to the rim.

Tap, tap, tap.

His stomach was taut—whether he had butterflies of excitement or anxiety he wasn't sure. He positioned the next nail carefully.

Tap, tap, tap.

"For the love of God, Jack!" Charles screamed.

"Yes," Jack sighed, "for the love of God."

Tap, tap, tap.

Charles coughed again, then fell silent.

Tap, tap, tap.

Jack pulled himself back over the wall. "Back in a moment, Charles."

He sprinted up the stairs and went out back. Behind the cellar was the *Montresor* garden. Usually pristine, the garden now ran with veins of mud and fertilizer. Plants sagged in the assault of the storm. Jack squinted through the rain and counted: six bags of dirt, six of sand. It would have to do.

He lugged them all inside, carrying two bags at a time into the cellar. Rain dripped from his hair, making rivulets along his skin, but he didn't stop to dry himself. He'd dry off in the basement and would wipe away the blood and footprints later.

One after the other he dumped the damp contents of the bags around the cask. He added what remained of the lime he'd used to make mortar, and tamped down the lime, dirt, and sand mixture. It didn't cover the lid, but it should help subdue any noise or smell. Besides, by the time they reopened on Monday, there wouldn't be any noise from Charles.

He tossed his tools back over the wall into the cellar and patted the lid before scurrying out of the tomb. *Time to finish this.* He took the remaining fieldstones and the mortar he'd made to repair the wall.

Charles called out, his yells and coughs barely discernible.

Jack said nothing. He worked steadily until after midnight, layer after layer. Mortar and stone. Finally, the wall was reconstructed.

Charles had stopped screaming.

"Charles?"

There was no answer, so he called again. "Charles?"

Jack listened. The rain pattered steadily, distant, on the roof and walls. He was glad it was raining. Rain washed away the dirt and grime and allowed new things to grow. He focused on the wall once more. Nothing. Not a sound.

No one would think twice about his finishing the work over the weekend. No one at all.

Jack's heart twinged, but he'd done what he had to do. Charles would never insult him again. And the walls would keep his secret.

*

Charles had not been missed—yet. It had only been two days, but Jack was nervous. He opened another bottle of Amontillado, and his hands trembled. He hadn't expected a private tasting in the cellar the evening the *Montresor* reopened. True, it wasn't the tavern's finest room—it was probably the draftiest—yet this was where Uncle Larry liked to entertain his friends, among his wine collection.

There they sat, three jovial couples tossing back the Amontillado by candlelight. Jack topped off the fat man's glass and smothered a nervous laugh. *If they only knew.*

Jack poured the redheaded woman another glass, set the bottle down, and turned to go check on the guests upstairs.

A muffled note pierced the candlelit air.

Jack's foot froze, poised on the first step.

More notes.

Jack's heart pounded in his ears.

Für Elise.

Charles's phone.

The ring tone stopped.

It started again.

He'd forgotten to take the phone from Charles's pocket. *Maybe they won't hear it. The battery must be almost dead.*

"I didn't know you had a sound system put in down here, Larry," the fat man said. "Turn it up. I like the classics."

"I didn't put in a sound system." Larry looked at Jack, then rose and walked toward the cellar wall. Everyone stared at the new patch of brick work. The place where the sound was loudest. The place where he'd buried Charles alive.

A warm drop of perspiration slid down Jack's forehead.

Für Elise rang out again.

And again.

And again.

217

Lauryn Christopher has written marketing and technical material for the computer industry for too many years to admit. In her spare time, she mostly writes mysteries—often from the criminal's point of view, as in her Hit Lady for Hire series. You can find information and links to more of her work, and sign up for her occasional newsletter at www.laurynchristopher.com

About this story, Lauryn says: "I first heard The Pit and the Pendulum *as part of a collection of recorded poems, and well remember the narrator's depiction of that yawning, punishing darkness. So when I approached the idea of presenting one of Poe's tales through a contemporary lens, my thoughts naturally turned to that old memory. In the original, the prisoner struggles desperately to avoid the pit. But what would he have found had he fallen in? In my reimagining of this tale, it is not the Inquisition that is the tormenter, but emotional abuse, which can lead you to doubt yourself, shake your grasp on reality, and slide into the darkness of the Pit."*

People aren't always what they seem, and that realization often brings pain and heartache. Too many people have been down the dark path of emotional abuse; few find their way back through the fear and pain...

THE WELL

Lauryn Christopher

I was strong once. There was nothing I couldn't do. It was as though I was a star, a bright, shining light, rising into the night sky, soaring, exultant, all the world spread out before me.

And then my star met yours and our two lights exploded into vivid, vibrant colors. Red and blue, green and yellow, purple and orange, lighting the sky in crashing waves that drowned out the naysayers. It was just the two of us, filling the sky in cascades of brilliant sparks, chasing away the darkness.

But your secret, inner darkness was not so easily overcome, and as the first sparks faded the ash began to fall, bringing your darkness with it like an unrecognized omen.

Was that when you began to hunt me? Or had I been your target from the very beginning, and simply failed to notice, blinded as I was by the combined brilliance of our light?

Was it all a lie?

*

Your darkness crept into our lives; a serpent, fed by your need to shine alone, unchallenged in the night sky, the sickly dull glow of your star casting deep shadows all around us. And when your darkness looked out of the shadows and saw me, it blamed me for disrupting its solitude and causing it pain.

You brought out your knives before we'd fully settled into our first home, and began to sharpen them, slowly, methodically.

I brushed off your sharp remarks like insignificant paper cuts; accidental, or so I thought. But even then, the scars began to criss-cross my psyche, their fine lines introducing almost insignificant weaknesses. I overlooked them, forgave the minor slights, not worth dwelling on, all in the name of giving you the benefit of the doubt.

But you had planted seeds of pain and doubt in the tracks of those first scars, and when the tracks weren't deep enough to promise a fruitful harvest, your words sharpened, becoming razors that sliced across tendons, shattering my strength; drops of acid weakening my belief in myself, while watering the tendrils of uncertainty winding through me. You nurtured my self-doubt until you had pulled my high-flying star to the earth, where it crashed like a meteorite that had strayed too close to the gravity well of your own insecurity.

My own light was dying rapidly by then.

It had been imperceptible, at first, then grew more noticeable, like the dimming and flickering and buzzing of an old fluorescent tube, trying to get my attention. By the time I was aware of the problem, it seemed that nowhere I looked carried the proper replacement bulbs. And when it finally winked out altogether, all that remained was the pale purple recollection of the once-bright light.

"You want this, you know it," you said, time and time again, and though I didn't really think that I did, each time you said it, I felt myself flinch, a little more unsure of myself, the roots of doubt winding their way through the meteorite's impact fractures and deep into the core of who I was, who I had been, feeding on my heart and draining it of life and color.

Your words became a near-Pavlovian trigger, the carrot offered before the stick, and with it, you altered my thinking, my beliefs, my interests, wiping them away and replacing them with your own. Skillfully, you erased who I was and shaped me into the uncertain, hesitant, fearful person you needed me to be.

Someone asked me once what my favorite color was, but I couldn't answer; by then my world had faded to shades of gray. I no longer recognized colors, and I shied away from the things that lurked in the shadows.

There were no safe places, except at your side.

Your hobbies had become mine, even activities that held little interest for me, because you told me that they did, and it was safer to agree with you than to argue. We ate the foods you liked, their seasonings like sawdust on my tongue, though I couldn't remember what flavors it was that I truly craved. We watched the movies you chose, listened to the music you enjoyed, avoiding my clearly unacceptable, unsophisticated selections.

And we only spent time with the people who you felt were sufficiently dim enough never to outshine you.

You isolated me from the light, wrapping me in darkness like a shroud and only allowed me to have the most superficial relationships with anyone outside your sphere of influence. With anyone but you. I was starving for contact, for connections, and you used that hunger against me, keeping me away from anyone who might share the tiniest spark, who might weaken the control you had on me.

I lost myself, and I had no idea what had happened. There were times I truly believed I was going mad, and like a drowning person, flailed wildly and ineffectually against it, feeling the tug of powerful currents pulling me under.

And all that time it was really just you, twitching the marionette strings you had attached to me, making me dance to your own macabre tune.

*

Sometimes, in retrospect, I have wished that you would have simply hit me. You would only have had to do it once, but I would have recognized that for the attack it was, and everything would have been different.

Instead, you chose a stealthier approach, and caught me unawares. Like an espionage agent biding his time, you ferreted out my weaknesses. Then you exploited them one by one for your own purposes.

And like the proverbial frog who trusted so much in the safety of the water in which it sat, I never realized that I was being boiled until it was too late.

Inch by inch you pushed me deeper into the darkness, as though lowering me into a well from which I feared I might never escape. Trusting you, I had walked blindly into the prison you built for me, thinking only of our next adventure. I allowed you to lower me into the well, never recognizing the squealing of the rusty pulley for the warning it was, blissfully unaware of the splinters I was getting from loose boards of the bucket in which I sat. I never saw the fraying rope tied to the bucket, until the last thread broke, dropping me into a pit, alone and afraid.

And I was always afraid.

I no longer trusted myself. Losing faith in myself had created a gaping, bleeding, festering wound, and I had nothing with which to heal it, nothing to replace my own faithless instincts. Even when I had been uncertain about what to do or what the outcome might be, I had always trusted myself to make, at worst, a fair guess which I might have to revise later.

But my instincts had failed to protect me from your darkness, failed to grab me by the throat and shake me into sensibility. I had lost faith in my own instincts, and saw the terror of that self-doubt reflected back at me every time I looked in a mirror.

I had trusted you with my hopes, my dreams, my secrets, my fears, and you had taken them all and sharpened them and turned them against me to cut out my heart, thinking that somehow that would ensure that it would always be yours.

Like a dog who expects to be kicked, I grew wary, slinking through edges of my life, hoping not to be noticed, I never knew when something I said or did would set you off. I began apologizing for every word that came out of my mouth, every decision I made, every action I took, in the vain hopes of avoiding the next attack. The apologies became automatic, a reflex, until I found myself apologizing for my very existence, wrapping the shroud of darkness you had given me even more tightly around myself in the hopes of avoiding your attention.

The shadows around me were filled with the demons of my own making, grown stronger and more powerful with your whisperings, made increasingly formidable as my light waned and the darkness overwhelmed me. I was sliding ever more rapidly down a slippery slope, with nothing to grab onto to slow my descent.

And as I slid deeper into the dark, I was afraid that I might never again find the light.

But mostly, more than anything else I feared, I was deathly afraid that you would discover my last secret.

I was afraid that one day you would realize that in wrapping the chains of your life so very tightly around me, you had failed to notice that I had wrapped the shreds of my own life around our children. That I had protected them from the darkness by giving them the last sparks I had been able to hold onto of our shared light, and then the last flickers of my own light before it faded altogether.

There are things we turn away from because of fear, and then there are things we do because we are more afraid of the consequences of not doing them.

What you might do to our children frightened me far worse than anything you might do to me.

So I stood in front of you, a willing target on trembling legs, shuddering under the onslaught of barbs, flinching as each dart pierced tender flesh. I withstood the knife thrusts, the sweeping cuts, though it took all my strength and more to keep from collapsing in a trembling lump at your feet. Through it all, I kept our children hidden behind me, the cloak of my own darkness spread wide, forcing you to focus the attention of your increasingly vicious attacks on me.

And they loved you.

Ran to you with open arms when you came home, laughing in delight as you scooped them up and spun them around, blissfully unaware of my heart racing in my chest, pounding like a drum until they were safely out of your arms and running off to play.

They never saw you for what you were, but I knew what you were capable of.

I berated myself constantly for staying, but I was too weak, my own injuries too severe to simply scoop up our children and flee with them to a place of light and safety, as my former, stronger, self would have done. But as long as you were attacking me, they were beneath your notice, they were safe.

Or so I hoped.

For so very long, I stood guard over them, going through the motions of living, caught in a strange sort of half-life that allowed me to disengage from even the harshest of your attentions.

The once-strong castle of my own strength fell into disrepair, crumbling from the inside, the bricks tumbling into the well with me until nothing was left of the castle but the façade.

Oh, it was picture-perfect, that Hollywood façade—the illusion of the happy suburban housewife who smiles at the neighbors before drawing the blinds and rocking her child to sleep even as tears of isolation and loneliness and desperation and confusion and fear and guilt rolled down her cheeks. I tried to understand why, having achieved the dream of home and family that I had always wanted, I still felt so desolate, so lonely, so sad, so afraid. Tried to understand why the person who was supposed to have been my life's partner harbored such an overwhelming need to keep me huddled in darkness at the bottom of a well of grief and despair.

The darkness drained me, then filled me. Like a person newly gone blind, denial and terror overwhelmed me at first, before giving way to a desperate, aching need simply to survive, if for no other reason than that I had no idea what else to do.

I crawled through the sludge and ooze at the bottom of the well, often floundering in the slop, my only companions the things that swam there, slithering around me, slimy creatures born of my own fears. Needle-sharp teeth tore into my flesh, while others stung me repeatedly with toxic, nearly invisible barbs. And when powerful tentacles wrapped around me and pulled me deeper into the muck, my screams echoed off the slimy walls of the well.

The bottom of the well was a vast, putrid swamp, filled with tiny things that buzzed around my head in blinding clouds, and other creatures that watched me from the shallows with beady eyes, waiting for me to make a misstep and fall into their gaping jaws. I waded through that swamp, towing my battered soul along behind me, until I found the walls—walls built from the bricks and stones that had once been the foundation of my strength, now overgrown with mold and crusted with filth.

I groped my way around those walls, but there were no doors, no windows, no passages. The well was as solidly built as the castle whose walls it was a reverse image of, and each time I found a once-familiar stone, it would vanish, making my prison that much smaller.

I was trapped in the darkness with my demons, and the walls of my prison were closing in around me.

At the bottom of the well, always at its very heart no matter how the walls shifted, lay a drain, covered with a metal grate. No slime coated that cold, dark metal. I was always aware of its presence. Of all the things in the well, that simple grid was the most fearsome to me, for while it offered the only possibility of escape, I seemed to instinctively know that the drain beneath led only to a deeper, more desperate darkness; an ultimate blackness where nothing survived.

You put that there on purpose, didn't you? Knowing I would try to explain away the usual things that slither and crawl and go bump in the night, you gave me something darker to fear.

And I did fear it. I wanted away from it, clawing at the slippery stones lining the sides of my dark prison, scraping my fingers raw and bleeding as I searched for even the smallest of handholds, hoping against hope that I could somehow find my way to the top of the wall.

But each time I pulled myself up by some meager fraction of an inch, the stone I gripped would betray me. Its false promise would crumble, the slime of lies coating it would move beneath my hand, and I would once again plummet into the inky darkness, splashing into water which did nothing to ease my thirst, warmed and salted as it was by my tears.

There is so much I don't remember of the years I spent in the well—the mind pushes the darkest of our demons into closets and bars the doors with locks, chains, and heavy boards nailed across them—but there are still nights when I hear my demons clawing at those doors and I wake, my heart racing, fearing that I will again find myself alone in the darkness at the bottom of the well where you imprisoned me, that you built to keep me all for yourself.

Even now, the monster sleeping coiled in the pit of my stomach still stirs at the sound of your voice on the other end of the phone, writhing and twisting in my guts, nausea rising as the creature wakes. Tentacles of remembered fears slither up my throat, stealing my breath, choking my voice, filling my mouth with the bitter taste of bile. The monster sleeps, but it is always ready to strike, waiting only for your whispered command to drag me back into that oh-so-familiar darkness.

Darkness that whispers to me, calls my name in my weaker moments. Darkness waits in the shadows for me to fall back into the well.

Damn you to hell.

Better still, to a slimy pit of your very own.

The most ironic thing of it all is that it was your own darker nature that inadvertently showed me the way out of my prison. When there was finally so little left of me for you to torment and your soul-sucking gaze saw through the shredded gauze of my feeble shroud and glimpsed our children—our precious, innocent children—your renewed hunger, your desire to feed on them, devour their bright little lights, ignited like a white-hot signal flare.

I saw that light, and I recognized it for what it was—but your attention was elsewhere, and you failed to realize that in that same moment you had dropped a rope into the well.

It is a long, difficult climb, coming up out of the darkness, when you are so weak that every inch gained makes you question your ability to reach your hand up to the next segment of the rope.

And then I heard your demon's voice at the top of the well, and my blood ran cold. Our children's tiny lights wavered, and they cried out in pain and confusion at the sharp barbs you flung at them, your words as subtle and insidious and damaging as the bite of a venomous serpent.

Looking up from where I hung, clinging to a rough, twisted rope in the darkness of the well, I saw their shadows, as you backed them toward the brink. What was left of my heart jumped into my throat in terror as they teetered, clinging precariously to the edge of the wall. Their fears dropped down on me like centipedes, crawling up my arms and wriggling down my back.

I was strong and you nearly destroyed me.

They were so young, with no resources to draw on to protect themselves. There would be nothing left of them when you were finished with them, when you pushed them all the way over and into the horrors of the well.

I could not let that happen.

I took hold of the rope and I climbed. One hand, then the next, little-used muscles straining with the effort of lifting myself out of the muck.

"There's no point trying," my self-doubt whispered as I slipped, the coarse rope sliding through my hand, tearing at my palms. "You're just going to fall back the bottom of the well."

I screamed back at them, drowning out the despair they sought to create with the sound of my own desperate fury.

"You're not going to make it," hissed my demons, their tentacles reaching up, wrapping around my ankles, trying to drag me back down. "The children belong to us."

Tears streaming down my face, I kicked myself free, sending the demons slithering back down into the sludge. I had failed myself, wallowing in the darkness as I had, giving in to the overwhelming hopelessness of the well. I could not fail my children

They would never survive the well.

I focused on those small bright lights at the top of the well…

Protect.

… and caught myself, stopping my fall.

My.

Clinging to the lifeline the rope offered…,

Children.

… I willed myself to try one more time.

*

And then one day I finally dragged myself over the rim of the well and fell to the ground at its base, gasping, almost choking in the sweetness of the cool, clean air after so long breathing only the foul stench of the well.

Once again I put myself between you and my children, presenting myself as the easier target. And as I knew you would, you immediately turned your bloody fangs and ravenous appetite on me, no longer trying to hide your demon behind the thin veneer of civilized behavior.

I clung to the edge of the well, determined never again to fall back into those murky depths. Though the climb had made me stronger, I was far from ready to do battle—if I had made an attempt then, you could have tossed me back into the well without giving it more than a passing thought.

But I had learned from watching you, studied your arsenal, and while you have always known how to be vicious, I had discovered ways to shield myself from all but the worst of your attacks.

The cloak I wore was still battered and torn, still made of darkness, but as I tended to my children, mending the wounds you had inflicted on them, they freely repaid me with bright colorful patches of light. I stitched those patches to the thin gauze of my cloak, covering the holes one by one, faster than you could tear new ones.

As you railed against me, I reinforced my tattered cloak with that brightly colored, heavily-layered patchwork armor, then painted it with a slick protective coating that deflected all but your best-aimed arrows.

I saw the moment you finally realized that I had covered my cloak with the well's own ooze; that the protective coating I had employed was the very muck you had cast me into, scraped from my battered soul and boiled until the darkness had evaporated, leaving only a clear, strong, flexible resin.

I pulled my hood up against your howls of anger and frustration and turned my back to you then, wrapping my children in the bright folds of the cloak they had helped me create, keeping them safe and warm while we healed.

There is still darkness in my cloak.

I am always aware of it.

I still fear it.

The darkness turned you into a demon, and left me little more than a shadow. And it will take but a moment's inattention for it to reassert itself with a vengeance.

But I have also found a use for that darkness, a use for that fear.

I changed during that long, painful climb out of the well, transforming into the mother tiger, with the single goal of keeping her cubs safe from your attentions.

It is the single mark in your favor that I have always believed that you loved us, in your own way, in the only way you knew how. The true tragedy is that the way you chose to express that love—through manipulation, intimidation, isolation—was toxic to us.

You chose to pit us against each other as predator and prey.

And while you may wander the deep darkness of the jungle in search of us, the lies you tell yourself pattering like rain on your pith helmet, the stock of your rifle slick in your hands, your weapon is loaded with ammunition that has long-since been rendered inert. For I am now the mother tiger, protecting her cubs, watching you through the tall grasses, silent and invisible.

I am strong again.

In many ways, stronger than I ever was, thanks to you.

And now you are the one who should be afraid.

Sonora Taylor *is the author of two short story collections:* The Crow's Gift and Other Tales, *and* Wither and Other Stories; *and* Please Give, *a novel. She is currently working on her second novel. She lives in Arlington, Virginia, with her husband. Visit her online at sonorawrites.com.*

About this story, Sonora says: "I love The Tell-Tale Heart *because most of the horror comes from the narrator's paranoia. I find it interesting how living our lives on social media creates the sense that we have to perform at all times in response to what we think people expect from us, which is its own form of paranoia. I wondered how someone who committed an atrocious deed would react, especially when they're always online and 'on stage' in their daily lives. That introduced me to Hailey, an influencer who doesn't crave 'likes' so much when she has something to hide."*

When every detail of your life is constantly photographed, filmed, and posted to social media, how is a person supposed to effectively get away with murder?

HEARTS ARE JUST "LIKES"
Sonora Taylor

Hailey's fingers trembled as she steadied her phone. It was always difficult to get her best side just right, but when she did, the result was beautiful. Her dimple appeared, her freckles shone, and her hair fell in a way that accented her eyes.

Of course, there were filters and Photoshop, but Hailey liked to keep her selfies as real as possible. Being real was what made her so popular online. Being real was what got her a like from Kim Kardashian when Hailey tagged her in a photo of her spritzing on Kim's new perfume. Being real was what made thousands of strangers flock to her account to fill her feed with likes, and what made hundreds of companies offer her samples of their own perfumes, or their foods, or their lotions, or whatever Hailey could promote on their behalf by being a real face for their real product.

Hailey had a job to do on Instagram, a job that brought in likes and money. She'd do anything to keep it. Fortunately, all she had to do was take her picture.

Before snapping her latest selfie, Hailey angled the camera a little more to the left. She didn't want the splash of blood on the wall to be visible. She smiled, then took her picture. It had 3000 likes within two minutes.

*

Hailey had many admirers who posted compliments both kind and lewd on her feed. TommyBoy89 was one she'd noticed amidst the din of all the rest. TommyBoy89 showered her with hearts, and liked every single one of her posts. It wasn't long before she noticed his photo next to his likes. She clicked through to his profile and saw a pair of beautiful eyes looking into hers, and a smile that was just as lovely.

Hailey liked his latest picture and added a comment: *You like so many of my pics. Why don't you say hi?*

TommyBoy89 didn't respond. Hailey shrugged and forgot about her comment until the next day, when she posted a selfie with a tamarind bubble tea from a new café in Georgetown—complimentary, of course, so long as she tagged the café and added #yum in addition to #ad. TommyBoy89 liked her photo within three minutes—and shortly after, he added a comment: *Hi.*

Hailey followed him and immediately sent a direct message so they could talk in private. They introduced themselves and found out the basics: they both lived in D.C., they both spent a lot of time on social media, they were the same age and liked the same restaurants. It didn't take long to meet at an Italian place they both liked, and because the internet helped them get small talk out of the way, it didn't take long for Hailey to invite TommyBoy89—who had asked her to call him Tom—to her apartment, where they spent the rest of the night and the better part of the morning having sex.

They became a couple and began to post online together. Tom had a bit of a following himself—not quite as large as Hailey's, but large enough to where they could be considered an Instagram power couple. Hailey's selfies were interspersed with pictures of Tom looking over her shoulder, and her comments were frequently littered with starry-eyed followers declaring the two of them to be #RelationshipGoals.

Hailey wondered if they'd feel the same if they noticed that Tom's likes had started disappearing in time with them becoming close. After they'd been together for some time, her likes—and subsequent offers from companies to promote their products and enhance her brand—continued to skyrocket. However, Hailey also noticed that she'd posted several pictures without a single like from TommyBoy89.

"Why aren't you liking my pictures anymore?" Hailey asked one day as they sat sprawled on her couch.

"I'm in a bunch of them," Tom answered as he scrolled through Instagram. "I feel weird liking my own face."

"There are plenty without you."

"I can tell you I like them in person." He leaned forward and kissed her cheek. "I *like* how your hair looks today, and those coconut pancakes you made this morning were delicious."

Hailey smiled, but didn't laugh. "I miss your hearts though," she said with a pout that was only somewhat fake.

"Hearts are just likes." Tom kissed her temple. "And I don't just like you. I love you."

"I love you, too." But her answer was distant, her thoughts lost in her feed as she scrolled through and saw he'd liked everyone's photos but hers. It was hard to ignore the way his hearts were speckled across other accounts, boosting their presence and lessening hers. Hearts were important. Hearts kept her in business. Hearts weren't just likes—they were what kept her alive.

Tom insisted, though, that they weren't a big deal. Their disagreement on the matter cooled things between them, though they were all smiles when they posted pictures online. Hailey wondered if he stayed with her to keep his gained popularity online, attaching himself to her influence. If that were the case, the least he could do was keep her afloat by liking just one of her damn posts.

"Jesus Christ, Hailey, will you lay off of me?" It was their third fight in two weeks. Hailey had posted several photos ahead of her weekly Instagram Live, and Tom hadn't liked a single one, not even the one where Hailey wrote, "I love you, Tom!" while making a heart with her fingers. "It's not that important!" he said.

"It is!" Hailey cried. "It's a video I want people to see, where we'll tell everyone we're moving in together for our six month anniversary! How's it going to look when you're not even liking my pictures?"

"It's going to look like we're filming a video together! You know a thousand people are gonna watch it anyway—"

"And we should get a thousand more, but I get drop-offs when people stop liking my posts."

Hailey wasn't exaggerating. She'd only gotten two offers from companies that week to promote their wares, and a photo of her breakfast that morning—an açaí bowl with homemade keto granola—had gotten a hundred fewer likes than a similar photo the week before. Hailey worried that she'd only continue to fall.

Tom, though, wasn't worried at all—which bothered Hailey more than any lack of likes. "It doesn't matter," he said.

"It does! How does it look when my boyfriend doesn't like my posts, when he goes around liking everyone else's pictures and not mine?"

"No one cares!"

"Everyone cares!" Hailey sped toward Tom and grabbed his phone before he could react. "Everyone watches us, and everyone can see when you don't give me likes."

"Give me my phone!" Tom wrestled with Hailey for the phone before she could get to her page from his account, where she planned to mass-like every post from the past week.

"They're not just hearts!" Hailey spun and yanked away from him, which caused Tom to stumble. He began to fall, and Hailey sent him down faster by hitting him in the chest with his phone. "They're likes—"

Tom's head struck the coffee table. The glass top cracked but didn't shatter. Hailey yanked him up by his shoulders.

"And when you don't like my posts—" Hailey slammed his face against the iron corner of the table "—you bury me!"

Hailey slammed Tom's head against the table one last time, then shoved his limp body against the wall. Blood smeared from his face onto the wall as he slid lifeless onto the floor.

Hailey stood still and waited for Tom to move. When he didn't, she walked to his body and placed her fingers against his neck. His heart didn't beat.

Hailey knew this was bad.

She also knew she was supposed to be live in ninety minutes. She'd find a better way to deal with Tom later. For now, she dragged him into her bedroom and shoved him under the bed, careful to bend in his feet so his shoes wouldn't be visible. She cleaned the trail of blood, then scrubbed the table and placed a colorful cloth mat over the crack in the glass. The wall would have to wait until she could buy paint. Wiping the blood would just make the stain worse.

Once she was done, she sat on the couch and tried to collect her bearings. Tom was dead. People would wonder where he was. People would ask about him. She wondered what she'd say when they noticed that Tom was no longer in her feed. Hailey wondered if she should begin scrubbing Tom from her profile now. She had relationship statuses to change, his accounts to unfollow.

But doing that too soon would only prompt more questions. Why had they disconnected? Did they break up? Where was Tom?

Hailey brought herself out of her thoughts, shook her head, and looked at her phone. She would have to buy time—and the best way to buy time was to act normal.

She picked up her phone. She'd do her live episode without him. She had before. And before that, she'd post a selfie.

*

"Hi everyone!" Hailey waved into the camera of her phone. Her laptop sat open beside her so she could monitor comments and likes on her feed while she recorded her Instagram Live on her phone. It was a lot of windows and a lot of people to watch, but Hailey was used to it. She smiled as she greeted her faceless followers. She couldn't see who she was waving to, but hearts swam around her face as her viewers liked that she was there.

"It's Thursday night," she continued. "And that means it's time to check in with you before my awesome weekend! As always, you can send me questions, and I'll answer them while I talk about what's been going on lately. So, yesterday I went to a really great sandwich shop in Dupont Circle, and—"

A question interrupted Hailey almost immediately. They always did, but while Hailey expected the question, it still caught her off-guard: *Where's Tom?*

Hailey smiled and looked back at her camera. "Someone's already asked me about Tom! He's not here tonight. He's out and about, but hopefully he'll be back for next week's video." She made a mental note to set the virtual stage for a dramatic exit on Tom's behalf, where, after months of love and joy and visiting the hottest places together, he'd straight-up ghost her. That was why he wasn't online through his various accounts: he was avoiding her. Maybe she'd get everyone to search for him. She tried not to chuckle at the thought of all of her followers going on a wild goose chase for someone who was dead—nor frown at the thought of all of them flocking away from her feed in search of his.

A swarm of typed sighs and sad-face emojis came through, and Hailey sighed as she slumped her shoulders for effect. "I know, you guys, I miss him, too. But we'll see him and his beautiful face again soon."

Hailey heard a ding, which signaled that someone liked one of her previous posts. She looked at her laptop and checked which post it was as she continued to speak. "Anyway, this sandwich shop, *Bahn Mots*, is a Vietnamese fusion place which offers new takes on the classic—"

Hailey stopped as she checked her notifications. Her breakfast that morning, the one with fewer likes than the breakfast she'd posted before, had one new like... from TommyBoy89.

Hailey blinked, then refreshed the photo. She didn't see Tom's username— just the thousands of likes that had been there before.

Hailey ignored it. It was probably a mistake. "Sorry guys," she said with a shrug. "I got distracted by someone liking my breakfast this morning. Did you all try that keto granola? I couldn't believe how good it was, especially since it didn't have any oats."

A flock of hearts flew through her screen. One follower wrote, *It looked so good! I'm making it tomorrow!* Another added, *I bet keto's why your face is so pretty.*

"Aw, thanks to the follower who said my face is pretty. It's just average, guys—" Hailey patted her cheeks as she looked from side to side "—and I keep it decent-looking with good food, good health, and this awesome oat scrub I just started using. It—"

Before Hailey could talk about the soap she'd promised the organic start-up she'd promote in exchange for free products and a boost on their channels, she got another like on an old post. It was a selfie she'd posted the day before to show off her new makeup, a blue eyeshadow that Tom said made her eyes look like an autumn sky over her freckles. Hailey had shared his comment in her post and tagged him, yet still, it had gone unliked.

Until that night.

TommyBoy89 liked the post.

"What the hell?" Hailey muttered. She didn't realize she'd spoken out loud until a series of questions came through from her followers, all various forms of *What?*

"Oh, nothing," Hailey replied with a smile, though it was weaker than it'd been before. "I just got distracted by another like on my makeup selfie from yesterday."

Another question came through, and Hailey readied a response on who the company was, or which colors would best suit which skin tones. The question, though, wasn't about her eyeshadow. *Hey, sorry I'm late. Where's Tom?*

Hailey kept her smile, but sighed through it. She hoped it was quiet enough to not get picked up on the mic. "I just got another question about Tom," she said. She knew avoiding questions about him would cause more suspicion than ignoring them. "You all must really miss him!"

Another cluster of hearts swam across the screen, and Hailey tried not to glower at Tom's popularity. She and Tom were popular. That was what the hearts were for: the two of them.

"Like I said before, I don't know where he is tonight," Hailey said with as much enthusiasm as she could muster. "But hopefully we'll see him soon."

Hailey heard another ding. She closed her eyes at the sound. All she'd wanted when Tom was alive was just one heart, one like to show her he was watching her online. Now that he was dead, his hearts were all she heard—and they were the last thing she wanted.

The sound of a question made her open her eyes. She read: *What's wrong?*

Hailey smiled again. She had to remember she was live. "Nothing, sorry," she said. "I'm getting a lot of likes again. Now, this scrub."

Another ding. Another like. Hailey ignored it. She picked up the scrub and continued, "It's from a new company called *Oatshine*, and—"

Ding.

"They use all organic oats and fruits—"

Ding. Ding.

"Which sounds like breakfast, and really, it is like breakfast, but for your—"

Dingdingdingdingdingdingding—

"WHAT?" Hailey slammed down the scrub and checked her notifications. She saw several likes, all of them for pictures she'd posted over the past six months—and all of them from TommyBoy89.

It couldn't be. Tom was dead beneath her bed, and his phone lay still on the coffee table next to her. Hailey checked each notification to see if he was indeed liking her pictures, but when she refreshed them, Tom's likes would disappear amongst the thousands of others, part of a number that Hailey lost count of within minutes of her pictures going viral.

But, as he had in life, Tom stood out from all the rest. His username clamored for her attention as she tried to keep up with his hearts. The likes became a steady beat that Hailey knew she'd have to ignore.

"It's a soap I've started using every day, and if you use the code HailStorm20, you'll get 20% off your first order."

The dings ceased. Hailey sighed with relief. "Now, this weekend," she continued. "I've got a lot of fun stuff planned—"

A follower asked her a question: *Didn't you have some big announcement with Tom?*

Hailey's grin stayed frozen in place as she replied, "Some of you remember that Tom and I were going to have a big announcement tonight." How could they forget? She'd talked about it for a week to get their followers excited. She'd talked about it, but Tom had not. Tom had posted pictures of his dinner, a couple selfies with her, and only one picture of her the night before, with a caption saying he'd have something special to share about a special someone very soon. It'd gotten lots of likes.

So had Hailey's announcements—but not one like from him.

Hailey seethed a little as she continued, "But, as I've mentioned a couple times now, he's not here, and I don't want to say anything without him."

Another ding, a single one this time. Hailey forgot her followers as she opened the picture that was liked. It was a close-up she'd taken of Tom after one month of dating, one that emphasized his eyes. The same beautiful eyes she'd seen when she clicked through to his profile all those months ago. Hailey bit her lip and tried not to hyperventilate despite her heartbeat climbing in time with her notifications. The thrum of dings thrashed in her ears as she stared at him staring at her.

One of her viewers asked, *What's wrong?*

"N-nothing," Hailey replied, though she couldn't smile.

You look awful, another follower wrote.

Eat more açaí bowls, a third one quipped.

A swarm of hearts flooded the screen. Hailey knew they weren't for her, but for the viewer's joke. She furrowed her brow and said as calmly as she could, "Really, I'm okay."

Ding. Ding. Ding.

"I'm just ready for the weekend, and—"

Ready for Tom to come back?

Hailey paused, then said, "Yes." She took a breath as she composed herself. A little vulnerability would make her story about being ghosted all the more tragic. "Yes, I'm more than ready to see him again. I miss him, even though it's only been a short while since I've—"

A ding snapped in her ears, and she looked at her laptop before she could stop herself. She clicked through when she saw that the notification wasn't just a like, but a comment. Hailey saw the first picture they'd taken together, one she'd snapped the afternoon after their first date. Tom kissed her cheek and she grinned at the camera. Underneath the picture, TommyBoy89 had written, *Hi.*

Hailey covered her mouth and tried not to scream. The dings became a steady stream once more—*dingdingdingdingdingdingding*—and she moved her hands to her ears to quiet their call.

A question popped up on her screen and glared her in the eyes: *Yeah, where's Tom?*

Their questions had to stop. Tom's likes had to stop. Tom had to be stopped. She'd stopped him before, and everyone would see it and know that they should stop, too, before she lost her mind.

"You want to know where Tom is?" Hailey snapped. She jumped up and stormed into her bedroom. Hailey dragged his body from beneath the bed and wrapped her arm around his shoulder to steady him as she held up her phone.

"Here he is! Here's Tom! So stop asking me, stop asking where he is, and for God's sake—" She stared into his open, lifeless eyes and his bloodied, broken face "—STOP LIKING MY PICS!"

Amelia Gorman writes horror stories and poetry in Northern California, when she isn't taking her dogs for long walks looking for tide pools. You can read her other horror fiction in Black Buttons 3: A Family Affair *and* Sharp & Sugar Tooth *and some of her poetry in* Undead: A Poetry Anthology of Ghosts, Ghouls and More.

About this poem, Amelia says: "This poem is primarily based on Berenice, *with general nods to Poe's fixation on unfortunate individuals being buried alive. The glut of patents for all manner of 'Safety Coffins' in the 18th and 19th century represents to me some of the most bizarre entrepeneurship in history. To take that absurdity even further and modernize it, I wanted to write about an attempt to sell those same products door-to-door."*

According to The Victorian News, *"…the phrases 'saved by the bell,' 'dead ringer' and 'graveyard shift' are believed to have come from the use of safety coffins in the Victorian era…" And while the prospect of being buried alive is no laughing matter, we are fortunate to live in a time when few need be concerned by such fears. But why let science get in the way if there's a sale to be made…*

SAFETY COFFIN
Amelia Gorman

"The whole thing is held together with 32 nails,"
he says, "that's one for every tooth."
I don't normally let salesmen in, but truth
is, I've been thinking hard about the future.

And his tongue is so silver, his teeth are so white.
And you love a good bargain, clearance sales,
kitchen gadgets, vacuums. All of that pales
in utility to something you will use this often and long.

And his coffin's so sturdy, the wood is so cherry.
I invite him in, make him tea and get him a bite
to eat, a plate of gingersnaps. If he just might
wait, my wife will be back from her appointment soon.

In fact, there she is, turning the doorknob now.
Berrie, meet the salesman, salesman meet Berrie.
Sit down together, let me grab some sherry.
My wife's been sick you see, she should get off her feet.

He starts: This coffin uses the best new technology.
See here, this little gold bell, and see how
it connects to the coffin? You can ring it to show
you've been buried alive, if you're so unlucky.

Not that you will be, but it's better to be wary.
Premature burial's not something you fix with an apology.
And after all, there's nothing more confusing than biology,
and sometimes what seems dead or dying isn't.

I ask: With all those clasps it looks too hard to lift,
help me bring it into the basement? We'll have to bury
it someday, makes sense to see if we can lift it. Scary
to buy it and not able to use it, you know?

And the bell rings almost every hour these days,
but I say better a bell than a hard-hearted grift.
When we dig up the safety coffin, I'll give my wife a gift
of thirty-two pearls and a silver tongue.

Sarah Murtagh is a fantasy writer with a fierce love of mythology, history, and cats. Her stories explore the darker aspects of life, often blended with gods and dark magic, but she promises she's friendly—just don't interrupt her when she's reading. Originally from Maryland, she now lives in Salt Lake City, Utah where she is a proud member of the League of Utah Writers. When she's not writing, or nose-deep in research and reporting as a data analyst, she spends time with her black cat and twin sister. You can find her on Twitter @sarahandstories

About this story, Sarah says: "Haunted characters from Poe's work always stuck with me, especially when their stories invited doubt: were they truly plagued by the supernatural, or were their ailing minds dealt a fatal blow by personal loss? In Medea, I wanted to instill that doubt and allow a visceral horror to arise from the narrator's feelings of powerlessness. Medea is written in a 19th century style to emphasize the timelessness of such human suffering and the intersection of mental illness and grief—and even though the perspectives of LGBT and women were rarely accessible, we have been present throughout history.

Even when reason tells us that what we believe is somehow questionable, dare we doubt what our senses assure us to be true? If we despair enough, believe enough, can we make our dream a reality, simply by sheer force of will?

MEDEA
Sarah Murtagh

My mind became my enemy when I was a young girl, and I inherited the struggle for stability that has characterized my bloodline for generations, perhaps for centuries. From when I was eleven, and the world opened its arms to communication through keystrokes instead of telephone wires, I contended for authority over my own thoughts. School days were punctuated by an overwhelming fatigue wrought by this conflict, or the insomnia that brought inescapable waking dreams. Worse than those symptoms, or perhaps caused by them, a paralyzing despair seized my constitution for weeks without end, such that my parents—rightfully concerned—forced me into the chair of a psychiatrist, and deposited into my hands the medication which would become the third regiment in my mental civil war.

All the following days of my adolescence were governed by the pull of one such force or another, but my parents' employment provided the steady supply of various treatments and the regular torment of each pill's effects, and if I was lucky, one of those might be relief. But I was rarely so lucky.

I was miserable, and thought I would be so forever—until I met Medea.

Named for the ancient sorceress and priestess of Hecate, she was the beloved daughter of a Classics professor with a curious sense of humor. We attended the same college, but did not meet until our sophomore year, at a gathering of occult enthusiasts to which I am reluctant to admit I belong, but it is true. While the motley assemblage in attendance traded superstitions and theories of magic and debated their corresponding interests, I was struck by Medea's singular beauty, as if Eros himself had pricked me. The black of her hair shone and cascaded around her like rivers of ink, and there was joy and powerful benevolence in her eyes, like secretive pools from which life might spring. When she spoke, her fingers danced as if to conjure a story all on their own, and my hands longed to receive that soundless tale. From the moment my eyes found hers, which shone from the face of heaven in that crowd as the moon's illustrious glory emerges from behind slumbering clouds, my attentions were concentrated on none but her.

I was bewitched by Medea's passionate theories of resurrection as an excitingly realistic prospect. She spoke at length of the possible incantations for spells that promised renewal of life, though whether the spirit must reincarnate into a new body or receive a blood sacrifice that would allow the decay of the original body to reverse, she was unsure. I countered with my own hypotheses in such studies and the hope that whatever previous illness we had suffered would be gone in the next life, and she bestowed upon me such attention and bold interest that after our conversation I requested to see her again. She smiled with a pleasure so rapturous that I feared my heart would burst with the agony of awaiting her response, but I was saved by her enthusiastic assent, and from that first glorious meeting I was incurable of my enamored state.

We met regularly on our campus, ate our meals together, and happily devoured the energy of one another's company. I reviewed my professors' assignments while I waited for her outside her classrooms, but it became impossible to assert my focus to them, as my mind and all my thoughts gravitated inevitably toward and around Medea. If I could have abandoned the unhappy commitment to my profession and become a student of Medea's innumerable miracles instead, I would have. Her remedying presence in my life marked the first occurrence in the last wretched decade where I was able to experience the unadulterated joy I imagined my peers were privy to. All the sadness that ruled me shrunk from the shining creature called Medea, and my spiraling thoughts, once oppressed by misshapen anxieties, instead spun eagerly around her. In addition to these manifestations of my bloodline and the erratic effects of my corresponding medications, I also feared the intensity of my affections would be a terror to her; but she assured me that my adoration matched hers for my person.

Emboldened by her proclamation, I laid upon her perfect lips a kiss equally desperate and worshipful. The anxiety sparked by my boldness metamorphosed to elation at the blessing of her own fervor, which should not have been so surprising, as each of her actions was awash with unashamed eagerness and the certainty of her intent. I adored her, and, beyond any reasoning I could comprehend, better than any situation I could have hoped for or expected, she adored me. If I was under a spell, and all my feelings had been falsely created and shaped to a reality of my own wishes, I would not have desired freedom if it meant parting from any version of my Medea.

For a time, all was as perfect as it could ever have been. We went everywhere together as the seasons passed in a golden hue, always delighted by one another's company, and the screens that connected us from afar brought us intimacy when we could not be close. At the beginning, if a stranger inquired upon our closeness, we claimed a recent discovery of being cousins. But as the seasons turned and turned, our courage in society's expanding perspective grew, until at every opportunity we proudly revealed the nature of our relationship. However, my family did not receive us so openly, a fact for which I grieved, and Medea's parents had long passed, but we were complete together and needed no other.

Only one nagging poltergeist remained and seemed only to grow with the years, as a storm gathers clouds, slow, gray, and ominous. The feeling remained that this beautiful treasure gifted to me was only temporary, and did not belong to me. I shared these anxieties with Medea, but she assured me this was another trick of my mind, that our happiness was hard-won in a life of loneliness; and that even if my fears came true, and we were somehow forcibly parted, it would do no good to dwell on it.

But I did dwell on it, as was my unfortunate nature even Medea could not entirely cure. Each morning when I saw her face, I no longer saw her beautiful shining one, but three: her loveliness as it was in the morning light, and as it might be in the golden age I hoped we would be blessed with, and her face as I feared it would become, cold, sallow, and lost to death.

Seized by fear of this potential misfortune, I would stare upon her face and watch the color of pleasant slumber in her cheeks. And when I could no longer trust the truth of the image before me, I would rest beside her and press my ear against her heart and count the steady beats—one, two, three—until I fell once again into the mercy of my dreams.

In Morpheus' realm, I was rarely safe. What used to be a visionless void when my body allowed me sleep became a persistent nightmare from which I would wake screaming. The demons of my dreams would conjure a thousand fantasies of the worst kind: Medea falling ill, Medea disappearing, Medea covered in the crimson of her own blood, the glory of her skin turned pallid, bruised, and rotten. To each of these visions of Medea I would plead—*don't leave me*—but they would. The terror of my beating heart would force me awake, and only Medea's soothing touch and loving voice could calm me and cool the heat from my clammy flesh.

These nightmares continued for months, worsening every night, until even waking would not relieve me of the insatiable fear. Shadows seemed to reach for Medea, and at times I saw a twin image of her, a fetch that followed her in the evenings. I felt again as a child at the mercy of tempestuous moods, except that this storm was unendingly and unrelentingly the same. All the hours of my day blurred into one terror: that I would lose her.

After the summer of our graduation, my anxieties materialized into truth. Medea's limbs weakened, her glowing skin paled, and her new, violent coughs filled our rooms night into day. I urged her to visit a physician, and he delivered to us the bleakest diagnosis: my Medea would not live to see another year. She was assigned the starch-white room of a hospital, and I sat at her bedside, sentinel and guardian, rarely departing from my duties. I slept seated by her side, my head rested by her arms.

I confess I sometimes could not bear to look upon her, and instead retreated to the vault of memories safely kept and played inside my mind. For once my thoughts allowed me a kindness: a compulsive, hopeful retreat. There, my Medea was glorious in her health, her smile eternal; but each time I was forced to open my eyes, the reality of her increasingly skeletal form jerked me from my reveries and into the helplessness of a waking nightmare.

Stubborn in my refusal to leave her at the mercy of mortality's feebleness, we sought the help of every physician accessible. Each visit prompted another steep request for payment in the post, until we could at last no longer pay and I shoved the rest out of sight. After months of treatment and the hounding of merciless collectors, Medea and all her doctors resigned themselves to the inevitable—and how I detested, *loathed* that word, the very idea that Medea's condition made any semblance of sense! But Medea would fight no further.

Bedridden and fatigued, Medea kept my hand always clasped in hers, so that she did not have to face the darkness of that eternal slumber alone. Whatever she asked for, I delivered. If she had proclaimed that she did not wish to pass onto the next world alone, I would have happily pulled out my own heart, for I would never see a world where our hearts did not beat together. But she did not ask this of me; of course she would not. She forced a promise from me instead that I would remain alive and strong. And then she resurrected the old discourse of our first meeting and vowed to see me again. Whether in a new body or in a bright new form a world away, Medea promised that I *would* see her again.

Her eyes closed, as if only to focus on the sound of her own breathing, and then she squeezed my hand—and released me. I screamed her name—*Medea!*—but her spirit had already departed and left me in the hospital room with only the electric hum that replaced her pulse, and her hollow skeletal body that bore so little resemblance to the goddess she used to be, but was still my Medea.

After Medea's passing, my life became a ruin. I slept little and swallowed my medication, and more, whatever I could find. The day of her funeral was covered in fog, as if a gray cloud had descended and never again moved. If the sun rose that day, I did not see it; my eyes never lifted from the place they had buried her.

Afterward, I retired to the house I had shared with Medea, paralyzed by the stillness and silence of my unwished-for solitude. Collectors sought their payment, and of course they cared little for my grief. I ignored all summons and requests to speak, disappearing instead into my sole world. Perhaps it was a blessing that my family did not bother me, but what good is there left in a world robbed of its meaning? There can be no blessings in such a world.

Alone in my house, my mind found cause to torture itself, and I fought back with drink, and in my efforts nearly drained the cabinets. But I could not banish the cycle of the two horrible visions that plagued my memory: first, the pale face of the corpse that had overtaken Medea's shining beauty, once so lush and lively, black lashes held still as if caught in a permanent, bittersweet tug from sleep into morning; second, the gray stone that had been laid upon the ground to mark the place of her body's eternal rest, the gray like fog in a winter sky, like storm clouds surrendered to breaking. These cruel images haunted my sight at all hours, no matter whether I set to lay in my bed and weep or to drink my cabinets dry with the hope of shifting my fatigue into numbing sleep. But the visions persisted, and indeed the drink did run dry, and I was left alone to bear the silence of my rooms and the aching beast of grief.

With no other options at my disposal, I set to employ my vision with the images of happiness archived so vividly on my screens. This was inevitably a fierce mistake, as each replication of Medea's unparalleled countenance stared back at me, eyes fixed toward me, reaching out from the glories of the past, her touch stopping cruelly at the glass screen. I seemed to spend days staring back, holding the endless archive of our memories in my palm and pleading silently for her return.

From then on I could not close my eyes to rest awake or to sleep, because Medea's *living* face would find me. Further attempts to numb my senses through misuse of medication and newly-bought drink were fruitless. I no longer sought the comfort of my bed. If I was to be plagued, it was worse to lie still; time slowed in the dark, where Medea's faint scent haunted the room. I paced instead, and with every step I discovered that moving brought not relief, but only a separate shade of madness. My footsteps echoed in their solitude, and my half-dazed mind swung between the ache that loneliness caused—*in* my body, *tangible*— and the faint imagining, half-hope and half-fear, that the echoes of my steps were Medea's footfalls. My soul was torn in two, between the wish to be rid of this agony by way of any possible solution, and the desperate need to receive some comforting feeling, however false, that she was with me still.

I could no longer remain stationary, even for a moment. I had to be moving, with my fingers because they were empty, or with my feet because they walked alone. So I walked. The city's rumbling dissonance promised distraction, so I set out when I could, caring nothing for the time of day.

But there *was* no escape, no refuge from my grief or from the image of a living Medea or a dead one. As if she had heard my desperate wish, she found me. Even though I left my screens behind so that I would not scroll through the captured images of our shared life, Medea was everywhere, not only in my cyclical thoughts of her, but out in the world, ashen with the end of autumn. I saw my Medea in the face of an advertisement, the five-foot-wide grin of her ghost towering over me, black eyes gripping. She became a woman in the grocery line, and I would stare, my gaze fixed upon her until I was forced to flee from the whispering crowds. And in passing through town, Medea stood across the street, skeletal form steady in the autumn gusts of wind, her white hospital gown billowing as she beckoned me to her. But still, she would slip from me when I ran to her.

No nights and no days was I safe from this taunting, this calling—I could not tell which. And nor could I tell whether I would have rather banished her, or else submitted to a life peopled by her ghosts. Had I not sworn that I would gratefully accept any version, any form of my angel named Medea? Was this haunting my price to pay for the delivery of my wish? And if I rejected it, if I denied that she had truly come to me, crossed the realms to find me, did that not mean my mind had sickened to the point of delusion? That the illness that ordered my thoughts had seized my vision as well? I could no longer afford the costs of what might have treated me, even if she *were* a delusion, the cruel creation of a lonely soul. The choice lay before me: to deny her and accept the cold reality that, with her passing, I also lost the meager stability that was protection against my own demons, or embrace her ghost and follow her wherever she might lead, to a heaven of pretty falsehoods or a taunting half-life ruled by her unreal presence.

Enough! I had had enough of fearing, enough of doubting. I opened my arms to her, however true she was or no, devil or witch, ghost or angel, she was my goddess and I would follow her, even into Hell.

This decision brought a kind of peace. Instead of fearful nights chasing a ghost through town and returning, damp and shivering, to find her waiting in our room, I lay back in her old chair in the study, and watched the ghost of my Medea dance. In life, her bones could not have borne her weight to support such an act, her muscles shrunken and tendons withered. Here she twirled in the moonlight of the study, and I sat dazed, drinking to bring some warmth back into my veins. And when she stretched her hand to me, I accepted with the abandon of a woman lost to the world, and danced into the night with my love, sure I could feel the cold of her skin against mine.

Once again I did not see the sun, for what need had I of society—or indeed of time!—when I had my love, who danced and held me in the dark? This I thought, until one night she bade me follow her out into the foggy streets. Of course I had to chase her; where else would I go but to follow her? But *where* were we going? I only asked in fear that, after my acceptance of her, she would leave me again. Then one word sighed from her lips into the damp air and repeated, until my ears heard no sound but Medea's ghost pleading: *Resurrection! Resurrection! Resurrection!*

Withered leaves crunched beneath my feet in my haste to follow her, and hope rose in my chest like a broken bird. *Could* it happen? *Would* it? She did not tell me, only echoed that one word, a command, a premonition. Understanding her intent, I confiscated a shovel and grasped it close to me. As I chased her through the cold night, the shadows of passersby cowered from me, blurring into creatures of silence, no doubt stunned by what must have been a grin of madness on my lips.

Where else would she have led me but to the cemetery where I had seen her lain to rest? Rest! If only it had been! Rest for her and rest for me, beside her; but no, she had forbidden it. Medea's ghost led me to her grave, and the horrible mundane stone, colorless as a cadaver. There could not have been a monument to her life more ill-fitting than that stone! And there beside that gray monstrosity she spread her arms and waited. I raised the shovel, pitched the blade into graven earth, and set vigorously to my task. Desperation fueled me, for I did not allow myself to hope—no, not yet, not until I could see my darling's health and life restored in bodily truth. Ignoring the chill of the starless night, I let nothing stop me. Each frozen mound of earth that resisted my tool, I pried apart with my hands. If my fingers bled and my nails cracked, I felt no pain from it, and Medea's ghost glowed brighter as I worked.

Then, when the edge of the horizon radiated dusty light and I had mere inches left to uncover, Medea extended her hands and produced a ghostly knife, the handle so white it could have been no more than a piece of her gown. To my horror, she pressed the blade to her white flesh. I sought to retrieve it before the edge could pierce her, but my efforts made no difference. Blood poured from her open veins as vividly as if she were still alive!

Doubt pierced me, horrible and sour in my chest. My kind Medea would never have brought me there to witness so gruesome a display; she would never have caused me pain even to save her own soul. Was this a demon wearing her countenance? A phantom sent *not* from my lost love, but from Hell itself? To what *end*? Medea's eyes—or a demon's—gazed not with mortal pain but with *expectation* at her bleeding skin. And then, with a will that was not my own, but that of the demon's, the apparition twisting my love of Medea—it could *not* have been her!—I accepted the blade, pressed it to my skin, and cut.

Crimson fell from my shivering flesh down to the remains of the earth beneath me. Above me, that horrible stone announced Medea's name in silence, and the black eyes of the ghost looked on hungrily. My eyes did not falter from her pale visage until my body, exhausted, collapsed atop Medea's coffin.

I hoped that Heaven had been kind, and my Medea had been allowed her return as Persephone from Hades. Upon opening the casket, I would discover Medea's lovely, healthy, living face ready to greet me. Instead, before even my eyes could open to see the result of the night, my ears were overpowered by a shrieking and howling so terrible I thought the dogs of Hecate had found me. I opened my eyes and beside me was a man, forcefully shaking me into consciousness. He held my arm in a punishing grip as he wrapped a tourniquet above my wound. My blood seeped between his fingers and onto the cloth. The bloody blade lay still upon the coffin, a knife I could not remember seeing before last night, but it mattered nothing at all, as he forced it away from my reach.

This was not *right*, I tried to tell him. I ordered him to let me go, pleaded that my work was not complete, but he hefted me from the grave and held me still. Behind the man's head, red lights flashed like the eyes of Cerberus against the gray sky. This was the source of the horrible noise, the sirens calling for me, but still I fought. Could they not see my darling's ghost, urging me to continue, her bleeding arms reaching toward me? The medics came to rush me away, and still I scratched and screamed, *no*, I would not leave.

Then I heard it: a rustling, a scratching from the casket, so muffled I almost did not hear it over the sirens' wretched cry. The shock overtook me, and in my awe I did not protect myself from the hands that sought to take me. They strapped me down before I had the presence to escape!

Listen! I cried to them. I shouted, but they shook their heads. They focused singularly upon *me*; they claimed what I heard was nothing but the branches rustling in the wind, when I knew that my Medea was trapped inside a wooden prison, clawing for release. The medics asked my name, but as they drove me away I could only repeat one which was not my own.

Medea! Medea! I screamed to the pale vision invisible to all but me: Medea, sickly and skeletal, panicking beside her gravestone; alone, translucent, and fading in the autumnal morning light.

246

Lawrence Berry sold his first story to Cavalier Magazine *and went on to have two 'best of' appearances in that publication. A founding member of HWAColorado, Lawrence originated the Yog:SEA award given to Colorado writers for service to the writing community, now in its sixth year. A specialist in horror fiction and the short form, a number of his new stories are included in anthologies scheduled for release in 2018 and 2019. Lawrence writes two national columns for the HWA:* Forbidden Words, *on the vocabulary of horror, and* Monstrous Friends, *monthly interviews with horror writers.*

About this story, Lawrence says: "Poe draws me to his work, usually in the autumn of each year, and The Fall of the House of Usher *is inevitably the first story I read. Everything that turned in Poe's heart is there—the spectral woman, tall and fair, vengeance and music, failed love and unquenchable hatred, all taking place in a ruinous mansion that is itself alive. I saw the twins first, working on a satanic song that would sear the hearts of the innocent. Then the personal shopper rode into my head on her motorcycle, Malone behind her. I've always seen it as a rock 'n roll story. It deserves rock 'n roll."*

No homage to Poe would be complete without a visit to the House of Usher. An isolated, brooding mansion, its inhabitants twisted by both nature and nurture, this contemporary version will lure you through the great doors, hold you captive, and endeavor to steal your very soul if you're not watchful. But don't be afraid; they say it's a nice place to visit...

A COLORADO WINTER SPENT IN THE HOUSE OF USHER

Lawrence Berry

Tempus edax rerum...
Time, the devourer of all things...

It had been a busy fall, and snow was weeks away. I worked with Eirian for a month, that singer from Wales who's tearing up the Billboard charts. Her publicity agent sent me a note saying she dresses like a poor fisherman that never met a gray she didn't like and a check for $100,000. I don't go to work, or think about working until I've been paid. If the synch doesn't feel right, I send the check back. Eirian had the height and thinness to wear great clothes and make them revolutionary. Like Twiggy. Like Bowie.

America's fashion was too busy with frets, bows, strings, and fringes—I went to France to ferret out silks, fabrics that flowed, and Eirian sold her first platinum album off the flash on the cover.

Eirian called me a bitch with a scary face. Later, she just called me Scary.

They paid another $100,000 for the Grammys, and she made the most beautiful women in the world groan with envy.

The label announced a second tour and the publicist sent the third check. By then it was easy. Eirian grew up hard and fame came too easy, giving her the malevolence of a vengeful spirit because she didn't really feel all that much alive. Her songs were about neuroses, alienation, self-harm and self-mutilation, playful explorations into death. I dressed her that way—as something undead that wanted to eat your heart.

They left on tour with six bags of new threads. A lot of kids were dressing like her, wrecking stores looking for knock-offs, and I received hate mail from half a dozen buyers wanting to know why I couldn't pick from what was *In*.

I went home and spent the money—on a Peter Max painting, a 14th-century dining room table. On old stone griffins and rare grimoires.

A CEO paid me to find him a car, and I sourced a new Bentley Continental with two thousand miles on it, plucked from a weird cat in Silicon Valley who'd recently discovered he really wanted a Bugatti. I also found the CEO a 26-year-old driver from Hong Kong skilled in Aikido. His company paid him a five million dollar bonus because of an article in Forbes. I spent that money, too.

So when August Valiant asked me to come to Leadville, Colorado, and decorate his personal home in a style worthy of Edgar Allan Poe's *House of Usher*, I had to say yes. After all, he did the necessary thing. He sent me a check for $500,000 with contact information.

*

The computer engineer I use for projects is Malone. He probably has a first name, but he answers the phone as Malone in a professional way that isn't over-friendly. His company is called *Malone*, which is how I write out his checks. His card displays his email, the single name, and phone number.

It isn't fair, but I make him do everything computer-related for me, including digging for hard-to-get information.

I called Malone and asked him to do a search of the Valiant family. Since it was Malone, he didn't ask why. He said, "Give me twenty."

When he called back I didn't have to speak, just pick up: "There were a lot of Valiants during the Gold Rush, but their thing was lead ore, not gold. The family hit a strike that produced several hundred thousand tons of lead—all this bad metal polluted Turquoise Lake, Leadville's water supply, and turned Valiant Lake, what the mansion fronts on, into a Superfund site. Big money, much like the Coors family."

"We're working for them," I said. Most of the time, even for clothes, always for houses and cars, I found something for Malone to do.

"Exposure to lead kills people. It took out nearly the entire Valiant clan, and they had enough people to wage a war. There's just two of them left. August, that's the brother, and December, she's his twin sister. Children in the family are always named after the month they were born in."

"They sent a lot more money than what it would take to hire us, but I don't know why."

"People don't like them. They're famous for it. Hotels won't give them a room, restaurants turn them away. They tend to overpay."

"I don't understand."

"You're going to the mansion?"

"Yes."

He sent me a photo of a colossus, huge enough to be a mountain hotel, sitting next to a span of water that was so aquamarine it gave off radiation. "This is the place. The family had it built in the 1800s after the mine made them a ton of money. Okay, so the first weird thing about the family is that they seem to have always lived together, even before they came west from Philadelphia, but back then they were symphony musicians. There's a lot of one-note music in that family. You see what I'm saying here, right?"

"No."

"For the last century, there have been rumors of the Valiant family having consanguineous relationships."

"Malone, I put clothes on people."

"First and second-degree incest. First degree is where you share fifty percent of your genes with your partner—children, siblings, parents. There's like a sixty percent chance of birth defects with this commonality, and looking at the old-time photographs from the Denver History Museum—which you yourself can access online—I'd say guilty as charged."

"What kind of birth defects?"

"Imagine the worst and then get radical."

"You said there are two Valiant family members left?"

"Right. Even though they were born with more money than they could spend, the brother and sister joined His Majesty's Satanic Orchestra and the band put out ten platinum albums in the Nineties before they split up, making them even richer. The same kind of rumors then. There was talk they had a baby that was born dead. A good thing for the kid, in my opinion."

"What about now?"

"Well, supposedly the two of them are putting together a new act called Satanic Beasts. They've announced a studio album called *A Colorado Winter Spent In The House Of Usher*. It's due out next summer."

"What kind of music?"

"What they invented with S.O., satanic rock."

I evinced some kind of surprise. Malone and I were both used to our employers engaging in unwise sexual unions, alcoholism, drug addiction, violence, mania, and just about every kind of mental illness. This was something new.

"Yeah, they're freaky. That comes across in nearly every account. And they really look like each other so much it violates most people's sense of taboo—they are, after all, fraternal twins, not identical. Let's just say people react in a negative fashion when they encounter the Valiant twins in the flesh."

"What should I expect?"

"I'm not even certain people like this can be considered human. Anything else?"

I hung up. Malone doesn't require goodbyes.

*

Valiant sent a car to my lodge in Evergreen and I read *The Fall Of The House Of Usher* several times on the way up to Leadville.

The house of Usher was an ancient pile of stones covered in fungus, sitting on the edge of a poisonous body of water called a "tarn." I had to look the word up. It means a bog; a lake-like body of water fouled with fetid, poisonous growth. The house is described as a place decrepit with shadows, full of expensive, aged, uncomfortable furniture. The study where most of the story takes place is cluttered with books, poetry, and musical instruments, yet the artistic mess lends little warmth or vitality. When you have clutter, your space looks lived in. With neglect, it can reach critical mass and soften into a kind of spiritual decay.

All in all, there's a kind of etheric pus pushing out against the walls of the house of Usher and equally swelling inside Roderick Usher and his sister Madeline. It made me remember arguing with my dentist about a cracked tooth that needed extraction and his weary description of an infected tooth swelling until the gum burst with pus, forming a life-threatening abscess.

*

It was a sunny day when we left County Road Nine and followed two miles of winding road into the estate through a primal forest. The huge trees created a twilight starred with green sunshine.

The huge, rustic manor had to go a 120,000 square feet, rough-skinned with acres of cedar and river stone.

We arrived at the house a few minutes later and seeing it up close did nothing to dispel the sense of giant wealth and the appetites that went with it.

I rang the doorbell and a man in his twenties answered. He had the preppy dress, the balding hair, and the clear eyes you see from Ivy League graduates. I told him who I was.

He let me in, saying, "I'm Evan, Dec's assistant. They're in the study rehearsing." Evan asked me about myself while we strolled, but I didn't answer, had nothing to say. I'd over-prepared with my morning microdose of LSD, and if my eyes lingered too long on a corner of the tile, the edge curled toward me. If I opened my mouth I might say anything. This is part of why I like being paid in advance—people overlook crazy if they've already spent the money.

We walked through passages cased in gleaming wood, galleries, comfortable great rooms, moving toward the end of the house. At last, we came to a corridor lined in funeral art, mostly ancient crypts, sheltered by ancient trees. Rock music drifted to us, strange subterranean rifts of an electric guitar, mixed with the tones of a flute. I heard them singing, but couldn't make out the words. August had a raspy voice like Axel Rose. December had an even more raspy voice like Bonny Tyler.

Three of the tall, wide paintings had been removed and a church pew shoved against the wall. Three men sat there. Two of them wore suits and had briefcases at their feet. The third man had on working clothes, a very long wrench laid across his legs. They glared at Evan and he glared back.

Evan opened the final double doors to a study-library that went three stories up. Evan introduced me and said, "August and December Valiant."

*

December Valiant studied my albino features without embarrassment, then tried to meet my cinnamon eyes through the charcoal lenses of my Santos De Cartier's. She was immensely tall and had to look down, her skin possessing the whiteness of someone intolerant of the sun, perhaps a shade more colorless than my own albino skin. Her eyes and hair were the blackest black imaginable, like a long straight fall of concentrated night. I'd been expecting some kind of Frankenstein, but she was beautiful in a way suggesting loveliness that went deep and was profound—with many hidden eddies and channels. There was a certain oddness of proportion, but nothing remotely unsightly.

"You came at once. We're honored," she said.

"How could I resist? You told me so little."

She laughed, genuine amusement that made her beauty light up, glancing in a loving way at her brother, who managed a smile. August Valiant was an exact copy of December, perhaps even taller, but equally monochrome in design, either white or a black without a trace of auburn lineage, with the addition of a full beard. If it weren't for breasts and facial hair, they could be the same person.

December took my hand, leading me toward her brother, talking as we went. "We're working on a new album."

"*A Colorado Winter Spent in the House of Usher*," I said.

As we came up, August murmured, "We love the story and we love the music of Poe."

Their gravity wasn't a pretense; it was what they were and had been for a long time now. Some families all talk the same. They were like that.

"But this room, it keeps the music from being good." December glanced around the vast library as if it had mischievous intent.

I wasn't the first decorator the room had seen. A lot of money had been spent and it showed in the fabrics, the rugs on the floor, the heavy drapes. There were galleries on the second and third floor, the four walls holding maybe a quarter-million books, reflecting generations of collecting. I thought of all the Valiants there once had been.

"But it must have the soul of Usher," August added.

"We've agreed on that," December said, giving me another amazing smile. All the good things and sunlight in the world lived in that smile.

"Do you always finish each other's sentences?" I asked, the stereo nature of the conversation disconcerting.

"We're twins, and we grew up here, just the two of us," August said.

"Silence in the mountains can be a savage thing," December added.

"Unendurable," August agreed.

"So it's best to be good companions."

The doors opened and I turned with them to see who it was—finding the man in working clothes nervously gripping the wrench. "Pardon, Mr. Valiant, but the dam, she is frozen up. I can't use the spill. If you could come."

"Pardon," August said, putting his guitar down. As he walked past us, December reached out and touched his arm, almost a soft caress.

"I miss him when he has to see to this old ruin."

How could I judge? Like all of us, she came from a people and a place impossible to imagine.

*

I could see she hated the library the way a woman will detest one room in a difficult house. There was no reason to inspect it, time enough for that later. I asked for a tour of the mansion and we set off, me hurrying to keep up with her long strides.

"Evan put this bench here because he hates the groundskeeper and the attorneys waiting and watching us in the study," December said as we walked down the long hall, past the two hopeful suits sitting on the church pew. She never glanced their way.

"It will need to go," I said. "The bench is like a doorbell always about to ring. You hear it when you're in the room." I just earned some of the money they paid me.

"That's unusually informed," December said, stopping at the end of the passage, thinking where to go.

"A second set of doors here, I think, so nothing and no one can reach you while you're working."

"Privacy is always an imperiled sanctuary at Valiant Manor."

She was like this, my entire stay. Half of a conversation whenever it was just the two of us together.

*

There were thirty bedrooms in one wing, and we circled around a squad of maids moving slowly along the wide hallway. They all smiled, local ladies from Leadville, and December flashed her amazing smile back. Five dining rooms. Two much smaller, more intimate libraries. A ballroom, which was getting set up for their use while I made the central library worthy of Roderick Usher. A billiard room. A sunroom the size of most houses, almost entirely overgrown with orchids and wild with their odor. The maids used the Westin Hotel's Signature Room Fragrance, so the hotel effect was pronounced walking through the house. I didn't judge the use of the perfume. The Villa La Cupola hotel in Rome used the same white tea scent and lodging there cost thirty thousand dollars a night.

*

December unlocked a steel door and led the way down to what I thought would be the basement. A great deal of money had been spent here. The walls were jet and jade tiles, pinstriped with citrine. The risers were set with fire opals and seemed to smolder with enchantment. She pushed through a viper wood door, and we entered a chapel, chairs grouped around a pentagram constructed from rubies, half-melted candles at the points of the stars. The upside down crosses mounted between rare oil paintings celebrating witchcraft seemed like decorations, but the effigy of a massive hooved and goat-headed beast behind the altar possessed a reality that was frightening.

"Do you indulge in religion?"

"I don't know," I said. I dodged joining clubs of any kind.

"This is the only religion that would have us."

Anticipatory silence followed—I wondered what August would have added.

"I would be willing to let all the demons there are drag me to hell for just one boon—do you know what that is?" December asked.

"No."

"Survival—so I might elude death's grasp for the fullest revelation of self-hatred."

She laid her hand on my shoulder, and I felt the great strength in her, well-laid madness, and the heat of fever. It was a demon that laughed far behind that fantastic smile, and I swear I heard the beast behind the altar move, begin to lurch forward.

December touched my cheek, her long finger gentle, but oddly wet. "You're bleeding."

I put my hand up and pressed a cut I didn't know I had.

She put the bloody finger in her mouth and sucked. "You have tasty blood."

In that instant, she switched with me somehow. I was her—high, proud, fair, and burning with fever—and she was me.

*

I came to myself again and we were in a gallery, high in the house, under a gilded round skylight of enormous girth. A stone sculpture of hunting dogs savaging a wild boar, slashing them with its tusks, occupied the circular room.

I felt like I'd been stepping in buckets.

"Donatello," she said. "*Cingale In Estremo.*"

I put my hand on the ancient stone, wanting to feel something real.

December took a man's heavy gold pocket watch from her pocket and checked the hour. "Almost four o'clock. Time for a treat!" She led the way to the stairs and I hurried to catch up.

"Why do you want the library to look like the *House of Usher*?"

December laughed, merry and seemingly without cares. "Why not?"

*

"This is doctor Deichmiller," December said, pressing a lace handkerchief to her forehead to blot a sudden sweat. "I do believe you've worn me out running around this old wreck."

We shook hands, the doctor's skin feeling scrubbed.

He turned to a medical table. Six or seven hypos were laid out. He took one, removed the cap protecting the needle, and December put her arm forward. He gave her an injection that sent a wave of pleasure across her features.

Dr. Deichmiller picked up a second syringe and turned to me. "It's a light energy cocktail of my own creation that will help you sleep later."

Before I could say no, December rolled up my sleeve. Dr. Deichmiller laid in the dose.

It wasn't transformative, but it was very good and played well with the LSD.

December went and stretched out on one of the medical beds—and just like that, she switched me off. I felt dismissed, no longer part of her wonderful glow. Dr. Deichmiller put a Bandaid on my cheek.

"I feel that fatigue again. I may be having another episode."

Dr. Deichmiller went to attend to her, and I went out, uncertain as to what had happened or why—glad to be alone again.

*

My first real home was the public library by my house where I went to escape the nightmare that was my family. A library was warm light, stacks of fragrant books with out-of-the-way places where you could be by yourself and peruse your finds. The first thing that was wrong with the room was all the open space. It was impossible to light and when I played some Alanis Morrisette, her voice echoed like she was singing in the Grand Canyon. If I hung absorbent panels wired with light and sound I could get a ceiling height of about twenty feet and make the divisions work. The furniture was Woodley and not bad, but I'd been using Waves, a modular leather system that was internally lit. It had hidden shelving, adjustable seating, and was an island to itself. Once a person got used to the modern lines and crazy comfort, the space became organic, fun to use. Books had been stacked against the walls to make room for tons of folios holding photos of the twins on stage. Shots of crowds, arenas, fan fights with the stage bouncers, August on electric guitar, December with a violin, a lute, a flute, instruments I didn't recognize.

The folios showed use. They looked at themselves as they had been. I could blow up the stills, cover the walls and the dropped panels making it a shrine to their art and style. After six hours, I had a plan and drawings.

*

I found a door that led out to the long emerald lawn that ran to the lake and called Malone. Other than the stubborn grass, the water killed anything that grew close—the trees were barren and gray, bushes like broken spines.

"You're at Valiant Manor?"

"Yes, and I need you to come up. Bring everybody." This meant the electricians, the carpenters, the painters.

"Is it weird?"

"No, it's good, but they definitely indulge." I watched an evening mist grow on the lake, amazingly white against the blue glow. Incandescent things seemed to exist in the deep water and move in the cerulean depths.

"There's always been rumors of drug use surrounding them."

"You're saying you'll live with it."

"You didn't throw up your hands in horror. When are the clients not crazed?" Malone changed gears. "When do you need us?"

"As soon as possible." I hung up.

The house was of such size it was on the same scale as the huge fir trees in the forest beyond the influence of the lake. With late twilight, the windows glowed with red energy, seeming to look down on me as December and August Valiant had, inquiring, picking at the corners, pulling the edges back to see what lived underneath.

I was about to go to my room when the electric guitar began playing, August singing with its shriek and grind. I didn't want to meet anyone just then, especially not a Valiant. I needed food and a bed. I hated it when people saw me the way I really am. Empty as a paper sack with nine times my share of crazy.

Even so, I walked part way back to the library to listen.

Skull House
Falls as dead angels fall,
Into sullen depths
Where Death itself
Has made a bed
Of broken teeth
And velvet sorrows.

It looms
Behind the most terrible
Nightmares;
A dim shape
Vast and heaving
With unspeakable horrors.

Skull House
Mad children whisper
That place built
On bones of sin.

You drive there
In your Inevitability Car,
The one that takes you
To the Dentist,
The Courthouse,
The Grave.

It has glossy black paint
And chrome door handles.
The seats are stitched

With red silk,
And there's a pillow
For your head.

You walk up steps
Each one carved of marble
With somebody's name cut in it,
Maybe your name,
Maybe all the stepping stones
Are chiseled with what somebody called you
When they threw you out.

The door opens
As doors open in dreams;
As if it was never really shut.

Skull House
Grins,
Sly.

It cuts open your head
With a gravedigger's shovel.

*

The bedroom doors each had their key in the lock, and I put mine on my dresser, not wanting any surprises. When people pay you a lot, they often dream up the concept of sexual bonuses. I haven't been avoiding sex. I just don't want it very often.

August opened my bedroom door and came in as far as the entry, which meant he had his own key. His clothes and hair were black and they merged into the deep gray of the bedroom. Only his skin showed, and it was like the tissue of a ghost, not flesh but a vague radiance. After what seemed like a very long time, he went out and closed the door.

The clients are the clients and they're all fucking serial killers. Money does that to a person.

*

The next day we had a consultation and December looked through the sketch boards, clearly surprised. August glanced up at the distant ceiling, asking himself if he'd miss it. "The damned place does look back at you. Sometimes it feels like nothing but eyes."

257

I wanted to follow his stare but was afraid I'd see something. You take a microbang of LSD every morning, anything is likely.

"I think the cavern harmonics have to go. I sound like Janis Joplin, belting it out from the grave."

August muttered an acknowledgment. "We stayed up for days working on the S.O. albums, taking meth, cocaine, and Oxycodone to stay awake and into it. Ivan used to call it a deadman's cocktail. You sand down your wiring and make it that acute, you don't come all the way back. You always hear too much, you hear what's not there."

There were nights I vibrated like a tuning fork. What could I say?

"Don't pay any attention to him. We did that once." December gave me a smile that had a gigawatt of wise humor. When she wanted to be normal, Opie would have believed her.

*

Day four I decided to skip my dose and tough it out. This meant I was a bitch all morning and tired as hell after lunch. I went to my room to find August and Evan going through my things, August picking my drug safe. They weren't embarrassed, and I was too fried to throw a fit.

"When we let a person in, we have to know them," August said.

"If you make a stink, it won't matter to him. He'll do it again." Evan seemed almost apologetic. "You know, it's okay to have more than a change of jeans."

August found my drugs and thumbed through them.

"Live man's cocktail," I said, trying for a joke.

"You're low. Go see Deichmiller, he'll resupply you."

"Deichmiller is a doctor."

"*Was* a doctor. He took someone's spleen out on Demerol and lost his license when they died."

*

The next day I gave up on being good. August was right. I wasn't out, but low is low. I went to see the doctor, coming in the medical suite to find he was reading Poe's *Spirits of the Dead* to December, unconscious, in a different bed.

He finished and put the book down.

"Does that help her in some way?" I asked.

Deichmiller laughed. "August's orders."

I told him what I needed, and he asked me to wait a minute, going to a drug safe the size of a vault. It was hard to look away from December, her unearthly beauty so potent it was godlike. She was more than asleep. She was totally out.

Deichmiller brought me a four-month supply, saving a lot of difficult conversations with illegal drug dealers.

*

The next night, after work, I went back to the medical suite, the nurse asleep at her station. December was still and rigid. I couldn't detect a pulse or feel her breath on my cheek.

I had a sound meter with me, hijacked from Malone, that had a full sensory array detecting sound across the entire spectrum. It was possible to have a vibration screwing up a room that went below the audible range, or high-pitched feedback you felt without being able to pinpoint.

I set up the machine and listened to December.

Not high, but way low, sepulchral really, I heard her murmur. What she was saying was obscene, intensely horrific. I recorded a few minutes and shut the machine off. Before I did this, I checked her heart and lungs which were thumping away, but oh so faintly.

Deichmiller kept legal drugs at the nurse's station, and I slipped in next to the sleeping woman to get some Excedrin PM, my head staying busy even when the work was done. Four o'clock treat announced itself in my brain daily, and sometimes I went up for a jolt, other days I gave it a pass.

August drifted in, maniacal in the dim medical light, giving off an aura of pain. He went to his sister. "I heard you, love. I hear everything you say."

His hands went under the covers and he did things I didn't want to see—I was terrified of being discovered, certain he'd kill me in the state he was in. Eventually, it was over, and he drifted out. The nurse woke up, seeing me kneeling by her hefty thigh. "Madre de Dios!" she cried, with a slight scream.

*

The ground floor remodel was complete after a month's work, the January winter on the house like an artic troll, shaking the structure down to its foundation with its winds, pushing sub-zero cold through the walls, releasing tons of snow. Malone needed to see August play live music to fine-tune the intelligent system's motion detectors. The system was voice activated—the entire room could be lit and have sound, if he wanted it so. If he didn't, the room detected where he was and what he was doing, directing light and sound to his needs, leaving the rest in a soothing half-light.

August played one of the dumber songs from their portfolio, *I Just Want To Have An Abortion*, striding around on long legs as he played and sang, the system right with him. It was like he was now able to wear the space, the very house, like a suit.

Uncanny, scary, truly voodoo-tech.

The groundskeeper came in through the new outer doors we'd put in, but left open, standing next to me. "The man, he will not listen. The valves in the dam are rusted and will not open."

"Is that bad?" I asked.

"You think maybe drowning in that blue sewage is a good thing, miss?"

August stopped playing. He could be loud when he wanted to be. "That's the interior decorator and you are the groundskeeper. Don't talk to her unless I tell you to."

The old man bowed and ducked his head, his hands shaking. He was still carrying a wrench that was three feet long. He went back out, but I stayed put, adding my attention to the ongoing work.

"You like that song?" August asked me.

"No, it's ugly."

"December wrote it."

I had to think about that. Malone put his hand to his head and wiggled his fingers, which meant things had gone past his sanity limit. Malone found it important to stay sane.

*

The construction crews were gone, the walls now a much more subdued tone of brown and gold. We installed rolling ladders on the library shelves, new furniture in the galleries, and the books that had given it life continued providing life support.

I had to walk around on drywall stilts while August played, making nutty sounds on a flute so Malone could calibrate the system to read two tall human beings playing music.

While August worked on *A Colorado Winter Spent in the House of Usher*, Malone and I lived it.

Somewhere in this time period, it began to snow again, huge flakes, filling the world, making dunes that grew to mounds. The grounds crew worked all day, every day, keeping the house clear, plowing the drive, but the rage of the weather was impossible to contain.

*

Each night I carried the meter up to December's room and listened to her, because her murmured confessions weren't always about the sin her brother had brought her to—sometimes she sang and the invisible music was incredibly pure. Sometimes she cried and I held her hand.

There were more times when we switched and she was me, I was her. I felt the heaviness of the disease that gripped her, despite the woman's uncanny strength. Somehow, some way, she rose out of it to sing, her voice a kind of spiritual power.

The transference wrecked a part of me I didn't know I had. When I went to bed after seeing her, it was like sinking into an induced coma, or floating with the corpses in a cruise ship lying on the bottom of the Pacific.

I came to one night and August was on me, grunting as he finished, his beard drawing blood from my breasts. I was filled with loathsome Valiant seed, the only thing worse than the water in the lake. When August suddenly saw it was me and not her, he slapped me hard, screaming, "Come back! It's you I want!"

The most terrible part, the unforgivable violation, was both of us laughing at him, our face a shifting torrent.

*

The next day I went to see the good Doctor and asked for Plan B, morning-after birth control. I wasn't using anything and hadn't in two years. There hadn't been a need for it.

"The Valiants don't allow birth control of any kind in the house. It's perverse in this modern age, but they're old people when you get to know them."

"I need Plan B. I'll take a car."

"The roads are closed. Come back at four. I'll come up with something special."

I wasn't sure how to feel. August had left in a fury. December had taken me again and soothed my tears. The violation felt like an engulfing madness I was not equipped to manage. I knew I was a crazy train, but I wasn't anywhere near as off the rails as she was. No one human went that far out. And there was still the question of exactly who was responsible for the sexual assault? Was it August, or December? Was there any real difference between the two of them?

*

I didn't stay away.

The next night I went again to see December, serene, deathly pale, covered to her neck in a hospital blanket, smiling, giving out a light. I felt that damned and demented part of her stroke my mind and desire to inhabit me.

The stars weren't in alignment.

Something wasn't quite right.

She fell away from my awareness, unable to complete the transference.

*

It was cold enough to freeze a person's eyebrows white, and I was sitting on the front porch, having a cup of coffee, not much to do, in no hurry to tidy loose ends. Eirian had called needing new outfits, which had given me the opportunity to fire her as a client. I was in a good mood. It was enough to sit, drink coffee, and watch it snow, the storm well into its second week. By this time I was nearly as crazed as the house and a mad hilarity had a grip on me.

In a way, the house was a larger silhouette of everything that was wrong with me, one that took my compulsions to the next level. The House of Valiant now felt like as much of a home as I'd see on this earth.

Even Malone, steady in his Malone orbit, had realized they were never going to let us leave. We'd joined the band. We'd become Satanic Beasts, and there was never going to be another innocent daybreak in our lives.

The groundkeeper's truck, loaded to the sideboards, his wife, and daughter next to him, drove out with the quiet stealth of a spy plane, pushing through spirals and waves of snow like a beat-to-crap fishing boat navigating a storm-torn bay. He was leaving, and that meant something that should have scared me, but I had become so attuned to the silent voice of December, the music of her lusts and agonies, that I couldn't even wave goodbye.

He couldn't either.

We exchanged glances, his carrying pity, mine wonder that he could escape. The Doctor had lied about the roads. The Valiant crews kept the access open, and it was possible to get away. It had always been possible.

Another earthquake rolled through the ground, making the trees shiver, the great desert of snow rising into flurries. We had over a dozen quakes a day now. Because seismic pressure was conducted through the ground itself, making the snowy fields rise and fall, I could tell the source was the town of Leadville.

I went in for another cup and when I came out, a Park Ranger was getting ready to knock. He handed me a notice about Turquoise Lake and possible dam failure.

"What does this mean?" I asked.

"Tell August to open his flood gates in case Turquoise starts to spill over. I think the dam will hold, but we have to warn you."

"What does that mean, spill over?"

"That the dam is running its outlets at the maximum bore and the snow is filling the lake faster than we can divert water. The estate here is downstream."

"Gotcha."

"You tell August."

"I will."

*

I took the notice to the library, Malone at work, no sign of August, thank God. Malone read the notice and asked me questions. I told him about the Groundskeeper. Malone was growing a beard and pushed his fingers through it. "It's the weight of the excess water in Turquoise Lake causing the quakes. The lake is maybe twice its normal size, maybe three times, and it's exerting force on the fault lines."

August came in and Malone handed him the notice, explaining what he'd just explained to me. My daily microdose had tripled and the air sparkled with corpse lights.

"This house has stood for over a hundred and thirty years, and it isn't in danger now."

The library woke when August entered, the voice of the room giant as the voice of the house itself, the lights creating a moving flow around him as if he'd become a deity and could summon a private sun.

I felt something shift in the house, a presentiment of the most uncommon thing in Valiant Manor—change. A wind came out of the west like a giant hand, shaking the house, rattling the windows in their frames. I have heard such winds called *furies* because they blast everything flat in their path. Valiant Lake washed against the house, suddenly much higher than the hedged bank. The water swelled until it was running just under the windows, a vicious current, carrying daggers of ice.

One great cry came to us from above in the medical suite, as December Valiant left this life.

For weeks, months, nothing had happened, and now the world ended in a flying span of seconds.

"I hear her," August said. "She's coming."

"Who is coming?" Malone asked, looking up from his gauges with mole eyes.

"I've heard her dying an inch at a time and made her sing in her coma, made her share herself with me." August stared at us with hysterical, white-ringed eyes. "You're deaf not to hear her up there, the slave I made her be."

The entire house creaked left, made a drunken slide to the right, and I saw the ghost of December Valiant swim into the room. In death, she was a feral thing, with jaws like a barracuda, the last woman of the Valiant line, here to end centuries of madness.

I grabbed Malone and some last, tiny, living spark in me pulled us both away. I made Malone rush through the long, wide room and not look back at how the Valiants came to their death, more of hell than heaven in the screaming, rending malice at our backs.

*

We ran through the house, pounding for the garage. The water covered the windows now and the entire structure shuddered under the weight of titanic waves. The Leadville dam had to be gone. All the frozen water in the world was coming in our direction. I pulled Malone through the final door, into the long garage, filled with vehicles.

"That one," he said. "The Hummer. The air flow to the fuel intake extends higher than the roof."

263

Malone was coming back from the spiritual abyss the Valiants had saturated into the beams of the house—the blinding fire and freezing cold of that eternal writhing darkness holding thousands of Valiants, all there had ever been.

He took the driver's seat as I ran around to the passenger side. "When we open the garage door, the water will roar inside, but not too much for the Hummer to take. This part of the house and drive is raised to protect it against flooding. That's how they build them in the mountains."

Then there was a great rending noise as the outer wall gave way and a great push of air boomed into the garage—half the house imploding. Hitting the garage door opener, Malone put the Hummer in gear, and we were moving as the door raised, two feet of water flowing past us, nearly lifting the Hummer. It rocked the heavy vehicle, but he kept his foot on the gas and followed the road out. The current was a terror and kept trying to pull us away, off the road, into the shaking, tumbling mass of the trees.

A hundred feet and we were above the worst of it. Another stretch of road and the tires were free of the flood.

There was a flare of blue light and I looked to see the lake take the house and tear it off its foundation, caked ice crashing through the endless expanse of the roof.

There was nothing to do but escape. Malone drove for all he was worth, following the drive out, turning up toward high ground. The strangest thing was a sound of wild music that followed us, rising above the tumult, a satanic litany celebrating the destruction of the House of Valiant.

Frank Coffman is a retired professor of college English, creative writing, and journalism. His speculative poetry and short fiction have appeared in a variety of magazines, journals, and anthologies. Founder and moderator of the Weird Poets Society *Facebook page, he served as the editor for the collection,* Robert E. Howard: Selected Poems. *His recently-published chapbook,* This Ae Nighte, Every Nighte and Alle, *is a collection of his own poems of the weird, horrific, and supernatural. A second tome, containing a broad variety of his speculative and traditional poetry, is scheduled for release in early 2019.*

About this poem, Frank says: "Certainly, Poe's most famous poem is The Raven. *Distinctive not only for its haunting story and captivating weirdness, the rare (and, in this instance, successful) use of trochaic meter in very long octosyllabic lines, rich with internal rhyme, adds to the memorability of the verses. Mulling over this verse on my umpteenth re-reading of the poem, it struck me that the story needed an epilogue. What happened to the plagued protagonist? To the raven? Since the poem is set in 'the bleak December,' I figured that the epilogue and final outcome of the tale should occur the following January."*

To close this collection, it seemed appropriate to pay honor to the man who inspired it, his most famous poem, and the tradgedy that lay at the heart of so much of Poe's work.

AT THE GRAVESITE

Frank Coffman

On the tenth of January, in an ancient cemetery
On the outskirts of the city of then snow-clad Baltimore,
Dead! Not one who was there buried, bitter cold of night had carried—
Another soul by Charon ferried, ferried 'cross the Styx to shore—
And the look upon his features was a death mask to abhor:
Staring wide eyes, caked with hoar.

As the legend is repeated: Dead he was—but he was seated
On the ground, his dead eyes staring at a gravestone—so they swore.
In his hand was clutched a feather, stark against that blizzard weather.
Black it was, and altogether curious. One could not ignore
It was trimmed out as a quill; ink-stained, had been used before.
And the dead hand black spots wore—

Showing clear a writer's trade; somehow this sad corpse had made
His livelihood; scrawled words or numbers were this grim one's daily chore.
Though, at first, they did not know it, he had some fame as a poet,
Had left tales and verse to show it—but, for now, they knew no more.
Those who did investigate, knew not just where to explore,
What 'round that scene they should look for.

Finally, from the man's coat pocket, a young policeman drew a locket,
And an envelope and diary *and more feathers?*—caked with gore!
The diary's ending wildly raved—clearly his mind could not be saved!
The letter proved he was depraved, a sane man nevermore.
And the grave those dead eyes gazed on but a short inscription bore:
Fair and Radiant Maid, Lenore.

About the Editor

Lyn Worthen has been reading since before she can remember, and began her career as a freelance writer and editor sometime in the previous century. And while creating technical training, product documentation, and marketing collateral paid the bills, her love for the written word ultimately led her to back to fiction. She currently divides her time between editing for indie fiction authors, building the occasional short fiction anthology, and writing fiction in multiple genres under various pen names.

Contact her at *www.camdenparkediting.com*

Camden Park Editing

About BundleRabbit
www.bundlerabbit.com

BundleRabbit is the premier DIY ebook bundling service. We help readers save money on ebooks by providing authors with the tools to bundle their books together and offer them at a discount.

BundleRabbit also provides an amazing service for multi-author projects: Collaborative Publishing. With collaborative publishing, co-author or multi-author projects can be created and published in both ebook and print formats and distributed through the major online retailers without the individual authors having to deal with the headache of tracking and splitting royalties among all participants.

Visit *BundleRabbit.com* to discover more.

Made in the USA
Columbia, SC
06 February 2020

87581647R00169